SURRENDER

He raised her wrist to his lips and lightly kissed the bruised flesh. "Better?" he asked softly.

It was much better than better, she thought with a sensuous little shudder. She nodded, and he gave her a slow smile. "What else, Jess?" he urged in the same low tones. "What else hurts?"

"My lips," she managed to reply, just before his mouth found hers.

His kiss was hot and demanding, yet she found herself responding with equal abandon as he tumbled her onto her sprawl of blankets beside the dying fire.

"Oh, Nick," she cried softly as his warm hands caressed her soft flesh.

"If you want me to stop, Jess," he said in a ragged voice, "tell me now. Otherwise, there won't be any turning back."

She slid her hands down his back, pulling him closer.

"If you stop now," she breathlessly told him, "I shall never forgive you."

DESERT HEARTS

Anna Gerard

Zebra Books
Kensington Publishing Corp.
http://www.zebrabooks.com

ZEBRA BOOKS are published by

Kensington Publishing Corp.
850 Third Avenue
New York, NY 10022

First Printing: September, 1999
10 9 8 7 6 5 4 3 2 1

Printed in the United States of America

In memory of my dad

Special thanks to Kathryn,
for keeping me on track . . .

and with love to Gerry,
who survived another one.

Prologue

September 1879
Dodge City, Kansas

Doc Holliday was an easy man to spot, even among the crowd in the smoke-filled Long Branch Saloon. With his pallor and his aristocratic features, he resembled nothing so much as the effigy of some long-dead young knight . . . that was, if the knight in question had been wearing boots and a dandified gray suit. His blond hair and mustache were almost as pale as his skin, giving him the look of a man near death.

Rumor had it, he was.

He sat with a rough trio of cowboys at a green baize–topped table, a deck of cards in his elegant white hands. A substantial hill of coins and cash tumbled in lazy disarray before him, testifying to his skill with the pasteboards. A young, dark-haired woman in a red satin dress was leaning over him, whispering in his ear. Whatever she said must have amused him mightily, for a faint smile played about his pale lips, a sure sign of strong emotion from the usually taciturn dentist-turned-gambler.

Too bad Holliday's pleasant evening was about to be spoiled.

Finishing off his whiskey, Nick eased away from the bar and started toward the table in question. He could have confronted Doc earlier, but he had dealt with the gambler before and knew that the man required careful handling. Even a perceived slight would be sufficient cause to rouse the man's cold temper and put an end to Nick's plan.

Holliday spotted him even before he reached the table, his pale eyes narrowing as he took in every detail of Nick's appearance. Last time they'd met, Nick had worn the simple, rough garb of an ordinary cowboy. Tonight, however, he had donned the austere black wardrobe affected by most gamblers who plied the western circuit . . . Doc excepted, of course. He took the single empty chair across the table from the gambler with only a curt, "Mind if I join you?"

The image he projected of a professional gambler apparently sufficed for the three cowboys. In rapid succession, they mumbled their excuses and threw in their cards, until Nick sat alone at the table with Doc and the woman.

Holliday gathered the discards and began to shuffle. "What a shame they left, since I was winning," he observed in a languid tone, coughing slightly. "Lucinda, darling, say hello to my old friend, Nick Devilbiss. An appropriate name, don't you think? He is a handsome devil, with that black hair and those cold blue eyes, and I understand he has quite a way with the ladies. Tell me, Lucinda, would you like to make a deal with this devil?"

"Send her away, Doc," Nick told him before the bemused female could make a reply. "We have business to discuss."

"Indeed?" The gambler swiftly dealt them each a hand, then glanced over at his companion. "You may go now, darling. It seems my friend would like a word with me . . . alone."

Nick waited until a pouting Lucinda had taken her leave, then coolly reminded the other man, "We're not friends, Doc."

"Oh, I know that, Nick," he drawled with a faint smile that didn't quite reach his pale blue eyes. "That was just a little conceit of mine. It sounded so much more polite than telling the poor girl you were a Pinkerton agent come to town to arrest me."

"That's not why I'm here tonight, and you know it. If I'd wanted to bring you in, you'd already be tied to your horse and we'd be headed out of town."

"I rather doubt that." With one slim hand, the gambler lightly fingered the butt of the nickel-plated Colt visible beneath his coat. "But do go on. I'm finding this conversation most fascinating."

"You spoke of deals. It just so happens that's why I'm here." Nick patted his coat pocket. "I would agree to forget the warrants I have here, in return for a bit of information from you."

"Why, Nick, I do believe that you have forgotten to ante up."

Nick clenched his jaw. *Play it his way, for now,* he reminded himself and plucked a dollar from his waistcoat. He tossed the coin into the center of the table, then picked up his hand. A pair of queens the jack of hearts, a red six, and a black nine. He pulled out a ten-dollar gold piece and added it to the pot.

"I'll need to get someone out of jail," he went on. "Short of breaking him out, the only way I can manage it is by negotiating his release with the local marshal. And that's where your information comes in."

"I see," Holliday murmured, calling his bet. "And this jailed someone is . . . ?"

"My younger brother, Rory."

Nick tossed aside all but the pair. Holliday dealt out three cards, face down, then discarded two from his own hand and dealt himself replacements. "And his crime?" the gambler asked as Nick looked at his cards, and then tossed another gold eagle into the pot.

"Attempted murder; fellow by the name of Pete Morgan."

Holliday called his bet and raised it, coughing slightly. "That presents a small problem, Nick. The man in question happens to be the mayor's future son-in-law. Releasing his would-be murderer would not be a politically expedient move for our good marshal."

"Damn it, Doc, there's got to be something you can give me that I can use," he persisted, calling the gambler's bet. "A name, something."

Holliday coolly laid out his hand, a flush, and waited. Nick spread his own cards—three queens, and a pair of fours—and then scooped up the pot. The gambler smiled just a little.

"Forgive me, Nick, if I put this bluntly. Your brother is not the sharpest knife in the drawer. Neither you nor I can offer the sort of help that he needs."

"Oh, he's smart enough," Nick countered with a wry shake of his head. "His problem is with the details. He's arrogant, but he's sloppy, leaves too much to chance. That's why he always gets caught. But if I can just get him out of jail this one last time, I think I can turn him around again."

"If you believe that, then you're a damned fool," the gambler drawled. "I can tell you it's already too late for that. Rory will end up either hanged or shot, and there is nothing you can do to change that fact. The most you can do is postpone the inevitable, so why even bother?"

Or, as Nick's father would have said, it's all over, except for the burying part. But it wasn't over, not by a long shot. Not if Nick had any say in the matter.

"The reason I bother, Doc, is because he's my brother."

"Why, Nick, I am quite touched by this show of fraternal affection. Very well, I will help you, but only because I am the sentimental sort . . . and because my luck seems to have gone sour with you sitting here."

He reached into his coat pocket for a stub of pencil, then plucked a bill from the stack before him and started writing. "Give the good marshal these two names and that date and I assure you he will be happy to make the exchange for you."

Nick stuffed the defaced currency into his pocket and rose. "I appreciate it, Doc. About those warrants . . . once Rory and

I have left town, I'll tear them up. In the meantime, I have to warn you that there are others out there besides me looking for you. You might want to consider pulling up stakes."

"As a matter of fact, I am headed for Arizona Territory tomorrow. I have plans to meet up with my old friend, Wyatt, and his brothers."

"Well, good luck to you, then."

He didn't offer his hand, knowing that the gambler wouldn't take it. Instead, he simply nodded and headed for the exit. Once outside in the mild night air, he drew a deep breath. Now he would learn just how deeply Doc's ties into the shady underbelly of Dodge City ran.

As the gambler had predicted, the marshal was glad to make the exchange, even though he had been rousted from a sound sleep to conclude the deal. It was just before midnight when Rory strolled out from the jail, a free man. His youthful features hardened, however, when he saw Nick waiting for him on the steps outside the jailhouse.

"Well, if it ain't big brother, come to visit," he said with a sneer as they started down the shadowed street. Here, away from the saloons and bawdy houses, darkness held sway without benefit of gaslights. "What the hell are you doing in Dodge?"

"Getting you out of trouble, as usual." He coolly met the blue gaze that was a mirror image of his own and asked himself for the hundredth time why Rory had chosen the path he had. Aloud, he merely asked, "So, was it self-defense again?"

"Hell, the fellow made me do it. I didn't have a choice."

"Right." Nick shook his head wryly, wondering if Rory truly believed that. "Come on; we're heading back to Kansas City."

"Now?" Rory's sneer became a snarl. "Are you crazy, big brother? It's dark out, or hadn't you noticed?"

"The moon's up, so it'll be bright enough if we stick to the trail. We'll ride for a couple of hours and then make camp. I just don't want to give the marshal a chance to change his mind and come looking for you again."

"The hell with that. I ain't goin' nowhere, and you damn sure can't make me." But in his voice, Nick heard echoes of other, long-ago protests. *I ain't goin' to school, and you can't make me. I ain't admittin' to that broke window, and you can't make me.*

"You don't understand, do you, Rory?" Nick halted in mid-step and turned to face his brother. "The only reason you're not still sitting in that jail cell is because I made a deal with the marshal. Now, you'll ride of your own accord or else I'll buffalo you and tie you to your saddle."

Rory gave a disgusted laugh. "Hell, you're plumb crazy if you think I'm gonna stand here and let you bust me over the head with that pistol of yours."

"Then I take it that means you've decided to ride. The livery is two blocks in that direction. You head on over and get the horses ready. I'll go back to the hotel for the rest of our gear and meet you back there in a quarter of an hour."

He expected another protest from Rory, but the younger man merely gave a sullen nod. "Whatever you say, big brother. I guess we're just gonna do it your way, like always."

Satisfied, Nick turned and started back down the street, a cool sense of relief sweeping over him at the knowledge that he had saved Rory from himself yet again. And, once they were on the trail together, things would be better. Rory would realize that Nick had done what he had out of concern, not in some misplaced attempt to run the younger man's life. By the time they made it back to Kansas City, Rory might be thanking him for stepping in as he had. Maybe he could even persuade the agency to give Rory an easy job or two. . . .

He heard the sound of footsteps behind him and instinctively turned. Whoever it was, he couldn't make him out for the shadows. All he glimpsed was the knife as it arced toward him, the blade glinting in the moonlight. It sliced into his right shoulder like cold fire, tearing flesh and then glancing off bone.

Nick staggered to his knees, disoriented by pain and shock.

Hell, someone had just tried to kill him, came the belated realization. It wasn't the first attempt ever made on his life, though all the others had come in the light of day, and over the barrel of a pistol or a shotgun. None had ever come this close to succeeding, however, so that surprise temporarily outweighed the pain. And since he hadn't seen his would-be assassin, he had no idea whether he had been a random victim or a deliberate target.

Blood was sliding down his back and arm in two warm, wet streams. Together, they formed a small but rapidly growing pool that gleamed black beneath the moonlight. It occurred to him that he would have to staunch the flow, before he bled to death. He slowly raised his free hand across his chest and clamped it over his shoulder, feeling the blood trickle between his fingers. Not good enough. He had to find help . . . had to find Rory.

"Goddamn it, Nick, look what you made me do," he heard his brother's furious voice from somewhere above him.

Nick blinked, trying to focus on the sound. A wavering image came into view, a knife in his raised hand, Nick's own blood dripping from its point. *Rory?* he thought in dull surprise. *Rory had done this?*

"And why the hell did you have to move?" the younger man raged on. "I could've got you in one try, but now I'm gonna have to hack you into pieces."

Christ, he really means it, Nick told himself, acceptance rapidly supplanting surprise. It occurred to him, too, that he should be trying to escape the younger man, but for some reason he was unable to move. He'd lost too much blood too quickly, he vaguely realized. And why in the hell were the streets so empty? There should be witnesses, people who could help.

If you don't move, you'll die. Get away from him. And then a familiar voice echoed in a mild drawl, "Get away from him."

A tall, thin figure now loomed behind Rory, and a nickel-plated revolver glinted in the moonlight. *Doc?* Nick squinted against the fog that seemed to have wrapped around him. But he'd left Doc back in the Long Branch. Maybe what he was seeing was simply Death, come to claim him.

And then he was slumping into the puddle of blood and dust, and it didn't really matter anymore.

Chapter One

Brimstone, Arizona Territory
September 1881

Jessamine Satterly had known Jacob Hancock for little more than an hour. It was sufficient time for her to be quite certain that she detested the man.

To be fair, he hadn't done or said anything that would have warranted anyone else's ire. In fact, he had been the soul of bland politeness. His offense had lain in implying that a woman was not suited to the task of running the First National Bank of Brimstone. And since Jess just happened to be the woman in question, she immediately found herself quite out of sorts with the man.

Unfortunately, Hancock was not only a misogynistic know-it-all, he also was a bank examiner . . . which meant that she had no choice but to be polite to him, since it was her bank that he was examining.

Not that they had started out at cross-purposes. In fact, Jess's first thought as he walked into the bank was that he must be an Eastern dandy, come to Arizona in hopes of making his fortune in gold and silver mining. Such men were the lifeblood of Brimstone's bank, so she always welcomed their arrival. Her second thought was that she had met this particular man somewhere before, though, for the life of her, she could not recall where. Odd, for he definitely was the sort of man that a woman—even one who had reached the advanced age of eight-and-twenty—was not likely to forget.

He was perhaps half-a-dozen years older than she and sported the tanned skin of a man who has spent time in the outdoors . . . this despite the fact that he was dressed like a Kansas City pimp. Indeed, with his gray suit, shiny black vest, and ruffled white shirt topped by a pearl stickpin, he likely would earn a bit of laughter from the locals. Lean and quite a bit taller than she, he possessed the strong and regular features she had always admired in a man. Unlike most of the men in this Western town, he was clean-shaven, while his dark hair had been pomaded until it glistened like obsidian. But his most striking feature was his eyes . . . cool, and the same deep blue as an Arizona sky.

Jess inwardly grimaced now at the memory. At the sight of the man, she'd suffered an uncharacteristic attack of feminine vanity. Its initial symptom had manifested itself in the absurd relief that she'd worn this outfit, a black-and-green-striped taffeta with just a hint of a bustle and topped by a short matching jacket, rather than the serviceable blue serge she'd first pulled from her wardrobe that morning. Those colors showed her pale skin, and dark eyes and hair—the same color as good Kentucky whiskey, her father always claimed—to advantage. As to the style, it neatly trod the line between fashionable and efficient.

The illness's next manifestation had occurred when he had asked to speak to the bank's owner. She'd been aware that her smile had held more than professional warmth as she admitted to being that person. The smile had held, even as he had plucked off his neat bowler and displayed an impressive sheaf of official documents. Those papers had testified to his identity and background, and had included an impressive-looking letter of authorization from the Territorial Bankers Association . . . the company that held her bank's charter.

The card he had presented her was equally imposing, with his name and title—JACOB E. HANCOCK, FINANCIAL CONSULTANT—and a Kansas City address engraved on heavy pasteboard trimmed in gold foil. Jess had studied everything with care, for this had been her first direct contact with someone sent from the association. Up until six months ago, her father still had remained an active partner in the bank and handled that end of the business. Before that, and until his murder more than a year ago, her late husband, Arbin Satterly, had served as the bank's contact with that group.

Satisfied that Jacob E. Hancock indeed had the authority he claimed, Jess determined that she had no choice but to answer his questions. It had been after his first query—"Have you considered hiring a male teller to handle the bank's more complicated transactions?"—that she had found herself abruptly cured of whatever temporary madness had possessed her.

Now, he was examining the bank's barred windows, one on either side of the door, which faced Brimstone's main street. A dozen sturdy iron rods were sunk vertically into the brick-framed, arched openings. Thick wooden shutters, fastened from the inside, offered both additional security and protection from occasional inclement weather. The white stuccoed walls were, themselves, almost two feet thick . . . as much protection from the brutal Arizona sun as from would-be bank robbers. He gave the bars an experimental tug, then lightly dusted his fingers on his coat front.

"Adequate," he murmured, though his expression said otherwise.

Jess gritted her teeth and nodded politely. "The same gentleman who designed Tucson's bank drew up the plans for ours."

He made a note in the small book he had pulled from his breast pocket, then turned his attention to the broad mahogany counter behind which the bank's teller worked. A matching mahogany partition pierced by a trio of arched and barred windows ran the counter's length, further separating the teller from the customers awaiting their turns.

It was there, at that counter, that the greatest portion of the bank's operations were conducted. Her father often bragged that the expanse of mahogany rivaled those elegant bars found only in the finest drinking establishments. Indeed, he had purchased the ornate fixture from the same St. Louis manufacturer who had furnished Brimstone's only saloon, the Lucky Nugget. Even Arbin once had joked that, should they ever grow bored with banking, they need only bring in tables and a few cases of whiskey to become saloonkeepers, instead. And with the counter's abundance of carvings and curlicues—including the front panel with its rendition of a life-sized eagle, wings spread in preparation for flight—Jess ruefully agreed with the men's assessment.

But Hancock appeared singularly unimpressed by the proliferation of gleaming mahogany and intricate carvings. Rather, he was studying the waist-high gates at either end of the counter, through which access to the narrow space behind it was gained. He stalked over to the nearest one and gave that gate a healthy shove. Unused to such treatment, it fluttered on oiled hinges for a few moments before finally subsiding with a creak.

"See here, Mr. Hancock, I must protest this—"

"Very unsatisfactory, Mrs. Satterly," the bank examiner cut her short, grimly shaking his head. "There is no latching mechanism or lock of any sort on either gate. A bank robber need merely stroll through the nearest one, empty your cash drawers in succession, and then walk right out the other side. I would judge such an operation to take thirty seconds, perhaps less. Let us hope that your vault is more adequately protected."

Not waiting for her reply, he gave its heavy steel door a considering look, stepping closer to examine its mechanisms.

"A combination lock," he said, with a frown that a horse breeder might reserve for a sway-backed nag. "You are aware, of course, of the advances in the field of locks and safes? Most modern banks employ some version of the time lock, which allows a vault to be accessed only at a preset time, meaning that unauthorized personnel—''

''I am well aware of how a time lock functions.'' Jess cut him short, grimly wondering if the Territorial Bankers Association would notice or care should Hancock just happen to disappear while in Brimstone. ''We have plans to convert to such technology in the next fiscal year.''

''I see. Very well, since we must work with what you have, how many people have access to the combination?''

''My teller, Lily Chwang, and I do, of course. My father, who was a partner in the bank until his health forced him to retire a few months ago, also knows it.''

Hancock lifted a dark brow. ''So three individuals are potential targets for any outlaw intent on opening the vault. Now, Mrs. Satterly,'' he interrupted as she started to protest, ''don't tell me that you would not readily divulge that combination if someone were holding a gun to your father or Miss Chwang. Yes, I rather thought you would.''

He scribbled in his notebook again while Jess waited for the heat in her cheeks to subside. Hancock must know as well as she did that a dozen time locks and a battery of armed guards would not keep out determined bank robbers, as proved by such outlaws as the James and Younger Gang. And surely he was not intimating that Arbin and her father were somehow responsible for the fact that the Black Horse Gang had held up their own bank a year earlier, absconding with the money and killing Arbin in the process.

''I know this must be difficult for you, Mrs. Satterly,'' Hancock went on, seemingly following her train of thought as he fixed her with his cool blue gaze. ''The company is not blaming you for the fact your bank was robbed. They only suggest that perhaps both the robbery and the, er, events that followed might have been averted had a few more security measures been in place that day.'' He paused, looking uncomfortable. ''My condolences, by the way, for your loss.''

''Thank you,'' she replied crisply, wondering as she did so how much time would pass before strangers no longer felt obligated to offer sympathy upon learning she was a widow. Every word of condolence, no matter how well meant, only served to revive the guilt she felt over her own part in Arbin's death.

To her relief, Hancock's lapse into humanity lasted only for the moment. Resuming his impartial manner, he asked, "Any other way out of here . . . through there, perhaps?" He pointed to the closed door that led to her office. "I noticed an alley behind the building, and a door. I presume access is gained through—"

"It is."

Jess hesitated, abruptly uncomfortable with the way this interview was proceeding. She had expected a discussion on her investment strategies and her customer base, not a debate on the merits of her bank's floor plan. Next, the man would be asking why she had chosen to leave the walls with their original whitewash finish!

Taking a deep breath, she planted herself between him and that door, arms crossed over her chest as she assumed her most frosty mien. "I was under the impression, Mr. Hancock, that a bank examiner examines the bank's bookkeeping practices . . . not the design of the bank itself. If you would care to have a look at my ledgers, or tour one of the mines in which we have invested, I will be more than happy to accommodate you, but I fear I have no more time in which to discuss my bank's architectural merits."

Her protest did not earn her the disapproval she expected. To the contrary, Hancock allowed himself the faintest of smiles, so that Jess was again struck by just how attractive a man he was. Thank goodness he'd not given in to a full-fledged grin, or she might well have wavered in her stance.

"Very well, Mrs. Satterly. We will dispense with further discussion on the physical aspects of your business; however, I would like your permission to spend a while observing the bank at work."

"I suppose there could be no harm in that," Jess pronounced with more enthusiasm than she felt. In the short time that the man had been here, her emotions had run the gamut from outrage to mild lust . . . quite an unsettling range for someone like her, who prided herself on her businesslike calm. The last thing she needed was to spend more time in Hancock's company.

"If you like, you may take a seat there"—she pointed to the far wall, where sturdy wooden chairs flanked a pair of waist-high tables—"and the rest of us will be about our business as usual."

Not waiting for his reply, Jess made her own way toward the teller window. Though Hancock had been relatively circumspect in his investigation, his presence in the bank was beginning to draw attention from the afternoon trickle of customers. A stranger in Brimstone always rated a second look, and she could ill-afford for people to begin speculating as to just what Hancock was doing in her bank.

She slipped past one of the gates he had found so inadequate, then waited while her teller, Lily Chwang, counted out a grizzled miner's bag of coins. As always while she watched the young woman work, Jess congratulated herself on the stroke of luck that had brought her and Lily together.

The prim, high-buttoned gown of brown calico Lily wore only emphasized the exotic Chinese beauty of her moon-round face. It also accentuated the dramatic tilt of her tiger-gold eyes, which color bore testament to the fact that her father had been a Caucasian businessman from San Francisco. Accepted completely by neither race, Lily had been destined for the same miserable existence as befell other women of mixed race in that city . . . that of a prostitute.

But the young woman had refused to quietly accept her fate. Instead, she and her five younger brothers had left California when she was but fourteen years old. They'd moved from southwestern town to southwestern town, never finding quite the right place to settle. A year ago, they had made their way to Brimstone, where their uncle, Chan, operated a successful restaurant not far from the bank. The easygoing Chan had taken them in, and the Chwang siblings settled into Brimstone to begin working for their uncle.

Lily, as a mere female, had been consigned to the meanest of kitchen chores, so that it was only by sheer chance that she and Jess had met. It had been in Barris's Mercantile, not long after the bank robbery. Jess was purchasing some thread for her aunt, while Lily had gone in place of her ill brother to pick up a few supplies for the restaurant.

When the time came to add the cost of those goods to the restaurant's monthly account, the young woman boldly had requested to see that list. As Mr. Barris sputtered, she swiftly added the figures without benefit of pad or pencil, and then pointed out to the man several errors in addition that inflated the total bill. The storekeeper tried to deny her claim, until he noticed Jess watching the unfolding incident with obvious interest. Grudgingly conceding that he might have made an error, he corrected the total to match the sum Lily had named.

Impressed by the young woman's demonstrated aptitude for numbers, as well as her polite if assertive manner, Jess had followed her from the mercantile. A few moments' conversation between the two women had revealed that Lily, while grateful to her uncle, nonetheless despised working in his kitchen. Impulsively, Jess had offered her a position in her bank as teller, replacing Willy Crume, who had resigned from that position in a panic the day after the robbery. Lily just as swiftly accepted the offer.

But Lily also possessed another, even more valuable talent than her skill with numbers . . . a way with even the most recalcitrant customers, eliciting confessions even from those who'd always sworn they would never have any dealings with a "Chinee."

Inscrutable, was the whispered opinion of many. *Plain nosy,* was Lily's own cheerful explanation of how she so successfully wormed information from others. Jess had long since stopped wondering how Lily seemed to know everything that went on in town and simply accepted the fact that such was the case. Even Ted Markham, publisher of the town's weekly newspaper, the *Brimstone Fire*, jokingly threatened to hire away the young woman as a reporter every time he stopped by the bank.

Now, preparing to take advantage of Lily's talents, Jess waited until the miner had departed the counter. "Whatever you do," she said softly, "don't let any of the customers know Hancock is a bank examiner. They'll think there is a problem, and it might cause a run on the bank."

"Do you think so?" the young woman whispered back in dismay. Though such a panic had never before been a concern for the First National Bank of Brimstone, it was not an uncommon occurrence elsewhere in the territory. "What should I tell them, then?"

"Don't tell them anything unless they ask . . . and then just say that he is consulting with us regarding, say, improved bank security. And if the opportunity presents itself, try to strike up a conversation with Mr. Hancock, as well."

"Should I ask him if there is a Mrs. Hancock?" she murmured, her earlier look of concern now replaced with a sly grin.

Jess refrained from rolling her eyes, aware that Lily was looking for a reaction from her. The younger woman's matchmaking efforts were becoming a joke of sorts between them. Eschewing sentimentality for practicality—for Lily knew that Jess and Arbin's brief marriage had not been a satisfactory one—she recently had decreed that Jess had been a widow long enough. Ever since, the young woman had taken it upon herself to weigh the merits of every unattached male between the ages of twenty and fifty as a potential mate for her friend.

Jess sternly shook her head. "Just see if he will drop any hints as to what sort of a report he intends to make to the home office."

Satisfied that Lily understood the seriousness of the situation, Jess left her to her duties and headed back to her own office. As for Hancock, he spent the next hour sitting with bowler hat propped on crossed knee, coolly observing the comings and goings of her customers. The ladies, in particular, returned his attention, shooting him sidelong glances . . . some merely curious, others more blatantly approving.

After a few minutes of internal sputtering, Jess managed to ignore him, for the most part, as she went about her business. Once, during a lull between customers, she glanced up through her open door to see Lily handing him a cup of her famous green tea. Lily was smiling as the pair exchanged a few words, while Hancock seemingly had unbent enough to favor her with the same hint of a smile she'd seen earlier. Reminding herself to quiz the young woman later regarding what she had learned, Jess returned her attention to her ledgers.

So intent was she in proving to herself that the man was no distraction that she did finally lose herself in her task. When the Regulator on the wall outside her office chimed five times, she looked up in surprise. Lily was escorting out the last customer, while Hancock was rising—rather stiffly, Jess was gratified to observe—from the seat where he'd been keeping vigil.

"I appreciate your patience in accommodating me on such short notice, Mrs. Satterly," he said as he started toward her. "And I must tell you that, from a service standpoint, I can find no fault with your system. From all indications, your business is conducted in an efficient and professional manner."

She stared at him in surprise, hardly believing that Jacob E. Hancock, financial consultant from Kansas City, was actually paying her and her bank a compliment. "Yes, well . . . thank you. And now I must help Lily finish up before we leave for the day."

"Certainly. And thank you again for your kind invitation to supper. I believe Miss Chwang said you dine promptly at six?"

Jess shot a quick, disbelieving look at her assistant, who still stood guarding the door. The younger woman's grin reflected only a hint of guilt as she said, "I told him what you said, Mrs. Satterly—that you would feel remiss in your obligations to the company if you left Mr. Hancock to fend for himself this evening. And I gave him directions to your father's house, as you asked."

"It seems you have taken care of everything, Lily," Jess

managed faintly, praying that her dismay did not show on her face. "Yes, Mr. Hancock, six o'clock will be just fine. I am certain my father and aunt will look forward to meeting you."

She waited until Hancock had left the bank and started down the wooden sidewalk, however, before giving rein to her outrage. "Really, Lily, whatever possessed you to foist off that impossible man on me? It was difficult enough being pleasant to him here at the bank, but to be forced to spend an entire evening pretending to be cordial . . . "

"Do not be upset with me, Jessamine," the younger woman coaxed with an impish grin. "I knew that if I didn't take a hand in the matter, you'd let him spend the night all alone in his hotel room . . . and then you never would discover that you and he are quite perfect for one another."

"Perfect?" The word rose on a disbelieving note. "You must have talked to a different Jacob Hancock than I. The man is obstinate and overbearing, not to mention arrogant—"

"See, a perfect match," she smugly proclaimed, even as Jess frowned. Surely *she* was none of those things, so what could the younger woman mean?

"And the fact that he is so handsome quite clinches it," Lily finished in satisfaction. "And if you don't believe me, why don't you ask Reba?"

Chapter Two

"Ask Reba what?" a woman's raspy voice demanded from the bank's doorway. "And who in the hell was that good-lookin' man that just left here?"

The speaker was Reba Starr, owner of the Lucky Nugget, Brimstone's only saloon. Though the older woman was coyly reticent about her age, Jess guessed her to be at least sixty. Reba was several inches shorter than Jess, though her artificially blond hair—"My own recipe, honey"—piled into a dramatic confection atop her head, added almost a foot to her height.

Her plump, grandmotherly figure was always squeezed into quite ungrandmotherly gowns of bright satin, such as the mauve one she wore this day. With its décolletage and exaggerated bustle, the fashion revealed a great deal of her pale, freckled bosom and added considerable breadth to her already wide backside, lending her silhouette a shiplike aspect. Now, she docked herself in the chair Hancock had just vacated and waited for an answer.

"His name is Jacob E. Hancock . . . Jake, he told me to call him," a grinning Lily hastened to answer the second question. "He's a bank examiner out of Kansas City, and I think he is the perfect man for our Jess. But she doesn't believe me, so I told her to ask you.''

''Bank examiner, is he?'' The saloon owner gave a ladylike leer, exposing a full set of store-bought teeth. ''Lawd, honey, he can examine my assets anytime.''

Jess rolled her eyes at the double entendre and suppressed an exasperated groan. It was not so much the woman's blunt sentiment as her timing. Now that her curiosity was piqued, Reba would not leave until she'd heard every detail concerning the man.

Normally, she would have welcomed a visit from the saloon owner. Given the fact that they were two females in businesses that traditionally were owned and run by men, it had seemed only natural that she and Reba had become friends. And because Reba's blunt, often crude manner hid a sentimental heart, she could not help but like the older woman. A down-and-out miner was always assured of a hot meal and a cot at the Nugget, once Reba learned of his plight. And Reba's friends knew they could always lean on the older woman's ample bosom for comfort in times of trouble, and could count on a lecture from her, as well, when the situation warranted it.

But now, it was Jess's turn to lecture. ''First of all''—she turned a stern glance in the Chinese woman's direction—''Lily wasn't supposed to breathe a word to anyone about who Mr. Hancock really is. And second of all, I have no interest in forming any sort of relationship with the man . . . especially one of a personal nature.''

''She and Jake got off to a bad start,'' Lily confided in a mock whisper to Reba, ''but I fixed things. I arranged for him to have supper with her and her father and Aunt Maude.''

''Good work.'' Reba gave Lily an approving nod, her mass of lacquered blond curls quivering in agreement. ''Now we'll just let nature take its course.''

''Really, you two are impossible,'' Jess interjected, her hands on her hips as she glanced from one to the other. ''And even supposing that I *did* have any interest in the man—which I do not—have you forgotten that Arbin has been dead barely a year? It wouldn't be . . . appropriate."

"Balderdash!" Reba gave an inelegant snort as she dabbed at her powdered bosom with a lace-trimmed handkerchief. The day was warmer than usual for September, so that even the bank's thick adobe walls did not deflect all of the heat. "Not to speak ill of the dead—hell, Arbin was a fine enough fellow, in his way—but everyone in town knew the two of you didn't suit."

"They did?"

Jess frowned. There never had been loud arguments between the two of them, for Arbin had been too dignified ever to shout. In public, they always had maintained a cordial air, with Arbin saving his disapproval of her too-forthright manner for when they were alone. Except for that time at the Gleasons' Fourth of July picnic . . .

Deliberately, she shook off the memory of Arbin's red-faced protests that no wife of his would be seen hopping about in a gunny sack race, no matter what the other wives did, and returned to the matter at hand.

"At any rate, I have no wish to remarry, so the two of you can stop conspiring right this minute. And, Reba, you surprise me. Surely you, of all people, aren't saying that a woman needs a man to have a fulfilling life?"

"Lawd, honey, no woman *needs* a man . . . but every now and then it's sure nice to have one under the quilts with you. Why else do you think I keep that no-account Bannister around?" she asked with a sly wink, referring to the Lucky Nugget's sour-faced bartender. A good ten years younger than she, the tall and poker-thin man was in both appearance and personality the opposite of his flamboyant employer.

Jess momentarily considered the woman's argument, then dismissed it. She had found that portion of her relationship with Arbin pleasant enough—at least, at first—though she never had quite understood what all the fuss was about. But later, when he had kept strictly to his side of their four-poster, she had not been unduly upset.

"Don't worry, Lily," Reba was saying, meanwhile. "I remember a couple of months back, when you convinced young Horace Woods to ask her to the town dance. She nearly snapped the poor boy's head off. A shame, too. Horace isn't half bad-lookin', even with those buck teeth of his, though he can't hold a candle to her Mr. Hancock."

"He's not 'my' Mr. Hancock," Jess protested curtly, feeling herself blush. "And while I admit that he may be handsome enough, he has the manners of—"

"—of Mr. Kirby's stable dog?" Reba helpfully suggested.

Jess nodded and allowed herself a wry grin. Her father's horse was stabled at Kirby's place, so she'd seen the beast in question any number of times. He was a sleek and handsome black hound, said to have the foulest disposition of any canine in Brimstone, known to bark and bite indiscriminately. It seemed an apt comparison.

Reba grinned back, then assumed a practical tone as she went on, "Now, honey, look at it this way. A slice or two of your Aunt Maude's chocolate cake should convince him to report only flattering things about the bank."

"I suppose you are right." Jess sighed and glanced at the watch pinned to her lapel. "I'd best hurry home, then, and warn Aunt Maude that he will be there. I don't suppose you might join us . . . help spread the misery thinner? I'd invite Lily, but that would be like asking the fox to guard the henhouse."

Reba shook her head and gave her familiar rusty laugh. "Lawd, honey, I'd love to be there, just to watch you and that Hancock man duel over the supper table, but that no-account Bannister is sick again, so I have to fill in for him tonight."

After extracting a promise from Jess to stop by the Lucky Nugget the next day with an account of her evening with Mr. Hancock, Reba sailed out the door once more, heading down Brimstone's dusty streets like a bright schooner.

"I'll lock up things here, Jess," Lily offered by way of apology, her mouth turned down in a rueful smile. "And I'm sorry if you're truly upset by what I did."

"I'll survive it," Jess grimly predicted, hoping she was right.

"And I'm sure by tomorrow I won't be mad at you anymore, either. But if you ever do anything like that again, I'll—"

"Fire me?" Lily asked with a grin.

Jess shook her head, feeling a wry smile twitch at her own lips. The day Lily ever left the bank would be a bleak one for Jess, indeed, and they both knew it. "No. I'll make Horace Woods ask *you* to the next dance."

"I know—I can say Papa is having a bad spell and send the man to Chan's, instead," Jess suggested. "The food there is quite good—though not as exceptional as yours, Aunt Maude—and it would save you the trouble of—"

"Please, Jessamine," Maude McCray interrupted in the pleasant accents of her native Georgia. "I am quite capable of handling a single guest, even at short notice. And I must agree with your friends that it could only be to your advantage to ply the man with a home-cooked meal."

"I'd rather ply him with a pitchfork . . . all the way out of town."

"Really, Jess." Maude moved the crystal fly-catcher from the table to the sideboard, then shook her head reprovingly at her niece. "Perhaps you just got off on the wrong foot with him. I am certain your Mr. Hancock will prove a nice enough gentleman when you get to know him better."

"He is not *my* Mr. Hancock," Jess protested yet a second time that day, wondering how he'd earned that appellation in such a short space of time. She wondered, too, how it was that the very mention of the man's name reduced her to the status of a belligerent schoolgirl. It wasn't as if she'd never dealt with difficult people, for she did so on a regular basis at the bank. Indeed, she had always prided herself on her diplomatic skills.

So why did even the thought of being cordial to Hancock make her grit her teeth in frustration?

She sighed and laid out the rest of the silverware on the snowy lace tablecloth, glancing over at her aunt as she did so. True to her word, Maude appeared unconcerned at the prospect of entertaining a stranger . . . but then, Maude never had been one to allow personal feelings to interfere with duty.

That was why Maude had refused several offers of marriage as a girl, claiming her first obligation was to take care of her widowed mother. Later, she had broken off her engagement to a dashing Confederate soldier to take care of Jess, left motherless when Lucinda McCray succumbed to a bout of influenza at the start of the war. She had remained with the family to nurse her older brother back to health after Harvey McCray returned from the war with a Union soldier's bullet in his leg.

She gave her aunt a fond look. Even after Jess was grown, Maude had continued on as the family's housekeeper. Her role once again had expanded to nurse two years ago, after Harvey McCray had been diagnosed with the lung ailment that sent the McCrays and Satterlys west to the Arizona Territory and the desert air. Now, at the age of forty-five, Maude retained much of her youthful loveliness, her porcelain complexion but lightly creased and her wheat-gold hair threaded with only a handful of silver strands. Trim and petite, Maude could pass for a woman many years younger, so that Jess always wondered why her aunt never had married.

Maude smoothed a final wrinkle from the tablecloth, then smiled at her niece. "We will be ready to dine as soon as your guest arrives. And I must say that you do look quite nice tonight, Jessamine, dear, though perhaps you might have chosen something a bit more . . ."

"Frilly?" Jess suggested with a wry smile in return.

She had exchanged the tight-cropped jacket she had worn earlier for a white, tailored shirtwaist, the substitution quite as frilly as Jess ever got. Maude, by contrast, was decked out in the palest of pink gowns, with lace and flounces enough to trim a dozen of her niece's dresses. While the older woman carried off the fashion quite well, Jess conceded, she herself would have looked and felt foolish in such an ensemble.

A sharp knock at the front door sounded, and Jess forgot about fashion. It would have been too much to hope for, she supposed, that the bank examiner had been taken ill or called away from town sometime in the past hour.

"I'll let Mr. Hancock settle in the parlor," she told her aunt as she started from the room. "Let Papa know he is here, if you would."

She spared a glimpse in the hallway mirror but forbore patting down the stray wisps of dark hair that had escaped the tortoise-shell pins keeping her chignon in place. She was not trying to impress the man, she reminded herself, but merely was showing him a modicum of civility in hopes he'd make a favorable report on her bank.

At the door, she halted, hand pausing on its knob. The wavering image of Hancock's tall figure, partly visible through the entry's small pane of bubbled glass, was distorted still further by the last of the sun's red-tinged rays. The sight sent a shiver through her, as if a goose had stepped upon her grave.

Then, just as swiftly, commonsense reasserted itself. The man might be overbearing, but he hardly possessed any unearthly powers. And, with luck, perhaps he would not linger long past dessert. Cheered by that last thought, she fixed a pleasant smile on her lips and opened the door.

Chapter Three

"Mr. Hancock," Jess murmured by way of greeting. "Please do come inside. I trust you had no difficulty in finding us?"

The man arched a dark brow. "Miss Chwang's directions were more than sufficient, especially since you live but one street away from the bank," he coolly replied as he handed over his hat. "In fact, I walked rather than try out the gelding I hired from one of the locals—I believe his name is Kirby, keeps a vicious dog."

He frowned in what Jess presumed was unpleasant remembrance of the beast in question, and she smothered a reflexive grin. She would have thought that Hancock and the hound would have found much in common with each other . . . that, or the dog would have been the one the worse for their encounter.

"Yes, I'm familiar with Mr. Kirby's stables," she managed in an even tone as she hung his bowler on the brass rack in the corner of the foyer. "Now, if you will follow me, the parlor is through here."

She led the way into a small if cheerful room with a view of the broad porch that ran the front of the house. Two black walnut chairs upholstered in horsehair-stuffed green velvet flanked a matching settee, the grouping interspersed by a pair of sturdy occasional tables. Along the far wall was a fireplace fronted by a pierced brass screen and topped with a simple oak mantelpiece. In one corner, a set of crystal decanters and a half-dozen glasses were arranged on a tall table that served as a makeshift sideboard. It was here that the McCrays entertained their guests, and here that Jess met with the occasional customer unwilling to conduct business in public.

Hancock fell into neither category, she reminded herself; still, she must show him a modicum of courtesy.

"Aunt Maude will join us in a moment. May I offer you brandy or a whiskey while we wait?"

"Whiskey will do just fine."

While she busied herself with pouring, Hancock moved about the room. He paused at the mantelpiece and indicated one of the pair of silver-framed photographs propped there. Its subject was a stiffly posed young woman dressed in a crinoline, her dark hair arranged in sausage curls about her pretty face. "A relative, I presume?"

"My mother, Lucinda McCray," Jess replied, smiling fondly in the direction of the picture as she handed the bank examiner his liquor. "She died of the influenza at the beginning of the war, when I was twelve years old. It was a very trying time. Papa had just been called up, which is why Aunt Maude came to stay with us."

"It was a trying time for many people," Hancock murmured, a note of irony in his voice. Then, returning his attention to the picture, he said, "She was a very attractive woman. You look much like her."

Jess glanced up to find the man's impassive gaze upon her as he accepted the glass. Was she imagining things, or had the imperious Mr. Hancock just paid her a second compliment this day? Feeling an unexpected blush heat her cheeks, she abruptly indicated the other photograph.

"That is my late husband, Arbin Satterly. The picture was taken by Mr. Fly in Tombstone just a few weeks before the bank robbery."

The familiar sensation of guilt nipped at her as she gazed at Arbin's tinted image. His thinning blond hair had been neatly pomaded, and his pleasant features were drawn into serious lines made sterner still by the spectacles perched upon his nose. He had just passed his thirtieth birthday, but his sober aspect was more appropriate to a man half again his age. The result was deliberate, as he had intended a larger copy of the picture to be hung on the wall of the bank.

It will reassure the customers that their money is in the care of a concerned, trustworthy gentleman, he had told her.

She had countered with her own opinion, that the photograph would announce to people that their money was in the hands of a self-important snob. It had been an unworthy sentiment, made in the aftermath of one of their increasingly frequent arguments. But, oddly enough, whenever she now tried to picture Arbin as he had been in life, her memories were always overlaid by the image of him as he appeared in this last photograph.

''A pleasant-looking fellow,'' Hancock murmured beside her. ''Quite the tragedy, for a man to be cut down so early in life.''

''Yes.'' Jess tore her gaze from the photograph and gestured the bank examiner toward a chair; then, managing a smile, she settled on the settee across from him.

Hancock was the first to break the uncomfortable silence.

''I suppose I should apologize, Mrs. Satterly, for the fact that the home office did not telegraph you in advance of my arrival.'' He took a sip of whiskey, then went on, ''Still, the purpose of my visit is to ascertain how your bank conducts business on a daily basis. Removing the element of surprise might have caused you to, shall we say, make certain adjustments in your activities for the duration of my stay.''

''Ah, yes,'' she replied, feeling her smile tighten. ''I might have decided to tally the day's deposits, or even lock the vault, for a change.''

''You misunderstand me, Mrs. Satterly. I merely meant—''

"Now, Jessamine," Maude's smooth voice interjected from the doorway, "let us not make our guest feel uncomfortable."

She glided into the room, ruffles whispering against the dark wood floors. Hancock set aside his whiskey and swiftly rose. Jess unclenched her jaw and grimly followed suit, making the introductions.

"Charmed, I'm sure, Mr. Hancock," Maude said and offered her hand.

He bent over the woman's slim fingers with a gallantry that Jess did not expect. "The pleasure is mine, ma'am. I trust your niece's invitation, welcome as it was, did not put you out unduly."

"One can never go to too much trouble for a guest, Mr. Hancock." Maude flushed becomingly, and Jess hid her surprise. Her aunt did not readily take to strange gentlemen, yet somehow Hancock had seemed to win her approval. In a warmer tone, the woman went on, "And now, sir, if you will join us in the dining room, supper is ready and my brother is awaiting us."

With Maude leading the way, they stepped into the adjoining room. Four places were set on the oak table, which was large enough to accommodate half a dozen more. At the table's head hunched a tall, gray-haired man who straightened in his chair as the trio approached.

"Hello, Papa," Jessamine said with a smile, hurrying forward to kiss his sunken cheek. "How are you feeling this evening?"

"About the same, girl . . . about the same." He raised himself a few inches from his seat and then sank back down again, the strain of even this small effort apparent in his taut features. "But never mind me, girl. Introduce me to your guest."

"Certainly, Papa. This is Mr. Jacob E. Hancock, sent to visit us by the Territorial Bankers Association. Mr. Hancock, may I present my father, Harvey McCray . . . founder of our bank."

While the two men exchanged pleasantries and Maude began transferring dishes from the sideboard to the table, Jess watched her father with carefully concealed concern. Harvey McCray had once been a bluff and beefy man, his square, flushed face reflecting his love of food and drink. But the illness that had settled in his lungs took its toll on the rest of him, as well. In the past two years it had pared his hefty frame nearly to the bone, while leaching the ruddiness from his cheeks and the rich brown hue from his hair. He moved more slowly, too, so that a stranger, upon meeting him, likely would have judged him to be a dozen years older than his true age of fifty-five.

But the one thing the illness could not rob him of was his focused mind and outspoken manner. Once both men had taken their respective chairs, Hancock seated between Jess and her father, Harvey shot the younger man a keen look.

"I suppose, Mr. Hancock, that you brought the appropriate documents from the home office authorizing you to look over our operation?"

"I certainly did, Mr. McCray, and your daughter examined them quite thoroughly; however, seeing that you still hold stock in the bank, I would be happy to bring by all the paperwork for you to look at, as well."

Harvey frowned over the offer for a moment, then smiled and shook his head. "If Jessamine is satisfied, Mr. Hancock, then so am I. Now, why don't you have a helping of Maude's pot roast and tell us the news from Kansas City."

Hancock obliged, regaling them for the next half hour with the doings of that town's politicians and socialites. As the meal progressed, talk turned to the situation regarding the gravely ill President Garfield, who had been gunned down by a would-be assassin two months earlier. The question had remained as to whether or not the vice president should take over for him.

Harvey leaned forward, a forkful of potatoes left hanging in midair. "But what of the rumors that the Cabinet finally convened to discuss the matter?" he wanted to know. "Last newspaper I saw from back East said that they agreed no action should be taken without the president's approval . . . which is not likely since, last we heard here in the Territory, he is near death."

"The rumors are correct, for once," Hancock said. "At this

point, Mr. Arthur can do nothing but wait in the wings, so to speak, until the president breathes his last. And in the meantime, politicians debate the constitutional issues and little is accomplished.''

''Then nothing much has changed over the past two years,'' Harvey confirmed in satisfaction as he finished off that last bite. ''Makes me almost glad that Arizona has yet to join the Union.''

''Now, gentlemen,'' Maude interrupted with a smile, rising from her seat, ''all this talk of politics has grown tiresome. Perhaps we might have dessert and speak of more pleasant topics. Don't you agree, Jessamine?''

''Yes, certainly,'' Jess murmured.

In truth, however, she had heard little of the evening's conversation. She had managed to nod and smile, at intervals, lest her father or aunt remark upon her inattention. Still, concern for her father mixed with uncertainty over Hancock's presence in her bank had served to keep her preoccupied throughout the meal. And while the question of where she had met the man before continued to nag at her, nothing in his conversation had stirred any memory.

Harvey, meanwhile, shoved aside his empty plate and leaned forward. ''Now, Jessamine, this is the first time I've ever heard you claim not to be interested in politics. What's the matter, girl . . . are you still upset with Mr. Hancock, here, for dropping by the bank like he did?''

''I'm not upset with him, Papa,'' Jess lied with a cool smile. ''Mr. Hancock is only doing his job. I suppose what I'm wondering is, what spurred the Association to send him down now? The letters made no mention of any irregularities . . .''

The question hung for a moment while Maude cut the rich chocolate cake for which she was famous. Hancock accepted his slice; then, clearing his throat, he turned toward Jess.

''You are quite right, Mrs. Satterly. There are no irregularities in your procedures.'' He paused, looking uncomfortable . . . which, for Hancock, meant he knitted his brow. ''I chose not to mention this earlier, not wishing to alarm you without due cause, but I suppose you should be told. You see, the Association has heard rumors that the Black Horse Gang has returned to the territory.''

The Black Horse Gang.

As always, when Jess heard that name spoken aloud, she shivered. Even a year before that terrible day of the Brimstone bank robbery, the mention of those outlaws had made the town's upstanding citizens frown in concern. Riding their trademark black steeds, and led by a brutal young man by the name of Rory Devilbiss, the gang had bullied and robbed their way through the county. Arbin's murder had been but a single vicious crime to be laid at their door.

''Those vile killers?'' Maude gasped out, dropping her serving fork with a clatter. ''Dear Lord, you think they'll try to rob the bank again?''

Harvey patted his sister's hand in a reassuring gesture, though his gaze rested on Jess as he spoke. ''Now, Maude, I'm sure he doesn't mean anything of the sort. It's not often that the same outlaws return to hold up a bank they've already robbed once. They would know that new security measures were probably put in place, and that the bank employees would be more watchful. And since they're wanted for murder, too . . . hell, they'd be fools to return to Brimstone.''

''Mr. McCray is quite right, ma'am,'' Hancock told her, though he, too, glanced at Jess as he spoke. ''We're just taking precautionary measures. I am certain your niece has nothing to worry about.''

Nothing to worry about.

Deliberately, Jess relaxed the grip on her fork that had caused her knuckles to go white. Of course, Hancock and her father were correct. Even if the Black Horse Gang had returned to the area, even if they were intent on robbery, chances were they'd set their sights on another town and bank.

But what if they didn't?

''Tell me, Mr. Hancock,'' she managed in even tones, ''has the marshal been informed of this?''

''I am certain he would have received the usual dispatches

that circulate among lawmen, but I've not spoken with him, myself. As I said, the gang's presence in this part of the territory is simply rumor, and nothing more."

Harvey frowned. "But if they *are* back, that means the law will have another chance at them. Hell, if my lungs weren't half gone, I'd have been after them, myself . . . not that Arbin should have tried to stand up to them in the first place. A nice enough fellow, but too meek for gunplay. Don't know what made him go for that pistol."

But I do. Jess took a deep breath, trying to ignore the fingers of guilt that clawed at her heart. *I know exactly why he did it.*

"It's always best for civilians to cooperate in such cases," she heard Hancock say, repeating the same sentiment both the marshal and the charter company had expressed to her even as they had offered their sympathy. "Any other course of action is far too risky."

"What's done is done," Harvey pointed out. "Those bastards who went and shot him damn well deserve to hang."

No, they don't, the thought drifted through Jess's mind with icy clarity. *They should be shot down on the street, just as he was.*

She glanced up to see that the others were looking at her, their expressions ranging from pain to embarrassment. Again, Hancock was the first to break the silence.

"Do forgive me, Mrs. Satterly," he said, and she thought she heard a genuine note of regret in his voice. "I never should have let the conversation take such a turn. Perhaps we might confirm tomorrow's agenda instead. As you earlier pointed out, the ledgers still beg to be examined. I trust ten o'clock tomorrow morning would not be too early for me to stop in again?"

She stifled the smallest of sighs and conceded defeat. "Ten o'clock would be just fine, Mr. Hancock."

His cool blue gaze lingered on her for a moment, and she thought she saw a glint of amusement in his eyes. No doubt the man knew exactly how exasperating she found him, and how eager she was to be done with the whole business.

"Very well," he replied and glanced about the table. "While

I've enjoyed your hospitality, I fear I must make an early evening of it. I have notes to make and a few dispatches to write. I am certain that you understand."

Maude and Harvey both made the expected polite protests, which Hancock rebuffed with equal civility, and the foursome rose. With the compliments paid to the supper and the company, Jess found herself with the dubious pleasure of showing the man out.

"Until tomorrow, Mrs. Satterly," Hancock said briskly as he took his hat. It wasn't until he reached the bottom step of the porch, however, that she impulsively called out to him.

"One last thing, Mr. Hancock," she began, then paused. *Blast it all, would he think her a trembling female if she asked it?* When he merely stood there, waiting expectantly, she forged on, "About the Black Horse Gang . . . do you truly think there is any danger they'll come back?"

"As I said, it is only rumor. I daresay you have nothing at all to worry about." He nodded and then clamped his hat upon his head. "Now, do try to have the ledgers ready tomorrow promptly on the hour, Mrs. Satterly."

"They'll be waiting for you," Jess managed through gritted teeth, her relief tempered by a return of her earlier annoyance. She refrained from slamming the door on his retreating form but did allow herself a few uncomplimentary words under her breath as she watched the shadows swallow him. Really, the man was quite impossible . . . and far too handsome for such a stodgy occupation.

Irked at the direction her thoughts were taking, she deliberately shut the door. Indeed, she was as bad as any man, letting herself be distracted by a pretty face. Had he buckteeth like Horace Woods, she never would have overlooked his overbearing manner to the extent that she had. As for his abilities as a bank examiner, she had only the company's word as to his qualifications . . . that, and his word that he was, indeed, the same Jacob E. Hancock mentioned in those letters.

She slowly turned and leaned against the door, hands behind her back, clutching at the knob. Perhaps she was just being overly cautious, or even petty. After all, the charter company did send its agents around on an annual basis. Hancock had seemed knowledgeable enough about banking protocol; besides which, the official lettering and seals on that sheaf of documents he had shown her was genuine, she felt sure.

But what harm could there be in telegraphing the main office tomorrow morning for confirmation, just to put her mind at ease?

The man who called himself Jake Hancock paused a few minutes later on the dark, dusty street in front of his hotel. The town had settled in for the night, but all was not still. The tinkling of an off-key piano drifted to him, the bright, discordant notes combining with the echo of raucous laughter. The sound was one he knew well, almost homey in its familiarity. But then, he spent a considerable amount of time in saloons.

For it was in such establishments that he sought them out . . . the drunken braggarts, unwittingly divulging their darkest secrets; the hard-faced saloon girls, eagerly betraying the cowboys who'd not paid them for their services; the lonely miners, wistfully seeking a bit of conversation. For the price of a two-bit whiskey, he could learn anything about anybody, and use that information to his benefit.

Deliberately, he turned his back on the hotel and followed the music. It led to the Lucky Nugget, whose brightly painted sign he had noticed that afternoon as the stagecoach rumbled past. He shouldered his way past the bat-wing doors, blinking against the haze of cigar smoke combined with the yellow glare of gas lamps, and took his measure of the room.

It was no different from the countless other saloons in countless other western towns through which he'd passed. A battered piano sat in the corner nearest the door, a dignified Negro with silver hair pounding away at its yellowed keys. A dozen round tables—the last three topped with green baize for playing faro and poker—ran parallel to the oak bar that took up almost one side of the saloon's narrow length. The long mirror behind the bar reflected back the twenty or so men who sat drinking and playing cards. One or two spared him a glance neither hostile nor curious. Acknowledging that lack of interest with a bland look of his own, he started toward the bar.

A stout, brassy-haired woman dressed in a low-cut gown of pale purple satin and old enough to be his mother stood behind the bar in animated conversation with another customer. Noticing him, she gave that grizzled man a rusty laugh and sidled over to where he now leaned, one new boot propped on the brass foot rail.

"Well, now, my good-looking friend, what can I do for you?" the woman asked, toweling an imaginary spot from the bar's gleaming surface.

He plucked a coin from his waistcoat and laid it on the bar. "Whiskey," he replied, and favored her with the slow smile that worked on women of all ages.

It worked on her, as well. She gave him a conspiratorial wink and then reached under the bar, withdrawing an unopened bottle whose label proclaimed its contents to be Kentucky's finest. Cracking open its seal, she caught up a glass and poured him a generous couple of fingers' worth of the liquor.

"My best . . . not like that cheap stuff the rest of them is drinking," she assured him in a stage whisper.

She slid the glass toward him and leaned both elbows on the bar top, the gesture affording him a better look at the expanse of her powdered bosom. It was a coquette's trick she must have learned years ago, long before the pale flesh now fairly popping from its confines of boned satin had taken on the delicately wrinkled look of tissue that had been crushed and then smoothed. The gesture must be habit; that, or she was under the delusion that she still was irresistible to men almost half her age.

He politely toasted her and took a sip, expecting to choke down a mouthful of burning liquid disguised as bourbon. Instead, it slid down his throat with a smooth heat he'd almost forgotten after weeks in this godforsaken country.

His surprise must have shown on his face, for she grinned.

"Didn't expect the good stuff out here, did ya? Name's Reba Starr, and I'm the owner of this fine establishment. Welcome to Brimstone, Mr. Hancock."

He took another sip, then lifted a wry brow. "You know my name."

"Lawd, yes. I make it my business to know every good-looking man that comes into town." Her grin never slipped, but he saw the shrewd glint in her pale green eyes as she went on. "I heard tell you're checking on things at the bank. Any problems a businesswoman like me ought to know?"

"Strictly routine, Miss Starr," he replied, smooth as the bourbon he was drinking. "But tell me, how did you know what my business here in Brimstone was? I've made a point of keeping matters confidential."

"Hell, Jess Satterly is a friend of mine. She told me what was going on."

She broke off abruptly as a bellow rose from the newcomers at the other end of the bar. "Hold your horses, boys, I'm coming," she shouted back, then turned to him again with a grin. "You'd best tell your boss to send around a more homely sort next time, if you're wanting to keep things under your hat. There wasn't a female in the bank all day that didn't notice you was hanging around . . . and I'm not just talking the customers, if you get my meaning," she added with a broad wink.

With a final flick of her towel, she sauntered back down the bar again. He took the opportunity to escape to an unoccupied table, aware of an unaccustomed heat rising along the back of his neck. *Just the whiskey,* he told himself, deliberately taking another swallow, and knowing his denial for the lie it was. Much as it pained him to admit it, from the moment he'd first laid eyes on Jessamine Satterly, he'd been hard-pressed to keep his attention on his mission.

It wasn't that she was a great beauty . . . though, to be fair, she was attractive enough. He took another drink, picturing her wide eyes the same golden brown as his whiskey and her mane of dark hair that would spill like molasses across a man's pillow, should she ever untwist it from its prim knot. Still, he'd known numerous women whose pale, chiseled beauty would make her appear dowdy by comparison. And it certainly wasn't her dulcet personality that drew him. Her tongue was as sharp as her mind, and he'd always preferred his women pleasant and pliant.

Perhaps what had distracted him was the simple element of surprise.

Prior to his arrival in Brimstone, he had known nothing more of Jessamine Satterly than her name and her marital status, save for the mental picture the word *widow* had conjured. He'd pictured her as a tough, middle-aged female who cared more for banking than babies, and whose attractions lay in her bottom line, rather than elsewhere. And as he'd always had a way with the ladies—particularly the less than attractive ones—he had counted on her not objecting to his prolonged presence in her bank. For once, however, he'd been wrong on two accounts . . . her lack of beauty and her susceptibility to his charms.

Still, he had accomplished much of what he'd set out to do, with time enough tomorrow to continue with his work. In the meanwhile, it would behoove him to glean a bit of knowledge regarding Brimstone's other citizens. Deliberately, he leaned back in his chair, the hard edges of the Colt peacemaker he wore tucked into the waistband of his trousers pressing into his spine. With a studied air of casualness, he let his gaze drift over his fellow customers.

They were cowboys and miners, mostly, with what looked like a merchant or two mixed among their number. Despite the flowing whiskey, they seemed a subdued enough lot, given that he'd been in the Lucky Nugget a good quarter of an hour and not yet witnessed a single fight. All were locals, he judged, content to swap stories and play a hand or two of poker for small stakes. On a Saturday night, when young bucks from the outlying mines and ranches drifted in, the atmosphere likely grew a bit rowdier; still, he suspected Reba had little more to contend with than the occasional brawl among her clientele.

He gave a satisfied nod. Experience had taught him that the local saloon usually was an accurate barometer of a town's temperament. Brimstone, despite its incendiary name, seemed a phlegmatic sort of place, the kind of town that he liked. Given a crisis, the locals would likely opt for talk rather than action.

And given a bank robbery, they'd likely not rush to form up a posse.

That last was a valuable bit of information to know, given that he had it on good authority that such a robbery was imminent . . . despite what he had told Jess Satterly.

Absently, he patted his shirt pocket to reassure himself that a certain piece of paper he'd been carrying about for a couple of weeks was still safely on his person. The information contained within it he'd long since consigned to memory; still, he might find that the written evidence of what he'd been told would come in useful in the future.

After a reasonable amount of time had passed, he set down his glass and got to his feet. Sometime tomorrow, he'd manage an excuse to check out the town marshal and whoever else passed for the law in Brimstone. Before that, though, he'd finish his inspection of the bank and mentally draw up the best ways out of town if one was in a hurry to leave. By the end of the day, he'd have all the information he needed and would be prepared for any eventuality.

He allowed himself a slow, satisfied smile as he made his way back onto the street. Save for his slight miscalculation regarding Jessamine Satterly, everything was going according to plan.

Chapter Four

"So, Jess, did you and Mr. Hancock have a pleasant supper last night?" Lily asked, looking up from the cash drawer she was arranging.

The young woman's words were casual enough, but her eyes sparkled with curiosity. A quarter hour already had passed since the two women had first entered the empty bank, and Jess had yet to bring up the subject. Now, her only reply was an expressive sound of dismissal as she pulled the last ledger from the locked cabinet beneath the teller counter.

She laid it with a thump atop the others already piled on the gleaming wood surface. A fine layer of dust promptly settled on the gleaming wood, and she sneezed.

Lily smiled. "A sneeze is a sign that one is thinking of romance. It is an old Chinese saying."

"Old Chinese saying, my foot," Jess replied with a scowl. She was more than familiar with the younger woman's habit of spontaneously concocting creative nuggets of wisdom, which she then attributed to her Asian forebears. "A sneeze simply means someone has forgotten to dust under the counter . . . again."

"Really, Jess, you have no sense of humor," Lily exclaimed, her smile broadening into a grin. "Now tell me, how did your handsome bank examiner enjoy his supper with the McCray family?"

Jess squared the pile of ledgers and shot her an impatient look. "Very well, I will tell all, if you'll promise not to bring up the subject again. Aunt Maude's cooking was excellent, as usual, especially the pot roast and chocolate cake. Father felt quite well, for a change, and seemed to enjoy having a visitor. The discussion was mostly about politics, with a few mentions of fashion for Aunt Maude's benefit. As for Mr. Hancock . . ."

She paused, searching for the right words that would not give Lily cause to pursue her role as matchmaker . . . or give her cause for worry, either. For Jess could not help but recall the man's mention of the rumor that the Black Horse Gang had returned to the vicinity. The possibility of a return visit from those killers left her with an uneasy feeling, no matter that she agreed with her father that such a likelihood was remote. Still, as a bank employee, Lily had the right to know of any potential risks to her safety. But perhaps it would be better to broach that subject later, once she'd had another chance to quiz the bank examiner as to what he truly knew.

"As for Mr. Hancock," she finally went on, "his company was tolerable, if not overly enjoyable. And he's not *my* handsome bank examiner, I'll have you know."

"As a matter of fact," a cool voice interrupted them, "I believe that I am. Your bank examiner, I mean," he clarified with a faint smile as they turned in his direction, "that is, unless the charter company has made an unprecedented mistake."

Hancock stood in the doorway, bowler hat in hand. His lean form was lit by the morning sun, giving him the dramatic appearance of a figure from some master's painted canvas. *Jacob E. Hancock, Come to Call.* Jess mentally dubbed that fictitious work of art, even as she felt twin spots of heat settle in her cheeks. What was it about the man that seemed to put her to a disadvantage?

"He's back," Lily murmured unnecessarily as he started

toward them. "Shall I take care of him or leave matters to you?"

"I'll handle him," Jess said with a firm nod and made her way around the counter. She'd not let the man intimidate her, or allow herself to give in to embarrassment. After all, it was his own fault he'd overheard her less than complimentary comments. He had slipped inside the bank even though the CLOSED sign in the window warned that the establishment had not yet opened for business.

She ostentatiously glanced at the Regulator on the far wall, which showed the time to be ten minutes until the hour; then, with the same show of innocent surprise, she checked the watch pinned to her lapel.

"A bit early, are you not, Mr. Hancock?" she politely observed. Not waiting for his reply, she indicated the stack of books on the countertop. "The ledgers are ready, just as you asked. You may use my office if you wish."

She folded her arms across her chest and waited expectantly. He was wearing the same gray suit of yesterday, though he'd exchanged both the black waistcoat and the ruffled white shirt for different garb . . . the former for a charcoal-colored vest and the latter for a high-collared shirt with a charcoal tie. He had a dusty look about him, as if he'd spent the morning wandering Brimstone's unpaved streets, not that such an occurrence was likely. In her experience, men like Hancock did not make extended forays on foot.

He gave her a crisp nod, seemingly unperturbed by her blunt manner. "Good morning, Mrs. Satterly . . . and thank you again for yesterday's kind invitation. I quite enjoyed making the acquaintance of your family. Now, if you do not mind, I think I would rather avail myself of one of those tables to go over the ledgers."

"Certainly."

Feeling oddly chastened, Jess helped him carry the books to the far table. By the time he had settled everything to his satisfaction, including the cup of hot tea that Lily had brought him, the clock was chiming the hour. Jess excused herself to prop open the heavy wooden door and turn the sedate window sign to indicate that the bank now was open.

The sounds of Brimstone promptly drifted in . . . the rumble of wagon wheels and clomp of horses' hooves; the jingle of tack and the shouts of drivers to their teams; the murmured greetings as friends and acquaintances passed on the street; even the faint tinkle of piano keys from the Lucky Nugget, which never shut its doors. It was a prosperous sound, Jess thought, the heartbeat of a town with a future. Used as she had been to the more sedate noises of a so-called civilized city like St. Louis, it had taken her some time to accustom herself to Brimstone's more raucous pulse. But now, even with the tragedy that had befallen her here, she felt herself quite at home.

She ushered the first of the day's customers inside and then joined Lily behind the closest of the teller counter's barred windows. "I'm afraid Mr. Hancock's presence will be far more noticeable today," she murmured with a sigh. "Just stick with yesterday's story about routine consultations, and with any luck, we'll be rid of the man before tomorrow."

"Don't worry, everything will be fine," Lily assured her in the same low tones. Then her tigress gaze drifted toward the man in question, and she frowned. "Really, Jess, I do think you could be a bit more cordial to him, even if you have decided he's not the man for you. After all, it's not his fault he has an unpleasant job, checking up on people. And I rather think that he likes you."

"You do?"

Clamping her jaw tight before it could drop open in surprise, she spared the man another look. He appeared absorbed in the figures before him, a slight frown creasing his brow . . . hardly the expression of a man contemplating a woman whom he liked.

Indeed, she'd seen no indication since yesterday afternoon that he thought of her with anything more than professional tolerance at best. To that end, she had come girded for figurative combat this morning, her tailored jacket and skirt of steel-gray poplin trimmed in black braid lacking any hint of feminine charm. The outfit gave her the look of someone's maiden aunt, Maude earlier had declared in well-bred horror as Jess prepared to leave the house.

Well, perhaps not an aunt, the older woman had conceded with a smile as she'd caught a glimpse of her own blue-ruffled figure in the foyer mirror. *Maybe a spinster cousin.* Jess, however, had been more than satisfied with the image she projected. If Hancock had any doubts as to her efficiency, her appearance alone should give him pause. And if it nipped in the bud any incipient feelings of ardor, so much the better.

To Lily, however, she merely said, "I promise, I'll try to do better. Now, both of us had better get to work."

She spent the next two hours conducting the usual business—making loans, offering advice on prudent investments—while Lily handled the withdrawing and depositing of funds. In between customers, Jess managed the paperwork that had accumulated in her office. For his part, Hancock left her undisturbed, keeping to his ledgers and glancing up only to request more tea.

"Quite excellent," he pronounced with a slow smile as Lily refilled his cup during a lull. "I must confess, Miss Chwang, that I have been only an indifferent tea drinker in the past, but I do believe you have converted me. Tell me, is this your own blend?"

"It's an old family recipe," she modestly admitted, though Jess glimpsed a spark of amusement in the young woman's eyes as the latter glanced her way. "We call it by a name that roughly translates to 'encouraging one to sneeze.' "

"Unusual name," he observed, even as Jess opened her own eyes wide in dismay. "Perhaps you might allow me to purchase a tin to take home with me?"

Assuring the man that she would make him a gift of it, Lily hurried back to her post behind the barred window. She adroitly avoided noticing Jess's attempts to gesture her over to one side, instead engaging herself in swift conversation with old Mrs. Pomeroy, who had come to make her regular deposit. Defeated, Jess returned to her office, consoling herself with the thought that, upon further consideration, she most certainly did not want to know any more about the infamous tea.

But when the clock chimed the noon hour, and Hancock still had not indulged in any spontaneous affectionate demonstrations, Jess happily concluded that it must not contain any mysterious Oriental love potions. That issue put to rest, she was able to face him with equanimity.

''I have a matter to which I must attend, Mr. Hancock, and so I must leave the bank for half an hour,'' she told him. ''But perhaps when I return, you might join Lily and me for a bite of luncheon. You see, Aunt Maude has offered to bring by a basket of last night's leftovers . . . including, I am certain, the remainder of her chocolate cake. Or, if you prefer something else, there is always Chan's—''

''My dear Mrs. Satterly''—he cut her short with a faint smile—''I certainly would not pass up another opportunity to sample your aunt's cooking.'' So saying, he shut the topmost ledger and rose. ''But I, too, have a matter beyond the bank's walls that requires my attention. If I might meet you back here in, say, three-quarters of an hour?''

''That would be fine. Do go on, and I shall advise Lily of our plans.''

As Hancock took his leave, Jess carried the books back to the teller counter, explaining to her assistant that both she and Hancock would return within the hour. ''And ask Aunt Maude to remain, as well. We'll close for half an hour and make a picnic of it.'' She paused, debating the wisdom of her next words, then blurted, ''Tell me the truth, Lily; was there anything . . . unusual about the tea you served Mr. Hancock?''

''It was only tea,'' Lily assured her, trying and failing to suppress a grin. ''Oh, Jess, you should have seen your face when I talked about sneezing. It was a wonder that I didn't burst out laughing.''

''What's a wonder is that I don't send you packing,'' Jess retorted, though a grudging smile now tugged at her own lips. ''Very well. See if you can't keep order around here for a few minutes while I'm gone.''

Jess left the bank and started up the street, blinking against the noon sun. The day had proved a pleasant one, so that she was not the only one abroad. In the months when the temperature soared well above the comfort zone, the townspeople ventured out onto the streets only in the morning or evening, when the heat was bearable. Now, however, people bustled about at all hours, relieved to be free of their self-imposed exile from the desert sun.

She smiled and nodded at her fellow passersby, her trim boots clicking purposefully along the sturdy wooden sidewalk as she made her way toward the telegraph office. Such walkways lined both sides of the town's main avenue and were no citified affectation, but a necessity. Despite the fact that Brimstone was a relatively sedate territorial town, its streets saw an inordinate amount of traffic . . . from the carts and wagons moving to and from the outlying mines to the steady parade of riders on horseback. A pedestrian on the unpaved road truly was at-risk, whether of falling victim to a runaway wagon, or of tromping through the inevitable mounds of horse droppings that dotted the thoroughfares.

A few minutes later, she reached the telegraph office. It was located two streets over from the bank, in the same building that housed the *Brimstone Fire.* Ted Markham served double duty as both telegraph operator and newspaper publisher. It was a serendipitous combination, he often assured her with a grin, since he was always the first in town to know everyone else's business. Now, the balding, mustachioed man in the ink-stained apron gave her a nod as the bell on the door tinkled out her presence.

"Be with you in a moment, Mrs. Satterly," he said, returning his attention to the bespectacled man with whom he'd been haggling over the wording of an advertisement.

While she waited, Jess amused herself by trying to read the backwards type already set up on the press in preparation for the *Fire*'s next issue. One headline expressed concern regarding the latest town ordinance covering the collection of liquor taxes. Another congratulated Marshal Crenshaw on his recent apprehension of a horse thief, and gave him equal praise for scaring off the population of stray coyotes that scavenged about town. When Ted limped over to her, she had just finished an article on the upcoming town social.

Contributors to the fund for this annual event include Mrs. Jessamine Satterly, owner of the First National Bank of Brimstone.

''Sorry for the wait, Jess,'' he said, dropping his earlier formality and giving her a wry grin. ''I tried to convince old Tom that he didn't need to list the entire pedigree of that sorrel he's trying to sell, but he had his mind set. So, what can I do for you today . . . another advertisement for the bank?''

She shook her head and reached into her reticule for the message she had composed to the Territorial Bankers Association last night.

Please confirm identity of J. E. Hancock, arrived Brimstone yesterday, claims is bank examiner authorized by charter company.

She felt a bit foolish for giving way to her suspicions regarding the man; still, the cost of the message was a small price to pay to satisfy her questions.

''Actually, Ted, I'd like to send a telegram. It's something of an emergency, so if you might—''

''Darn it, Jess, I can't,'' he interrupted her, a sour expression settling over his mild features. ''The telegraph lines are down again. Probably the same thing as last time . . . some damn-fool drunken miner took a potshot at a buzzard perched on one of the poles and ended up hitting the lines instead. I sent Jamie to check things out, but it might be late this afternoon before he can finish any repairs. If you want, I can hang on to your message until then.''

Jess hesitated, then crumpled the paper into a ball. ''Perhaps it wasn't as important as I thought, after all,'' she replied, wondering if this was some sort of divine sign that her suspicions had been unfounded. "If I change my mind, I'll stop by later."

"Whatever suits you. Sorry for the inconvenience." He hesitated a moment, as well, then blurted, "Listen, Jess, about the town social next week. I was wondering if . . . well, if you might want to go with me."

Jess took a deep breath. She'd known for some time that the newspaper editor's interest in her went beyond that of a business relationship, though she had never considered him to be anything more than a friend. Still, he would not be entirely unacceptable as a suitor. Though several years older than she, Ted possessed a wit and intelligence that she appreciated. As to his appearance, he was a pleasant-enough-looking man, his limp the result of a war wound he'd suffered years before as a young cavalry officer. That last was quite a romantic detail, according to a number of Brimstone's unmarried women, who considered him imminently eligible. But she could hardly say yes to him now, after yesterday's melodramatic declarations to Lily and Reba.

"If you don't mind, Ted, I'll let you know tomorrow," she temporized. "I have a few matters concerning bank business that I need to handle first, before I worry about my social life."

"All right, but I'm warning you, Mabel Willingsworth has her eye on me," he answered with a grin, naming one of those same females who Jess knew had declared the man a prime matrimonial candidate. "She's sent over two homemade pies already this week and hinted there'll be more to come if I do the right thing."

"I consider myself forewarned," Jess said with a laugh and headed toward the door. Perhaps she should accept his invitation, and see where matters led from there. *But he's nowhere near as handsome as Mr. Hancock,* she could hear Lily's teasing voice in her ear.

And then a series of sharp booms stopped her in her tracks. *Gunfire?* But a recently passed ordinance prohibited the discharge of any weapon within the town limits. *Perhaps it's just the coyotes come back, and the marshal is scaring them off,* came the fleeting hopeful thought. And then the pounding rhythm of hoofbeats interspersed with the distant sound of women's screams drifted to her.

The Association has heard rumors that the Black Horse Gang has returned to the territory.

"Dear God, the bank!"

She started down the sidewalk at a dead run, barely hearing Ted Markham calling after her, barely noticing other townspeople poking their heads from their homes and shops. How many shots had been fired . . . a dozen, perhaps more? From the pattern of sound, she guessed there had been more than one shooter, though whether they were aiming at the same target or returning each other's fire, she could not guess. Neither could she be sure without seeing that the shots even had come from her bank.

She clung to that last hopeful thought for as long as she could, until she reached Main Street. By the time she halted there, she was gasping for breath; still, the sight that greeted her made her cry out in horror.

A faint drifting of dust and black smoke clung to the street like a malevolent ghost, while the smell of discharged gunpowder filled the air. The screams she'd heard earlier had long since died, replaced by the wails of frightened children and the frantic shouts of men. While the women, for the most part, remained on the sidewalks comforting their offspring, a score of men huddled in a loose knot on the street in front of the mercantile.

Two or three of their number bent over what Jess could only guess was a fallen man. That guess was confirmed when Doc Caldwell, jacket askew and black bag in hand, rushed down the wooden stairs from his second-story office over the haberdashery. With Jess close on his heels, he hurried as quickly as his stout form would allow in the direction of the crowd

They parted for him, only to close ranks again as Jess approached.

"You'd best stay back, Miz Satterly," warned a rail-thin

young miner whom she knew as Billy Barton. Turning his back on the cluster of men, he held out a warning hand. "There's men been shot, and it don't look good."

"Who's been shot, Billy? What happened?" she demanded, trying to peer past his skinny shoulder.

Billy shook his head and spat a brown stream of tobacco juice. "It was them, the Black Horse Gang," he confirmed. "They robbed the bank again. From what I hear, Miz Chwang's just fine, but they shot the marshal and Deputy Bowser, both."

"The Black Horse Gang, you say?" Ted Markham exclaimed in grim tones, rushing up behind them.

Billy nodded and stepped aside to let him join the huddle of men. This time, Jess caught a glimpse of the two men sprawled in the dirt. Doc Caldwell had been bent over one. Now he shook his head and turned his attention to the other victim; then, raising his head again, he shouted, "He's still breathing! Get him to my office, quick!"

Abruptly, four men broke from the group, carrying the limp form of Deputy Bowser. Jess glimpsed a bloodstained arm dangling as they moved at a half-trot in the direction of the haberdashery, the doctor right behind them. The remaining men stayed behind, gathered in a grim half-circle around the fallen figure of Marshal Crenshaw.

"Oh, no," she breathed in dismay, taking a few reflexive steps back. She'd been through this same tragedy once before . . . yet, horrible as it was, she seemed suddenly unable to avert her gaze.

Thankfully, Crenshaw's face was turned away from her, but Jess could see the bright blood that had soaked his shirtfront crimson and had spread in a dark puddle beneath him. Ted was kneeling beside the man, gripping a faded blue horse blanket that someone had handed him. Gently, he draped the length of pale wool over the marshal's face and torso, then awkwardly rose again. At his murmured words, two men stepped forward, one bending to take hold of the dead man's feet and the other supporting his shoulders.

Jess shut her eyes and turned, memories of Arbin's death

washing over her. In a flash, she saw it happen again . . . Arbin picking up the derringer, the outlaw's cool blue eyes gleaming above the dirty red bandanna tied over his face. *Say your prayers, partner,* that man had proclaimed. *It's over, 'cept for the buryin' part.*

Then the outlaw's pistol roared and Arbin fell, clutching his chest. He had lived long enough for her to rush to his side and, kneeling, lift his head into her lap. He had stared at her in confusion and then, with a strangled gasp, he had gone limp, the uncertainty in his hazel eyes fading to dullness.

Abruptly, a woman's frantic voice broke in on her grim memories and made her open her eyes once more. "Jess! Jess, where have you been?" Lily cried, rushing through the bank's open doors and out into the street.

Sidestepping a small, crushed willow basket and the yellow pup that was greedily eating whatever it had held, Jess hurried the short distance to meet her there. "Oh, Lily," she softly exclaimed as they walked back inside the bank together, "I'm so glad you are all right. I'd never have forgiven myself if—"

"Jess, they robbed the bank," the young woman tearfully broke in on her words, "but that's not the worst of it."

"I know. I saw Marshal Crenshaw. He's dead, and Deputy Bowser is shot as well. They've taken him to Doc Caldwell's office, and—"

"No, you don't understand!" Lily broke free from her grasp and took a step back, her tiger-gold eyes dark with emotion. "Before the gang rode out of town, they took a hostage. I tried to stop them, but there was nothing I could do."

She paused to swipe at her damp cheeks, then wailed, "Jess, the Black Horse Gang has taken your Aunt Maude!"

Chapter Five

"Taken Aunt Maude?" Jess echoed numbly as a wave of light-headedness swept her. "Dear Lord, why?"

"As insurance, of course."

The crisp words belonged not to Lily, but to Hancock, who had entered the bank unnoticed by either woman. Striding toward the same table where he'd earlier been working, he went on. "If the gang finds themselves cornered by a posse, they'll use her as a bargaining chip . . . but in the meantime, her presence makes it less likely some overly enthusiastic lawman will take potshots at them."

With that dire pronouncement, he grabbed up one of the chairs, then set it down with a thump behind Jess and unceremoniously pressed her into its wooden embrace. "Here, sit down before you fall down," he bluntly ordered, then turned his attention to Lily. "Now, Miss Chwang, why don't you tell me what happened here."

Jess straightened in her chair and shot him an outraged look. "I'll tell you what happened. The Black Horse Gang robbed my bank and kidnapped my Aunt Maude!"

"I am quite aware of the basic facts," came his cool reply.

"What I'm asking for are details that might help us determine just exactly where they have taken Miss McCray. I do have some experience in these matters, you know."

"As much experience as you have in predicting bank robberies?"

At her caustic tone, he raised a cool brow. "I'm not sure what you mean, Mrs. Satterly."

"Damn you, Mr. Hancock, you know exactly what I mean!"

Jess sprang up again, ignoring the wobbliness in her legs. "You told me not to worry about the Black Horse Gang, and I believed you. If you'd even hinted there was a chance of this happening, I would have warned the marshal and posted some guards, and I never would have left Lily and Maude here alone. But now, because of you, a good man is dead and another one seriously hurt . . . and my aunt has been kidnapped by killers!"

Those last words trembled dangerously on the verge of tears, and Jess broke off, not trusting herself to say more. As she started to turn away, however, she felt Lily's soft touch on her arm.

"Wait, Jess, you're not being fair to Mr. Hancock," the younger woman protested. "Even if he *had* told you to worry, and you took every precaution, that doesn't mean the Black Horse Gang wouldn't have tried to rob us anyway. And it might have been worse. . . . they might have killed even more people."

Her grip on Jess's arm tightened. "I know you are terribly distraught right now, but please don't blame Mr. Hancock for all of this. It wasn't like he helped the Black Horse Gang rob us."

Jess took a deep breath. Lily was right, of course, though the knowledge did nothing to lessen her resentment of the man. Had the entire town been forewarned, they might have been forearmed and, at the very least, inflicted equal damage on the Black Horse Gang. Equally distressing was the way the man now seemed to think he was in charge of investigating the robbery. It was her bank, after all, so the questioning of Lily rightfully should be left to her.

Hancock, meanwhile, had levelly met Jess's accusing gaze.

"Actually, you are right," he agreed in what was, for him, a humble tone. "I realize now I should have been more direct in my suspicions, but that does not undo what has already happened. Now, if you don't mind, Miss Chwang"—he turned again in Lily's direction—"why don't you take Mrs. Satterly's chair and describe exactly what happened."

"Wouldn't it be better to form a posse and ride after the gang instead?" Jess pointed out, trying one last time to take charge. "Every moment we delay puts them farther from Brimstone, and my aunt in greater danger."

"To the contrary, if we first have some idea of where they are headed, it will be easier for a posse to catch up with them. Now, go ahead, Miss Chwang . . . Lily. Tell us exactly what happened from the moment the gang stepped inside the bank, every word you can remember them saying, even if it doesn't seem important."

Lily took a seat and shot Jess a questioning look. At least her assistant knew who was in charge there, Jess thought wryly, as she gave the younger woman a grudging nod of approval. Clasping her hands tightly in her lap, Lily focused her gaze on the open door, as if picturing the outlaws standing before her again.

"It happened about fifteen minutes after you and Jess left. The only people in the bank besides me were Mr. Tilton and Maude. I heard them before I saw them. . . . the sound of hooves as they rode up, the jingling of their spurs. Four men came inside, though there were others waiting on the street."

Hancock gave her an approving nod. "You're doing fine so far. Now tell me, what did they look like, what were they wearing? And did one or another of them seem to be in charge?"

"One man was about your height, Mr. Hancock, and I think he was their leader. Another one was much taller, and the other two were shorter. But they all wore light brown dusters and tan pants, so it was hard to tell them apart . . . especially since I couldn't see much of their faces," she admitted. "They had red bandannas tied over their noses and mouths, and straw hats pulled down low on their brows.

Just like the first time, Jess thought with a shiver, recalling the man who had shot her husband. Only his cold blue eyes had been visible over the bright cloth that obscured the rest of his features. Otherwise, he had been as anonymous as the others of the gang.

Lily didn't seem to notice her distress, however, her attention still focused on the past as she continued. "They came in single file and spread out across the bank. The two shorter men took up positions at the front of the bank, one at the door and one at the window. The other two walked up to the counter. The very tall man stood there holding a crowbar in one hand and some sort of leather satchels—or saddlebags, perhaps—in the other. The one who was their leader shoved old Mr. Tilton to the floor and told him to lie there . . . and then he caught hold of Maude."

She hesitated again and turned a miserable look on Jess. "It all happened so fast, I didn't have time to think. He put a gun to her head and said he'd shoot her if I didn't open the vault. I-I didn't know what else to do. I didn't want to give them the money, but I couldn't let them hurt your aunt."

Jess bit her lip at that plaintive confession and reflexively glanced in Hancock's direction, remembering his prediction of the day before. *Don't tell me that you would not readily divulge that combination if someone were holding a gun to your father or Miss Chwang.* Of course she would open the vault . . . just as Lily had opened it when the gun had been turned on someone else.

"You did what you had to," she assured the younger woman. "Now, what happened once you opened the lock?"

"They made me lie on the floor alongside Mr. Tilton. Then the tall man went inside the vault."

Though she'd been told to keep her head down, Lily still had kept track of the outlaw's progress by dint of listening. Briefly, she described the metallic shrieks that rose from the vault as he methodically pried open steel drawers and boxes, and the echoing clatter that followed as he tossed aside those now-emptied containers. The rush of footsteps beside her had been the man at the window abandoning his post for the teller counter. The slamming of the cash drawers told her that he was emptying them with the same hurried efficiency as his confederate was employing in plundering the vault.

"It took only a minute or so," she continued. "When they were finished, the man holding the gun to Maude said, 'Let's go, boys.' Then the last man—the one who had been at the door the entire time—yelled back that the law was coming . . . and that's when the shooting started."

She'd not seen much of the gun battle, Lily confessed, nor had she any idea that the marshal had been killed and the deputy wounded as a result. Instead, hands clamped over her ears against the deafening sound, she choked on the acrid smoke of discharged weapons and prayed for it to end quickly. And, indeed, the entire incident had taken less than a minute . . . this she knew for a certainty, for she had dared to glance up to watch the seconds tick past on the Regulator outside Jess's office. The last thing she saw was the outlaw leader using Maude as a shield while he and the other three fled the bank.

"Did you hear anything else," Hancock asked, "anything that might give a hint as to where they were headed?"

"Really, Mr. Hancock," Jess interjected with an inelegant snort. "do you honestly think the Black Horse Gang would go to the trouble of robbing a bank only to conveniently tell their victims the location of their secret hideout?"

A cold smile twisted his lips, so that he suddenly looked nothing at all like a mild-mannered bank examiner. "Actually, it has been known to happen. Most criminals of my acquaintance are, shall we say, not good with details."

"Their leader did say something," Lily exclaimed, drawing both their attention back to her. "He yelled it out to the others right after the shooting stopped. It was quite odd . . . something about meeting a dead squaw."

She shook her head helplessly. "My ears were still ringing when he said it, so perhaps I misunderstood . . . no, wait, I remember! It wasn't a person, it was the place where they were supposed to meet if they had to split up. Dead Squaw Canyon!" she exclaimed, triumph lightening her youthful features.

The same look of triumph burned more coolly in Hancock's eyes. "Excellent work, Lily. Now tell me, where is this Dead Squaw Canyon?"

"I-I don't know," she answered, the bright look fading from her face. "I've never heard of it before . . . have you, Jess?"

Never, Jess started to reply, then paused. Oddly enough, the name had a niggling ring of familiarity about it. Of course, with all the peaks and arroyos and gulches in Arizona Territory—most of them bearing two names, one English and one Spanish—it was easy enough to lose track. Finally, she shook her head.

Lily's gaze dropped dejectedly. "I'm sorry, Mr. Hancock. I wish I could have told you more."

Hancock gave the younger woman his slow smile . . . the same smile that, under different circumstances, would have set Jess's own heart to beating faster. "You did quite well, Lily," he told her, "both in your account of the incident and the way you handled the outlaws. You kept your head and cooperated with them, which was the safest thing to do. I'm sure Mrs. Satterly will agree."

"Of course," Jess hastened to reassure her assistant. "It's just that I'm so worried about Maude—"

She broke off at the sound of footsteps entering the bank. It was a grim-faced Ted limping toward them, with a haggard-looking Reba clinging to his arm. Ted's ink-stained apron now bore fresh smears of crimson in addition to the usual black . . . the wounded men's blood, Jess realized with a shiver. As for Reba, the once-jaunty green plumes that she'd pinned into her mass of brassy hair now drooped woefully over one red-rimmed eye, while her powdered features had sagged into lines that made her look a decade older.

"Lawd, I can't believe it!" the older woman cried, rushing to embrace both Jess and Lily. Then she stepped back, dabbing at her eyes with a lace-trimmed handkerchief. "I've known Kenny Crenshaw for almost ten years, ever since I first came to Brimstone. H-he was a good man. And poor Maude! Jess, does your father know yet what happened to her?''

Dear Lord, she'd forgotten about Papa! He'd have to be told, and quickly. She could only pray that the shock of the news would not be an unbearable strain on him, given his fragile health.

Guiltily, she shook her head. ''I'm sure he heard the shots, and he must be worried sick. I'll go home and tell him, just as soon as the posse rides out after her.''

''You might not want to wait that long,'' Ted warned her. ''I've sent someone else to help Jamie, but it might be another hour or two before they have the telegraph wires repaired. I'm thinking it was the Black Horse Gang that cut the lines in the first place, so they'd have a head start on the law. Anyhow, the minute I can, I'll wire Sheriff Behan in Tombstone so he can put together a posse to go after them.''

''Sheriff Behan . . . Tombstone? But Ted, aren't the men here forming a posse themselves?''

''No, Jess, they're not,'' he replied, dropping his gaze with a sigh. ''We did talk about it, but we all agreed that it's a job for trained lawmen. If Marshal Crenshaw and Deputy Bowser couldn't handle the Black Horse Gang, what makes you think any of us could stand up to them?''

What made Arbin think he could stand up to them either?

The guilty whisper of unwelcome conscience burned within her head. Shoving aside the thought, Jess concentrated on her anger instead. ''So are you telling me that we should just leave Maude to her fate? I can just see the headline you'll write for that story. *Outlaws Rob Bank, Town Too Frightened to Rescue Abducted Woman.*''

Ted jerked his gaze upward again, his pale features reddening. ''Damn it, Jess, that's not fair! None of those men are cowards, and neither am I. But forming a posse of merchants and miners to chase down a band of killers is madness, pure and simple. The best thing we can do is wait for the lines to be repaired and then wire Tombstone for help.''

''I hate to say this,'' Reba chimed in, stuffing her damp

handkerchief back into her bosom, "but I have to agree with Ted.

"Now, wait," she went on, raising a hand as Jess opened her mouth to protest, "you remember how it was when Arbin was gunned down. Folks were angry and wanted to do their part, so Kenny and the deputy took a dozen of them out after the Black Horse Gang."

Jess nodded, recalling the way the town had rallied that day, and Reba continued. "They tracked those sidewinders for six days and never found more than hoofprints. In the meantime, Mickey Streeter managed to shoot himself in the foot, Cliff Bender's horse pulled up lame, and old Joe Riley about got bit by a rattlesnake. That's what happens when you send townfolk that ain't never shot anything meaner than a desert rat out after outlaws."

She broke off with a large sniff and whipped out her handkerchief once more. Jess, meanwhile, took a shaky breath and tried to sort out her thoughts. Perhaps it did make more sense to let professionals take on the job of finding her aunt. The town of Tombstone lay some miles to the southwest of them, in the same general direction as the Black Horse Gang had headed, a good half day's ride from Brimstone. And while the place was renowned for its gambling and rowdy characters, it also boasted the rough-and-tumble Earp brothers, who had gained a reputation in this part of Arizona as peacekeepers. If they could get word to Sheriff Behan and the Earps soon enough, those men might intercept the outlaws as they rode south.

But what if it took hours to repair the telegraph lines . . . or what if the gang turned off the main road long before they reached Tombstone? The trail might be lost, and Maude as well.

"There's something else, Jess," Ted interrupted her grim musings. "We all know the Black Horse Gang are killers, so we have to face certain possibilities. Once they are well into the desert again, they might decide . . . well, they might decide that they don't need a hostage anymore. Best case, they might simply turn her loose, and maybe we'll be lucky enough for someone to find her in time."

Worst case, they'll just shoot her, Jess silently finished for him. Unbidden came the image of her aunt sprawled upon the desert floor, the vivid fabric of her blue ruffled gown splashed with crimson, her dead eyes staring heavenward.

"Lawd, Ted, do you have to be so blunt about it?" Reba demanded. "Why don't you just tell us we ought to be planning to bury her, same as Kenny?" Then, glancing in Jess's direction, she tearfully exclaimed, "Look what you've done to the poor girl, Ted. She's gone pale as a ghost."

Indeed, another wave of light-headedness had swept Jess, though this time it was not shock but excitement that sent her reeling. The mental picture of her aunt lying dead had abruptly dissolved from her thoughts, replaced by a vision of fine black lines etched with delicate precision upon a ragged sheet of yellowed parchment. Suddenly, she knew how to find this canyon that was the Black Horse Gang's destination . . . that was, if the Black Horse Gang hadn't stolen the information out from under her.

Ignoring the others' questioning looks, Jess rushed into the open vault. Her determination momentarily faltered, however, as she took in the havoc wreaked by the outlaws. It was just as Lily had described it. The rows of metal boxes that once had neatly held her customers' cash and other valuables sat askew on their shelves or else littered the vault floor, their lids gaping like so many astonished mouths.

Reminding herself that the destruction paled before the wounding and loss of life the town had suffered, she hastily searched for one particular box. She finally found it, forced open as most of the others were. Its contents—the bank's own papers of collateral—were intact, however. She pulled forth the particular document that she sought, then carefully unfolded it.

It was a map of the land that had once belonged to the Apaches, but now was the southeastern-most quadrant of Arizona Territory. Given the way that the mountains and trails scrawled off the page, she suspected the map had been cut from a larger work . . . perhaps a military map that had hung on some Spanish officer's wall. The black ink with which it was drawn had long since faded to brown, while the parchment itself was ragged from the countless hands through which it had passed over the years.

A hunnerd an' fifty years, give or take a few, the old miner had assured her that morning almost four months earlier. He'd been waiting at the door well before she'd opened for business that day. A bearded man of perhaps sixty years, he had been dressed in the fashion of many a miner she'd seen: a ragged, once-white shirt; a grimy vest of tan canvas; and army-issue gray trousers so worn that he likely had worn them new during the War Between the States.

Mr. Johnson, as he had given his name, had been distressed to learn that there was no banker of the male persuasion with whom he could discuss his business. But being reminded that the First National Bank of Brimstone was that town's sole bank, he finally had condescended to speak with Jess.

What he'd wanted, she swiftly learned, was a loan . . . a grub stake of sorts so that he could finally return to his grandchildren in South Carolina and settle down for the remainder of his years. The progeny in question, he'd assured her, would wire repayment just as soon as he'd made his way safely to them. As collateral, he would leave her this map, which led to a lost cache of Spanish gold, which document she could mail back to him once the note was paid in full.

Spreading the map on her table, he'd traced out the cryptic notes and arrows that led to a point south and to the west of Brimstone, just above the border with Mexico. While the trail and landmark names all were set down in an ornate Spanish hand, someone in more modern lettering had penciled in the English translations and versions.

One place name, in particular, had caught her eye . . . that of an arroyo not far from where the usual *X* marked the treasure's resting place. The Spanish name for it was the relatively sedate Arroya del Sol.

The more dramatic English appellation was Dead Squaw Canyon.

At the time, the morbid name had been but a mere curiosity, and Jess's attention had been focused on the old miner. Politely, she had inquired why he had not recovered the treasure if the map was, as he implied, the genuine article. *Too old an' stove up,* had been his blunt reply.

More won over by that admission than by a belief that the map was anything other than a hoax, she had made old Mr. Johnson the loan. The supposed treasure map she had filed away with other deeds and documents she held as collateral, certain the map would never be reclaimed . . . and never dreaming she might one day have need of it, herself.

Now, Jess stepped back out of the vault. She glanced in Hancock's direction, only to discover that he was no longer in the bank. *Probably gone to write up a report,* she thought sourly, not that it made a difference. He'd only want to take over for her, and she certainly did not want or need his help in this matter.

Maude was her responsibility. She'd do it alone.

"Lily, I'm leaving you in charge here," she swiftly told the younger woman. "Bring in some of your brothers to help clean up the vault, and then get out the books and see if you can determine what is missing. Ted, Reba"—she turned to the pair—"please keep an eye on my father until I get back."

"Get back?" Reba echoed uncertainly. "Lawd, Jess, just where do you think you're going?"

Jess carefully folded the parchment, tucked it in her shirtwaist, and then met Reba's worried gaze. "Why, I'm going to rescue my Aunt Maude, of course."

Chapter Six

More than a year's worth of dust covered the flat leather box . . . hardly surprising, since it had lain at the back of Arbin's wardrobe, untouched, ever since the day of his death. Jess had thrust the box, along with the rest of his personal belongings, into the wardrobe's camphor-y depths right after she had chosen the clothes in which to bury her husband. Pulling forth the same somber black suit he had worn in his last photograph, she'd then shut the mirrored doors on his life.

A fortnight later, when the excitement surrounding the robbery and his murder had settled down, she'd hired a pair of husky town boys to haul the wardrobe—contents intact—from their bedroom and up into the attic. She often told herself that, one day, she would get around to disposing of Arbin's things, but that day had not yet come. *Sentimentality,* she always explained her hesitation to her father and aunt.

Guilt, her inner voice more accurately told it.

Now, however, Jess hesitated only a moment before plucking the box from its hiding place and closing the wardrobe once more. Downstairs in her bedroom again, she moved aside a silver-backed brush and comb, then set the box on her oak dressing table. Fastidiously, she swiped her pocket handkerchief across its brown leather surface. The motion set a small billow of dust onto the lacy white runner that covered the table, but she barely noticed, intent as she was on opening the lid.

Within lay a double-barreled derringer, its nickel finish gleaming dully in the afternoon sun. Arbin had bought the pocket pistol soon after their arrival in Brimstone, deeming it a suitable weapon for a businessman such as he. Even now it looked innocent enough, nestled on a simple bed of green felt . . . yet, indirectly, the weapon had caused the death of her husband.

If only he'd not carried it with him to the bank that fateful day, if only he'd not pulled it from the cash drawer when the Black Horse Gang demanded money, then perhaps he would be alive still.

Someone should do something about those outlaws, Jess remembered proclaiming in disgust one night at the supper table. It had been just days before the robbery, following on the news that a miner had been robbed and shot at his claim just outside Brimstone. *I don't understand why the marshal doesn't go after them. Surely he must know the entire territory would think him a hero if he stopped them.*

But it had been Arbin and not the marshal who had tried to stop them, and he had died for his trouble. If only she hadn't said what she had, perhaps he never would have made the attempt.

Grimly, Jess snatched up both the derringer and the small pasteboard box of ammunition that lay beside it. Fumbling only a little, she loaded the weapon. While she prayed she'd have no reason to fire it, prudence dictated that she travel armed. After all, one could hardly stand up to a gang of brutal outlaws empty-handed.

Jess tucked the loaded pistol into one of the sturdy black boots she'd pulled on just a few minutes before. She also had exchanged her gray poplin for a more appropriate riding costume: a divided skirt of tan duck topped by a simple white cotton shirtwaist and belted in black leather. It was an outfit she wore but rarely, given her preference for riding in a cart or carriage, rather than bounding about on horseback. But given the urgency of the situation at hand, she was more than willing to mount up.

A quick glance in the cheval glass confirmed that her skirt hem brushed well below her boot tops, concealing the derringer from any casual glance. The mirror also reflected the room and its furnishings . . . a pair of windows hung with lace curtains that matched the dressing table runner; a four-poster, large enough for two and still draped in the pale yellow quilt that had been a wedding gift from Arbin's late mother; a tall oaken wardrobe that matched the one stowed away in the attic; a washstand with a yellow-flowered china basin and pitcher to match the quilt.

Jess grimaced. It was a pleasant enough room, unchanged since Arbin's death, save for the faint outline on the sun-faded wallpaper that showed where his wardrobe had stood, and the fact that his personal belongings no longer lay in neat precision on the washstand. One day—perhaps the day that she finally sorted through his things—she'd also rearrange the furniture, and maybe purchase a new quilt for the bed.

Abruptly, Jess turned from the mirror and walked over to the bed, where her paisley carpetbag sat gaping. She added the box of ammunition to the change of clothing and few supplies she'd hastily packed. She'd already sent word to Mr. Kirby requesting that he have her father's gelding, Old Pete, saddled and ready for travel. All that remained now was telling Papa good-bye.

Snapping shut the bag, she grabbed it up and hurried downstairs. Her father was waiting for her, propped in his chair in the parlor . . . the same chair into which he had sagged in despair a few minutes earlier, when she'd told him about the bank robbery and Maude's kidnapping. To her relief, however, he had raised no opposition when she told him of her planned ride to Tombstone to inform the authorities what had happened in her town.

Indeed, he had agreed with her argument that the repair

of the telegraph lines might take longer than Ted Markham anticipated, so that it made sense to send ahead a rider—her—with the news. What she had not shared with him was the information contained in the parchment she'd recovered from the bank vault, fearing to waste valuable time explaining just how the page had come into her possession.

Neither had she told her father that Tombstone would not be her final stop . . . that, posse or no, she intended to ride in search of her aunt.

Now, Harvey struggled to his feet and held out a bony hand. "Jessamine, girl, be careful," he rasped out, drawing her into his embrace. "Once you reach Tombstone and talk to the sheriff, I want you to send me a telegram letting me know you are safe. And if you have any news of Maude—"

He broke off, his eyes suddenly damp. Jess gave him a reassuring kiss, hating the fact that she must lie to him.

"I'm sure Sheriff Behan's posse will find her, safe and sound," she replied, managing a smile. "I'll wait in Tombstone until they ride out after her, and then I'll start for home again. In the meantime, Reba and Ted have promised to check in on you, so you'll be just fine while I am gone."

"Just fine," he echoed, frustration twisting his already haggard features. "Blast it, Jess, I'm the one who should be riding after her. If not for my lungs—"

He broke off on a fit of coughing, and Jess saw in concern that the handkerchief with which he dabbed his lips came back spotted with blood. She pretended not to notice, however, and he quickly tucked away the evidence of his illness in his waistcoat pocket. Then, lightly patting her on the cheek, he gave her a smile.

"Remember, Old Pete needs a firm hand, so be sure you let him know who's boss from the start. Now hurry along, and I'll wait to hear good news back from you."

With a final hug for her father, Jess snatched up her bag and grabbed her old black felt hat from a peg near the door, then hurried from the house in the direction of Kirby's livery. The owner's infamous black hound was no where in sight, though

Old Pete—a sturdy piebald—was saddled and waiting for her in the corral. He rolled a baleful eye in Jess's direction but stood quietly enough as she strapped her carpetbag and canteen to the back of his saddle. He remained placidly chewing a wisp of dried grass even while she tied on the worn bedroll she'd borrowed from the stable boy. It wasn't until she'd gingerly swung herself into the saddle and, with a tentative kick, urged him forward that Old Pete made his first protest.

Skittering forward a few steps, the paint abruptly halted again, then turned and nipped at her leg. Fortunately, his large yellowish teeth connected with boot rather than flesh; even so, Jess squeaked in surprise and almost dropped her reins. Her momentary distraction was enough for the gelding. With a nicker of satisfaction, he broke into an ungainly canter and headed for the street.

"Blast it all!"

Her hat now dangling by its ties down her back, Jess struggled to get the beast back under control. By the time they'd reached Main Street, she'd managed to plonk her hat back atop her coil of braids and rein in Old Pete to an even less comfortable trot. Remembering her father's advice about a firm hand, she kept him to that pace as they continued down the dusty road.

It was a somber sight that greeted her as she rode through town. Less than an hour had passed since the Black Horse Gang had made their murderous foray into Brimstone, and an almost palpable sense of shock still clung to the town. Jess could see it in the faces of the people, the day's business long forgotten as they huddled in small groups and talked with one another.

She noticed, too, that the fatal gun battle had had an impact on the town's structures, as well as its citizens. Here and there a merchant stood outside his shop, sweeping up broken glass and boarding shut the windows that had been shattered by stray bullets during the gun battle. The Lucky Nugget's piano was silent, for once, and the usual traffic of carts and wagons had come to a halt, so that the clomp of Old Pete's hooves echoed off the buildings. Even the horse trough outside the mercantile had not gone unscathed. At least one bullet had pierced its thick wood, so that water seeped from it like blood, creating a muddy stream that crept halfway across the broad street.

A restless group of men still huddled on the street, though the marshal's lifeless body had long since been moved to the back room of Doc Caldwell's office. Someone had spread sawdust across the spot in the unpaved street where he had fallen, but the bloody puddle had saturated the wooden shavings before drying beneath the desert sun. The result was a grisly splotch of color, like rust-colored ink spilled across the pale sand.

Giving both the mud and the stained bit of ground wide berth, Jess spared a glance for her fellow townspeople. The men, especially, seemed dismayed by her presence, and she realized Ted or Reba must have spread the word as to what she planned. She could see on their faces a common expression of mingled anger and embarrassment little different from the look Ted had turned on her in the bank. Though they'd claimed to be too intimidated by the Black Horse Gang to give pursuit, they seemed equally uncomfortable with the idea of a woman riding off after outlaws alone.

Perhaps it wasn't too late, she thought with a resurgence of optimism. Maybe the sight of her would be enough to spur them to form that posse, after all. And with her parchment, even a handful of untrained men might well succeed in tracking the outlaws to their lair and rescuing Maude!

But her hope for this mass change of heart promptly died as, one by one, the men dropped their gazes before her searching look and turned away. By the time she reached the edge of town, with its neatly lettered sign that welcomed visitors to stay awhile, she knew with certainty that there would be no posse from Brimstone . . . not today.

And then she heard the sound of hoofbeats behind her.

Jess knew instinctively who the rider would be; still, she glanced behind her, just to be certain. Her guess confirmed, her first impulse was to dig her heels into the paint's broad sides and gallop off. Knowing he'd only follow her, she accepted the inevitable and reined in Old Pete to a walk.

"Going somewhere, Mrs. Satterly?" the familiar voice asked coolly.

She shot him an equally frosty look before deliberately fastening her gaze on the open country beyond. "As a matter of fact, Mr. Hancock, I am . . . not that it is any of your business."

"To the contrary, if it has to do with the bank robbery, it *is* my business."

Abruptly, he maneuvered the large roan he was riding so that it blocked her way. Old Pete snorted in dismay, while Jess gasped in outrage. This was carrying his role as bank examiner too far!

"You have no jurisdiction over me, Mr. Hancock! If I want to leave town, I shall," she sputtered, sawing on the reins as she tried unsuccessfully to move past him. Every time Old Pete nosed past the mare, however, the man would bring his mount around again to block her path. After a few seconds of fruitless sidestepping, she finally jerked the paint to a halt and glared at the man.

"Blast it all, what do you want?"

"I want you to leave chasing outlaws to the posse."

"What posse?" Jess demanded. "Now that the marshal is dead and the deputy is wounded, there's not a man in Brimstone who'll dare go after the Black Horse Gang. And with the telegraph lines down, who knows how long it will be before the sheriff in Tombstone can send out riders? If I don't ride out after Aunt Maude, then who—"

"I will"—he cut her short, then went on—"not that I don't admire your bravery, or understand your concern for Miss McCray's safety. But the truth of the matter is that, if you should accidentally stumble across the gang, all you'll accomplish is getting yourself killed."

"And you'll do better?"

"I could hardly do worse. For one thing, I'm much better armed."

And he was armed surprisingly well for a man who spent

his days adding numbers, Jess grudgingly admitted to herself. True, he still wore his same gray banker's suit, but his open jacket revealed strapped around his waist a Colt peacemaker, the same revolver that newspaper accounts claimed the Earps favored. And though the black bowler set with businesslike precision atop his pomaded dark hair gave him the look of an Eastern dandy, tied to his saddle was an efficient-looking rifle of the sort suited to buffalo hunters and lawmen.

Jess inwardly cringed, thinking of her own minuscule arsenal. Though she was dressed more appropriately for travel in the high desert, her own weapon would be of use only if she was within a few feet of her target . . . and even then, its accuracy would be challenged by her minimal skill with a pistol.

Even as she silently conceded that argument to him, he went on. "As I said before, I feel that I bear some responsibility for what happened. And since this whole business happened on my watch, so to speak, it seems only appropriate that I be the one to go after the outlaws."

"So you intend to capture the Black Horse Gang single-handedly? That's quite a heroic goal for a mere bank examiner, Mr. Hancock."

"Heroic? Hardly," he replied with a wry twist of his lips. "I fear my motives are much more pragmatic. If I can manage to recover the money—and, of course, your aunt—things will go a bit easier on me when I return to the home office. I *am* up for a promotion, you know."

Jess choked back a caustic reply. The charter company might tar and feather him, for all she cared. Still, her Brimstone posse *was* woefully short of volunteers.

"Very well, Mr. Hancock, you've convinced me. Oh, not to return home," she clarified in honeyed tones as she saw the flicker of satisfaction in his blue eyes, "but to allow you to accompany me to Tombstone."

"Accompany you to Tombstone?" he echoed, the question rising on a note of outraged disbelief. An instant later, however, he had regained his usual air of cool composure. "Very well, that seems a reasonable enough compromise. We'll ride to Tombstone together, and once you've told the sheriff there all you know, you'll turn back. But might I suggest we depart immediately? The Black Horse Gang has an hour's advantage on us by now."

Not waiting for her reply, Hancock abruptly spun his mount about and started off at a fast clip. Jess hesitated only an instant longer; then, gritting her teeth, she sank her heels into Old Pete's sides and galloped after him. No doubt he thought to leave her in his dust and discourage her from making the journey. Little did he know that Old Pete—in addition to being one of creation's orneriest four-legged creatures—was accounted one of the swiftest steeds in town.

By the time the broad road leading to the hills beyond Brimstone had narrowed into a scrub-lined trail, Jess easily had caught up with Hancock on his borrowed roan. Her triumph came at a price, however, as she fought to settle into her gelding's rhythm . . . not an easy task for one who rode but infrequently. She'd be bruised and battered by nightfall, she glumly realized, but she'd rather be trampled beneath Old Pete's hooves than ask Hancock to slow their pace.

She did ask him one other question, however. "Tell me, Mr. Hancock, why is Kirby's black hound following us?"

He glanced back at the sleek dog in question, which had been padding after them ever since they left Brimstone, and shook his head. "This roan was not the original horse I hired. When Mr. Kirby learned I was headed out after the Black Horse Gang, he insisted I take her, claiming she was his best mount. He did mention, in passing, that his dog was rather attached to her. I presume he'll tire after a bit and turn around."

But the hound persisted after them, falling back at times and then rushing to catch up. Jess wondered if the beast was as uncomfortable as she. The sun was still high in the sky and, save for the brim of her hat cocked rakishly over her eyes, no shade was to be found there on the trail. Already the dry air had begun to parch her lips, and she thought longingly of her canteen, strapped on behind her. But she'd lived long enough in this territory to know that one did not heedlessly gulp down one's water supply at the first twinge of thirst.

To her relief, Hancock did slow, periodically, and not just to rest the horses. Rather, he appeared to be quite ostentatiously tracking the gang . . . an unnecessary waste of time, she thought, as she watched him pull out a compass. Though the road itself was little more than a rutted trail, it was obvious even to Jess's untrained eye that a group of riders had recently passed, given how the rocky path was churned. The occasional clear print of a shod hoof on a patch of sand also confirmed the fact.

What exactly Hancock searched for, she could not guess. She rather suspected he did not, either, and that the demonstration was simply that . . . a show of male competency put on for her benefit. Whatever his reasons, he was slowing their pursuit, so that she chafed impatiently each time they reined up.

She finally said as much an hour later, breaking the silence that had held between them since they had left Brimstone. Hancock eyed her coolly from beneath the brim of his bowler.

"Unfortunately for us, Mrs. Satterly, outlaws have a disconcerting way of not following established protocol . . . including not sticking to the main road. I'm merely attempting to make certain that we're still headed in the right direction."

"But you can see for yourself that their trail leads that way," she countered, pointing down the narrow path as she climbed down from her mount. "The hoofprints quite clearly show that several horses have recently passed."

Not waiting for his reply, she reached for her canteen. Old Pete's spotted sides were dull with dried sweat, and he'd already begun to blow. After taking a small sip herself, she poured a handful of water into one palm, and the gelding drank noisily. She splashed a few drops on a concave rock for the hound, who waited until she had mounted up again before deigning to drink.

Hancock, meanwhile, had finished his examination of the trail before them. Climbing back onto his roan, he favored her with a cool look. "As you say, it's obvious several people have ridden by today. But supposing the gang split into two groups just to throw us off, and the one with the money—and your aunt—left the trail and headed out across the desert? Or suppose they've been traveling cross-country the entire time, and we're following the wrong group of riders toward Tombstone?"

Jess had no answer to that argument, for the scenarios he had conjured up held more than a note of unsettling possibility. True, she had the parchment, so she would find Dead Squaw Canyon sooner or later. But in the time it would take to track the outlaws to their lair, anything might happen to Maude.

Chastened for the moment, she set off after Hancock, who'd already spurred his roan and was several lengths ahead of her. She drew up alongside him and kept to his pace, while the black hound remained a silent presence behind them. She let Hancock scan the trail while she squinted against the afternoon sun and watched the distance for the telltale cloud of dust that always accompanied a group of fast-moving riders.

All she saw were ragged, blue-tinged hills interspersed with the tans and browns of the desert. It was no barren spread of rock and sand, however, for green patches of cacti and scrub liberally dotted the desert. Their swift passage flushed the occasional plump, pale brown dove from its hiding place within a spiked crown of yucca, and startled numerous sandy-hued lizards from their perches atop outcroppings of matching rock. Here and there, a mottled brown squirrel scampered across the trail, pausing to stare, bright-eyed, at them before ducking behind a sparse clump of grass. Once, the black hound gave chase, running the hapless rodent to ground before resuming his march.

As the day wore on and the sun dropped lower, the hills took on a pink blush. The terrain grew rockier, so that following the outlaws' trail grew more difficult. Now, Jess did not protest every time they halted, but studied the surrounding landscape as keenly as did Hancock. She began to fear that the Black Horse Gang might indeed have left the main trail. Still, she had no choice but to forge on to Tombstone, where she would find the sheriff and tell him what she knew of the outlaws' destination.

It was almost sunset when the ragged silhouette of that brawling mining town finally came into view.

Chapter Seven

From a distance, the town of Tombstone appeared to be little more than a sprawl of wood, brick, and adobe buildings scattered on a hillside. Once they reached its outskirts, however, Jess could see that it actually was a prosperous and well-kept town. Indeed, it was a much larger version of Brimstone, boasting several more hotels and far many more saloons.

And while the sight of a stranger would have been remarked upon in Brimstone, it seemed no one paid them any heed as she and Hancock rode through Tombstone's broad dusty streets. Even the black hound drew no notice as, apparently disconcerted by the unfamiliar sights and sounds, he padded through town practically on the roan's hooves.

By dint of questioning several passersby, they learned it would be in one of those saloons that she and Hancock might find the local sheriff. Dusk had faded into nightfall by the time they tied up their horses outside the Crystal Palace, at the corner of Fifth and Allen streets. Raucous laughter and bright music spilled out into the street, testifying to the saloon's popularity among Tombstone's gaming crowd.

Jess stifled a groan as she gingerly climbed down from Old

Pete and then turned to Hancock. Illuminated by the yellow gaslight that haloed the saloon doorway, he looked quite as dusty and travel-worn as she expected she did herself. He swung down from his saddle with far more ease than had she, however. Pulling off his bowler, he raked a hand through his dark hair, then lightly slapped the hat against his thigh. A fine cloud of dust rose between them.

He raised a wry brow. "One of the hazards of desert travel, I expect," he observed in his usual detached tone. "Now, may I suggest that you wait out here with the horses, Mrs. Satterly, while I track down our Sheriff Behan?"

"Nonsense."

She pulled off her own dusty hat and hung it from her saddle horn, adding, "I am sure you're about to explain the proprieties to me, Mr. Hancock, but let me assure you that I have been inside a saloon before. I hardly think that my presence inside this particular one would cause a stir. Besides, I want to speak with the sheriff myself."

"As you wish."

He stepped back and indicated that she was to proceed him, the courtly gesture containing more than a hint of irony. Swiftly embracing that unspoken challenge, Jess took a deep breath, then pushed past the bat-wing doors and into the smoky light.

Inside, the Crystal Palace reminded Jess of Reba's establishment, though it was far larger and more luxuriously appointed than the Lucky Nugget. A carved and mirrored mahogany bar twice the size of Reba's stretched for almost an entire wall, with men crowded elbow-to-elbow down its gleaming length.

Opposite the bar, gamblers filled tables offering faro and poker, their expressions of grim concentration a contrast to the tipsy revelry of those patrons simply there for the drink. Adding to the gaiety was the birdlike voice of a fresh-faced young woman standing upon a small wooden platform in one corner. Dressed demurely in white, she warbled a genteel ballad while accompanied on the piano by a balding, black-suited Negro. A bluish haze of cigar smoke overhung it all, dulling the bright yellow glow from the row of ornately globed gaslights that dangled the length of the tinned ceiling.

Jess gazed about the crowd, which ranged from suited, mustachioed gentlemen of obvious means to beardless young cowboys still dressed in the sweat-stained garb of the range. Patrons freely milled about, so that standing room was at a premium. How in the world would they find Sheriff Behan in such a gathering?

''I suggest we ask the bartender,'' Hancock answered her unspoken question, raising his voice to be heard above the din.

Jess nodded, sticking closely behind him as he elbowed his way through the press to find a gap along the bar's gleaming brass foot rail. The bartender—a short, clean-shaven man wearing a white shirt and a black bow tie—swiped the bar top with a damp rag and gave them a harried look. ''What'll it be, sir?''

''Two whiskeys . . . the good stuff,'' Hancock ordered. Then, as the man expertly poured the amber liquid into two crystal glasses, the bank examiner added, ''And could you point us in the direction of Sheriff Behan?''

''Over there by the last faro table, wearing the green waistcoat.''

Hancock nodded his thanks, laid a few coins on the bar, and took up a glass. He downed the one whiskey in a single swallow, then handed Jess the other tumbler.

''Drink it,'' he instructed when she just gazed at him quizzically. ''It'll help ease your sore muscles. Otherwise you'll be stiff as a ramrod come morning.''

Given that she already could feel every inch of her body painfully knotting in the wake of her unaccustomed ride, Jess did not hesitate, but drank it down in one swift gulp, just as he had done. The whiskey scalded its way down her throat, bringing tears to her eyes. Aware of Hancock's amused gaze upon her, however, she managed not to choke or grimace at the liquor's fiery taste.

''Quite . . . refreshing,'' she lied with a ragged smile. ''Now, let's find Behan.''

The lawman in question stood chatting with a handful of

other men. He was tall and slim, his receding dark hair and neatly trimmed mustache emphasizing his handsome, finely boned features. Nattily dressed in a dark gray suit and a contrasting vest of forest green, he had the sleek look of a professional politician. A lovely dark-haired girl wearing a low-cut blue silk dress clung to his arm, her possessive smile leaving no doubt that she considered the sheriff her property.

Hancock did not wait for an invitation but joined the circle of men, coolly introducing himself and Jess as he explained to the bemused sheriff what had brought them from Brimstone. At his mention of the Black Horse Gang, Behan's tight social smile dimmed.

"Yes, Mr. Hancock, we just received that telegram less than an hour ago," he confirmed in a self-important tone, then turned to Jess. "I am sorry to hear about your bank's misfortune, Mrs. Satterly. But I'm forgetting my manners. Let me introduce the both of you to some of Tombstone's finest citizens."

In the same polished tones that must have helped elect him, he ran through the names of the men—merchants and professional men, all three—before turning a fond look on the girl at this side. "And this is Miss Josephine Marcus. She is a renowned thespian who has condescended to make Tombstone her home . . . at least, for a time."

Jess wryly noticed that, even entwined as she was with the sheriff, the girl still spared a seductive pout for Hancock. The brief look she turned on Jess was far less friendly, though it softened into a pitying smile as she took in Jess's travel-rumpled appearance.

"Pleased to meet you, I'm sure," she said in the harsh accents that betrayed her New York upbringing, then returned her attention to Hancock. "If you're in town for a few days, perhaps you'll have the opportunity to see me perform."

"A rare treat, I'm sure," the bank examiner murmured before addressing Behan again. "If you don't mind, sheriff, Mrs. Satterly and I would like to discuss the particulars of the robbery with you."

"Certainly. Josie"—he smoothly detached himself from the

girl's slim-fingered grasp—"why don't you entertain the boys for a few moments while I chat with these fine people? Mr. Hancock, Mrs. Satterly, if you'll just follow me."

A few moments later, the trio had made their way up a narrow wooden staircase to the second floor of the Crystal Palace, where a series of small offices overlooked the street below. In the dim light, Jess made out several of the occupants' names painted on the windows: MARSHAL VIRGIL EARP, JUDGE WELLS SPICER, SHERIFF JOHN BEHAN.

The latter led them into his office and lit a lamp. "Actually, it's quite a convenient location for a man of my position," he explained with a self-deprecating smile. He gestured them to a pair of chairs, then took his own seat behind his desk. "After all, the sheriff is, first and foremost, a man of the people . . . and where better to find people than here at the Palace? But on to more important topics. I understand from the telegram that not only was your bank robbed, Mrs. Satterly, but that a female bystander also was kidnapped?"

"It was my aunt, Miss Maude McCray," Jess replied. "She was in the bank at the time. The Black Horse Gang took her hostage."

Behan gave a sage nod. "Unfortunately, that sort of thing is becoming more and more common these days. And it makes what I'm about to tell you that much worse. You see, much as I'd like to help recover your bank's money and find your aunt, I'm afraid our posse is already occupied searching for another group of malefactors."

"Then you have no one else to send?"

The sheriff shook his head. "Marshal Virgil Earp, his brothers, and my other deputies all rode out just this morning. With luck, they will have apprehended the men in question and be back in Tombstone by tomorrow evening . . . or the following day, at the latest. Once they return, I'll be happy to send them out after the Black Horse Gang. In the meantime, the best I can do is wire the territorial governor and see what other arrangements he can make."

"But you don't understand," Jess exclaimed, leaping to

her feet. "My aunt's life is in danger. If we don't find her soon—"

"I'm sure the sheriff realizes the gravity of the situation," Hancock smoothly broke in, then turned to Behan. "I believe our best course of action is to stay here for the night and determine what to do in the morning. Perhaps you might recommend a suitable hotel."

"The Occidental is the next block over. They boast comfortable beds and serve mighty fine food, as well," the sheriff said with the smile of a man anxious to promote the local businesses. He rose and gave Jess a nod. "Don't worry, Mrs. Satterly. I'll make arrangements in the morning with the governor's office . . . and in the meantime, I'll keep you and Mr. Hancock here abreast of everything that goes on."

"We'd appreciate that, sheriff," Hancock replied. Then, almost off-handedly, he added, "I don't suppose you've ever heard of Dead Squaw Canyon, have you?"

"I can't say that I have. And now, if you don't mind, I should return to my friends downstairs."

With that polite if blunt dismissal, Behan escorted them from his office. Barely had they made their good-byes and gone outside in the street again, than Jess started for her horse. She had one foot in Old Pete's stirrup when Hancock grabbed her arm and pulled her around to face him.

"Going somewhere, Mrs. Satterly?"

His voice sounded as if it came from far away . . . or perhaps it was simply the sudden ringing in her ears that made it seem that way. Vaguely, she realized that the whiskey she'd drank earlier had proved quite potent on an empty stomach, so that she now was a bit tipsy. Lest he guess that her senses were, for the moment, slightly muddled, she turned on the man as cool a look as she could muster.

"I'm riding out to find my aunt, Mr. Hancock," she told him in lofty tones, "or didn't you hear what Sheriff Behan said? The posse won't return to Tombstone for another two or three days. By that time, it may be too late."

"Agreed; however, I see no point in your heading off like this in the dark."

"But the Black Horse Gang—"

"—will have to make camp, as well. You can hardly have a dozen riders thundering about at night, not in this part of the country. Someone is bound to ride off into an arroyo."

He paused, lifting a wry brow, then went on. "Besides, they've probably concluded by now that they're not being followed, so they have very likely slowed their pace. We'll lose no ground if we start again tomorrow."

"We? Then you and I will be riding together?"

Jess frowned, uncertain how to take this change in plans. It occurred to her, too, that Hancock continued his firm grip on her arm. His only motive, she felt sure, was to keep her upright; still there was an intimacy about the gesture that, intentional or not, abruptly made her uncomfortable.

As if the same thought had occurred to him, the man abruptly loosed his hold on her and took a step back. "Yes, we'll ride together, Mrs. Satterly. I see no hope for it otherwise. And now, why don't you procure us two rooms at the Occidental, while I take the horses down to the livery for the night."

So saying, he removed her carpetbag from Old Pete's saddle and handed it to her. That accomplished, he untied the roan from the post; then, surveying her with much the same critical eye as Miss Marcus had, he added, "I suggest we also take Sheriff Behan's advice and try the dining room there. You might wish, however, to freshen up a bit, first. I'm certain the Occidental's maitre d'hotel does require a certain standard of cleanliness for his patrons."

He left a momentarily speechless Jess staring after him as he led their mounts down the street, the black hound trotting after him. By the time a suitable retort occurred to her, the moment for rebuttal had passed; still, she gained a small bit of pleasure in watching Old Pete bare his yellow teeth in the bank examiner's direction.

Her satisfaction was short-lived, however, when Hancock casually flicked him on the muzzle with the reins before the piebald could take a nip. The surprised gelding snorted and meekly lowered his head.

"Better luck next time, Old Pete," she muttered in sympathy before beginning the short walk to the hotel.

Night had completely engulfed the town, though one would hardly know it for the blaze of gaslights and lanterns spilling from the nearby establishments, which lit the street almost as bright as day. She'd long since heard rumors that Tombstone boasted a saloon for every hundred of its citizens, and she could well believe it. If the town's other businesses multiplied at the same rate, she wryly thought, Tombstone might soon rival St. Louis for size.

By now, the ringing in her ears had begun to subside, so that she was aware of other sounds . . . music from the dance halls and saloons; bursts of feminine laughter; the gruff sounds of men's voices rising and falling. The uneven clump of boots and jingle of spurs accompanied tipsy cowboys as they made their way up the wooden sidewalks, singly or in groups. Here and there, a stray dog barked, adding a more domestic note to the hedonistic rhythm.

Though, once during her brief walk, a passing cowboy slurred an ungentlemanly suggestion her way, Jess reached the Occidental Hotel without incident. She registered them both; then, catching a glimpse of her bedraggled state in the lobby mirror, she wryly decided to take Hancock's advice. Once she reached her room, stripped down to her undergarments, and splashed half a pitcher's worth of water into its matching basin so she could scrub off the worst of the trail's grime. Then, having shaken the dust from her clothes, she dressed once more and made her way back downstairs to meet Hancock.

He arrived in the lobby a few minutes later, looking as if he'd just been plucked from the window of a man's haberdashery despite their long day of travel. The considering gaze he turned on her hinted that she had not fared nearly so well, even with the hasty bath, though he was too polite to comment. Reminding herself that her goal was to find her aunt and not to impress a snobbish bank examiner, she merely gave him a cool smile in return as they started for the dining room

"I trust you settled in the horses without a problem?"

"They're safely stabled at the O.K. Corral. I gave instructions for them to be saddled and ready at dawn." He paused before the bill of fare posted outside the dining room door. "Loin of beef, Westphalia ham, Columbia River salmon, asparagus points," he read off in satisfaction. "It would seem that Sheriff Behan did not exaggerate."

And, indeed, he had not, Jess decided an hour later as, comfortably ensconced at a corner table, she finished off a slice of custard pie. Her aunt's cooking notwithstanding, she'd not tasted cuisine this fine since leaving St. Louis. Even Hancock seemed impressed by the fare, to the point of remarking once that he had to keep reminding himself that he was in an Arizona mining town, and not Kansas City.

And discussion of the food seemed the limit of their dinner conversation, for which Jess was glad. The tragic events of the day combined with the hard ride and the glass of whiskey she'd imbibed had left her bereft of pleasant conversation. Hancock seemed equally caught up in thought. With any luck, he'd prove an equally silent travel partner tomorrow . . . that was, if she did not simply leave Tombstone by herself before dawn. After all, she had the map leading to the outlaws' hideout, so why did she need Hancock?

But three guns *were* better than one, she grimly reminded herself, reluctantly abandoning that last plan. So long as Hancock realized that she was in charge of their expedition, and not he, they would make tolerable enough companions. And given his concern with recovering the bank's money, lest his employer pass him over for advancement, he'd likely dance to her tune once he knew she held the map.

By now, he had stirred from his reverie and returned his attention to her. "We have an early start tomorrow," he reminded her, quite unnecessarily. "I believe I shall make a night of it, and suggest that you do the same."

"Actually, I had planned to take in the sights . . . perhaps stop back by the Crystal Palace for another whiskey,'' came her coolly ironic reply, though inside she silently fumed. Blast it all, would the man never learn that he had no authority over her?

Her deliberate challenge seemed not to have the quelling effect on him that she'd intended. He merely shrugged and rose from his chair. ''As you wish. I would, however, avoid the Oriental. The livery man advised me that it has a rather unsavory reputation, even for a town like Tombstone.''

''In that case, then perhaps I'll simply retire to my room,'' she said in the same frosty tone as she followed him out of the dining room.

But barely had they reached the doorway when Hancock halted abruptly. Jess, who had been on his heels, all but stumbled into him. Regaining her footing just in time to avoid an unseemly collision, she heard another man comment in a cultured Southern drawl, ''Well, I'll be damned three ways, if it isn't my old friend—''

''Jake Hancock, of Kansas City,'' the bank examiner swiftly introduced himself, stepping forward so that Jess's view of the other man momentarily was blocked. ''But I'm afraid you have mistaken me for someone else. I don't believe that we have ever met, Mister—''

''Holliday,'' he supplied, ''John Henry Holliday . . . though most persons of my acquaintance feel compelled to call me 'Doc.' ''

Chapter Eight

Her curiosity piqued, Jess moved alongside Hancock, so that she now stood practically face-to-face with the newcomer. The first thing she noticed about him were his eyes.

Pale, they were, and of a shade somewhere between blue and gray, lit by a cool, intelligent fire. He was hatless, revealing a neatly pomaded thatch of ash blond hair slightly lighter than his long mustache. His handsome features were almost as pale . . . and haggard, she noted, as if he'd been recently ill. He was younger than Hancock and far leaner, dressed in an elegant dove gray suit that lent him an aristocratic air.

He was studying her in equal interest, so that she realized she'd been staring for far too long. His gaze flicking momentarily to the bank examiner again, he added, "I believe you are forgetting your manners, Mr. Hancock. You haven't yet introduced me to this vision of tawny loveliness."

"No, I haven't."

With those curt words, Hancock took Jess's arm—less in a gesture of courtliness, she suspected, than as a show of solidarity—and started to move past him. Holliday was swifter than he, however, and with a graceful move once again blocked their way.

"I do beg your pardon, Mr. Hancock," he said in that same smooth drawl. "It's just that you quite reminded me of an old friend, so that I have a hard time believing we don't already know one another. Perhaps I might make my apologies by buying you a drink at the Oriental . . . that is, if Mrs. Hancock does not object."

"I'm not Mrs. Hancock!"

"She's not my wife!"

The twin denials—Jess's voiced in a tone of horror, Hancock's clipped with impatience—brought a suggestion of a smile to Holliday's pale lips. "Indeed? Then I owe you yet another apology. Now, Mr. Hancock, about that whiskey . . ."

Jess expected the bank examiner to make another curt refusal. Instead, releasing his hold on her, he replied, "On second thought, Mr. Holliday, I do believe I will take you up on your offer, since my companion had already indicated that she wished to retire early. If you'll allow me to escort her to her room, I'll meet you in, say, a quarter hour."

"I look forward to it," he replied and stepped aside with lanky grace. Only Jess saw the ungentlemanly wink he gave her as he murmured, "And perhaps, dear madam, our Mr. Hancock will feel more inclined to introduce you to me at a later date."

Jess waited until they were upstairs and out of earshot before she turned to the bank examiner. "Holliday," she murmured. "I believe I've heard that name before. Isn't he a gunman of sorts?"

"I'm sure I can't say," was Hancock's cool reply as they halted before her door. "I'd rather pegged him for a gambler. If he is, then he likely travels about quite a bit, so no doubt he'll be a good source of information. He might even know the location of Dead Squaw Canyon."

Let's hope not, Jess thought in consternation. If Hancock was to travel with her, she needed the bargaining chip of being the only one to know their exact destination. Otherwise, he surely would try to take control of the situation.

Aloud, she merely said, "It's worth a try. Very well, Mr. Hancock, I shall see you at dawn at the O.K. Corral . . . that is, if you are still quite certain you wish to continue on."

"I'll be there, Mrs. Satterly. Good night."

She frowned thoughtfully as she watched his retreating figure. Was he indeed interested in this Holliday person merely as a source of information, or was there another reason why he sought the man's acquaintance? Odd, too, how Holliday had made the same mistake as she, thinking that he knew the bank examiner from somewhere else. Whatever the situation, she fully intended to quiz Hancock on the subject come morning.

But her thoughts as she settled into the narrow if comfortable bed were not of the two men, Hancock and Holliday. Rather, she lay in the dark listening to the sounds of Tombstone drifting through her open window and thinking of her aunt. She pictured Maude as she'd been that morning, dressed in a blue flounced gown and smiling a little self-consciously at their dual images in the foyer mirror. And now that fragile, smiling woman, who'd clung to her gracious airs even through a war, was a hostage of perhaps the most vicious men that the territory had ever known.

Was she hurt? *Perhaps.*

Was she frightened? *Almost assuredly.*

Was she even still alive?

"Of course she is!" Jess answered that last question in a vehement whisper, sitting up in bed and pillowing one damp cheek on her knees. She'd be doing nothing to help Maude by speculating on her fate. Better that she manage a few hours' sleep so that she would be ready for the next day's ride.

But even with that last directive echoing in her head, Jess did not immediately settle back down. Rather, she climbed out of bed and turned up the gaslight so that the room was suffused in a faint glow. Then, reaching into the boot where she'd tucked it for safekeeping, she pulled out Mr. Johnson's map.

Neither Tombstone nor Brimstone was marked on the parchment . . . hardly surprising, since the document had been drawn numerous decades before either of those fledgling towns had been founded. Even so, several of the trails and passes, as well as mountains and peaks, were landmarks that she recognized from modern maps.

Studying the parchment more closely now, she saw that what she'd thought were arrows pointing the way along the trail were instead cleverly etched serpents. One of those inked snakes slithered its way from a spot she judged to be just west of what was now Tombstone. That would be their starting point tomorrow, she decided, from which place they would head south.

Carefully, she refolded the parchment and returned it to its hiding place. Then, turning down the light again, she slipped back into her bed. This time the question that nagged at her was of a more mundane nature . . . was Hancock still tilting up whiskey glasses with Doc Holliday? She laid awake a few minutes longer, listening for the sound of booted footsteps passing her door that would signal his return.

When another quarter hour passed and the hallway without remained silent, she rolled over and buried her face in her pillow, determined not to spend a moment longer wondering about the man's activities. *Dawn, indeed,* she thought with a sniff and scrunched her eyes more tightly shut. Chances were she'd be forced to pound on his door at first light . . . and there'd be no sympathy to spare from her if he found himself waking with a pounding head after a night out on the town with the gambler!

The Oriental Saloon resembled its nearby neighbor, the Crystal Palace, in its outward appointments . . . the carved mahogany bar, the tasteful wallpaper, the faro and poker tables. But while the latter attracted the town's more prominent citizens, the Oriental's clientele was drawn from the rougher edges of Tombstone society. The atmosphere was sullen, aggressive, as were the men who drank and gambled there. Little wonder, he thought wryly, that Sheriff Behan had not mentioned the Oriental as one of his recommended places.

He found Doc Holliday seated alone at a corner table, an open bottle and two glasses before him. The gambler gestured to him to take a chair and poured out a measure of whiskey for them both, then reached for the card deck before him. Idly, the man began to shuffle.

He took the seat indicated, as well as the half-full glass Holliday slid toward him. "You're looking well, Doc," he observed, holding a steady gaze on the man. "It seems the desert air agrees with you."

"So the doctors all claim. As for myself, I'm optimistically predicting that I'll die of lead poisoning long before my lungs give out." He paused, pale eyes narrowing. His tone was affable, however, as he went on. "I must confess, I rather feared you might pass on my invitation, after all, Mr. . . . Hancock, was it? Or, now that we're alone together, perhaps I might just call you Nick Devilbiss?"

"Call me by that name again, and I'll start remembering those warrants that I forgot back in Dodge City."

"Why, Nick, I do believe you are threatening me," the gambler mildly countered. "That's hardly a way to talk to the man who kept your own brother from killing you."

Nick Devilbiss grimly nodded by way of reply, the scar along his right shoulder twinging at the recollection. Even after two years, the memory was fresh in his mind. He had wakened the morning after the attack to find himself in a hotel bed, his torn shoulder bandaged and himself liberally plied with laudanum. The room had proved to be Holliday's, though the gambler had already departed for Arizona. Lucinda, Holliday's companion of the night before, had remained behind to offer her own brand of comfort.

Unfortunately, the prostitute had known nothing more about the attack than what Doc had mentioned to her in passing. Indeed, her understanding was that Doc had been forced to kill Rory to save Nick. A few days later, when Doc's money ran out and Lucinda departed to offer comfort elsewhere, Nick finally dragged himself out of bed. It was then that he had learned that Rory had only been creased by Doc's bullet, and that the younger man had fled town.

Now, Nick sighed inwardly. Holliday was right, and on all counts. The gambler *had* saved Nick's life, and Nick *was* threatening him . . . not that it would do much good. The tubercular dentist-turned-gambler had more lives than a cat, and more nerve than a dozen men. All the warrants and wanted posters west of the Mississippi wouldn't do more than raise the man's aristocratic brow.

Holliday said, "Now let me guess. You must be on another job, and Mr. Pinkerton has insisted that you travel incognito."

"I *am* working undercover," he conceded, taking a sip from his glass, "but I'm not on company business, Doc, not this time."

He settled back in his chair and debated just how much to tell the other man about the circumstances that had brought him to Arizona. Running across Holliday here in Tombstone had been a piece of bad luck, since the man was one of the few people outside the company who knew his true identity. On the other hand, he knew Doc was not prone to idle gossip, so any information Nick shared with him would not go beyond this scarred oak table. And, almost as importantly, it was a relief to shed his prim bank examiner's role . . . at least for a time. But how much could he say, and not compromise the situation?

Holliday, meanwhile, with his usual shrewd grasp of a situation, saved him the trouble of deciding what course to take. He gave Nick a faint smile and began dealing out the cards, saying, "I don't suppose it would have anything to do with that rapscallion younger brother of yours, now would it?"

Nick took a deep breath, then replied, "That's not exactly what lawmen in these parts call him, but, yes, I'm looking for Rory. I suppose you've already heard that the Black Horse Gang is back from Mexico, or Montana, or wherever they've been holed up since the Brimstone robbery and murder last year?"

"News like that does get around in these parts."

"Word reached our Kansas City office, as well. The wanted posters were all changed to 'Dead or Alive' and the reward was doubled. I took a leave of absence hoping I could find him before someone killed him, or he killed them."

"Indeed. I must assume from your bleak expression that you did not succeed in at least one of those endeavors."

"I didn't."

It had been the Territorial Bankers Association that had ponied up the extra reward money and pushed for Rory's apprehension. Warned by his supervisor that no quarter would be given the younger man just because he was Nick's brother, Nick had decided to take matters into his own hands. Inspired by the charter company, he had conceived the idea of making his investigations in the guise of a bank examiner.

As for the alias, the name Devilbiss was too well known in Arizona Territory these days not to draw undue attention. He'd simply borrowed the name and corresponding letters of introduction from one of the charter company's actual bank examiners. The real Jacob E. Hancock, meanwhile, currently was taking the waters in Eureka Springs, Arkansas, with a comely young woman who was not his wife.

He felt his lips twist in a bitter smile. Paying a prostitute to lure the real Hancock into adultery and out of reach was the least of Nick's sins. It was this day's events that weighed upon his conscience, though he had done what he could to prevent them. Or had he?

You told me not to worry about the Black Horse Gang, and I believed you, Jess had declared. *But now, because of you, a good man is dead and another one seriously hurt . . . and my aunt has been kidnapped by killers!*

His fingers tightened on the whiskey glass as he shoved aside the memory of those accusing words and met Holliday's pale gaze. "Rory and the others rode into Brimstone this afternoon and robbed the bank again . . . but this time they didn't just kill a bank teller. They murdered the local marshal and shot the deputy, then took a hostage with them. A woman."

"A troubling scenario, to be sure. But where does your lovely companion fit into all this? Surely she is not an example of Mr. Pinkerton's more cunning forays into undercover detection . . . oh, and do take a peek at your hand."

Nick idly glanced at his cards, discarded a couple, and then shook his head. "Jessamine—Mrs. Satterly—owns the bank in Brimstone. Since none of her fellow citizens elected to form a posse, she decided to take on the job of tracking down the Black Horse Gang herself. When I tried to convince her to turn back, she informed me that she would allow me to ride along with her, if I wished."

"Splendid woman," came Holliday's approving murmur.

The gambler had always had a penchant for bold females, Nick knew. He recalled a certain hard-drinking prostitute by the name of Kate who'd lived with Holliday during his Dodge City days, even claiming on occasion to be his wife. Though another sort of female entirely, Jessamine Satterly still would be the kind of woman to hold the tubercular dentist's fancy.

Aloud, Nick merely said, "It's not just the money she's after. You see, the woman who was kidnapped just happens to be her aunt." He hesitated, then grimly finished, "And her husband was the man killed in the first robbery."

Holliday again favored him with his faint smile as he dealt out two more cards, then replaced his own discards. "You do get yourself into the most interesting scrapes. I presume Mrs. Satterly has no clue yet that she's riding about the territory with the brother of the man who killed her husband?"

"She doesn't, and she won't. I intend to ride out after Rory before dawn tomorrow . . . alone."

It was, after all, the only logical solution. He'd make better time without her, and he'd be spared worrying that she might be shot, or thrown from her horse, or suffer some other disaster while in his charge. And under these circumstances he could not afford the distraction—not if he wanted to bring back both Maude McCray and Rory alive.

Instead, Jess could wait here in Tombstone for the Earp posse to return, then pass on to them what information she had about the gang's likely destination. Such a plan would afford him the head start he'd wanted, while still giving him a few more guns on his side once he was ready to confront Rory. To be sure, she'd be furious with him for leaving her behind . . . but, given that he'd likely never see her again, he could live with her outrage.

"What will happen once you and your brother meet up again?" the gambler wanted to know.

Nick shrugged. "That's up to Rory. I'm going to try to convince him to head west with me to California, and let him emigrate from there to Australia. It would give him a clean start, a chance to make a life of his own, without either of us constantly looking over our shoulders for the other. My only other option is to try to work out some sort of amnesty agreement with the governor . . . maybe bring in the rest of the gang in exchange for a pardon for Rory."

Holliday, meanwhile, had assumed the thoughtful look that always preceded one of his more outrageous statements. This time was no exception.

"It occurs to me, Nick—or should I say Jake—that you might need some help in tracking down your brother," he observed, reaching for the bottle to refill his now empty glass. "I think I shall ride with you tomorrow."

The hell you will, was Nick's first reflexive thought.

Fortunately, he knew the gambler well enough to be certain that such a response would only spur him on. Instead, he contented himself with a bland warning. "It'll be a dull ride, Doc."

"It's damned dull here. My friend Wyatt and his brothers are out playing lawman, so I have absolutely no one of any consequence to talk with. One can only listen to Clifford"—he gestured at the massive blond dealing faro—"complain about his corns so many times."

He paused to cough in a way that Nick remembered from the last time they'd been together. Apparently the desert had only slowed the progress of his disease, not cured him.

Recovering himself, the gambler said, "At least with you, I'd be assured of intelligent conversation for a few days. Besides, if you don't take me along, I'll be obliged to tell Mrs. Satterly that you are not, shall we say, the man you represented yourself to be."

Nick lifted a wry brow. "Why, Doc, I do believe you are threatening me," he coolly echoed the other man's earlier observation.

Rather than deny Nick's words, the other man took a sip of whiskey and said, "Do you know, Nick, I find something quite fascinating about you and your brother. You're like two dark angels . . . one long since fallen from heaven and happily carving out his new niche in hell, and the other still clinging to those pearly gates, too stubborn to admit that the Almighty has booted him out of Paradise. In some ways, you both remind myself of me."

Nick suppressed a wry grimace. The truth was, he had patterned his prim Hancock persona after Doc at his most exasperating. As for the gambler's reference to dark angels, Nick could only dismiss it as the whiskey talking. Rory might be one of the fallen, but Nick was not. And he was Rory's only chance to find salvation somewhere other than at the end of a rope.

But the more immediate problem lay in dealing with Holliday.

Stalling, Nick reached for the whiskey bottle and splashed another inch of the reddish brown liquid into his glass. On the one hand, he always worked alone when in the field. On the other, he had seen Doc's skill with both rifle and gun, had witnessed his spit-in-the-eye-of-death attitude in the face of danger. Besides, the man likely had some knowledge of the surrounding countryside, which Nick did not.

"All right, Doc, you can ride along," he surprised himself by saying, "but just so long as we're in agreement that I call the shots . . . and that you'll back me in whatever course of action I take."

"Agreed," the gambler replied, satisfaction lighting his pale eyes. "And now that we have that settled, I don't suppose you'll change your mind about our riding out at an ungodly hour?"

"No, I won't." Nick finished off his whiskey and stood. "My horse is stabled at the O.K. Corral. I'll be ready to ride at first light. If you're not there by then, I leave without you."

"Oh, very well," he drawled. Then the gambler frowned. "Why, Nick, you never even looked at your cards."

Nick reached out and flipped the pair over, revealing an ace and a king of spades. Then he tossed down the remaining three in his hand . . . the queen, jack, and ten of the same suit.

Doc tossed down his own hand, which consisted of a pair of fours, beside Nick's cards. "Straight flush," he murmured approvingly. "Looks like your luck just might be starting to change, after all."

Chapter Nine

Maude McCray huddled on the rocky ground beneath a sliver of moon and a thin blanket that stank of male sweat, and wondered just how soon she would die.

She had expected death from the first terrifying instants of her kidnapping, when a masked man had seized her in a crushing grip and pressed a cold steel gun barrel to her temple. Just moments before the gang burst through the bank's entry, she'd been standing inside that very doorway, a cloth-covered basket of food in the crook of one arm. The clock inside the bank had just rung the quarter hour as she arrived with the promised luncheon for her niece and that handsome Mr. Hancock. But it happened that both he and Jessamine had stepped out on errands, so that Maude had had no choice but to chat awhile with Lily until the pair returned.

Not that the half-Chinese young woman had not been pleasant company, Maude bleakly recalled; it was just that she never felt entirely comfortable in her presence. She never was quite sure how to treat Lily . . . certainly not as a servant, but not exactly as an equal, either. Still, they had conversed pleasantly enough for a few moments, until Lily excused herself to take care of an old gentleman who had tottered in.

Maude had heard the thunder of approaching horses long before she saw the riders themselves. Oddly enough, she'd felt no shiver of alarm at the sound, for it had been more than a year since Brimstone last had been terrorized by the Black Horse Gang. . . . more than a year since her nephew-in-law's tragic death. She had assumed the horsemen to be a group of cowboys, arrived early from one of the nearby ranches.

And then four masked men brandishing pistols had rushed into the bank and barred the door behind them.

Of the robbery itself she recalled but little, save for Lily Chwang's frightened face as the young woman hurried to do the outlaws' bidding. Then the shooting had begun, an explosion of sound ripping through her ears and drowning out her own thin, frantic cries of fear. Just as swiftly, the shooting ended . . . and Maude abruptly found herself dragged into the street.

Her next memory had been less coherent, that of the headlong flight from Brimstone. The riders had numbered several more than the four robbers—perhaps as many as a dozen—though she had been hard-pressed to make a count. It had been a hellish journey that found her slung facedown over the pommel of one outlaw's saddle, clinging feverishly to the leather even as every hoofbeat battered her midsection. Dust thrown up from the other riders parched her lips and throat until she thought she'd surely expire of thirst, if she did not first lose consciousness and then slide to her death beneath churning hooves.

The gang kept up that brutal pace for hours, stopping but twice to rest their blowing mounts for a few moments. Both times she'd been too overcome by the pounding and sheer terror even to consider trying to escape. Instead, she'd managed to drag herself upright in the saddle for a few moments and claw her snarled hair—its confining pins long since strewn across the desert sand—from her wind-burned face.

By the second time they'd halted, she dared a glance at the

men who had abducted her. They were a savage and filthy lot . . . young, most of them, including the man who had held her captive during the robbery. She gathered from his manner and the way the others deferred to him that he was their leader. If so, than that made him the infamous Rory Devilbiss, the man whose name was anathema to the decent, God-fearing people of Brimstone.

He might have been accorded a handsome man, if not for the cruel twist to his lips and the soulless chill to his blue eyes. His gaze had flicked across her once as she'd looked about, and she had gasped, as if struck, before hurriedly dropping her own eyes. It was then that she had concluded that, though they were keeping her alive for now, sooner or later they would have to kill her.

Why else would they have let her see them without the concealing red bandannas that had covered their faces during the robbery?

With the coming of nightfall, the outlaws had finally stopped to set up a hasty camp. Where they were by then—or even if they were still in Arizona—she had no idea. All she could tell was that the relatively flat terrain near Brimstone had given way to rocky foothills. The florid orange sun had dipped all too quickly beneath the distant line of mountains, but Maude barely noticed. Instead, she had huddled where her captor had unceremoniously dropped her from the horse, hovering on the edge of consciousness and too exhausted to crawl from that spot.

Sometime later, a sharp kick to her thigh roused her to wakefulness. Stifling a cry of mingled fear and pain, she had managed to pull herself into a sitting position. It had been fully dark by then, though a nearby campfire poked fingers of yellow light into the shadows. Through her tangle of hair she could make out a pair of black-booted, trouser-clad legs before her. She'd not dared to gaze higher.

Abruptly, a canteen had landed with a metallic thud before her. She grabbed for it, fumbling for what seemed like hours to unscrew its lid. As the tepid water splashed over her cracked lips, she almost sobbed in relief, not caring that fully half of that mouthful spilled down her chin and onto the bodice of her silk gown.

"Don't waste it, you stupid bitch."

She recognized the harsh voice by now; still, she gave a fearful cry as Devilbiss snatched the canteen from her hands, then reached down and caught her by the torn ruffle of her high collar. What his intentions had been she'd dared not guess . . . nor did she learn, for another male voice had interrupted them.

"Rory, you'd best take a look at Mackey. He ain't good."

"Shit," the outlaw leader had breathed in disgust, releasing his grip on her as he turned away.

Cautiously peering up, she saw him head toward the small campfire. The rest of the gang was gathered there, and the horses were tied beyond. Perhaps if she remained where she was, she would go unnoticed in the shadows for the rest of the night, even though it meant she did not dare inch closer to the campfire.

For though the earth still held some of the day's earlier warmth, the chill of a desert night had begun to settle over the land. She realized that she was cold . . . shivering, in fact, and not only from fear. Her thin silk gown, its side seams partially split from her brutal ride, would soon prove scant protection as the temperature continued to drop.

But her fear of freezing to death was supplanted by more basic fears as she heard the men begin to argue. Their voices grew louder and they periodically glanced her way now, a few chilling words drifting to her.

Woman. Why else we brung her? Break 'er in for ya. She'd not needed to hear more to know what it was that they planned for her.

Abruptly, one of the men broke from the group and started toward her. Maude clutched the torn ruffle of her collar together, willing herself not to scream, not to whimper. Whatever they said to her, whatever they did, she'd not let them know how very frightened she was.

The man halted before her, a tall and menacing silhouette wrapped in shadows. The flickering glow from the campfire lit him just enough for her to tell he was blond, and that he was holding something in his hands. *Dear God, don't let them tie me,* had been her sudden, frantic thought.

Yet even as she cowered on the rocky ground, he leaned over and draped a worn woolen blanket over her shoulders, then shoved a piece of dried beef into her hands. "Here, you'd best eat something, ma'am."

The voice had belonged to the same man who earlier had called Devilbiss away . . . the same one, she recalled, who had plundered the bank vault. He, too, was young, but far more massively built than the gang leader. And, unlike Devilbiss, this man's words held a note of concern so unexpected that her eyes suddenly welled with tears. Gathering her courage, she clutched at his hand.

"Please," she choked out in a frightened whisper, "tell me what will happen to me."

He had pulled from her limp grip and taken a step back. "We're holding you hostage, ma'am, that's all I know."

"B-but I heard them talking . . ."

"Rory says we're to leave you be tonight," he told her, sounding oddly uncomfortable for a vicious outlaw. "Now, you'd best get some sleep . . . and don't think about tryin' to run off, ma'am. Even if you made it out of camp, you'd probably fall down a gully and break your neck, if the rattlers and wolves didn't get you first."

With that grim warning, he had turned and headed back to the campfire. She waited awhile longer, her gaze fixed warily on the men gathered there, in case any of them decided to seek her out despite Devilbiss's orders. Only when it seemed that she truly would be left in peace this night had she relaxed her vigil enough to huddle more deeply into the fetid blanket and gnaw at her jerky.

Now, as the moon rose higher and the outlaws bedded down

around the dying campfire, Maude settled herself as comfortably as she could on the rocky desert floor and wondered how much longer the gang leader intended her to live. She must yet have some value as a hostage, she told herself, or else he would not have stopped his men from using her. But what about tomorrow night, and the next?

She drew the blanket higher around her, so that its shapeless folds better disguised her form. No doubt she looked quite as miserable as she felt, but her disheveled state would mean nothing to a man intent on rape. Surely her best course was to stay in the shadows and not draw attention to herself. As for escape . . .

She muffled a hysterical giggle that ended on a sob. Even if she had been capable of wandering about the desert under her own power, instead of barely able to crawl after the day's rugged ride, the blond outlaw's warning about snakes and other predators would have sufficed to keep her where she was.

The time she had found a rattlesnake coiled on her front porch had been a traumatic enough experience to make her permanently terrified of those reptiles. As for wolves, she'd heard enough tales of their bloodthirsty ways from Brimstone's old-timers to be frightened of those creatures, as well. And considering that she had no water, no supplies—did not, in fact, even know where in the territory or how far from Brimstone she was—she'd surely be dead within a day should she manage to flee her captors. For now she had no choice but to remain where she was, until the Black Horse Gang either killed her or freed her.

Or until help arrived.

Maude drew a shaky breath and dashed the tears from her eyes. Until that moment, it had not occurred to her that riders would be in pursuit of the gang, yet surely they must be. After all, the outlaws had robbed Brimstone's bank and kidnapped her, and they were still wanted for Arbin's murder and the previous robbery, as well. No doubt Marshal Crenshaw was leading the posse that would rescue her . . . if not tonight, then perhaps tomorrow. Certainly, Jessamine and Harvey would have seen to it that help was on its way.

Clinging to the first bit of hope she had found since the ordeal began, Maude peered into the deepening shadows for any sign of wayward snakes and wolves. Finding none, she spared a final, fearful glance for the outlaws, then slipped into an exhausted sleep.

Chapter Ten

Blast it all, where was the man?

Jess glanced in the direction of the stairway, then frowned when she still did not see Hancock's familiar figure making its way down to the lobby. Shaking her head in disgust, she turned back to the hotel desk and showed the sleepy, red-haired youth behind it two folded pages. ''Please see that this one is telegraphed immediately,'' she told him, indicating the brief note to her father she had just written.

Tombstone posse delayed, Hancock and I gone in search of Maude. Home soon. Love, Jess

A moment of guilt assailed her as she pictured her father's reaction at reading the telegram. He would be upset that she had taken on such a mission, she was certain, but he also had known her long enough not to be surprised at her decision. If not for his illness, he would have been the first to pursue the Black Horse Gang, so surely he could not fault her for the same sentiments.

Squaring her shoulders, she shrugged off her doubts and then slid the other paper across the counter to the clerk. ''And this other must be delivered to Sheriff Behan first thing this morning.''

The note in question actually was a tracing of her map that she had made while waiting impatiently for Hancock to join her in the lobby. On its reverse side, she had penciled for Behan's benefit an explanation of the Black Horse Gang's likely destination. She had also noted her own intention to follow them, and her request that Marshal Earp's posse be sent in that same direction to lend assistance once they returned to Tombstone.

When the desk clerk stared at her blankly, she reached into her drawstring purse and plucked out a few coins. ''This is important. You won't forget, now, will you?''

The heavy-eyed youth brightened perceptibly. ''No, ma'am . . . I mean, yes, ma'am . . . I mean, I'll see everything is sent,'' he agreed, gathering up coins and papers and tucking them into his checkered waistcoat. ''Now, ma'am, if you'll just sign yourself out,'' he added and opened the register to the page where she had written her and Hancock's names the night before.

She reached for the pen, then paused in dismay as she saw a careless, angular signature already inked in beside the bank examiner's name. ''Mr. Hancock has checked out? When?''

''He left about five minutes before you came downstairs,'' the desk clerk replied. ''Sorry, ma'am, I didn't know you were waiting on him.''

''Never mind that. Just tell me how to find the O.K. Corral.''

A few moments later, Jess was rushing down Allen Street, her carpetbag clutched in both arms. She was wearing her same split skirt and a fresh, tailored shirtwaist, so that her progress was unimpeded by a tangle of petticoats; even so, she did manage to catch her boot toe a time or two against the uneven boards of the sidewalk, which only added to her irritation with the bank examiner. Not that she should have been surprised that he changed plans on her, she told herself. Really, the man had the most unfortunate need to be in charge of a situation!

Early as it was, a hint of morning sun tinged the broad road with pale pink, so she could see that it was empty, save for herself. In the distance, however, she could hear faint echoes of a western town's familiar morning sounds . . . the restless stamp of sleepy cart horses; the thud of goods being unloaded onto wooden sidewalks; the lazy crow of a lone rooster. By the time dawn was in full bloom, every street would be alive again, she knew.

Her concern now, however, was with finding Hancock. The livery proved to be less than a block away, its sign with the oversized O and K prominently advertising its location. Panting, Jess slipped past the pair of tall wooden gates and into the corral area, then stopped. Hancock's roan, flanked by the black hound, and a large gray gelding were saddled and waiting; Old Pete was not. At the sound of her approach, however, he stuck his white muzzle over a stall door and whickered.

''Blast it all,'' she muttered and hurried over to the gelding, her exasperation with Hancock swiftly turning to puzzlement. Her saddle and tack hung nearby, which meant that she had no choice but to saddle Old Pete herself . . . not her most favorite of chores.

Setting aside her carpetbag, she bridled the gelding and led him from his stall. Barely had she hefted the bulky saddle onto the paint's back, however, than she heard the door to the livery office creak open behind her.

''Well, I'll be a daisy,'' a lazy male voice drifted to her. ''if it isn't the lovely Mrs. Satterly. I thought you said it was to be just the two of us traveling together, Hancock.''

''It was.''

The reply held a note of repressed irritation. Quite irritated herself, Jess gave the cinch a final tightening yank and then turned to face the two men. Doc Holliday, wearing a handsome gray suit and carrying a sawed-off shotgun, coolly met her angry gaze with a faint smile of amusement. Hancock, dressed in black trousers and a white shirt topped by a black waistcoat, wore an expression as stark as his garb. With a muttered epithet, he strode past her and untied his roan.

Jess promptly was on his heels, biting back curses of her own. "What happened to our meeting in the lobby of the Occidental at dawn . . . and what is this about you and Mr. Holliday traveling together, without me?" she demanded heatedly instead.

Her accusing look also took in Holliday, who appeared far too ill to be out that early in the day, let alone traipse across the high desert in search of outlaws. Even as she watched, he briefly bent double with a cough that reminded her of her father's symptoms. A flash of sympathy for the younger man momentarily cooled her anger. Holliday, like Harvey McCray, must have come west in hopes of stemming the inexorable tide of his consumption. And, like her father, he would soon find out that the desert air was no match for his disease.

Hancock, however, seemed unconcerned either by her anger or his travel companion's poor health. "Our original agreement was that we would ride together to Tombstone, after which you would turn back," he countered, swinging into his saddle so that he now gazed down at her from a lofty height. "I kept my end of that bargain. Regarding our riding together today, I made that ridiculous agreement only to prevent you from heading out alone last night. Certainly you can't believe that I had any intention of tracking down outlaws with a woman in tow?"

"What I can't believe is that I ever rode this far with so pompous an ass as you!"

She turned and stomped over to Old Pete, fastening her carpetbag and canteen onto his saddle, then untying him and grabbing up his reins. The paint rolled a wicked eye but, sensing her mood, wisely refrained this time from nipping her as she climbed somewhat stiffly into the saddle.

"Very well, Mr. Hancock," she continued, "you may ride with whomever you wish, but that certainly does not mean I intend to give up my own search for my aunt. I'll simply travel alone."

"As you like," came the bank examiner's clipped reply. He turned to Holliday who, having tied the shotgun onto the gray and gracefully mounted, was watching their exchange with coolly amused interest. "All right, Doc, let's ride."

The latter gave Jess a courtly nod, and the pair headed for the wooden gates. Squaring her black hat firmly over her neatly pinned crown of braids, Jess put her heels to Old Pete and followed. She made no comment, however, until after they were back on Allen Street, and the two men had urged their mounts into a trot. Then she called after them in a deliberate afterthought, "Oh, Mr. Hancock, I do believe I forgot to mention that I have a map showing the way to Dead Squaw Canyon."

Hancock abruptly reined up, so that the roan snorted in protest. Wheeling about, he waited until she had caught up with them before he demanded, "You have what?"

"A map to Dead Squaw Canyon," she repeated and halted beside them. "I suspect it will come in handy in tracking the Black Horse Gang, don't you?"

The bank examiner gave her a cool look. "That's rather convenient, your suddenly having a map. Tell me, where did you find it . . . surely not tucked under your mattress in the hotel?"

"As a matter of fact, I brought it with me." She reached into her boot, where she had stashed the folded sheet of parchment, and casually waved it in his direction. "It just happens that I took it as collateral from an old miner a few months ago."

"I doubt it's genuine. Let me see it."

He abruptly made as if to snatch it from her, but Jess was quicker. Reining Old Pete back a few paces, she tucked the parchment back inside her boot top and shook her head.

"I think not, Mr. Hancock. This map is bank property, which means I am responsible for its safekeeping. If you wish to take advantage of the information I have, you may ride with me, and I will consult the map as we travel; otherwise, you and Mr. Holliday must track the gang on your own."

"Damn it all, if you think this is a game—"

"It's no game, Mr. Hancock," she grimly cut him short. "The Black Horse Gang has my aunt, and I intend to see her brought safely back . . . with or without your help. And since you seem eager to ride without me, I have no choice but to keep control of the map if I wish to accomplish what I've set out to do."

"She's right, of course," Holliday interjected in his lazy drawl. "You'd best throw in your hand, because the pot is hers . . . at least this go around."

The bank examiner favored them both with a dark look. When he spoke, his tone was that of a man controlling himself by dint of great exertion.

"Every minute we spend debating this means that the Black Horse Gang is putting that much more distance between us and them. Very well, we'll ride together, and if Mrs. Satterly feels the need to hold on to the map, then so be it. But it will be her responsibility to keep pace with us and keep us on track."

He paused, his frown deepening as he turned his entire attention to Jess. "And if you fall behind, even once, I reserve the right to take that damned map from you, no questions asked. Agreed?"

"Agreed," Jess replied with a curt nod, tapping her heels into Old Pete's side to urge him forward. Behind her, she heard the cool drawl that was Holliday's voice.

"Why, Mr. Hancock, I do believe that you lied to me. You said this would be a dull ride, but we're not yet out of Tombstone and already I find myself vastly entertained."

By the time they did leave Tombstone behind them, it was almost full light. Once again, the road out of town narrowed to a trail that, in spots, was nothing more than a set of wagon wheel ruts carved from the rocky terrain. There in the high desert the morning air was cool, so that the rising sun on Jess's back as they rode in a westerly direction was welcome.

Less welcome was the company of the men riding with her . . . at least, one of them.

She had no time to brood over events, however, for they traveled at a brisk pace until they reached the San Pedro River a few miles from town. Here, the terrain dipped from rocky hills down to a small, lush valley dotted with cottonwoods and willows in addition to the ubiquitous desert scrub. Birds abounded there, as evidenced by the random flash of feathers and soft bursts of trilling song that heralded the riders' approach. The river itself had dried to a modest stream with the summer months, but Jess could see from the oxbows and exposed rocky banks that the waters often ran much higher.

They halted at the water's edge, and Hancock immediately swung down from the roan. "No one has crossed here in the last two days," he determined after a glance at the bank. "Are you certain we're on the right trail?"

"The river is clearly marked on the map. If the outlaws are headed to Dead Squaw Canyon, they have no choice but to cross it."

Still, it was just as obvious to her that the muddy riverbed had not recently been chopped by the passing of hooves. But perhaps the gang was following a slightly different trail than the three of them were, given how close they were to town.

Holliday, meanwhile, had urged his gray off the trail to a point several yards downstream, where he now halted.

"I do believe, however, that several riders have recently crossed here." he coolly observed, riding his own mount across the shallow waters at that same point. Reaching the other side, he turned back and called to them, "I venture to say that if I follow these tracks a bit farther, they will lead back to the main trail."

"We'll meet you at that point," Jess called back and promptly urged Old Pete into the stream.

Unused to wetting his hooves, the gelding splashed about rather more than was necessary, sending muddy droplets flying.

Jess heard the bank examiner's muttered epithet behind her as he swiftly remounted and followed after her. Suppressing a triumphant smile—not only had he been wrong, but now he was wet—she and Old Pete clambered back onto the bank and onto the trail again.

She kept Holliday and his gray easily in sight as he moved in a parallel fashion through the scattering of cottonwoods that gave the area an almost parklike feel. The river was perhaps a quarter of a mile behind them by the time his path converged again with theirs.

"It appears that our outlaw friends decided it was safe to return to the main road," he drawled, even as Hancock halted his roan and climbed down to study the trail before them.

The bank examiner made a curt sound of agreement, and Jess rolled her eyes. Since when did bank examiners from Kansas City become expert trackers? She kept such uncharitable thoughts to herself, however, as he turned to her and demanded, "Now which way?"

"We'll keep headed west," she said, pulling out the map again to confirm her memory. She traced the inked lines with a finger, stopping at the snake symbol she had made note of last night, and then nodded to herself in satisfaction. "West," she repeated, "and in a mile or so another trail should intersect this one."

"The pass to Charleston," Holliday confirmed, naming the small mining town to the north of them. Jess had often heard it called a smaller version of the rowdy Tombstone, though she had never set foot in the place.

Doc, however, had. "I've passed quite a bit of time in Charleston, myself . . . though not in recent months. A few of the more prominent citizens there took a sudden dislike to me, so that I found it prudent to conduct my business elsewhere."

"Indeed? Not that it matters, since we will be turning south at that point," Jess told him, wondering what he'd done to deserve the townspeople's enmity.

As if reading her thoughts, Holliday gave her his faint,

amused smile. "Poker, my dear," he drawled. "I had the bad manners to win . . . too often and too much to suit the locals."

Hancock snorted as he climbed back into the saddle. "In case you didn't know, Doc Holliday is a professional gambler. He's also quite proficient with that nickel-plated Colt of his."

"I do have that reputation, though I'm not sure why," that man conceded with a shrug, looking more amused than put out by Hancock's jibe. "Rumor credits me with dispatching many more men than I actually have. At last count, I believe it was only six . . . or perhaps seven, though one of those was with a knife."

Jess stared from one man to the other, uncertain whether or not to give credence to what she was hearing. On the one hand, they might simply be trying to unnerve her, given this morning's failed attempt to leave her behind in Tombstone. On the other, Arizona was filled with men who had a reputation with a gun. The dapper Doc Holliday could easily be one of them.

Which might be the reason Hancock had convinced the man to ride along, came the sudden flash of insight. Perhaps the bank examiner realized his own limitations in pursing outlaws and decided he needed a hired gun to help him carry out the job.

Thoughtfully, she tucked away the parchment again and forged ahead, the two men behind her and the black hound trailing after them. They reached the crossroads more swiftly than she anticipated. She called a halt long enough for Hancock to again satisfy himself that the Black Horse Gang had passed that way before them, and then started south.

This trail proved even less well traveled than the road on which they'd begun, and Jess found herself longing for the comfort of her tall leather chair behind her desk in the bank. That seat, at least, was softly padded. Her aching hindquarters attested to the fact that her saddle was not.

In her anger over Hancock's treatment of her, she had managed to ignore the bruises and stiff muscles that were the result of yesterday's unaccustomed ride. Now, however, the further pounding of the rough trail reminded her why she never had been an enthusiastic horsewoman, and she prayed she'd have no reason to dismount again before day's end. Of course, she'd never admit her discomfort to either man, lest they use it as an excuse to try to abandon her in the next town they passed.

But there were no other towns, and with the rough terrain their pace proved slower than any of them had hoped. Twice they crossed paths with lone horsemen coming from the south, though neither man admitted to encountering a group of fast-moving riders in the past two days. As for the Black Horse Gang themselves, the only sign of them was the occasional hoofprint on a sandy patch of the trail.

Conversation with her travel companions proved equally sporadic and desultory. Once, while they were waiting for Hancock to conclude his examination of a suspect trampled bush, Jess asked Holliday if he truly was a medical doctor.

"A dentist, actually," came his cool reply. "Unfortunately, my patients all decided to take their business elsewhere. It seems they objected to my constantly pausing to cough in the midst of filling their teeth."

After that, Jess refrained from making any more personal conversation. As the day progressed, she reined in half a dozen more times to consult her map. Each time, the bank examiner sharply questioned her choice of direction, until she would have shoved the map in his face and told him to read it himself, had she not known that was just what he wanted. As dusk came upon them, however, it was Hancock who called a halt to the day's journey.

"We'll camp there," he said without preamble, indicating a spot a few minutes' ride beyond, in the upper reaches of a small wash.

The site in question was quite suitable . . . concealed enough so that they could light a campfire without giving away their location, yet high enough above the desert floor that the unlikely rainstorm would not send a torrent through to sweep them away. Even so, given that it was Hancock's suggestion, Jess would have felt duty bound to suggest an alternate, had she been a little less saddle sore. Since she wasn't, she approved his decision with alacrity.

As she had feared, climbing out of the saddle proved an arduous undertaking; still, she bit her lip against her reflexive groan and managed to dismount without calling undue attention to herself. Once she had determined that her legs would hold her, her first task after she'd tended to Old Pete was to take inventory of her food. The results were not encouraging. In raiding Aunt Maude's kitchen before she'd left Brimstone, Jess had availed herself of the staples—flour, coffee, beans, a bit of bacon—and just enough to last a single person perhaps a week. Now there were three of them, so that her food would last two or three days at most.

"Don't worry, Mrs. Satterly," came Hancock's clipped voice behind her. "Before I left Brimstone, your Miss Chwang was kind enough to prevail upon her uncle to provide me with a few staples, as well. If we pool our resources, we'll have more than enough until we can restock. Now, would you care to try your hand at cooking a meal, or should I?"

Pride and weariness battled, but only for a moment. "I'm not quite as skilled as the chef at the Occidental," she loftily told him, "but if you can start a tolerable cooking fire, I think I can manage something halfway edible."

And the meal did prove quite tolerable, Jess decided with satisfaction sometime later, sitting beside the flickering fire as she finished off her last bite of biscuit. To her surprise, the two men with her seemed quite at home in the wilderness . . . certainly more comfortable than men accustomed to city living should be. Had their mission not been such a grim one, she might even have thought the arrangement cozy. Making certain now that sufficient biscuits and bacon remained for a cold meal in the morning, Jess settled the coffeepot at the edge of the fire ring, then settled back with a sigh.

The moon had risen high above the rugged horizon, bright as Brimstone silver against the obsidian gleam of the desert sky. Other than the crackle of the dying fire, the only sound to break the silence was the cool night breeze that wound its way through the rocks in a mournful whisper. Like the distant cry of a frightened woman, she thought with a shiver, abruptly trying to imagine how her aunt might be faring. A night bird called in the distance, and she started.

"Nervous?" came Hancock's wry question from the shadows beside her as he leaned forward and reached for the coffeepot.

Jess shot him a disapproving look. "Certainly not," she lied, shaking the last drops of coffee from her own tin cup. Then, giving way to honesty, she went on in a tight voice, "I'm just thinking about my aunt. You've met her, Mr. Hancock, so you've seen the sort of woman she is . . . gracious, soft-spoken, always finely dressed. She's not the sort of person to do well under harsh circumstances. Do you think . . . that is, surely the Black Horse Gang would not . . ."

"I suspect that your aunt is a stronger woman than you give her credit for being," he cut her short as her thoughts began to stumble over increasingly frightening scenarios. "Assuming she has made it this far with them, she has a chance to survive the ordeal. If you're asking if she will remain unmolested in their company, that is highly unlikely . . . but if you want my opinion as to whether or not we will find her alive, I will give you better odds on that."

Jess nodded, uncertain whether he intended his words as reassurance, and then glanced over at the other man. "What do you think, Dr. Holliday?"

"Do call me Doc," he murmured from his spot across the fire.

She nodded. "Then you must call me Jess . . . and do tell me your view of the situation. You do have some knowledge of outlaws, after all."

"Very well. If you are asking my opinion as a gambler concerning our chances of finding your aunt alive and tolerably well, let us just say that I would not take your Mr. Hancock's bet."

Even as she made an involuntary sound of protest at that statement, he continued, "As a student of human nature, however, I might be inclined to agree with him. In my time here in the west, I've seen strong men crumble under adverse conditions and watched weaklings rise to heroic heights. As a result, I have learned never to predict how my fellow man—or woman—will react in a given situation."

And he was right, of course. She could never have guessed that Arbin would try to confront the Black Horse Gang, just as she would never have believed that no one in Brimstone save she and Hancock would dare to track down those outlaws. Perhaps Maude *was* made of sterner stuff than she'd imagined.

Somewhat more cheered than she had been a moment ago, Jess stood. "Thank you for your honesty, both of you. And now, since we have an early start in the morning, I believe I will get some sleep. Good night, Mr. Hancock, Dr. Holliday . . . Doc."

"Pleasant dreams, my dear Jess," Holliday drawled from across the fire, his pale face thrown into even harsher planes by the flickering shadows.

Hancock offered no such comforting platitudes. "I recommend that you sleep with your boots on," was his parting suggestion. "That is, unless you want to be shaking out spiders and scorpions from them in the morning."

Jess glanced reflexively at her feet, steeling herself against the impulse to kick at imaginary, multilegged creatures crawling across her boot toes. *Blast the man,* she thought with a shiver, even as she gave a grateful shake of her head for his advice. Still, sleeping soundly was now out of the question, as was a final private visit behind the rocks for a few moments before she retired. And perhaps she should arrange her blankets a bit closer to the fire . . . or maybe she should just make this journey by herself, as she'd intended.

But as she settled into her borrowed bedroll, trying not to groan when the rocky ground beneath her prodded every bruise and pulled muscle, she found herself glad that she was not alone in the desert night. True, her companions were an overbearing bank examiner and a caustic dentist, but one could not always be particular in the choice of one's posse. And knowing they were there, she could shut her eyes and be assured that, should man or beast approach in the dead of night, someone would be there to help her defend the camp. In an odd way, it was like being back in her old room, with Arbin stretched out in the bed beside her.

Well, not exactly like that, her inner voice amended in a shocked tone, even as she felt herself blush. Luckily, neither man seemed inclined to view her as a potential bedmate, for which treatment she wasn't sure whether to be complimented or insulted. Holliday, she felt sure, had his share of women despite his ill health, but she envisioned him as too fastidious to indulge in such activities around a campfire. and certainly not in the company of another man. As for Hancock . . .

Jess frowned to herself, forgetting her embarrassment as her previous uncertainty about him returned, an uncertainty that had nothing to do with his interest in her, or his lack thereof. For the most part, he was the epitome of the irritatingly prim and polished city gentleman, a stickler for minutiae who likely had counted every sheet of paper and bottle of ink in her bank.

But more than once she'd glimpsed behind his cool blue eyes a heated and single-minded impatience quite foreign to his usual manner, so that she wondered yet again if he truly was who he claimed to be. If only the telegraph lines had not been cut the day of the robbery, she would have had her answer from the charter company and long since put her suspicions to rest.

It does not matter, anyway, she firmly told herself as her eyelids began to flutter and the fire's soft crackling sounded more distant. What was important was that, of all the people in Brimstone, only he—a stranger—had come to her aid, albeit for reasons of his own. For that, she would overlook the worst of his flaws since, come to think of it, perhaps he was not quite as exasperating a man as she had first pegged him.

But even as she started to drift off, the memory of an earlier comment of Hancock's made her eyes fly open again. Lily had helped gather his provisions, he had said. First thing tomorrow morning, Jess vowed, she would check to make certain that no suspicious tin of tea was tucked among them.

Chapter Eleven

Nick waited until he heard the regular breathing of the woman curled up just a few feet away before he reached for his saddlebags beside him. By now, the fire had burned down to coals, so that most of the illumination came from a bright half moon hanging high above them. Wrapped in the familiar cloak of shadow, and with Jess sleeping, he could once again shed his Hancock persona for a time.

Untying one saddlebag, he withdrew a slim metal flask. He unscrewed its lid and splashed a bit of whiskey into his coffee, then swallowed down that fortified brew in a few swift gulps. Slowly, the liquor's warmth spread to his aching muscles, and he sighed. "Damn it all," he muttered, "I'm getting too old for this."

Beside him, he heard Holliday's soft laugh as the man proffered his own half-full cup of coffee. "Why, Nick, as I recall, I am just a few years younger than you. Surely you can't mean that I am getting old, too?"

"It's the job, Doc," he said, topping off the other man's cup with whiskey and then pouring himself another splash, straight. "I've spent a dozen years riding hell-bent all over the countryside, chasing men down, shooting them, getting shot at . . . and for what? Sometimes I wonder why in the hell I didn't find myself regular work.''

''You mean, like a job as a bank examiner?''

With those ironic words, the gambler took a large swallow of his own whiskey-laced brew. ''Men like us, Nick, are not meant for regular work,'' he went on. ''Could you picture yourself scooping out flour at the mercantile, or adding columns of numbers all day? I daresay you'd die of boredom . . . that is, if you didn't shoot yourself, first.''

''But what about you, Doc? Hell, you used to be a dentist.''

''I was a skilled member of the medical profession, a field requiring several years of training,'' Holliday coolly clarified. ''As such, I performed delicate surgical procedures and eased men's pain . . . besides which, I had the luxury of setting my own hours and hanging out my shingle wherever I pleased. I do suspect, however, that even had I not been forced to abandon my practice, I might eventually have grown weary of pulling teeth and sought a greater challenge.''

The gambler fell silent for a moment, taking up his cup again. Nick used the silence to ponder the other man's words for a moment. He *would* be bored senseless with stepping into the same shop or office, day after day, and returning home to the same place, night after night. His long-ago stint in the army had planted the seeds of wanderlust in him, while his years working as an operative for Mr. Pinkerton had nurtured those seeds into a sprawling vine. Taking up a routine job would, for him, be akin to trying to grow a rambling rose in a pot on the windowsill.

But that did not mean that the ground wasn't growing colder and more rocky beneath his bedroll with each passing year.

Nick stifled a sigh and tucked the flask back into the saddlebag, then glanced Jess's way again to make certain she had not stirred. Assured that she still slept, he said, ''We've got another hard ride ahead of us tomorrow if we expect to catch up to Rory and his men. I just hope to hell we're headed in the right direction.''

"If you're not certain, then why haven't you relieved the lovely Mrs. Satterly of the map that she so jealously guards and lead our expedition yourself?"

Why not, indeed? To be sure, he had contemplated doing just that all during the day's ride. The cleanest way to lay hands on the map, he'd finally determined, would be to wait and snatch it as she slept, then steal with it from camp before she awakened. Unfortunately, Doc seemed taken with the woman, which meant he'd probably warn her. That, or he'd try to stop Nick . . . which would result in minor unpleasantness, at best, or in one or both of them dying as they shot it out, at worst.

"Because I'm not anxious for you to put a bullet in me, Doc," he replied. "or am I just imagining that you've developed a liking for her?"

"Why, Nick, you wound me with your lack of trust. Surely you know me well enough to realize I am too much the gentleman to try to put my brand to a woman when another man has already laid claim to her."

"Laid claim to her? What the hell are you talking about?"

"Nick, it's my lungs that are bad . . . not my eyes," Holliday drawled with a faint smile. "I've seen the way you watch her, like a stallion eyeing a mare. I'd even lay odds that, if you put your mind to it, in another twenty-four hours she'll be handing that map over to you, pretty as you please."

Stinging from the gambler's unexpected—and unjustified—accusation, he allowed himself to consider that option. Finally, he shook his head. He'd have to make due with physically wresting it from her, or else waiting until she relinquished it voluntarily.

When he told Holliday as much, however, the gambler shook his head. "I cannot believe, Nick, that you are agonizing over something so simple. What it boils down to is that Jess wants to find her aunt, you want to find your brother . . . and you'd both like to recover the stolen money. You've already lied to her about who you are, so why draw the line there? All that matters is that you both get what you want, in the end."

"Hell, Doc, don't you have a conscience?"

"I can't say that I do," the other man drawled. "I believe that I coughed it up with my lungs long ago."

So saying, Holliday drained his cup and gracefully stood. "I believe I shall retire, as well. And if it turns out that you and the map are missing in the morning, I will simply throw in my lot with the lovely widow . . . which doubtless means that the two of us will be riding out after you."

With that wry promise, the gambler took himself off to his bedroll. Nick remained where he sat for a few moments longer, sipping his whiskey and wondering how the hell he'd gotten himself into this situation in the first place.

What he should have done as soon as he reached Brimstone was coordinate his efforts with the marshal. That way, they could have had a contingent waiting for the gang to ride into town . . . that was, if Crenshaw had been willing to give credence to rumor. But someone might then have tipped off Rory, so that he would have chosen another town and bank to rob. On the other hand, the outlaws might have ridden into the trap, and Rory might have been gunned down before Nick ever had a chance to talk to him.

"Hell," he muttered, finishing off his whiskey and trying not to groan as he unfolded himself from his position crouched by the fire. He could spend all night running various scenarios through his mind, or he could do the sensible thing and get a few hours' sleep, like the others.

But as he spread out his bedroll, he spared a lingering look at Jess curled up in her own blankets. Sleeping on the ground would be a damned sight more comfortable wrapped around some soft female curves. And if Holliday hadn't been with them, he might have been tempted to say the hell with his conscience, as the gambler had suggested, and taken a more direct approach by sliding under the blankets with her and seeing what happened. But even if she proved willing, such a tack would inevitably lead to his having to explain who in the hell he really was.

And he rather suspected that Jess Satterly was not the type

of woman who would take kindly to sharing her bed with the brother of her husband's killer.

"Hell, he's dead."

The blunt words cut through Maude's weary haze, and she knew a moment of pure terror. Dear God, what if they blamed her? But surely they could not have expected a wounded man to have survived the break-neck pace the Black Horse Gang had kept up for a day and a half. Had they truly cared that he lived, they would have left him behind in Brimstone, or else sent someone on with him into Tombstone for a doctor, instead of strapping him to a saddle and forcing him to endure such punishment.

She huddled in the shadows of this night's campsite, every muscle in her body aching as she recalled the day's hellish ride. Rory Devilbiss himself had dragged her from her blanket that morning as the first gray fingers of dawn had crept over the jagged horizon. He had hoisted her onto a tall black gelding, so that she perched on the saddle behind the wounded man, whose name she had heard but promptly forgotten. He had clung, half-conscious, to the saddle horn, his once-white shirt stiff and dark with dried blood.

Devilbiss had mounted his own jet black steed and grabbed up the reins of their mount. "Keep him in the saddle," was all he'd rasped out as he abruptly kicked his own stallion into a swift canter.

The wounded man swayed like a stringless marionette, and she had been forced to wrap her arms around his waist. He stank of dried sweat and blood and urine, so that she had thought for a time she might swoon from the smell. Almost as bad was the fact that she'd had no choice but to ride astride. Her blue silk gown, now sadly stained and torn, was hiked well above her ankles, revealing her nether limbs in a scandalous fashion.

After a few minutes of galloping over the rocky terrain, however, she had forgotten both propriety and squeamishness in her need simply to hang on. They rode that way for hours, stopping once to water the horses and slowing every so often to rest them before thundering on again at a swift pace. Her blond hair, now snarled into an ungainly curtain, whipped painfully across her face, even as the sun and dry wind parched and burned her pale skin. This, too, she soon learned to ignore.

Soon after the sun reached its zenith, Devilbiss had called another brief halt in the shade of a small wash. Maude had slid from the saddle and gratefully accepted a sip of water and another sliver of jerked meat from the blond giant who had shown her the same kindness the night before. Two other men, meanwhile, had lowered the wounded man from his horse and propped him against some fallen rock, where he groaned and muttered incoherently.

"Wouldn't it be kinder just to leave him here?" Maude had whispered, feeling a flash of sympathy for the injured man despite the fact that he was a member of the hated Black Horse Gang.

The blond man shook his head. "No, ma'am. Some varmint would be after him while he was still alive. At least, with us, he'll die in one piece."

They had remounted a few minutes later and continued the frantic race through the high desert. The wounded man subsided into unconsciousness, his head lolling on his chest. He did not rouse again.

How long they continued to ride she could not say. Time passed in a blur, marked only by the pounding of hooves and the inexorable progress of the sun moving across a distant blue sky. It wasn't until darkness fell that they finally stopped for the night. Maude realized then, and quite belatedly, that her charge had died sometime earlier. Too tired to care, she had done nothing more than tumble off her horse and collapse some distance from the men as they made their camp.

And then she had heard Devilbiss's voice. "Hell, he's dead."

The murmur from the other outlaws had reflected neither sorrow nor outrage; still, Maude had seen for herself the gang's viciousness. Perhaps now that one of their own was dead, they would kill her to even the score. But as the minutes passed and no one sought her out, her terror slowly leached away until only exhaustion remained.

She must have succumbed to that weariness, for the sudden crunch of boots against rock brought her fully awake. How long she had huddled there in the darkness, she could not guess. All that mattered was the horrified realization that she was no longer alone.

There were nine or ten of them surrounding her, the light from the flickering campfire behind them transforming them into identical, ominous silhouettes. Biting back a moan, she scrambled awkwardly to her feet, clutching the ragged edges of her gown's flounced neckline in a reflexive attempt at modesty. "Pl-please," she whispered, and took a step back.

One of the gang, stout and curly-haired, gave a guttural laugh. "Hear that, Rory? The little lady's beggin' for us to show her a good time."

"Well, Carson, that's just what she's gonna get."

Abruptly, Devilbiss stepped forward and caught her arm, dragging her to his chest. Maude gasped, then cried out as his grip on her arm tightened. He stank of horses, sweat, and lust, and in the darkness his blue eyes looked black.

Evil, the frantic thought flashed through her mind as he leaned closer and murmured, "Well, lady, I like 'em younger and prettier . . . but, hell, you'll just have to do."

After a single, shrill cry of fear, Maude made no other sound as Devilbiss dragged her away from the others and raped her with a brutal efficiency that made a mockery of her struggles. A few minutes later, he was standing over her again, coolly refastening his trousers. She watched him through dry, dull eyes, wondering if he would kill her now or leave her for the others . . . and wondering if she cared.

"All right, Carson," she heard him say, "you're next."

She shut her eyes as the second man shoved between her legs. She smelled his foul breath in her face as he leaned forward and pinned her wrists above her head. "C'mon, little lady, beg again," came his urgent words while he fumbled with one hand between them, trying to free himself from his pants.

A moment later, he was panting and rubbing his flaccid organ across her belly. "C'mon, beg," he demanded again, his grip on her wrists tightening, so that she bit her lip lest she cry out in pain. "You know I can't do it, 'less you ask for—"

He broke off abruptly, his words ending on a yelp even as the pressure atop her eased. She heard Carson curse, heard the soft thwack that was the sound of a fist landing into flesh. Then another man's rumbling voice said, "This ain't how you treat a woman, even one that's a hostage . . . and anyone who thinks different has to go through me."

Surprised out of her lethargy, Maude opened her eyes again to find two men looming over her now. One—short and stout, clutching the waistband of his trousers in one hand and nursing his jaw with the other—she knew must be Carson. The other was the same blond giant who had become something of her rescuer these past two days. A flicker of hope rose in her, and she slowly dragged herself to her knees.

"Len, ya son of a bitch, what the hell do ya think yer doin'?" Carson meanwhile whined in outrage. "Ya heard Rory say I could poke her. Why don't ya wait yer turn?"

"There ain't gonna be no more turns."

Len stood with his arms crossed over his broad chest, looking even larger than he was in the flickering light from the campfire. Carson, who stood a head shorter than he, hesitated; then, as Maude fearfully watched, he pulled from his boot something that glinted in the moonlight. *A knife.*

"Damn ya," he snarled and lunged.

Had she not been breathless from the effort of choking back her cries, she might have called out a warning. As it was, she could only gasp as the blade arced toward the larger man. Len, however, was prepared. Moving gracefully for a man his size, he easily sidestepped the attack and brought his fist crashing onto the other man's arm. Carson shrieked, and the knife skittered from his grasp.

It was Devilbiss who broke away from the other watching

outlaws to scoop up the dropped weapon. Coolly, he tucked the blade into his own belt, then turned to the blond giant. "So, what the hell *is* going on, Len?"

"I don't like it, Rory. It's bad enough that we took her hostage, but this . . . this just ain't right."

"It ain't right," Devilbiss slowly repeated, shaking his head. "Well, Len, I don't quite know how to tell you this, but robbing banks and shooting people ain't right, either . . . and I damn sure didn't hear you protesting then."

The other outlaws chuckled at that, though they swiftly subsided as Devilbiss raised a silencing hand. "Now, Len," he went on in a softer tone, "we've been friends a long time, and it hurts me to think you might be challenging my authority. So tell me . . . are you challenging it?"

A sudden crackle of danger passed between the men before Len shook his head. "You know I'd never challenge you, Rory. I'm just asking you for a favor. Tell the men to let her be."

"I'd like to oblige you, but I think the other fellows would object"—he paused as a murmur arose from the rest of the outlaws—"and it seems to me they'd be within their rights. Everything we take, we divide up equally . . . including the hostages. So I don't see much hope for—"

"I'll trade them," Len cut him short. "My share of the loot for her."

Devilbiss laughed softly. "Why, Len, that's a right generous offer, but it's not too often that we get ourselves a genuine female out here. The boys still might prefer a turn with her to the money."

"And my share of the next job, too," he persisted, glancing over at the others now. "Go ahead, Rory; put it to a vote."

The outlaws remained silent for a moment. Then a voice spoke up. "Hell, with the extra money, I could buy myself two or three gals next time we're in town."

"Yeah, and purtier ones than her," another man added.

Devilbiss listened to the murmur of approval before nodding his own head. "Okay, Len, looks like she's yours . . . unless the law catches up with us and we have to use her to make a deal. And in the meantime, you're responsible for feeding her and making sure she stays up with us on the trail. She lags behind even once, and we shoot her. She tries to escape, and we shoot her. Agreed?''

Maude barely heard the outlaw's reply, swept as she was by a sudden fit of trembling. By now, the knifelike agony between her legs that she had felt when Devilbiss thrust into her had dulled to a burning ache; even so, the pain still was such that she feared the stickiness she felt on her thighs was blood. She also was aware of other sensations: the gritty dirt beneath her bared legs and buttocks . . . the cool night air rippling over breasts exposed by the shredded fabric of her gown and chemise . . . the throbbing of flesh bruised from fingers cruelly prying her legs apart. Still, she had endured it once and survived.

If it had to happen again, she told herself, better it be the same man, again and again, rather than a succession of them.

Abruptly, she was dragged up from where she crouched. ''C'mon, ma'am,'' Len said, gripping her by one arm and pulling her behind him as he headed back toward the campfire. She stumbled after him, clutching the bodice of her torn dress together as best she could with her free hand and trying not to trip over the trailing ruffles that had been half-ripped from her skirt.

''Go on, Len, get yer money's worth outa her,'' one outlaw roughly called out as they passed the group.

Another man guffawed. ''Hey, Len, least ya could do is let the rest of us watch while ya poke her.''

Two days ago, Maude knew, she would have blushed or gasped in outrage at such vile talk. Now she simply closed her ears against the foul words and breathed a silent prayer of relief that she was still alive—at least for tonight.

They walked past the campfire and halted at a spot to one side of where the rest of the outlaws had spread their gear. ''Wait here,'' was all Len said before he loosed his grip on her arm and started back in the same direction.

She did not see where he went, for her trembling legs gave way and she sank ungracefully to the rocky ground. She scraped back her tangled hair from her face and tried to gather her thoughts. It seemed now that, so long as she kept apace of the other riders and did not escape, the only outlaw she needed to please was Len. And while a criminal, like the others, he had shown a spark of humanity that separated him from them. He might not treat her kindly, but perhaps he would not abuse her. And, at this point, all that mattered was staying alive until somebody came and rescued her.

Rescued her.

A reflexive sob rose in her chest. Dear God, *was* anybody looking for her . . . or did they just assume that the Black Horse Gang must have murdered her somewhere in the desert? Perhaps Jessamine and Harvey already had packed away her things, maybe even made plans to leave Brimstone, where so much tragedy had befallen their family.

She shut her eyes, bleakly picturing how she would live out her days with these killers, acting as the concubine to one, until the desert sun and wind turned her haggard and he finally abandoned her in disgust. The coyotes and wolves would scatter her bones, and her family would never know her fate. She'd be dead, leaving no children behind, no proof that she had ever existed.

''Here.''

A pair of saddlebags landed before her with a thud, distracting Maude from her morbid contemplation. Puzzled, she looked up to see Len looming over her again.

''The bags . . . they were Bert's,'' he explained, crouching beside her and unfastening their buckles. ''He wasn't a big fellow, so maybe there's somethin' in here that'll halfway fit you . . . a shirt, maybe some pants. You can't go around wearin' that torn dress, and he won't be needin' these duds, that's for certain.''

As she watched, he dumped out from one saddlebag a crumpled blue shirt and a pair of brown trousers—both of which looked relatively clean—and a set of men's underdrawers. But what caught Maude's attention was a small, flat object that had tumbled out with them . . . a wooden comb.

Greedily, she snatched it up as if it were made of gold, then waited as he emptied the second bag. It held a battered tin of tobacco, a sticky twist of peppermint candies, a dirty red bandanna like those the other men wore, and, surprisingly, a small Bible. *Too bad I can't send it to his mother,* was her first fleeting thought as Len shoved it all back into the leather pouch.

"Not much to speak of," he said.

She wondered for a moment whether he was being literal or philosophical, and then swallowed back a reflexive, half-hysterical giggle at the absurdity of it all. A philosophical outlaw, indeed. Next she'd be expecting him to quote Aristotle and Shakespeare while shooting at lawmen.

But that momentary flash of grim amusement promptly faded as she realized he was staring at her. The comb dropped to her lap as she instinctively clutched at her torn dress again. *Just one more time,* she faintly thought. All she had to do was endure it one more time.

"I'll rustle us up some food," he abruptly said, nodding back in the direction of the campfire. "If you want, you can change into those clothes while I'm doing that." He paused and grabbed up his canteen from his own stack of gear, then handed it to her. "And you can use some of this water to wash up with, if you like."

"Why waste the water, when I'll just have to do it again later?" came her bitter reply . . . and then she gasped as she realized what she had said.

If she had been shocked by her words, the outlaw appeared acutely embarrassed. "Now, ma'am, let's get this straight," he said in a rush. "No matter what the boys said, I don't have any intention of dishonoring you."

"You—you mean you're not going to . . . that is, you don't want to . . ."

"I ain't never had to force a woman, or pay for one, neither . . . and I ain't about to start now," he informed her in stiff tones, sounding even more embarrassed, if that was possible. "My late mama raised me to treat ladies like ladies, and hurting you would be an insult to her memory. So why don't you put on those duds, and I'll be back in a few minutes."

It was Maude's turn to be embarrassed as he stalked off toward the campfire, though why she should be, she was not certain. After all, what else was she to assume of him, buying her from the others like he would a horse or a saddle? But for now, she would just be grateful for her reprieve.

"Thank you, Len's mother," she whispered with a glance up at the stars. They glinted back at her like a handful of tiny diamonds strewn across a black velvet cape, and she blinked back a sudden rush of tears as she took in their stark beauty. There were worse places to die than here in the desert, she told herself.

And, certainly, there were far worse places to live.

Chapter Twelve

''I've always found whiskey . . . to be a great restorative . . . in the morning,'' Doc Holliday observed between coughs and swallows from the bottle he had pulled from his saddlebag. ''In fact . . . it's an excellent restorative . . . any time.''

Watching him down the whiskey on an empty stomach, Jess could not help but wince. In the dull gray light of the predawn hours, he looked thinner and more sickly than ever, so that she wondered again what had possessed him to join their little posse. A man in his condition should be propped on a settee sipping tea, instead of pickling his innards with Kentucky's finest. Of course. after a day and a half of hard riding, and a night curled up on the cold, rocky ground, she almost wished she'd had the foresight to bring her own flask of something slightly more potent.

She settled, instead, for a tin cup of boiled coffee and one of last night's biscuits wrapped around a well-cooked chunk of bacon. A few minutes earlier, she would have traded both food and drink for a hot bath, or even a basin's worth of wash water. Since such civilized amenities were in short supply on the trail, she had made due with dampening her handkerchief with a bit of her precious drinking water and scrubbing down as best she could.

Her clothing had fared even less well, a layer of dun-colored sand giving her once-white shirt a hue closely matching that of her tan skirt. Her hat had fared equally ill. No matter how many times she slapped the worn Stetson against her thigh, it continued to release billows of desert sand and remained a disconcerting shade somewhere between charcoal and brown.

Hancock, however, appeared almost as fresh as if he'd spent the night in a Kansas City hotel. She sourly wondered just how much of his water he'd squandered in the process of restoring himself to that state. She was gratified, though, to note the lines of weariness around his eyes that had not been there yesterday. Perhaps by tomorrow he'd even have an unwanted crease or two in his trousers.

He caught her appraising gaze over his own tin cup, and he frowned slightly. Then, dashing what was left of his coffee into the cooling remains of their fire, he stood and settled his bowler atop his neatly combed dark hair. "Time to head out," was his only comment, however, as he stuffed the cup into his saddlebag.

Holliday, who had eschewed both food and coffee, merely restoppered his bottle and returned it to his own gear, then fastened his gun belt back around his waist. All three horses already were saddled and waiting, Jess saw, and she wryly wondered which of the two men had dealt with Old Pete. Without his ration of oats in the morning, the paint tended to be even more foul-tempered than usual.

She hurriedly finished her own coffee and stowed the remainder of her belongings; then, tucking her derringer back into one boot, she reached into the other for the map and shook it open. She'd not been quite able to pinpoint the spot on the trail where they had made camp, forcing her to guess just how far they would have to travel this morning before they reached a recognizable landmark. Still, the map had proved relatively accurate thus far, she thought in satisfaction.

The line of snakes continued their southward path, heading

ever closer to the Mexican border and Dead Squaw Canyon. She traced that line with one finger, noting the faded penciled comments regarding landmarks and distances for what she judged would be the next leg of their ride. If the map continued correct, the rocky terrain would soon be transformed into the foothills of the Huachuca Mountains, making their progress that much slower than yesterday. Of course, the Black Horse Gang's journey would be equally hampered.

"I don't suppose you've decided yet to share with the rest of us," came the bank examiner's voice unexpectedly from behind her.

She started and promptly refolded the parchment, then spun about to favor him with a quelling look. How had he done that, walking around behind her as silently as a desert rat? "Really, Mr. Hancock, it is quite impolite to sneak up on people like that."

"No more impolite than keeping our destination your own personal secret," he coolly retorted. "Now, how about pointing us out in the right direction . . . unless you'd rather just hand over the map to me?"

"I would not."

She stalked over to Old Pete and swung stiffly into her saddle, swallowing back a yelp as the gelding nipped in her direction. "I'm afraid you'll just have to continue to trust my judgment," she went on. "According to the map, we continue south until we reach a fork in the trail. At that point, it appears we move off the main pass and follow a less traveled route toward the west. We'll know we've reached the right turnoff by a formation there called Las Tres Cabezas . . . the Three Heads."

"Charming," Holliday interjected as he mounted his own gelding and urged it around. "I, for one, quite look forward to viewing this quaintly named landmark."

Hancock did not reply outright, but muttered a few words that Jess presumed would be considered unseemly for a man of his professional standing. Unaccountably cheered, she gave Old Pete a swift jab with her heels. Followed by the two men, she made her way back to the spot where they'd left the trail the previous night.

She sensed a greater sense of urgency about Hancock this morning as they started at a swift pace down the trail. He stopped less often to examine tracks, seemingly convinced that the Black Horse Gang was following the same route laid out in the map. His apparent confidence in their destination reassured Jess, so that she forgot her aching muscles as she kept her gaze fixed on the jagged mountains that loomed increasingly closer. Today might be the day they finally tracked down the outlaws and rescued Maude.

But as morning edged its way toward midday, her watchfulness was rewarded by a disturbing sight as they breached a low rise . . . a dozen or more vultures wheeling lazily against a cloudless blue sky. A chill fist of dread clamped over her heart, and she abruptly reined in Old Pete.

"I see them," Hancock grimly confirmed as he and Holliday halted beside her. "They seem to be concentrating on a spot near that outcropping. It's not much farther a ride, perhaps another quarter hour."

Jess shot him an uncertain look. "Do you think it's—"

"It could be anything . . . a stray cow brought down by wolves, a dead rabbit. Let's take a look first, before you start worrying."

But both men's expressions were grim as they urged their horses into a gallop. Jess followed swiftly behind them, fearing what they might find, yet unable to stand the uncertainty of not knowing what—or who—had attracted those desert scavengers. And if someone *was* dead, it did not have to be Maude. It might be a miner fallen victim to outlaws, or a rustler shot down by a rancher.

A few minutes later, they reached the spot where the vultures were gathered. The sweet odor of decay hung in the dry air, removing any doubt that the object of the birds' interest might still be alive. A few of the large black birds continued their graceful circles above, their wide shadows rhythmically skimming the ground and sliding across the outcropping. The remainder had gathered on the ground, jostling for position atop what first appeared to Jess to be a discarded bundle of clothes. At the sound of the approaching riders, however, the vultures awkwardly scattered, revealing in their midst a crumpled human form.

Jess gave a choked cry and abruptly reined in Old Pete. "I-I can't look," she confessed in a small, tight voice.

Holliday, who had halted beside her, shot her a surprisingly sympathetic look. "Do not worry, my dear," he murmured. "Your Mr. Hancock and I will take care of the necessary unpleasantness."

The bank examiner, meanwhile, had spurred his roan closer. The hound followed, as usual. A few feet from the body, both man and dog halted. By now, the birds had begun hopping back toward the body, wings spread for balance as they moved in their characteristic lopsided gait.

Holliday joined him, and both men dismounted. Snatching off his bowler, the bank examiner roughly shooed those shaggy black birds, while the gambler merely watched and the hound loosed a few rusty barks. Amid indignant cries, the vultures abruptly became airborne again, transformed from ghoulish, capering clowns to graceful aerial acrobats once more.

The bank examiner knelt beside the body, joined by Holliday, who fastidiously put a handkerchief to his lower face as he, too, bent for a look. Jess averted her gaze from the grisly sight and climbed down from her own horse.

Old Pete, seemingly subdued in the presence of death, for once refrained from nipping as she kept to his far side and busied herself with inspecting her stirrup straps. She heard the murmur of male voices for a few moments, followed by the rhythmic crunch of rocky ground beneath boots as they headed back in her direction. Only when they stood beside her did she glance back up again to meet Hancock's grim gaze.

"It's not your aunt," he bluntly informed her, "nor anyone else we recognized. But as his clothing does match your Miss Chwang's description of the garb worn by the outlaws who robbed her, I rather suspect he is one of the Black Horse Gang."

"But how . . . how did he die?"

"Gunshot wound," was Holliday's cool assessment of the situation. "Given that he's probably been dead since sometime last night, and the buzzards have been at him all morning, I can't guess at the caliber. But from the size of the hole in his back we saw when we turned him over, he was done in by a pistol, and not a rifle or shotgun."

"So he must have been hit during the shoot-out in Brimstone." Jess shivered. The marshal's killing by the outlaws had been followed by the brutal death of one of their own. Not an even exchange, certainly, but a small balancing of justice's scales, perhaps. "I wonder why they didn't leave him behind, where Dr. Caldwell might have saved him."

Holliday raised a wry brow. "I fear the outcome would have been the same. Even had he survived the bullet, he'd have soon found himself on intimate terms with the hangman . . . as will the rest of the gang once they are finally apprehended."

He glanced Hancock's way, and an odd look of challenge passed between the two men. Before she could guess at its meaning, however, Hancock spoke.

"I suggest we take a look around," he said and clamped back on his bowler. "Chances are this is where the gang slept last night, so look for footprints, bloodstains, any gear they might have left behind. Maybe we can get some idea of how many of them there are, how long ago they broke camp . . . anything that will give us an advantage in tracking them."

Not waiting for a reply, he abruptly started back in the same general direction as where the buzzards once more were gathered. Holliday veered off in a slightly different direction, whistling softly as he scanned the ground. The hound, obviously satisfied he had done his share of investigating, trotted back over to where the roan waited and stretched out beside her.

Jess tied Old Pete to a nearby scrub and, giving the corpse wide berth, started for the most prominent group among the scattering of rocky formations. *Three of them,* she noted in satisfaction as she approached the rounded boulders that were twice as wide as she was tall. With luck, this was the landmark on the map that indicated where their trail intersected another . . . Las Tres Cabezas. Once they had learned all they could from whatever signs the gang had left behind, she would determine if another pass did indeed veer off from the main trail.

For the moment, however, she concentrated on the ground around her. The dirt was chopped and scuffed, as if a number of riders had passed by. The drone of flies drew her attention to pungent piles of horse droppings a short distance away, where doubtless the outlaws' mounts had been tied for the night. She carefully sidestepped that area, as well, while allowing herself a grimly amused look in the bank examiner's direction. Hancock probably could formulate an equation based upon the number of mounds and each one's relative position that would help him calculate how many horses had been corralled there. She would content herself with counting hoofprints.

The campsite, she swiftly found, was abandoned, but not entirely silent. Amid the buzzing of insects and the crunch of footsteps—hers and the men's—came the occasional hoarse protest of a vulture as it squabbled with its fellows. A hint of a breeze had risen, wafting the pungent odor of decay in the opposite direction and rattling the scrubby bushes that dotted the area. A lonely sound, she decided, once again glad that she was not alone in her travels through the high desert.

So intent was she on searching out prints, both man-made and equine, that she almost missed the brilliant flash of blue behind the largest of the three head-shaped boulders. The last time she had seen that same color, it had been reflected back at her in her foyer mirror as she and her aunt had bantered that one last time. She willed herself to calmness, though she could not suppress a small sound of dismay. What else besides a portion of Maude's blue silk dress could she now be seeing?

"Find something interesting, my dear?"

Holliday's cool drawl made her start, and she realized that she must have been staring quite helplessly in that direction for some moments. She nodded without a word and pointed toward the sliver of bright color.

The dentist frowned slightly. ''I shall check it out,'' he said and vanished behind the rocks.

He was gone for what seemed an eternity, though it could only have been for the space of a few heartbeats. Still, Jess was almost prepared to chase after him when he finally reappeared, a bundle of blue silk in his arms. He shook it out, and the remains of what once had been a woman's stylish gown cascaded from his lean white hands in a ragged torrent of torn flounces and ripped sleeves.

Jess did not realize her knees had buckled beneath her until she felt the sudden pressure of Hancock's arm around her waist. He had pulled her to him, so that she sagged in a most mortifying fashion against the firm support of his lean torso. She swiftly struggled to regain control, concern over her aunt compounded with a far more personal dismay. Doubtless her momentary show of weakness had confirmed both men's conviction that a woman was not suited to ride with their little posse, her inner voice scolded her.

Another far more frivolous corner of her mind noted that the bank examiner's chest was quite as solid as the rock formations that surrounded him . . . and that perhaps he was holding her more closely than the situation warranted.

Hancock must have thought the same thing, for he abruptly hoisted her upright again and gave her a shake. ''If you've decided not to swoon after all,'' he coolly told her, ''perhaps we can get on with our investigation. I presume from your reaction that this gown belongs to Miss McCray?''

''Sh-she was wearing it the morning of the bank robbery.''

With that ragged reply, Jess closed the short distance to where Holliday still stood, the dress hanging limply from his grasp. He handed it to her, his pale gaze revealing no emotion as he met her eyes. ''I suspect that much of the damage might be attributable to the tribulations of a cross-country ride,'' he offered with surprising delicacy for one who had carelessly admitted to killing half a dozen or more men.

Jess nodded wordlessly as she examined the tattered yards of silk. If Maude had been forced to ride astride, that could explain the torn flounces and the split side seams. The torn bodice, ripped with force enough to have popped off a score of sturdy bone buttons, was a different story. It took little imagination to guess how, or why, the dress had suffered such damage.

Hancock, meanwhile, had joined the pair. He took the length of blue silk from Jess and gave it a cursory look. "At least this proves we are on the right track," he said, and then turned to the gambler. "Was that all you found back there, Doc?"

"No other clothes or any gear . . . and no other bodies besides that of the unfortunate wretch feeding the buzzards. I would venture to say that Miss McCray is still alive and traveling with the gang."

"And from the looks of the camp, they're only a couple of hours ahead of us." The bank examiner nodded in satisfaction. "If we pick up our pace, we have a chance of catching up with them by nightfall."

His gaze dropped again to the gown, and Jess saw his grip on the fabric tighten. Whatever emotion was reflected in his eyes was hidden from Jess, however, by the shadow of his hat brim across his face. When he glanced up at her again, his features were arranged in the same cool lines as usual. "What do you want to do with the gown . . . leave it, or take it with you?"

Jess's first impulse was to bundle it into her saddlebag so that the once-elegant fabric would suffer no more ravages from either man or nature. Then she shook her head. The dress was far beyond repair; besides which, when they did find Maude, it would serve only as a cruel reminder of the fate that had befallen her.

"Leave it," was her blunt answer, though she bit her lip as he let it slide from his fingers to puddle in a brave flash of color between them. Had her aunt also lain crumpled at someone's feet, tossed aside like this discarded gown? Still, the fact that Maude had made it this far into her ordeal spoke eloquently for her bravery. Jess could only pray that the older woman's courage remained intact even after the brutal treatment she must have suffered.

But even as she struggled with such thoughts, she suddenly was aware that the mournful murmur of sound around them had taken on a new, rumbling note. Hancock and Holliday heard it, too, she saw, for they had halted and were gazing at a spot to the east of them, where a dun-colored cloud of dust was rising. The hound, meanwhile, had sprung to his feet and now stood at attention, growling softly deep in his throat.

"Riders," Hancock unnecessarily said as the figures of five men on horseback came into view. "It looks like they're headed straight toward us."

"Surely it's not the Black Horse Gang." Jess shaded her eyes with one hand, trying to make out more detail. "All these mounts are bays or duns, and there's not enough of them."

"It's not Wyatt and the boys, either," Holliday confirmed. His drawl held the usual note of unconcern, but he eased back his gray jacket in a practiced move that revealed his holstered pistol. "I wonder what it is that they want."

"The buzzards must have drawn them, just as they did us," the bank examiner replied. "They're probably just a group of cowboys from some nearby ranch . . . nothing to worry about." But Jess saw that he, too, rested one hand on the butt of his pistol.

The horsemen rapidly drew closer, only to halt some distance away when they finally noticed the trio and their mounts waiting in the rocks. They were too far away still for Jess to make out any conversation, but their actions spoke quite plainly. Abruptly, they drew rifles and pistols, then moved forward again, but at a slower pace.

"Trouble," Holliday murmured and moved casually toward his own rifle, still tied to his gray. Hancock did likewise, then glanced over at Jess.

"Wait behind the rocks, until we know what's going on here . . . and take that damned dog with you, too."

For once, Jess found herself willing to comply with the man's orders, politely phrased or not. She knew that, should matters degenerate into a gunfight, she'd be less than useless there in the open, though perhaps she could lend assistance from a position of cover. Convincing the black hound of the plan's merits, however, proved more difficult.

She snapped her fingers and softly called to him, without result, then made as if to grab him by the circle of rope that served as his collar. At that, he briefly bared his teeth in her direction before turning his attention back to the approaching riders.

"Blast it all," Jess muttered before leaving the beast to its own devices and scurrying to the rocks. If the dog bit someone or got itself shot, that was just too bad.

She wedged between the two largest boulders, so that she had a clear yet protected view of the scene, then drew her own pistol from her boot. Her gun hand, she noted in dismay, was sweaty and shaking. If she was forced to fire her weapon, heaven only knew what she might hit.

By the time she settled herself, the riders were almost upon them. They had been clustered together at their first approach, but while she'd been struggling with her pistol, they had spread out to form a single wide line, one man deep. Now, Jess could see the metallic glint from what had to be badges pinned to their chests, and her apprehension lessened. *Another posse, perhaps.*

Still, she remained where she was while the horsemen halted at the edge of the campsite. The black hound gave a warning bark but, quite surprisingly, subsided at a stern word from Hancock. Four of the riders, meanwhile, remained where they were. All were perhaps Hancock's age, and wearing identical expressions of grim resolve. *Deputies,* Jess guessed, and likely newly sworn.

The centermost horseman was older and stockier than the others, and had a larger star pinned to his dusty brown vest. A rifle was balanced across his ample lap. He nudged his mount forward a few steps more, then halted and tipped back his hat to reveal a fringe of red hair.

"Afternoon, gentlemen." His nasal twang marked him as originally having hailed from Texas. "I'm Marshal Chapel, from San Luis, just east of here. You mind telling me just who you are, and what's your business in my part of this here county?"

Chapter Thirteen

''I'm Jake Hancock, out of Kansas City.'' The bank examiner's tone was equally cordial, though he did not bother to hide the rifle he held loosely at his side. ''I'm employed by the Territorial Bankers Association. My friend and I are in pursuit of the outlaws who robbed the Brimstone bank a couple of days ago. We tracked them to this spot and—''

''Friend, you say?''

The marshal's shrewd gaze narrowed as it flicked from the two men to the trio of horses tied nearby. Certain she was well hidden but not wanting to take any chances, Jess eased back behind the rocks so that she could only hear what was happening.

''If you're tellin' me it's just the two of you boys,'' Chapel went on. ''I'd say you got yourself an extra mount . . . lessen it belongs to that dead fella over there. Trouble is, he looks like he's been dead awhile, but them horses of yours look like they've been rode hard all morning.''

''We just found the man, ourselves . . . and, yes, he does appear to have been dead for some time,'' she heard Hancock say. ''Our best guess is that he was one of the gang we're pursuing. There was a shoot-out after the robbery, and Brimstone's marshal was killed. We assume this man was wounded at the same time."

Hancock's reply had been couched in the same smooth tones as the marshal's, though Jess noted that he did not address the other man's observation regarding numbers. Now, however, she heard the faintest note of impatience in his words as he continued, "If that's the last of your questions, Marshal, we'd like to be on our way. Every minute we delay puts us farther behind the bank robbers."

"Does it, now?" Chapel's voice had taken on a sharper tone as well. "You know, Mr. Hancock, you ain't introduced me to your friend there. I'd be a mite offended, 'cept it happens I already know Doc Holliday."

Sensing trouble, Jess peered around the rocks again in time to see the gambler give a mocking nod. "The pleasure is once again mine, Marshal."

"Bullshit!"

Abruptly, the lawman swung his rifle about so that it was trained on Holliday. Jess smothered a gasp as, simultaneously, the deputies brought around their weapons to cover Hancock as well. The black hound, who had been watching the proceedings with distrust, gave another warning bark and then began to growl low in his throat again. He subsided at a sharp command from Hancock, though he remained at his post alongside the roan, who absently nibbled on a nearby scrub.

For her part, Jess sank back into her hollow between the two largest boulders. Blast it all, what was she supposed to do? She had been listening to the unfolding drama in growing dismay, wondering whether or not Hancock and Holliday expected her to try to rescue them from the situation. But even from her position of concealment, she could hardly disarm five trained lawmen. Indeed, any attempt at doing so would likely have resulted in a full-blown gun battle . . . though, now, it was too late to try such a move, even had she dared.

Chapel, meanwhile, had clambered down from his horse. Not taking his eyes or weapon off either man, he started toward them. "You mighta got off scot free on that murder charge back in Dallas, Holliday, but that don't mean you wasn't guilty. And even if you didn't do that killin', there's a bunch of other fellows that died with their boots on because of you."

He paused and gestured with his rifle. "Now, why don't you two put down your weapons, real careful-like, and we'll have us a little chat. And, boys"—that was directed at his deputies—"be sure one of you checks out the good doctor. He usually carries a knife and a derringer, along with that shotgun and nickel-plated Colt of his."

"How kind of you to remember, Marshal Chapel," Holliday drawled as he casually began divesting himself of said weapons. "I regret to say that there's very little I recall about you."

One of the deputies, meanwhile, had dismounted and started toward him, apparently intent on carrying out his boss's orders. The lawman in question—a brown-haired, mustachioed young man in a sweat-stained white Stetson—was twice the gambler's size, and a few inches taller than his lean height. A cold glance from Holliday, however, abruptly stopped him in his tracks.

Chapel gave an impatient snort. "He ain't gonna bite you, Reeves," he urged on the deputy. "Now search him, like I told you."

Reeves edged closer. "Er, Mr. Holliday . . . Doc," he ventured, "I'd appreciate it if you'd open up your coat."

The gambler, with an expression of cool disdain, spread his lapels to reveal nothing tucked in his trousers's waistband. Reeves moved a bit closer and gingerly patted him down, then took a step back. "And I need you to raise your pants legs, sir, so I can see there's nothing in your boots."

Holliday gave a genteel sneer as he reached into one boot and withdrew a derringer similar to Jess's, then plucked a buck knife from the other. "I do expect everything to be returned to me, undamaged, once we've resolved this little misunderstanding."

"It will be," Chapel interjected, while Reeves gathered the discarded weapons into a small pile several feet from the gambler. Then Chapel nodded at his deputy. "All right, boy, check out the other fella."

Hancock had already laid down his own rifle. As Reeves approached, he began unbuckling his gun belt. "Misunderstanding is right," the bank examiner clipped out as the other man repeated the same ritual he'd employed with Holliday. "If you want to arrest someone, Marshal, I suggest you try the Black Horse Gang."

The lawman chuckled. "Well, sir, it just so happens that's who me and the boys is after. Someone from Silver Pass rode in this mornin' with a telegram from Sheriff Behan outta Tombstone tellin' us to look out for them. He didn't say who or how many, just that they'd probably be headin' toward Mexico."

He paused and glanced toward the rocks in Jess's direction, and she flattened herself against them that much more. "But the wire did say somethin' about they had a lady ridin' with them. Ma'am, why don't you step out from behind those rocks with your hands raised, so the boys don't have to go lookin' for you."

Jess bit back a cry of dismay. Obviously, the lawmen had spotted her earlier, when they had poised some distance from the camp to reconnoiter. There was no point pretending otherwise, she knew. She shoved her pistol back into her boot, then raised her hands and edged out from behind the boulders.

"Thank you, ma'am," Chapel gravely greeted her, gesturing her closer with his rifle. "Now, I can either have Reeves search you, or you can give up all your weapons on your own."

Jess glanced at Reeves, who had perked up at this possibility, and then reached into her boot. "This is all I have, Marshal," she said as she handed the derringer over to the deputy. "And Mr. Hancock is quite correct. There *has* been a misunderstanding. I am Mrs. Jessamine Satterly, owner of the First National Bank of Brimstone . . . the bank that was robbed," she emphasized when Chapel appeared unimpressed. "Those outlaws also kidnapped my aunt, and Mr. Hancock and Dr. Holliday are attempting to rescue her. I'm afraid time is of the essence here, so if you would just return our weapons and let us be on our way—''

''That's a real interestin' story, Miz Satterly.'' Chapel straightened his hat and then gestured her toward the two men. ''Unfortunately, all I have to work with is what I know; namely, we got ourselves a bank robbery and the outlaws—one of them a lady—that done it. You folks are ridin' in the right direction, travelin' mighty light except for your guns . . . and one of you is a lady, and one's a known killer by the name of Doc Holliday. Now, until I know different, what am I supposed to think?''

''That we are who we say we are,'' Hancock answered for her, a note of barely checked impatience coloring his words. ''Let me point out that we are only three . . . pretty sparse numbers for a gang of bank robbers. And if you check our saddlebags, you won't find any stolen cash. Beyond that, the outlaws you're looking for are known as the Black Horse Gang. I believe you'll notice there's not a black horse in that bunch,'' he finished, with a gesture toward Old Pete and the other two mounts.

Chapel grinned, exposing two rows of tobacco-stained teeth. ''Hell, you folks can call yourselves the Purple Horse Gang and ride pink ponies. It don't make me no never mind. As for the money and how many you are, a smart group of bank robbers would split up, one half to carry the money and the other to throw the posse off the trail. I figure you folks for the second group.''

Holliday, meanwhile, took a step forward. ''If it will make you feel better, Marshal, I'll be glad to let you take me back to San Luis, so long as you let my friends go on their way. Mrs. Satterly is quite correct. Her aunt's life is in great jeopardy, and every minute we waste here makes it less likely she will survive her ordeal.''

Jess shot the gambler a grateful look. It was a generous offer, more than she had the right to expect from a man she hardly knew . . . and especially a man of his reputation. Chapel, however, seemed less impressed with this display of self-sacrifice.

''Well, Doc, I can't rightly do that. What I will do is telegraph

Brimstone and Tombstone to see if someone can back up your story. If they do, you'll be free to go, but until then you'll be sitting in the San Luis jail. Now, mount up, folks."

"But, Marshal—"

"See, here, Chapel—"

"Mount up!" the lawman bellowed, effectively halting Jess and Hancock's protests. By way of emphasis, Reeves—who had stashed away their weapons and remounted—and the other deputies abruptly urged their horses a few steps closer, rifles at the ready.

"Do as he says," Hancock muttered, disgust evident in his voice as he stalked over to the roan. "Once we get to San Luis, we'll get things cleared up. With luck, we won't have lost more than a few hours."

"But what about Aunt Maude?" Jess gave her two companions a desperate look as she untied Old Pete. "We can't just forget about her."

"Don't worry, my dear," Holliday coolly declared and lightly swung into the saddle. "At this point, a few hours more or less probably won't make much difference. If the gang has kept her alive this long, I would venture to guess that they don't intend to kill her . . . at least, not unless someone forces their hand."

Which was not quite the reassurance that she wanted, Jess grimly thought, but it was better than nothing. At Chapel's direction, she and her companions urged their mounts east, hemmed in on either side by the rifle-toting deputies and followed by the marshal. The black hound trotted behind.

The trail along which they rode had intersected their earlier route, confirming to Jess the fact that they had reached the landmark on her map that she earlier had sought. Once they resolved the issue of their identities with Marshal Chapel, they need only retrace their ride back to Las Tres Cabezas and pick up the trail again from that point.

The ride to San Luis took almost two hours. Chapel and his deputies were not inclined toward conversation . . . but then, neither were Jess or Hancock and Holliday. The latter man, surprisingly, seemed more reconciled to the delay than did Hancock, whose set jaw indicated that he'd have much to say once they finally were released.

It was midafternoon by the time they reached their destination. San Luis proved a town much smaller and shabbier than either Brimstone or Tombstone; still, Jess noticed at least two saloons, in addition to the usual livery, mercantile, and assay office. Their progress down the single main street was noted by a dozen or more of the locals, all of whom gaped in interest.

They halted a moment later in front of a long, narrow building of white adobe that was half the size of Jess's bank. Two crudely lettered signs—one of which proclaimed MARSHAL'S OFFICE and the other JAIL—were nailed alongside a sturdy, unpainted door.

"This here's the place," Chapel cheerfully told them as he dismounted. "Reeves, you bring those weapons and their gear, and come with me. You other boys take these horses down to the livery, and then you're free to go home." Then he turned to Jess and the two men. "You folks climb on down, and I'll show you the accommodations."

While the black hound followed the roan and the other two mounts off to be stabled, Chapel ushered the rest of them through the door. The accommodations within proved to be a single room, the front half of which served as the marshal's office. A wooden desk and two uncomfortable-looking wooden chairs, along with a pot bellied stove and a glass-fronted gun cabinet, made up the furnishings. The back half had been converted into a two-bunk cell separated from the office by floor-to-ceiling black bars that ran the width of the room.

The cell already held two other prisoners—cowboys, Jess judged from their garb. Both youths gazed up morosely at the newcomers' entrance. A third youth, who obviously had been left behind to guard them, looked up in equal consternation at this sudden influx of people.

"Davey, I got you some new boarders," the marshal said as he pulled a large key ring from a nail on the wall. "Might even be bank robbers, if we're lucky." To Jess, he said as he unlocked the cell door, "I'm right sorry, ma'am, but we've only got the one cell. I'm afraid you'll have to squeeze in here until we can make other arrangements."

"Don't worry, Marshal Chapel," she answered in a lofty tone as she marched past the iron bars. "I am certain we will be detained here for only a short while."

"Well, ma'am, it might be longer than that." He waited until Holliday and Hancock had followed her inside, then shut the door with a resounding clang and turned the key. "You see, the telegraph lines haven't made it out to San Luis. I'll have to send Reeves to Silver Pass and let him send the messages from there."

"How long do you estimate this will take, Marshal?" Hancock coolly demanded from the corner of the cell where he'd propped himself. Holliday, meanwhile, strolled over to the single barred window and silently stared from it.

Chapel shrugged. "It's a good hour's ride to Silver Pass, and then the waitin' time 'til someone replies. Comin' back, it'll be gettin' onto dark, so the ride would be slower. I'd guess seven or eight o'clock tonight."

"So you're saying we'll be stuck here in San Luis overnight?"

"That's assumin' someone backs up your story, so I suggest you folks make yourself at home. Mrs. Meeks—Davey's mother—will be bringin' by supper in a couple of hours." He hung the key back on its nail and then turned to the deputy. "C'mon, Reeves, let's go write us some telegrams."

Jess had listened to this exchange in no little alarm. They'd be losing almost a day in their pursuit of the Black Horse Gang . . . even longer, if Chapel had cause to doubt the veracity of the telegrams he'd be getting in reply. And though he'd done no more than relieve them of their guns, what if the marshal decided to take their personal possessions as well? Indeed, he might decide that her map was some sort of evidence and confiscate it! But that was not the least of it.

Frowning, she gave the cell a closer look. Almost as bad as the delay itself was the possibility that she might be forced to spend the night here with four men. Not only were there not enough beds, but there was no privacy at all. And, doubtless, the available blankets were dirty and crawling with multilegged creatures. As for facilities of the more personal sort, the only concession to such bodily functions was an offensive-smelling slop bucket in the far corner. Jess shuddered inwardly. No matter how pressing her need, she never could avail herself of that!

So caught up was she in such concerns that it took her a moment to realize someone was addressing her. " 'Scuse me, ma'am," a soft twangy voice ventured for a second time, "but would you like to sit on this here cot? Truly, I don't mind standin' for a spell."

The question came from one of the two young men with whom they were sharing the cell. Blond and freckled, he looked no older than eighteen or nineteen, far too young to have committed any sort of serious offense. Of course, there was William Bonney, who had begun his murderous spree at a tender age . . .

Shaking off such unproductive thoughts, she gave the boy a polite smile. "Why, thank you—"

"Jimmy," he supplied.

"—Jimmy, but I've been riding all day. I do believe I shall stand for awhile longer. Perhaps later." Then, seeing his crestfallen look at her refusal, she went on, "Tell me, what are you doing in here? You seem too polite a gentleman to be guilty of a crime."

He hung his head. "Well, ma'am, me and my brother, Pat"—he gestured at the other youth—"got drunk last night and shot up the town a bit. Oh, we didn't hurt no one, but we made a lot of noise and broke a few windows."

"It was just one window," Pat supplied in a sullen voice. He shook his shaggy brown hair out of his eyes. "But since we can't pay for the damage, we have to stay here 'til tomorrow. What did you folks do?"

"We're here by mistake. Marshal Chapel is under the misapprehension that these gentlemen and I are bank robbers." Jess ignored the disgusted snort from Hancock's direction and deliberately changed the subject. "Tell me, boys, what do you do to pass the time in here?"

"Play poker, mostly." Jimmy reached into his vest pocket and pulled out a ragged deck. "The marshal let us keep a deck. But it's kinda dull, just me and Pat, here."

"Poker?" Holliday drawled, rousing himself from his self-imposed silence and turning from the barred window. "Perhaps another player or two would make it more interesting. Hancock, are you in?"

"Hell, Doc, why not? We don't have anything better to do," the bank examiner muttered in disgust.

The youths, who had brightened at this prospect, now glanced uncertainly at each other before staring back at the gambler. "Excuse me," Pat spoke up, "but you wouldn't be *the* Doc Holliday of Tombstone, would you?"

"I am. I trust you gentlemen have no objection to playing with me."

"Oh, no, sir . . . Doc," came Jimmy's eager reply. "Heck, no, we'd be honored, sir. It's just that, well, me and Pat don't have any money, like I told the lady. We've just been playing for fun."

"Then that is how we shall play . . . just for fun." He turned a cool smile on Jess. "Mrs. Satterly, would you care to sit in, as well? Since no money will change hands, it would be strictly an educational experience for you."

Jess allowed herself a smile despite her worry. Apparently, playing cards with John Henry Holliday, alias Doc, had a certain cachet to it. Who was she to pass up such an opportunity, especially when it was the sole means of passing the time? Coolly, she seated herself on the bunk and gave the gambler a wry look. "As Mr. Hancock so eloquently put it . . . hell, Doc, why not?"

The five settled down to a serious round of poker, pausing only when Mrs. Meeks brought the promised supper at dark. Jess, whose sole experience with the game came from peering over her father's shoulder as he played, had found herself quite out of her league for the first hour. Hancock merely snorted inelegantly at each untutored play she made. Doc and the two young brothers, however, gallantly offered advice after each hand. By the time they had finished off Mrs. Meeks's tolerable meatloaf and quite passable biscuits, Jess had managed to win three imaginary pots on her own. She had just celebrated her fourth win of the evening when the door to the marshal's office opened and a dusty Reeves clomped in.

The poker game came to an abrupt halt. The five cards—three queens and two eights—that Jess was holding fluttered from her grasp, unnoticed, as she stood and hurried to the bars. Hancock joined her a moment later, his expression grim. From behind her, Jess heard Holliday's murmured observation, "I presume both of the others have folded . . . which means, young Patrick, that I call you."

For his part, Marshal Chapel had been sitting at his desk all evening, boots propped up before him and red brows furrowed as he squinted at a dime novel. At the deputy's entry, he set down the book and lurched to his own feet. "Well, boy?"

Reeves plucked off his stained Stetson and slapped it against his thigh to rid the hat of trail dust, then reached into his pocket and withdrew two folded papers. Handing them over to Chapel, he merely said, "Here you are, Marshal. I got them answers to your telegrams, like you asked."

Chapter Fourteen

A plump yellow moon, bright as the crackling campfire, peered through the jagged mountaintops. Maude clutched a dead outlaw's wooden comb in her hand and gazed up at that celestial body with an inner sigh. Was anyone she knew watching that same moon? she wondered, not that it truly mattered. She was certain by now that nobody would ever find her . . . almost as sure that no one even was looking for her.

A great wave of self-pity swept her, and for several moments she let herself be buffeted by it. Just as she was in danger of drowning, however, her pride reached in and slowly dragged her back to emotional high ground. After all, she reminded herself, she had suffered before and come out the stronger for it. Indeed, she had survived a war, when so many others of her acquaintance had not.

Memories that had lain dormant for so many years abruptly shook off their cobwebs and marched through her mind just like soldiers from that frightening time. She recalled how, as a young woman of five-and-twenty, she had held her dying sister-in-law's hand. Prayer and hard work had been the only curatives left to her, for she'd long since exhausted their small supply of medicine . . . but prayer and hard work had proved useless, at the end. When Lucinda finally slipped away, Maude could do nothing more than comfort her motherless niece, left a virtual orphan now that Harvey had gone off to war.

She had remained with her niece in the months and years that followed. Alone, she had fought frightened crowds for her family's share of scarce rations and kept the young Jessamine safe. Later, when her wounded brother returned home from the war, it had been she who'd nursed him back to health.

By the time the war finally ended, she judged that her duty to her family was completed. She had been prepared to resume her own life . . . and then the letter that changed everything had come.

The missive had consisted of but a few blunt lines. Written by his mother, it had informed her that Lt. Ronald Haggerty, the man she had promised to wed once the war was over, had been shot and killed by Union forces two months earlier. Implicit in the letter was the accusation that, had he not so hurriedly enlisted in response to Maude's rejection of him, he might have been elsewhere during that battle and so survived.

Maude had known this angry letter to be but a mother's desperate need to blame someone for her son's loss. True, she had told Ron that she could not marry him, but that had been only because her family needed her more than he did at that moment. With Lucinda desperately ill and Harvey in the midst of the fight, she was the only one left to take care of things. Later, she vowed, when the war ended, she would gladly be his wife.

Ron had understood and agreed. In fact, he confessed to being relieved, for he had been torn between her and his need to serve the cause in which he believed. He, too, saw no reason they must wed until after life returned to normal. When that day came, they could freely dedicate themselves to one another, unencumbered by other obligations save their love for each other. Thus, together, they had agreed to the wedding postponement.

But Ron had died and, in the years that followed, Maude

had never married, though why that was, she was not quite certain. True, Jess needed a motherly influence during her youth, but Maude could have served that role while raising a family of her own. As for Harvey, he could as easily have hired a housekeeper, or even remarried himself. Not that she regretted her decision, Maude reminded herself. She had spent fifteen interesting and productive years in her role, and could take pride in what she had done. But that did not stop her from wondering how different things would have been had she made a life together with Ron.

Ron. Her mental picture of him had faded over the years, just as had the photograph of him that she kept tucked in her handkerchief drawer. Frowning, she tried now to conjure his image in her mind . . . blond, handsome, laughing. But, quite disturbingly, the face that appeared in her thoughts was not that of her lost love.

Rather, it was the face of her captor, Len.

She gave a guilty start and glanced in the direction of the campfire, where he and the other outlaws had gathered. Perhaps it was not so odd, after all, she reassured herself. Len was tall, blond, and roughly handsome, just as Ron had been . . . though the former was quite a number of years younger than she. And, for the moment, he was the man who stood between her and death.

Maude allowed herself a shaky sigh. Who knew if she might still be alive, had he not stepped in last night to spare her from the rest of the gang's lust? He had kept a discreet distance from her as she pulled off her tattered gown and washed away the evidence of the rape. Both her dress and petticoat had been beyond salvage. Her camisole and pantalets had sustained less damage than she had feared . . . luckily for her, since she was not yet desperate enough to wear the dead man's change of drawers!

She'd been fortunate, as well, in the fact that the late Bert Mackey had been a relatively small man; even so, she'd had to roll up both pant legs and shirt sleeves and use a strip torn from her petticoat to cinch the trousers around her slim waist.

The result had been functional if not fashionable, especially when she had topped the garb with the dead man's battered Stetson. Not that she was complaining—the less appealing she looked to these outlaws, the better.

Later, Len had brought her a plate of food and had eaten silently beside her. He had slept beside her, as well, though sleep was all he had done. Aching and exhausted from all she had been through, she had not thought to do more than doze, herself. Oddly enough, however, with Len's long frame stretched between her and the other outlaws, she had fallen into dreamless slumber.

With morning had come a resumption of the rough riding she had endured the past two days. With a horse of her own now—also courtesy of the deceased Bert—and dressed in men's garb, with her hair shoved under a hat, the ride had proved easier. This day had progressed much like the last one, though all her energies now were concentrated on keeping up with the others. With the coming of nightfall, they'd made camp, as before. Len had brought her food, again, sitting silently if companionably beside her while they ate, before leaving her again to join the others. And, as promised, she had suffered no further abuse at the other outlaws' hands . . . though Devilbiss, in particular, continued to watch her with cold interest.

Now, she lifted the comb once more and resumed trying to unsnarl her tangled curtain of blond hair. A few minutes later, she had made little progress, save to knot it more tightly, if that was possible. Tears of frustration welled in her eyes. Muttering Jessamine's favorite oath—"Blast it all, anyway"—she flung down the comb and watched it skitter across the rocky ground.

Then a shadow fell over the spot where it lay, and a beefy hand picked it up again. "I think you dropped this, ma'am," Len gravely said as he squatted down beside her and proffered the discarded comb.

Embarrassed, she snatched it from his hand. "I might as well cut it all off," she muttered, lifting a tangled lock to show him.

He smiled, his expression quite boyish in the moonlight.

"Now, that would be a right shame, cutting off such pretty hair. Why don't you let me help you?"

So saying, he took the comb back from her and scooted behind her, then lifted a few tangled strands. At his touch, she flinched. She promptly regretted that reflexive act, however, when she heard the offended note in his voice. "Now, ma'am, I told you I wouldn't hurt you. I surely would appreciate it if you'd believe me."

"I-I do believe you," she replied in a small voice, surprised to realize that she truly did. Feeling suddenly bolder, she added, "And I'd appreciate it if you'd call me 'Maude' instead of 'ma'am.' You make me feel like an old woman."

She heard his soft chuckle behind her as he lightly ran the comb across those snarled strands. "Now, ma'am—I mean, Maude—you're not old, at all . . . leastaways, not to look at. Surely your husband tells you that you're pretty."

"I'm not married. I was engaged once, but he—he died."

The comb momentarily paused. "Well, that's a right shame," he finally said, "but I'm sure you'll find yourself a nice man, one day. Now, try to relax, so I don't have to tug too hard."

Maude smiled wryly into the darkness. "Len, you act like you've had a lot of practice at this . . . combing hair, I mean."

"I have. When I was just a little boy, I used to help my mama comb out her hair. Hers was as long as yours, but more yellow, like sunflowers. Yours is pale like moonlight." Then, giving a rueful-sounding cough, he added, " 'Course, when I got a little older, I gave that up and spent my time riding and shooting with my brothers."

As he spoke, the comb moved surely through her tangled locks so that, bit by bit, the snarls straightened into silky strands again. Maude felt herself begin to relax, soothed by the motion of the comb and the rumbling timber of his voice as he told her stories about roaming the Tennessee forests with his brothers. Perhaps an hour had passed when the last tangle had been defeated, and her silvery hair flowed past her shoulders in its usual silken stream.

"There, that's better," Len declared in satisfaction. "But

it's just going to tangle up again if I don't plait it for you. Now, don't worry none," he added when she would have protested. "I used to braid up rawhide to make my own tack . . . bridles, quirts, all sorts of things. Can't be much different with a lady's hair."

And, indeed, a few moments later he had efficiently twisted her hair into a neat if complicated tail, the end of which he tied off with a bit of ribbon she had salvaged from her petticoat. Then, scrambling to his feet, he pulled her upright and turned her around to face him.

"There, pretty as a picture," he said with another grin, his hands lingering on her shoulders as he studied his handiwork. "Now, don't undo it until we get someplace where you can scrub up. Then, if you want, I can fix it for you again."

"I won't undo it, I promise," she replied with a soft smile, all too aware that his hands still cupped her shoulders. She should have felt uneasy, even repulsed. For some reason, however, she was finding his touch comforting, almost enjoyable.

Enjoyable?

Feeling herself flush, she took a swift step back, so that his hands awkwardly dropped to his sides. As if just realizing what he'd been doing, Len retreated a few steps, as well, and abruptly dropped his gaze. "Guess I'd best check the horses again before we bed down," he muttered and turned to leave.

Maude watched him stride off into the shadows and waited for the night breeze to cool her cheeks. Whatever had possessed her to think such thoughts? she sternly demanded of herself. For one thing, the man was a brutal outlaw. For another, he was far too young a man for a woman of her age. Why, she could almost be his mother . . . almost.

But the sudden heat that had suffused her had been anything but motherly. Of that much, she was certain. She gave herself a sharp mental shake, telling herself that these odd feelings had been but a momentary aberration, certainly nothing to ever be repeated. Besides, should Len ever guess the direction her thoughts had turned, he'd either be embarrassed or else horribly amused by the idea that a woman her age could have designs on him. And right now she could not afford to lose his protection just to indulge some long-dormant passion.

But as she settled down into her blankets, she felt that earlier heat return, burning now between bruised thighs that suddenly ached in quite another way. She'd felt this way only one other time before, and that had been with Ron. She had given herself to him, before he had left for the fighting, wanting him to have one last precious gift from her before he went away. No one knew she had done that, and never again had she been tempted in such a way.

That was, until now.

Mortified, she buried her face into her palms, not daring to stir when she finally heard Len crawl into his own blankets barely an arm's length away from her. Dear Lord, what was happening to her? If she didn't know better, she would say that she had begun to think of him in the same way that a woman in love thinks of a man . . . though surely that was not possible. She hardly knew him, and what scant knowledge she did have was that of a lawless man who robbed and killed for a living. The fact that he had treated her well, thus far, meant little. Indeed, it might all have been a cruel act on his part to lull her into complacency before he abused her, just as Devilbiss had done.

But as she lay there on the hard ground, listening to his even breathing, she was certain she had not misjudged him. Whatever he was or had been, he had shown her a kindness that none of his fellows had. Perhaps it was because she reminded him of his mother, she wryly thought, which was all the more reason for her to suppress her unseemly urges and pray that, one day, he might feel compelled to set her free.

Jess stared up at the plump yellow moon hanging high over the streets of San Luis and silently uttered an unladylike oath. Aloud, she said, "Blast it all, there's no possible way we can pick up the trail again until tomorrow. Because of that pompous Marshal Chapel, we've lost an entire day."

"It could have been much worse, my dear," Doc Holliday drawled beside her. "A less reasonable man might not have believed the answers our good Sheriff Behan and your Mr. Markham sent in reply to his telegrams . . . or he might have refused to send the telegrams in the first place."

Hancock, who had gone to check on their horses as soon as they'd been released, now gave an inelegant snort as he rejoined her and Doc. "And a more reasonable man would have seen there was absolutely no cause to haul us in, in the first place."

Not that Marshal Chapel had any intention of pursuing the true culprits, Jess thought with a sniff. The lawman had made that fact quite clear as he'd opened the jail cell and ushered them out. "Guess the gang's long gone out of my jurisdiction," he'd allowed without any visible sign of embarrassment. "I reckon it's up to the territorial officials to send someone out after 'em."

Now, Jess and the two men halted outside the door of the Silver Mule, one of San Luis's two saloons. "I do believe this is the place our overly enthusiastic lawman said we might find rooms for the night," Hancock wryly observed and pushed open its swinging doors.

Accustomed as she now was growing to saloons, Jess looked over the Silver Mule with what she fancied was a practiced eye and found it distinctly lacking. Dark and smoky, with few tables and a rough oaken bar behind which bottles and glassware were stacked on crates, it possessed neither the comfortable atmosphere of the Lucky Nugget nor the elegant ambience of the Crystal Palace.

The patrons appeared neither comfortable nor elegant, either, and the mumble of voices rising from them held a distinctly sullen note. As for the bartender, he was a forbidding-looking young man with mutton-chop whiskers who, Jess surmised, likely watered the whiskey. The requisite music was supplied by a drunken cowboy in the corner mournfully warbling "Oh, Dem Golden Slippers" several notes off key.

Holliday, who had followed behind her, met her dismayed gaze with an ironic smile. "Believe me, my dear, I have seen much worse. But do shake out your bedcovers before you attempt to sleep. For my part, I think I shall eschew sleep and instead spend the night at the poker table, relieving these good citizens of their hard-earned cash."

"If that noise keeps up"—she rolled her eyes and nodded toward the cowboy, who now was mangling yet another popular tune—"I doubt any of us will get much sleep, anyhow. Mr. Hancock, do you very much mind seeing what sort of accommodations this place offers?"

While the bank examiner did just that, Jess watched with interest as Doc Holliday made his casual way to the nearest table. There, five sour-faced cowboys gathered around a surprisingly large pile of cash. They immediately made room for Doc, though whether they recognized him or simply thought him a newcomer to fleece of his cash, she could not tell. If it was the latter, she thought with a smile, they were in for a surprise. She knew, firsthand, the gambler's skill with the pasteboards.

A touch on her arm brought her back around to face Hancock once more. "We are in luck. They do have a room available for the night, and there's a bathhouse around back."

"*A* room?" Jess repeated with a frown. "Do you mean just one?"

"Just one. Luckily, this is the sort of place that makes no distinction between ladies and females of another sort, so I rather doubt anyone here will much concern themselves over the niceties."

She shot him an appalled look. "*They* may not concern themselves over the niceties, but *I* certainly do. Really, Mr. Hancock, you cannot expect the two of us to share a room, no matter how innocent the circumstances."

"Suit yourself, then," he replied with a shrug. "I'll take the room, and you can have the empty stall in the livery. That's the only other available spot, according to the proprietor . . . unless, of course, your friend the black hound is already occupying it."

"But I . . . you—"

She broke off with an exasperated shake of her head. A

gentleman would have offered to take the stall, but then, she had long since concluded that Hancock was no gentleman. Of course, he'd been sleeping on the ground these past two nights, just as she had, so she could hardly blame him for opting for a bit of comfort this one night. Certainly, she would prefer a bed over a pile of straw. And, with luck, the room might even have a comfortable chair or couch upon which one or the other of them could curl up for the evening.

Grimly, she met the bank examiner's cool gaze. "Very well, Mr. Hancock, I will spend the night with you."

Chapter Fifteen

By the time they reached the upper floor, however, Jess began to wonder if she should have opted for the livery, after all. The murmur of male voices and the smell of cigarette smoke wafted through the rough-hewn planks beneath her feet, those boards so uneven that she could glimpse light from the saloon below. If this did not immediately disabuse her of any notion that she'd get a peaceful night's rest, then the sounds emanating from the rooms around them did. From behind four of the five doors—two on one side of the hall, and three on the other—came a veritable cacophony of grunts and moans, leaving no doubt as to the activity occurring there.

Cheeks flaming, Jess stalked over to the particular room assigned her and Hancock. A crooked "3" was chalked upon its door, which sagged open a few inches. Clutching the bundle of clean linen that she had insisted the proprietor supply them, she nudged open the door the rest of the way, then stepped aside so that Hancock could turn up the gaslight.

"Oh, my," she murmured a moment later and almost dropped the blankets.

The yellow glow revealed a room so small that it barely

accommodated the narrow bed and rickety table that were its sole furnishings. The wooden walls were splintered, one pocked with half a dozen bullet holes. As for the floor, it was stained with tobacco juice and an old rust-colored stain that looked suspiciously like blood.

Hancock nodded toward the far wall. ''At least we have a window,'' was his wry assessment of the grimy pane perhaps a foot square that gave a shadowy view of the building next door.

To Jess's mind, this was no mean amenity, given that the smell of sweat and lust permeated the air . . . and, likely, the very walls and floor. Thank goodness she had thought to insist upon the new bedding, she thought faintly, for who knew what the existing blankets were like?

Hancock, meanwhile, had set down the gear he'd been carrying and edged his way past her to the narrow framework of dirty glass. By dint of a few moments' struggle, he managed to open it a handbreadth. Cool night air drifted in, dispelling a bit of the stench.

Breathing a bit more freely, she turned back to Hancock. ''Could the bathhouse be as bad, do you think?'' she ventured in a small voice.

He flashed her a grin. ''I would lay odds, my dear Mrs. Satterly, that it is considerably worse. Shall we go see?''

She barely heard his words, for his grin had set her heart abruptly thumping faster. This was the first time that she'd seen a look of genuine amusement cross his features, she realized. The emotion revealed a dimple in one cheek that she'd never noticed before and crinkled his cool blue eyes with unexpected warmth. All at once, he appeared less the handsome if dour bank examiner and more the dashing and quite devastatingly attractive adventurer. The transformation would have been quite debilitating to a less high-minded female than she. As it was, Jess did find herself momentarily breathless, and fervently prayed that she did not look quite as travel weary as she felt.

She gave herself a sharp mental shake as she set down the bedding and gathered up her carpetbag. If the two of them were to share quarters this night, she had best keep a firm rein on such wayward thoughts.

"Yes, let us take a look," she finally managed. "In fact, we probably should avail ourselves of the bathhouse before we settle in here. Given the nature of the Silver Mule's clientele, I'd prefer not to leave anything of value lying about unattended, since it appears this door has no lock."

"A sound suggestion," he replied, taking up their saddlebags and his rifle. "If you would care to lead the way . . ."

The bathhouse proved to be little more than a walled-off section of the blind alley in the shadows directly behind the saloon. A modicum of privacy was provided by a pair of shoulder-high swinging doors; otherwise, the top was open to the moonlit sky above. A lantern conveniently glowed within, revealing a wooden platform built above a graveled surface. In the center of the platform sat two tin hip baths. Draped over either was a threadbare towel while, beside each, two wooden buckets of water steamed gently in the night air.

Appalled, Jess turned to Hancock. "I can understand we have no choice but to share a room, but surely you cannot expect us to share a bath as well!"

"Actually, I expected to stand guard while you bathed first. But if you prefer, I can wait up in the room for you," he coolly replied and turned back toward the saloon.

In a flash, Jess had weighed the two evils—Hancock, standing just outside the slatted door as she crouched naked in the tub, scrubbing the trail dust from her; or some drunken, unknown cowboy barging in on her under the same circumstances—and made her decision.

"Wait, Mr. Hancock. I-I would be very grateful if you would stand guard for me."

At her plea, he turned back around. Shadows obscured his features, but she gathered from his tone that he was not smiling now. "If you are certain you can trust me not to peek, I'll see that no one intrudes on you. But if you don't mind, I'd like to take a bath of my own before the hot water cools completely."

"I'll hurry," she promised as, bag in hand, she scooted inside the enclosure and closed the twin doors behind her.

A series of wooden pegs protruded from the wall where the lantern hung. Setting her bag on a dry patch of gravel, she hurriedly slipped off her boots, then unbuttoned her skirt and shirtwaist, hanging both items on the pegs. Before she unlaced her camisole top, however, she glanced back toward the swinging doors. She could hear both the soft crunch of Hancock's boots against the alley's unpaved surface as he idly moved about, and the faint, almost tuneless whistle of a man impatiently marking time.

And what would you be doing if the situation were reversed . . . peering over the doors at him?

She ignored the inner voice that impishly whispered, *perhaps,* and instead divested herself of stockings, pantalets, and camisole. The cool night air raised gooseflesh on her naked limbs and made her nipples tighten. Shivering, she tiptoed across the gravel and onto the platform, halting before the nearest tub. A sliver of yellow soap lay propped on its lip, and she bent to retrieve it.

As she did so, the faint whistling abruptly halted, only to resume as she swiftly straightened and glanced back toward the doors. The tune, she realized with a smile, was the same one the drunken cowboy in the corner of the saloon had been singing earlier. The sound of footsteps continued as before, and at a safe distance, she satisfied herself. She climbed into the tub and reached for the first bucket and gingerly tipped a bit of it over her crouched form.

A trickle of blissfully hot water spilled down her weary flesh, and she sighed in pure joy. Then, remembering her promise to Hancock to hurry, she dipped the soap and managed a bit of lather, then began to scrub. A few minutes later, she had emptied most of the second bucket over her head, splashing the remainder of the soap from her hair so that, as she squeezed the water from them, her brown locks now squeaked cleanly. A bit of soapy water still remained in the first bucket, so she caught up her discarded undergarments. It might be some time before she'd next have the chance to do laundry, she reasoned as she gave them a quick wash and rinse, as well.

Those clothes wrung out as best she could manage, she reached for the towel and patted herself dry. Still naked but far cleaner than when she'd started, she tiptoed back across the rough gravel to her carpetbag and pulled out fresh undergarments, then redressed in the same skirt and shirtwaist. That accomplished, she ran a quick comb through her still-damp hair and hurriedly braided it into a loose twist that hung over one shoulder. Not exactly a style one would see in *Godey's,* she wryly thought, but it would do for now.

Perhaps twenty minutes had passed by the time she gathered up her carpetbag and damp laundry and stepped back out from behind the swinging doors. Accustomed as she had grown to the lamplight, it took her a moment to make out Hancock in the shadows. The bank examiner stood a quite respectable distance from the bathhouse, she saw, his back turned toward her as he scanned the night sky.

"I am quite finished, Mr. Hancock," she announced, feeling infinitely refreshed . . . and far more trusting of the man than she had since their journey together started. Indeed, he had proved the perfect gentleman in what could have been an awkward situation. "Shall I wait here for you, or—"

"Go on up to the room," he cut her short, glancing back around. "You'll be safer there than wandering around out here. Just be sure to prop that table you saw by the bed beneath the doorknob, so no one can get in. And leave it there until you hear me at the door."

"Very well, if you are certain—"

"I am."

His tone did not brook argument; besides which, she had no true desire to stand about in the alley while he performed his ablutions. *Afraid you might be tempted to peek?* an inner voice softly jeered. Avoiding the answer, she instead summoned a polite smile. "Very well, Mr. Hancock. I will set the room in order while you're gone."

"You can strew lace doilies about, if you wish, just so long as you promise to keep the door shut,'' his wry words drifted to her as she stepped back into the noisy saloon.

Nick waited until the door closed firmly after Jess; then, with a groan, he grabbed up his belongings and moved stiffly toward the bathhouse. His discomfort had nothing to do with the hard day's ride, however . . . and everything to do with an ill-timed glance in the wrong direction. As a result, he'd spent the past quarter hour in an embarrassingly noticeable state of arousal.

He pulled the swinging doors shut behind him, wryly aware of the need to make certain that they aligned completely. He hung his gun and holster on the nearest peg, then began stripping off his clothes. Jess had not been as careful in guarding her privacy, a fact he had discovered as she was preparing to step into her bath. Safely alone now, he indulged himself in the tantalizing memory.

His intention had indeed been to make certain that no one—including himself—would disturb Jess at her bath. His concern had been genuine, for he had earlier noticed what he was almost certain that she had not . . . one of the drunken cowboys eyeing her with interest while he, Nick, had been making their arrangements with the Silver Mule's proprietor. And while he had made a point of intercepting that cowboy's lustful gaze with a cold stare of his own, he was not about to risk Jess's safety by assuming that a single chill look had been sufficient to diffuse the other man's interest.

But from the moment he first saw what the saloon offered by way of a room, he'd known that his idea of their sharing sleeping quarters would likely prove uncomfortable in more ways than one. He might have reconsidered taking that stall in the nearby stables, save for the fact that he was even more uncomfortable with the idea of leaving Jess to sleep alone. Given that the room was little more than a whore's crib, it took little imagination to picture that same drunken cowboy shoving his way past her door in the middle of the night. And though Doc would be playing poker all night long just a floor below her, he had the professional gambler's unfortunate tendency to become engrossed in a game to the exclusion of every sight and sound around him. Thus, Nick had steeled himself to remain and play the role of protector.

At the memory, he wryly shook his head at his own naïveté as, naked and still exhibiting the lingering effects of his earlier arousal, he climbed into the other tub. Hunkering down, he dashed a bucket of water over his head. It had cooled considerably in the time it had taken Jess to finish her bath; still, he welcomed its bracing effects on both body and mind as he recalled the events of the past several minutes.

Pacing about the darkened alley, he had whistled a few tuneless bars while congratulating himself on his professionalism in handling the situation. After all, he'd asked himself, how many men could wait there while an attractive woman bathed without succumbing to the temptation to spy on her as she did so? His downfall had come when he innocently turned in the direction of the bathhouse's slatted doors. They gaped no more than an inch . . . but from where he stood in the alley, that small gap had been sufficient to afford him a most interesting view of what lay within.

The yellow glow from the lantern had clearly outlined Jessamine Satterly's naked body as she stood beside the hip bath. Hers was neither the thin, almost sexless form of an unmarried girl, nor the doughy, wide figure of a woman who'd already borne her babes. Instead, her curves had the full yet satisfying firmness of a woman at the brink of her sexual maturity. He had taken in the sight with a masculine appreciation that generated a reflexive if impersonal tightening in his loins. And then she had gracefully bent toward the tub, affording him an unimpeded view of her buttocks.

The sight of that softly rounded cleft invitingly pointed his way had sent him into an immediate and almost painful state of full arousal. Abruptly, he could picture himself slipping quietly past the bathhouse doors so that he was standing behind her. He wouldn't bother undressing, but would just unfasten his trouser buttons and free his aching organ to the cool night air. Before she could protest, he would clutch her hips and pull her to him, thrusting himself into the inviting warmth between her thighs. She would give a single, soft cry of protest . . . and then she would be moving with him, her cry giving way to a moan of desire as he rode her like the roan mare.

His mental flight of carnality had come to an abrupt end, however, as Jess straightened and turned around. He realized that he'd stopped whistling, and that those few instants of silence had aroused her suspicions. Guiltily, he promptly resumed his whistling with the chorus to the first song that popped into his head, "Oh, Dem Golden Slippers."

The tactic seemingly allayed her concerns, for she turned around again and climbed into the tub. What she did next he could not say, for he had turned his back on temptation and headed in the opposite direction down the alleyway. By the time she stepped from the bathhouse again, fully dressed, he'd had his thoughts, if not his body, back under control. Despite the shadows, he'd not dared turn to face her lest she notice his state and realize that he had peeked, after all!

Now, however, as he sluiced the soap and trail grime from his torso, he mentally berated himself for indulging in such juvenile behavior. Too much lay at stake with this job—his brother's future . . . Maude McCray's life—for him to risk jeopardizing it all. From here on out, his demeanor toward her would be nothing less than professional. Even if she decided to sleep buck naked in their shared bed tonight, he would act as if nothing was amiss.

Nick splashed the last few tepid inches of water over his head, then set down the empty bucket and climbed from the tub. In another few days this would all be over, he told himself as he reached for the remaining towel and began to dry off. Depending on how it all worked out, Jess would return to Brimstone—with her aunt, if they were lucky—and he'd either be escorting Rory to prison or California. In another two or three weeks, Nick would return to his usual duties with the agency, this chapter of his life permanently closed. As for

Jessamine Satterly, the lovely widow would be a tantalizing memory, and nothing more.

Oddly enough, however, he did not feel the usual sense of satisfaction that came from knowing he had a particular matter back under control. Frowning, he pulled on his underdrawers and trousers, then raked his fingers through his damp hair before reaching for his boots. Perhaps once they were on the trail again tomorrow, he would be able to shake that unsettling feeling. For tonight, however, he would—

The faint echo of a woman's scream abruptly rippled through the still night. Nick dropped the boot he was holding and froze, every sense alert. The sound had come from the upper floor of the Silver Mule, he was certain. As to the identity of the woman who'd cried out, she might have been any of the several females who serviced the saloon's clientele. Why, then, did a sudden sense of foreboding grip him?

Nick grabbed up his rifle from the corner of the bathhouse, then yanked his gunbelt from the peg and looped it over his head. Not bothering with boots or shirt, he shouldered his way past the bathhouse's swinging doors and raced for the saloon. Once inside, he spared a quick glance for the gaming area and bar. None of the patrons seemed aware of any disturbance taking place, which meant either that he had imagined the sound or that screaming women were commonplace at the Silver Mule.

A few heartbeats later, he was taking the splintered back staircase two steps at a time, until he reached the landing above. Swiftly, he took stock of the situation. No one lay murdered in the hall, he saw in relief, and no trail of incriminating bloody footprints walked their way along the rough-hewn boards. As for the scream, while it had not been repeated, he obviously was not the only one to have heard it. Curious faces peered expectantly from around the doorways . . . that was, from around all save one.

The door to Room Three remained quite firmly closed, while the muffled sound of an angry male voice issued from within.

Chapter Sixteen

Nick drew his pistol and, moving silently on bare feet, made his way to the room that was his and Jess's for the night. The male voice he had heard issuing from it grew louder now. Of Jess's voice, however, he heard nothing.

Which might not mean a damn thing, he harshly told himself as he squelched an instant of alarm. She might either be talking softly, or else she had chosen not to speak. It didn't necessarily indicate that she'd been bullied or pummeled into silence.

Easing to the far side of the door, he reached across for the knob and carefully turned it until the cylinders clicked; then, keeping clear of the entry, he gripped his rifle in both hands and kicked the door open.

A pistol shot blasted past him and buried itself into the hall's opposite wall. He had just time enough to register the sound of a choked, frightened cry—this one most certainly Jess's—before he flung himself sideways through the doorway. With the ease of much practice, he swiftly brought his rifle to bear on the pistol-waving cowboy who swayed drunkenly in the center of the room.

"Drop your gun and throw up your hands or I swear to God I'll shoot you where you stand!"

At Nick's harsh command, the man blinked and then gave him a leering grin. "Ain't no reason t'shoot," he slurred, swiping with his free hand at the blood that welled from a fresh scratch on his pockmarked cheek. "I'm just havin' me a talk wit' the lady. Now, why don't you go on 'bout yer business."

It was, indeed, the same cowboy whom Nick had noticed watching Jess earlier. He was perhaps forty, with a small, mean look about him . . . like a dog that would take a bite from a man, just for the hell of it. Sober and armed, he'd likely be smart enough to give up his weapon and make a strategic retreat. Drunk and brandishing a pistol, he might well kill someone if he felt threatened.

Slowly, Nick lowered his rifle so that he now held the weapon in his right hand, barrel pointed toward the ceiling. Spreading either hand toward his shoulders in a conciliatory gesture, he took a step closer and assumed a neutral tone. "Sorry, friend. I must have misunderstood the situation. I thought you were frightening Mrs. Satterly."

"I wasn't frightenin' her . . . was I, li'l lady?"

For the first time since he'd entered the room, Nick flashed a look in Jess's direction. What he saw sent a wave of cold anger washing over him and almost broke his deliberate air of unconcern. One sleeve of her shirtwaist was torn at the seams, and her damp hair had come unbound. Obviously, she had struggled with the intruder and was no doubt responsible for the welts across his face. What damage, if any, the cowboy had inflicted upon her, Nick could not tell. She stood now with her back against the far wall, looking pale but relatively composed for a woman who had just faced down a gun-toting drunk with rape on his mind.

Then she met Nick's gaze, and he saw the flicker of fear in her eyes before she turned back to the cowboy.

"You are wrong, sir," she countered in a voice that trembled only slightly. "You did frighten me, and I want you to leave my room. Now."

"An' I will, jus' as soon as I get what I came for. Hell, you let this fella have his," he added with a nod in Nick's direction. Then, as Nick took another casual step forward, so that he was separated from the antagonist by only an arm's length, the man's features tightened with belligerence.

"See here," he sputtered, and pointed his gun in Nick's face. "I tol' ya to go on 'bout yer business, an' I meant it. Now git out, or I'll put a hole in ya."

"All right," he softly agreed, "I'll go about my business, if that's what—"

He broke off abruptly, simultaneously twisting to one side and slamming his free fist against the cowboy's gun hand. The pistol flew from the man's grasp, but even before it skittered to the ground, Nick had swung back around and twisted the butt end of his rifle up so that it connected with a crack against the cowboy's skull.

"—you want," he finished in satisfaction as the unconscious man slumped to the floor at his feet.

A faint chuckle drifted to him from the doorway, and he spun around, ready for another round. Then, recognizing the newcomer, he relaxed.

"Well done, Nick," Doc Holliday murmured in approval from where he leaned against the doorjamb, his own pistol drawn. "I heard the shot and came to help, but it seems you've handled matters quite handily by yourself. Though, if I might point it out, you do seem a bit underdressed for the situation," the gambler added, reholstering his pistol while his pale gaze took in Nick's bare feet and chest.

Nick allowed himself a wry half-smile. "I guess next time I'll just have to tell the bad guys to wait until I've finished my bath." Then, his amusement fading, he turned to Jess. "Are you all right?"

"I-I'm fine," she answered in a small voice. "He bruised my arm when he grabbed me, but it's nothing much." Then, glancing down at the unmoving cowboy, she added, "You-you didn't kill him, did you?"

"If he did, he's going right back to my jail," broke in

another, familiar voice. Marshal Chapel crowded his way into the room, thumbs hooked into his belt loops as he stared down at the man sprawled on the floor. Then, reaching for the fallen pistol and tucking it in his waistband, he went on. "I hear tell there was some gunplay here a few minutes ago. You mind tellin' me what happened?"

Nick gave him a brief chronicle of events from the time he'd heard Jess's scream until he felled the drunk. Frowning, Chapel listened to his account, then turned to Jess. "All right, ma'am, if you're not too shaken up to talk, why don't you tell me your version of what went on here?"

The only sign Nick saw of her earlier fright was the way she clasped her hands tightly before her. Otherwise, her voice was steady as she said, "I came back to the room alone after my bath. As Mr. Hancock had suggested, I wedged that table"—she indicated the rickety piece of furniture overturned near the door—"beneath the doorknob, since the door itself has no lock. A few minutes later, I heard a knock. When I opened the door again, this man shoved his way in and tried to force himself on me. I screamed, and Mr. Hancock came to my rescue. Everything else happened just as he told it."

"All right. That sounds likely enough."

With a snort of disgust, Chapel gave the drunk a none-too-gentle kick in the ribs. The man stirred and began to groan. "This here fella's name is Bill Slaton," the lawman went on. "He's got a bad habit of gettin' drunk and disorderly, 'specially toward the ladies. If we can get him on his feet, I'll take him on down to the jailhouse."

"Here, let me help you," Nick offered coolly. Handing his rifle to Holliday, he squatted behind the man, who had dragged himself into a sitting position. He grabbed Slaton beneath the arms, then hoisted him upright and gave him a small shove in Chapel's direction.

The marshal caught hold of the staggering man and pinned his arms behind him. "All right, Bill, let's go." Glancing back at Nick, he sternly added, "And why don't you folks see if you can't stay out of trouble, least ways until morning."

''We'll do our best, Marshal,'' was Nick's ironic reply as the lawman marched his unsteady prisoner from the room and down the hall.

Holliday, who had stepped aside to let the two men pass, now resumed his earlier lounging pose in the doorway. ''Well, that was quite entertaining,'' he drawled. ''It almost makes up for having to fold a winning hand in my rush to assist you two.''

''I do appreciate your help,'' Nick answered, quite sincerely. Matters could easily have gone far less smoothly than they had, and he might well have needed the gambler as backup. ''Now, if I could ask you one last favor . . . could you wait here with Jess while I retrieve the rest of my gear from downstairs?''

''It would be my pleasure, but do try to hurry. One of those enterprising fellows downstairs might try to abscond with my winnings while I'm occupied elsewhere.''

With a quick nod of thanks, Nick strode back into the hall and toward the stairs. The curiosity seekers who had earlier been watching from their respective doors had long since grown bored and shut their doors again . . . this to Nick's relief, since he now felt conspicuous wandering about in his state of half-dress. He made his way swiftly downstairs again and out into the alley, following the lantern's yellow glow back to the bathhouse.

His saddlebags and clothes were still where he'd left them, he saw in relief. He shrugged on his shirt, debating as he did so whether to bother with his boots. He decided against it, since he'd only be pulling them off again in a few minutes, and gathered up the rest of his gear. Turning down the lantern, he padded back out into the now-dark alley.

And then a delayed reaction to what had just happened abruptly hit him, so that he sagged against the bathhouse wall. Shutting his eyes, he let out a shuddering breath and waited for the pulse that rapidly beat in his ears to slow.

It wasn't the fact that he'd been shot at, or had a pistol shoved in his face that unnerved him. He'd faced down far worse in the past and survived . . . hell, that was what he did for a living, after all. What left him weak-kneed was a far more chilling realization than the fact that he might have been killed tonight. Because he'd been so wrapped up in his own needs, Jess Satterly had almost been raped, maybe almost murdered.

Hell, you hardly know her . . . so why do you care?

The harsh words rang in his ears even as he sought an answer to that question. Perhaps the answer was that he *did* know her, and far too well for his own comfort.

If he was honest with himself, he would admit that those traits of hers that irritated him the most were the same ones that he, himself, had in spades. Stubbornness, for one . . . a conviction that she was always in the right, for another. And loyalty. How many other women would have the nerve to saddle up and ride after a gang of outlaws, even to rescue someone they loved? When she wasn't being a royal pain in the ass, she was someone whom he admired . . . hell, even liked.

But this bit of insight did nothing to change what had just happened. Nick raked a weary hand through his hair and opened his eyes again. In his single-minded goal to save his brother from himself, he'd almost sacrificed someone else again. Already, he had Marshal Crenshaw, the wounded deputy, and Maude McCray on his conscience . . . not to mention Arbin Satterly, and who knew how many other people Rory had killed or injured. Now, Jess had almost been added to the list.

So maybe it's time to let Rory pay for his crimes and be done with it.

It was a tempting course of action, and for a moment Nick pictured himself saddling up the roan and heading back to Kansas City. Let the posses and bounty hunters do what they would. He would no longer be his brother's keeper, not anymore. If Rory hanged, so be it.

Then, slowly, he shook his head. No matter what Rory had done, no matter that Rory had tried to kill him, they were still brothers. He had no choice. He had to keep trying.

* * *

Jess waited until Doc had closed the door, so that the two of them were alone. Then, moving carefully, lest her carefully maintained control shatter, she walked to the bed and perched on its edge. Then she shut her eyes.

"My dear Jess, you look quite pale," she heard Holliday say, his voice laced with a note of genuine concern as he moved closer. "Would you like me to bring you a restorative whiskey?"

"No. I'll be fine in just a moment. Besides, there's something I need to ask you before he gets back."

Jess opened her eyes again and met the gambler's pale gaze. Odd, how that single word had stuck in her mind, when so many other frantic, frightening things had happened in such a short space of time. But then, she'd had her suspicions from the beginning, so that what she needed now was Holliday's confirmation of them . . . that was, if he would give it. Knowing she had but a few minutes to learn what she needed, Jess opted for bluntness.

"His name isn't Jake Hancock, is it?"

Holliday quirked a wry brow. "I'm not certain that I know what you mean, my dear."

"Yes, you do, Doc."

She paused and took a deep breath, then went on. "That night at the Occidental Hotel, when we first met . . . you started to call him by another name, and he stopped you. And then, just a few minutes ago, you did it again. You called him 'Nick.' "

When the gambler made no reply, she persisted. "Is it true, then, what you claimed at the time . . . that you really did know him before? And his name isn't really Jake Hancock, is it?"

"Oh, dear," he drawled with the faintest of smiles. "It does appear that you have found us out. Very well, since I already have been indiscreet once tonight, I will go out on a limb and admit that his name truly is Nick. But anything beyond that you will have to ask him directly."

"But what if he won't tell me the truth?"

"Then I suppose you will just have to live with a lie."

He paused and plucked out his handkerchief, giving way to a short bout of coughing. When he recovered himself a few moments later, a sheen of perspiration dampened his brow.

"We all lie, you know," he went on in a weaker voice, "to other people . . . to ourselves. And usually, when we do lie, we also manage at the same time to convince ourselves that we are justified in what we've done."

Jess gave him a skeptical look. "So what you're trying to tell me is that Hancock—or, rather, Nick—thinks he has a good reason for pretending to be someone he is not?"

"What I am saying, my dear, is that sometimes a lie may be preferable to the truth."

Jess would have persisted, but the door opened just then, and the man she had known as Jake Hancock stepped back inside. "Thanks again, Doc," he said without preamble. "I can take care of things from here on out."

"I am certain that you can," the gambler murmured. "And now, I believe I shall return downstairs to my poker game. I don't know about the two of you, but I feel quite lucky tonight." A moment later, the door clicked shut behind him, leaving Jess alone with a stranger.

For the man standing before her was not the same man who had stepped into her bank just a few days ago. That man had been well-dressed to the point of being a dandy, and precise in his manner to the point of fussiness. He had been a fine-looking man, but in a well-bred, citified fashion. In point of fact, he had been a taller and more handsome version of her late husband.

This man, however, reminded her nothing at all of Arbin.

When he had burst into the room, half-dressed and brandishing a rifle, she momentarily had mistaken him for an outlaw or a bounty hunter. When she finally recognized him, her shock had been replaced with awe as she watched him dispatch the drunken Slaton. Swift and efficient in his actions, and dangerously attractive in his appearance, he had sent her heart racing with more than gratitude, even as the logical portion of her mind registered the fact that something was amiss. Now, seeing him standing before her again, she knew what it was.

In a glance, she took in his well-muscled torso, visible beneath his unbuttoned shirt. Dark hair generously covered his chest and vee'd down to the waistline of his trousers, so that her gaze reflexively dropped lower. Hurriedly, she jerked her gaze upward again, noting the way his dark hair spilled rakishly over his brow, and how his handsome features were set in cold, uncompromising lines. It was as if he finally had stripped off his civilized mask to reveal the dangerous male who had been lurking beneath all along.

If he noticed her scrutiny, he gave no sign. Instead, he abruptly dropped his gear and stalked toward her, cool blue eyes narrowed. ''Why in the hell did you open that door for someone besides me?''

His tone was controlled, but the note of suppressed anger in his voice was obvious. The unspoken accusation—that she had disobeyed his command—set her own anger to simmering and dispelled her uncertainty. Whoever he was, he had no right to order her about as if she were a child!

She scrambled to her feet and met his gaze with a heated look of her own. ''I had no intention of opening it, but this Slaton person claimed you had been injured. I was concerned for your safety . . . though why, I don't know.''

To her dismay, those last words trembled slightly, so that she found herself dropping her gaze as she recalled those few frantic moments. Upon her return to the room, she had duly wedged the doorknob, seeing the sense of that advice. That accomplished, she'd gone about changing the bed linens, bundling the old ones in the far corner and replacing them with the new. Then the knock had come, too soon for it to have been he, followed by the sound of someone rattling the knob.

Yer man's done taken a fall, Slaton's rough voice had claimed in response to her nervous demand to know who was out there.

The words had sent a wave of fear through her as she pictured the man she knew as Hancock sprawled at the bottom of the stairs, bruised, most certainly . . . unconscious, perhaps . . .

bones broken, quite likely. Why she cared so much she could not explain, not even to herself. Not thinking of her own safety, she had tugged aside the table to throw open the door. And then a grinning Slaton had shoved his way in and seized her arm.

Shaking off the memory, Jess squared her shoulders and gazed up again. Hancock—no, not Hancock, Nick—was staring down at her. His expression remained forbidding, but the grim look in his blue eyes had softened slightly. Even so, his tone was curt as he said, "That's the second oldest trick in the book, Jess. Don't fall for it again."

"Believe me, I won't," she shot back. Then, as he turned away, she added, "Tell me, what's the first oldest trick . . . claiming to be someone whom you are not?"

Slowly, he turned back around to face her, his expression neutral now. Very softly, he asked, "What are you trying to say, Jess?"

With one corner of her mind, she noted that, twice now, he had dropped the formality of her surname and addressed her with a familiarity he had never before taken. What it meant, she wasn't certain . . . nor did she care. For the moment, all she wanted was to get to the bottom of his deception.

Tamping down her anger, she met his look with a cool gaze of her own. "What I *am* saying is that I know your name isn't Jake Hancock. It's Nick."

"I see. And what else do you think you know?"

She took a deep breath. "I also know that you're not a bank examiner."

"You saw my letters of introduction, and my authorization from the territorial bankers," he replied with a wry quirk of his brow. "You believed me then, so why don't you believe me now?"

She could have offered other reasons: the fact that he had used a false name; that he was an intimate of the gun-toting gambler, Doc Holliday; that he had joined her in her search for Maude, when no one else would. To her dismay, what she blurted out was, "Because bankers don't face down killers and disarm them. Instead, they try to be heroes and get themselves murdered for their trouble.''

Tears of angry guilt momentarily blinded her as the image of Arbin's dying moments again played out in her mind. After tonight, she could better imagine how he must have felt in those last few instants, facing down the gun-wielding masked outlaw just as she had faced the drunken Slaton. The same pistol Arbin had reached for that fateful day had been tucked into her boot tonight, but she had not dared draw it while Slaton still held his own gun. Had her hesitation stemmed from fear, she wondered, or from common sense? For surely she would have died at Slaton's hands had she attempted to shoot it out with him.

By the time she blinked away the dampness, Nick was watching her with silent consideration. When he finally spoke, it was in the measured tones of a man humoring a troublesome child.

''Very well, Jess, you're right. My name isn't Hancock, and I'm not a bank examiner. Now, why don't we forget all about this and try to get some sleep? We've got another long ride in front of us tomorrow, and I—''

''That's all you're telling me, that your name's not Hancock and you're not a bank examiner?'' Jess stared back at him, not quite believing she'd heard rightly. ''After all that we've been through together thus far, surely I have the right to know what's going on here.''

''There's nothing more you need to know. Believe me.''

''Fine.''

With that eloquent retort, Jess marched over to where her carpetbag and saddlebags lay and snatched them up. ''The room is yours, Nick. I'll stay in the stable tonight, and tomorrow I'll continue on . . . *alone,*'' she clarified with cool emphasis on the last word. ''I'm sure that whatever scheme you're involved with can be concluded quite satisfactorily without my help.''

''Damn it, Jess, this isn't necessary.''

''Yes, it most certainly is.''

Chin held high, she stalked over to the closed door, but Nick was swifter than she. Before she could protest, he was blocking her exit, arms folded over his chest as he glared back at her.

"Do you honestly think I'd let you sleep out there, alone in the stables, especially after what just happened with Slaton?"

"Do you honestly think I'd sleep in the same room with a man who has lied to me repeatedly, and who won't tell me why he really came to Brimstone?"

Anger warred with indecision in his blue eyes for a few moments, before he slowly nodded. "All right; you have a point. If you'll put down your gear and promise to stay here for the night, I'll tell you what I can."

Chapter Seventeen

Jess set down her bags and folded her own arms over her chest, copying his aggressive stance. ''Very well, Nick. I'm waiting.''

''What I'm about to tell you is said in strictest confidence. I'm trusting you not to breathe a word of this to anyone else . . . do you understand that?'' At her impatient nod, he went on. ''I'm here in Arizona for one reason: to track down Rory Devilbiss and the rest of the Black Horse Gang. As you've guessed, my name isn't Jake Hancock, it's Nick . . . which is all the name you need to know for now. And, as I already told you, I'm not a bank examiner. What I am is a Pinkerton detective.''

''A Pinkerton detective?''

Jess stared at him with true surprise. Of any scenario she might have conjured, this was one that had never occurred to her. ''So the bankers' association hired you to track down the bank robbers. But why couldn't you just tell me that was the reason you were in Brimstone?''

''They hired *Pinkerton* to capture the gang,'' he corrected her. ''I'm not connected to the case in an official capacity, which is why I didn't identify myself to you. I've taken a short leave of absence from the agency to pursue the matter on my own."

He paused, his expression carefully guarded. As Jess waited in growing consternation, she could almost see him picking his words as carefully as an artist might choose colors from his palette.

"I'd heard rumors that they might strike your bank again," he went on, "so I thought that Brimstone would be the best place to start looking. I even had the notion that maybe I could stop the robbery before it happened. The only way I could keep an eye on things without arousing suspicion was to set myself up as a bank examiner. Unfortunately, the gang managed to ride into town and commit the robbery while I was busy checking the layout of the streets for possible escape routes."

Jess frowned, more confused than before by his role in this drama. "What you are saying makes no sense," she exclaimed with a shake of her head. "If the Pinkertons were already on the case, why would you be involved in it on your own?"

His blue eyes took on a shuttered expression. "That's something I can't tell you . . . at least, not yet. But I can assure you that my reasons will not interfere with my rescuing your aunt and recovering your money for you."

"And what about the gang? How can you possibly hope to capture them on your own, one man against so many?"

He favored her with a slow, humorless smile. "I'm a professional at this sort of thing, Jess. Believe me, I can handle them."

Had any other man made so bold a claim, she would have dismissed it as pure folly. But the chill confidence he wore like a mantle did not brook failure, so that she found herself believing him. But belief was not trust . . . at least, not yet.

She frowned. "I suppose if I asked for proof of your *real* identity, you'd give me another sheaf of papers, like the ones that showed your name as Hancock?"

"As a matter of fact, I do have official Pinkerton identification, but it's in a safe deposit box in Kansas City." He gave her a wry smile. "Carrying around that sort of thing when one is working undercover rather defeats the purpose of a false identity, don't you agree?''

Jess ignored the sarcasm. ''And if I wired Mr. Pinkerton to ask if you worked for him, I presume he would claim not to know you?''

''Unless you were the one who hired me in the first place, you'd get neither a denial nor a confirmation that I worked for the agency.''

Which meant he could insist all day that he worked for Pinkerton and she'd have only his word for it. A tendril of doubt curled in her chest. He had lied to her once before, she knew. Who was to say that he wasn't lying now, as well?

He must have read her uncertainty in her face, for his expression hardened. ''I've told you everything I can, Jess. Doc is the only other person to know who I am, and that wasn't by my choice. Believe me, what little you do know would be quite enough to get me killed if you told it to the right people. You'll just have to trust me on this one.''

Jess took a deep breath. Belief might not be trust, but surely it was a step in the right direction. ''Very well. Where do we go from here? Just because I know who you are doesn't mean I intend to give up the search for Maude.''

''I didn't think you would. We'll ride out tomorrow, just as we planned. That part won't change . . . but beyond that I'm not at liberty to say.''

For a moment he sounded like Hancock again, so that she almost smiled. Then, as another thought came to her, she sobered. ''I won't ask you any more questions, then, but only if you promise me one thing.'' She paused for a deep breath, then went on. ''When we do track them down, I want you to help me find out which one of the gang killed my husband. The rest of them, I don't care about, so long as he—whoever he is—is brought back to be hanged.''

Something flickered in Nick's cool blue gaze and then was gone. ''I promise you that I'll see he gets what he deserves.''

A tone of flat finality colored his words and sent a reflexive shiver through her. She would not want to be that man when

Nick found him. His answer, however, was what she wanted to hear.

He gave her a considering look. "You know, it occurs to me that since I shared some of my secrets with you, I think it would be only fair for you to do the same. This might be the time to let me take a look at that map you've been so jealously guarding."

The map! She'd almost forgotten about it, though the faint crackling in her boot reassured her that it was still safely tucked away. As for showing it to him, that *would* be the fair thing to do . . . so why, then, did she hesitate? But hesitate she did, and long enough for that earlier hardness to settle again over his features.

"So it only works one way," he murmured. Abruptly, he abandoned his post at the door and headed for the bed. "Stay or leave, Jess . . . it's up to you. In the meantime, I'm going to get some sleep."

As she watched in dismay, he stripped off his shirt and tossed it in the direction of his saddlebags. His trousers followed, leaving him wearing nothing but a tight-fitting pair of underdrawers. While one frivolous corner of her mind noted in approval the firm play of muscle in his buttocks as he bent to pull back the blankets, another noted the wicked-looking red scar that sliced down his right shoulder blade and wondered how he'd been injured.

The rest of her thoughts centered on the fact that she'd just put several cracks in the fragile bridge of trust they had begun to build between them. It was apparent that she had offended him by not handing over the map; however, it was too late to rectify that situation tonight. Perhaps tomorrow, when they were on the trail again, she would let him take a look.

While she conducted this mental debate, Nick had climbed beneath the blankets and settled in to sleep. She waited until he had remained unmoving for some moments, and then she took a steadying breath. If he had no qualms about sharing a room, she stoutly told herself, than neither did she. Unfortunately, the bed appeared barely large enough for one person, let alone two.

Unless those two would be lying entwined all night long.

Shaking off the quite unsettling mental image that sprang from that unbidden thought, Jess turned down the gas lamp. Now the only illumination came from the moonlight that filtered in through the single window. The resulting shadows allowed her a modicum of modesty as she began unfastening the buttons of her shirtwaist.

The room held a bit of a chill now, so that gooseflesh marched up her bared skin as she slipped off the torn garment and then stepped out of her skirt. She slipped off her boots and added them and her stockings to the pile of discarded clothes. The map crackled in her hand as she debated what to do with it. After what had just happened, she wouldn't put it past Nick to go searching for it after she'd fallen asleep. Finally, she folded the parchment another time and tucked the square into the waistband of her pantalets and arranged her camisole over it. Uncomfortable the result might be, but it was the only way she could ensure that the map would remain in her possession.

A moment later, clad only in her chemise and pantalets, she tiptoed to the bed. Nick had not moved . . . nor, did it appear, was he feigning sleep while actually taking advantage of her dishabille to peer at her from over the tangle of blankets. Even so, she hesitated. Innocent or not, as the circumstances might be, the fact of the matter was that she was about to climb into bed with a man who was not her husband.

You're being foolish, her inner voice chided her as she stood there shivering. Truly, what difference did it make? Had she not already spent the past few days traveling through isolated territory in the company of not just one man but two? If Nick had any intention of forcing himself upon her, surely he would have done it then. Steeling herself, she took a deep breath and then eased beneath the topmost cover.

The relief of settling into a bed instead of the rocky ground made her sigh in contentment. Unfortunately, the bed's rope slats were not knotted as tightly as they might be, so that the mattress sagged in the center . . . a fact she swiftly discovered as she collided with a muscular masculine form.

Biting back a gasp of dismay, she hurriedly inched her way back to her side of the bed, only to find herself sinking toward the center again the moment she relaxed. Twice more it happened, and twice more she squirmed her way back to her own side of the bed. The fifth time she slid into him, Nick's curt words abruptly broke the silence.

"Damn it, Jess, just lean up against me and go to sleep."

Mortified, she turned so that her back nestled into his side and obediently sagged against him. The heat of his bare skin radiated through the sheer fabric of her camisole, the sensation promptly easing the chill that had settled into her. Pressed as she was against him, she could breathe in the very scent of him, a faint mingling of soap and leather and the comforting smell of clean male flesh.

She'd quite forgotten what it was like, sleeping with a man, she thought in surprise. Now, lying next to Nick, it dawned on her how much she had missed the simple pleasure of cuddling up to a warm male body on a cool night. *Enjoy it while you can,* her inner voice urged her as she slowly relaxed. Unless she remarried one day, she'd never have another chance again to sleep with a man . . . and, certainly, never again with Nick.

Which was too bad, she thought with a regretful little yawn, since with him she might be tempted to do more than sleep.

If she'd been less tired, the unseemly direction that her thoughts had taken might have shocked her. As it was, exhaustion swept her in a sudden wave, so that she regarded the notion with sleepy interest and nothing more. She'd have time enough tomorrow to be shocked, she told herself as her eyelids flickered a final time and she gave herself up to slumber.

He'd been trying to sleep for a good hour now, but with no success. With a muffled curse, Nick propped himself against the splintered headboard and listened to the soft, regular sound of Jess's breathing. She had been asleep almost from the moment she crawled into bed while, once again, he simply lay there. At first, he had tried to tell himself it was the confrontation with Slaton and the resulting unpleasant memories that kept slumber at bay. Finally, he conceded the truth, that his wakefulness stemmed from the fact that Jess was sleeping right next to him . . . and that her presence there was working on him like a tonic on a sick man.

It wasn't as if she were naked beneath the bedclothes. Indeed, her undergarments covered her quite thoroughly, so that only her arms and her feet were bare. And his senses weren't overwhelmed by potent perfumes, for the only fragrance that clung to her was a clean whiff of soap mingling with the faint, sweetly female scent of her skin. Somehow, this lack of coquetry was more compelling than had she been awake and deliberately trying to seduce him.

Making it worse were the sounds that emanated from the parchment-thin wall beside them. For the past several minutes, he had been treated to the rhythmic thumping of the neighboring bed, accompanied by the expected grunts and groans. Try as he would to ignore them, the relentless bumps and cries soon had worked on his imagination. Once again, his erection strained painfully against the confining fabric of his drawers as he pictured himself and Jess contributing their own sounds to the general cacophony.

He endured the torment for some minutes, when Jess lightly stirred and turned so that she now lay facing him. Her breasts now pressed with tantalizing softness against his ribs, while one hand rested on his belly.

He bit back a groan, all too aware that her fingers lightly rested but a few inches from the hot bulge of his erection. He knew that he had to resolve this problem immediately. He also knew that, if her hand moved any lower, he might not be in any position to deal rationally with the situation. All this, he knew . . . yet rather than sliding her hand away, he left it where it was. Almost of their own volition, his fingers reached over to stroke the silken warmth of her breast.

She sighed and snuggled closer to him. Emboldened, he slid

his other hand down her back, cupping the firm curve of her buttocks. His caress drew another soft sigh from her, heightening his own growing excitement. It would be an easy enough matter to draw her atop him, so that he could better explore the soft lines of her body while his own throbbing flesh pressed against her yielding warmth. If she did not protest that liberty, he would continue his exploration until she was thoroughly aroused, as well. From there it would simply be a matter of awakening her and continuing what he had started.

But even as his thoughts moved in that direction, it occurred to him that he was planning something dangerously akin to rape. The realization promptly dampened his desire. Here he was, using a sleeping woman to ease his needs, taking advantage of her involuntary actions to trigger some voluntary reactions of his own. Hell, he was as bad as Slaton . . . worse, actually, since unless she awakened, Jess would never even know what he'd done.

With a muttered curse, he abruptly rolled away from her and climbed out of the bed, then padded toward the open window. By now, the occupants of the adjoining room had ceased their previous exertions, so that the only other sound was the occasional voice drifting from the saloon below. Lulled by the silence, he let the trickle of cool night air slide over him, until his need had burned itself out again and he could once more think clearly.

At the very least, what he'd been contemplating a few minutes earlier had been unprofessional, if not outright unethical. Grimly, he shook his head. He had accused her of not trusting him, when apparently she had a very good reason not to do so. And he needed her trust if he was going to get his hands on that map and find Dead Squaw Canyon before much more time had passed.

Hell, why not look for it now? He glanced over at Jess to reassure himself that she remained sleeping, then moved quietly over to where she'd stowed her gear. A quick search of her saddlebags and discarded clothes did not yield it, nor was the map stashed in one of her boots, as it was during the day.

She must have it on her, he realized with mingled anger and amusement. Apparently, she'd also not trusted him not to search for the map while she was asleep, and she had been right in this, as well.

Chances were he could locate the place without Jess's help, if he had the luxury of time . . . but time was one thing he sorely lacked. And though their journey, thus far, had been relatively easy, that would change once they rode deeper into the mountains. Without that parchment of Jess's, he might spend days or even weeks tracking Rory through the maze of washes and foothills just above the border.

He thought fleetingly of his own map that he'd been carrying these past few weeks. Scribbled on the back of a complaint issued against one Whitey Kilroy, it had been drawn by the man in question as he lay dying in a Dallas alley. Nick had learned of the outlaw's whereabouts from an informant soon after he first had begun his search for Rory, just a few weeks earlier. Knowing that Kilroy had been a member of the Black Horse Gang at the time of the Brimstone robbery, Nick had hoped that the outlaw might be persuaded to tell him what he knew of Rory's whereabouts in the interim.

Unfortunately for the outlaw, whose pale blond hair was responsible for his sobriquet, he'd had a run-in with a Texas cowboy who'd objected to his cheating at cards. Kilroy had ended up with a bullet in his belly only hours before Nick had tracked him down. In agony from his wound, the outlaw had gladly traded information for a bottle of numbing whiskey. He had told Nick everything he knew about the gang's operation, including one particular item of interest. But the map he had painstakingly drawn with a stub of pencil beneath the glow of a gaslight was useful only if one knew where Dead Squaw Canyon was to start with . . . which was the problem that had dogged Nick from the first.

Weary all of a sudden, Nick stood and turned back toward the bed, then hesitated. He'd proved already that, when it came to Jess, he had the unfortunate habit of forgetting he was a professional. Better not to put it to the test again, lest he fail even more miserably than he already had. Instead, he would do what he should have done from the first: spend the night on the floor.

The blankets that Jess had earlier stripped from the bed lay bundled in the corner. Since his bedroll was in the livery, still tied to the roan's saddle, he'd have to make do with them, instead. He spread out the threadbare bedding, which was redolent of numerous past occupants, then pulled up his saddlebags to use as a pillow. At least the floor was far smoother than the rocky ground upon which he'd been sleeping these past nights, he wryly thought as he settled on his makeshift pallet. He could only hope he had shaken out whatever vermin might have lingered within the blankets, themselves.

As he waited for sleep to claim him, however, his thoughts tumbled back to his earlier conversation with Jess. A few odd words that she had said had stuck in his mind, and he heard them again now in the darkness.

They try to be heroes and get themselves murdered for their trouble.

She had referred to bankers, in general, but she had been speaking of her husband. It was as if she blamed herself for his death, though why she would feel that way, he could not guess. Still, it helped to explain why she was so intent on finding her kidnapped aunt. Perhaps if Maude was rescued, that would partially counterbalance the tragedy of Arbin Satterly's murder.

He felt an instant's envy for the dead man. What would it be like, he wondered, to have someone cherish his memory as Jess obviously did her husband's? For why else would an intelligent and attractive woman such as she never have remarried . . . and why else would she want to be seeking vengeance for his murder?

Maybe she feels guilty that she's happy he is dead.

The notion sprang unbidden to his mind, and he frowned into the darkness. Not happy, he amended, but possibly relieved that her husband was no longer in her life. Perhaps they hadn't been suited, or maybe he even abused her, and widowhood had proved an easy escape from the misery. Maybe she had wondered what her life would be like without him, and then convinced herself that her innocent speculations had somehow conjured up the tragic fate that had befallen him.

If so, then she would not be the first person to lash herself with that particular whip of guilt. He'd felt an instant's guilty relief the morning after Doc had saved his life in Dodge City, when he had thought the gambler had killed Rory in the process. When he'd learned that Rory still lived, his guilt had been all the greater for that moment of disloyalty.

Shifting about on the hard floor for a more comfortable spot, Nick sighed and shut his eyes. Soon enough, he would be battling even more guilt, and he did not look forward to that particular war. Since Jess still refused to turn over the map to him, he would have no choice tomorrow but wait until they were away from San Luis, then wrest the parchment from her and abandon her on the trail.

He pictured her reaction of outraged hurt at this betrayal, and he inwardly winced. *She won't soon forgive you that one, Nick,* he grimly told himself. Or maybe she would, if she ever learned that stealing her map was the lesser of the two evils he intended to employ in resolving his particular situation.

For he had let her believe that his plan was to bring the Black Horse Gang—and, most particularly, its leader—back to Tombstone for a quick trial and even speedier hanging. The truth was that he had lied. He had no intention of bringing Rory back. Arbin Satterly's murder would go unpunished, as a result, and Jess would never be free of her self-imposed guilt.

He wouldn't soon forgive himself for this betrayal, either, Nick knew . . . but not even for Jess would he sacrifice his own brother.

Chapter Eighteen

The black hound halted in mid-lope to plunk himself down on the rocky trail and scratch at a flea bite behind his ear. Nick, riding on the trail behind him alongside Jess, surreptitiously followed suit. In fact, he had been itching almost from the moment last night when he had abandoned the bed in Room Three of the Silver Mule for a pallet on the floor.

The action drew Jess's attention, and she glanced over at him.

"I still don't know why you insisted on sleeping on the floor, and on those blankets," she exclaimed with a shudder, repeating the same sentiment she had voiced when they'd risen at dawn, almost two hours earlier. "God knows what you might have picked up from them."

He grimaced, wondering the same thing himself. "It's just a couple of bites, nothing more. And I already told you that I would have been in worse shape if I'd spent all night on that sagging mattress."

That had been the best excuse he'd been able to offer when she had awakened to find him curled uncomfortably in the corner . . . that the years of riding after criminals had taken their toll on his back. Better she think him old and decrepit than to know the truth: that he'd not trusted himself to lie in the same bed beside her.

"I slept there all night in perfect comfort," she countered with a small frown. Then, changing the subject, she asked, "What about Doc? Are you certain he'll be all right, staying in San Luis alone? You saw how he looked . . . far too ill to be playing cards all night. He should be resting in bed, and sipping tea instead of whiskey."

The motherly censure in her tone drew a wry smile from Nick as he idly scratched a flea bite on his wrist. Once they had dressed and gathered their gear, he and Jess had made their way back down to the saloon to find the gambler still at the same table where he'd been playing the night before. Two other bleary-eyed men had kept the vigil with him, their haggard, unshaven countenances overlaid with desperation. By contrast, Doc had appeared cheerfully alert, his pale eyes burning feverishly against the chalky hue of his face, and a half-full bottle of whiskey at his elbow. An impressive stack of bills and coins was arranged before him.

"You'll forgive me if I decide not to accompany you on the remainder of your little journey," the gambler had drawled by way of greeting. "As you can see, I have had a profitable night and am now in the process of winning two small mines and a share in a racehorse from my friends here, Big Al and Chinless Eddie."

"Damned lunger . . . he's about cleaned us out," muttered the larger of the aforementioned pair, whom Nick presumed to be Big Al. His doughy face took on a glum expression as he squinted at the cards he'd just dealt himself.

The other man, whose receding chin doubtless was responsible for his unfortunate nickname, slapped down his own cards in disgust. "He ain't goin' nowhere, that's for damn sure, not 'til I've won back some of my money."

"You can see how my friends clamor for me to stay," Doc had amiably addressed him and Jess. "I did enjoy our short time together, however, and I wish you the best of luck in tracking down your outlaw gang. I trust that the missing lady will be found safe and sound."

"We'll let you know how things turn out," Nick had assured him as they bid the man farewell and made a swift departure from the doubtful hospitality of San Luis.

Now, as they retraced their trail from that town back toward Las Tres Cabezas, he wondered if the gambler's defection had been deliberate. Had Holliday continued on with them, his presence might have complicated Nick's plans to seize the map and travel on alone. As it was, his decision to remain behind served to ease Nick's conscience on one score . . . Jess's safety. Once he'd left her behind, she could simply ride back to San Luis and let Holliday escort her home as far as Tombstone.

But trust Jess to be worried about a man whose reputation was such in this part of the country that the mention of his name often was sufficient to avert a confrontation.

He gave her a reassuring smile, telling himself that the odd emotion now clawing at his gut was not jealousy. "Don't let his appearance fool you, Jess. Doc Holliday is one man who can take care of himself. I daresay he'll let Big Al and Chinless Eddie win back a few hands, just to keep the peace, and then find himself a couple of other pigeons to pluck."

"But he looked so ill—"

"He should have been dead years ago . . . or, at least, that's what he claims the doctors told him. If the late nights and whiskey haven't killed him yet, I doubt they'll do so anytime soon."

She nodded and fell silent again, but as they rode on through the cool morning breeze he noticed that she kept glancing his way. At first he was certain she knew what had happened—or almost happened—between them last night, and he waited uneasily for her to confront him. But then, after her half-dozenth frown of consternation, he realized in relief that what must be bothering her was his appearance.

For, last night, when he had left her and Doc to check on the horses, he impulsively had bartered a portion of his wardrobe with the stableboy. Luckily, the young man had proved to be much his same size, and eager for some fancy go-to-church clothes, as the youth had put it.

Now, instead of the ruffled shirt and fine wool vest and trousers he'd been wearing the past days, Nick was dressed far more comfortably in denim pants and a plain white shirt topped by a worn leather vest. He'd also traded his crisp bowler, so that a battered brown Stetson was now pulled low over his brow.

Given the contrast between these clothes and his "Hancock" wardrobe, it was not surprising that Jess found his appearance unnerving. Even Doc had remarked upon the transformation, though his final wry parting words—"Wherever did you find those clothes . . . the local stable?"—had been both unsettlingly accurate and for Nick's ears only. Hell, he'd glimpsed his own reflection in the mirror hanging behind the Silver Mule's bar and been taken off guard, himself, though for far different reasons.

For, with his cowboy's wardrobe and two days' worth of whiskers, he was a disconcertingly similar if slightly older version of his younger brother as he had seen him that last time in Dodge City.

Shaking off the uncomfortable comparison, he instead concentrated on how best to proceed with getting his hands on the map and leaving Jess behind. Ahead on the rocky trail lay a tangle of scrubby trees that he recognized from yesterday. He could leave her there, tied safely beneath a shelter of sorts, while he continued on alone to Las Tres Cabezas and then south in search of Dead Squaw Canyon. And better he do it now, while the day was still early, so that she'd have plenty of time to free herself and ride back to town during daylight hours.

He waited until they were almost upon the spindly stand, then slowed the roan to a walk. "About that map of yours," he said without preamble, and without much hope, "I'd like to take a look at it. Now that we're this close to finding the gang's hideout, I think I should know just where we're headed . . . just in case."

To his surprise, she nodded and reined in Old Pete. "You're right."

As he halted the roan beside her, she reached into her boot. She paused for a quick flick of her reins at the paint's muzzle as he nipped at her, then withdrew the folded parchment. *This is going to be simple, after all,* he tried to tell himself in satisfaction, even while he felt his gut clench as she handed the map to him.

His fingers brushed hers as he took it, the brief contact sending a warm, familiar jolt through him. *You're a professional . . . do your job.* Avoiding her gaze, he spread out the map and studied it.

"I guess I've been foolish, thinking that I couldn't trust you," he heard her admit as he mentally retraced the route they had taken these past days, "but after last night, when you rescued me from that man, Slaton, and before that, when you stood guard over me in the alley . . . well, I've changed my mind."

"Have you, now?" he murmured as he visually followed the inked trail that continued down the page toward Dead Squaw Canyon. Another landmark drawn near the arroyo caught his interest, and he allowed himself a thoughtful frown.

Casually, he reached into his shirt pocket and pulled out the makeshift map scrawled by Whitey Kilroy. A glance from it to the parchment of Jess's confirmed that Kilroy's crude drawing had been based on more than just a dying man's drunken ramblings, and might prove to have the value he had hoped. Satisfied, he refolded the map and paper, and tucked both in his shirt before returning his attention to her.

Jess stared back at him, her expression reflecting uncertainty. He shoved back the inconvenient voice of conscience that told him there must be a better way, and drew his gun.

"You weren't foolish, Jess. You were right not to trust me, not that it mattered in the end. I would have taken the map from you if you hadn't handed it over to me." He pointed his Colt at her and casually gestured with it. "Now, get down off that horse . . . slowly."

Her eyes, the color of fine whiskey, widened under the shade of her hat brim, and then narrowed. "Blast it all, Nick, this isn't amusing. Now, put that pistol away, and—"

He pulled back the hammer, the resulting metallic click stopping her in midword. Her dark eyes widened again, and now he saw a flicker of fear in them. Ruthlessly, he tromped on his conscience again as he said in a quiet voice, "I'm not trying to be amusing, Jess, I'm deadly serious. Now, dismount before I have to shove you off."

Her full lips thinned into an angry, frightened line as she complied. Easing the hammer back into place, Nick climbed down from the roan. He pulled a length of rope from his saddlebag, then walked around to where Jess stood staring defiantly at him, arms crossed and two patches of color burning on her now-pale cheeks.

"What are you going to do now, Nick Whatever-your-real-name is . . . shoot me?"

"Hell, no," he replied in disgust. Shoving his pistol back into his holster, he advanced on her. The black hound, which had flopped to the ground during their exchange, now sat up and growled a soft warning.

Nick glared at the beast until it subsided, then turned his attention back to Jess. Despite her bold stance, she was shaking, and he felt another moment's qualm of conscience. But which was worse, he grimly asked himself . . . seeing the hate in her eyes now, or watching her be shot down by the Black Horse Gang later?

"I don't want to see you hurt, Jess, and that means I can't let you go with me to Dead Squaw Canyon. Yes, I know Maude's your aunt"—he cut her short when she opened her mouth to protest—"and I know you want to help rescue her. But this is a job for a professional. You try to stand up to them and they'll shoot you down, just like they did your husband."

It was a cruel truth, and she jerked at the words, as if he had slapped her. "You bastard," she whispered in a stunned little voice.

He silently echoed that sentiment, even as he pressed his

advantage. "I've asked you before to turn back, and you always refused. I know damn well that, if I asked you again now, you still wouldn't . . . or else you would pretend to go back and then turn right around again. So I have to make sure you won't follow me."

As he'd been talking, he had tied a loop in one end of his rope. Now, abruptly, he caught Jess by the arm and slid the rope over her one wrist, then looped the loose end over the other, so that in a matter of seconds her hands were tied firmly before her, with one end of the rope dangling to the ground.

With a gasp of outrage, she flung her bound hands upward. She would have landed a blow squarely to his chin had he not anticipated her reaction. He sidestepped her swinging fists, so that she caught the brim of his hat instead, sending the battered Stetson tumbling. The motion overbalanced her, and she almost stumbled. He reached out to steady her, but before he could do so, she regained her footing and started down the trail at a dead run.

"Shit," he muttered in disgust and promptly took off after her.

Their brief race ended a moment later as he swiftly closed the distance between them and seized her arm. This time she did fall, pulling him onto the rocky trail with her. Nick hit the ground with a muffled curse that was echoed by her cry as she wrestled to break free of his grasp.

A moment later she was on her back beneath him, her bound hands pinned between them as she glared up at him. Nick glared right back, though his outrage was tempered by grudging admiration. An amateur when it came to tracking outlaws she might be, but she certainly did not lack for courage.

"Damn it, Jess," he gritted out, "you're making this harder than it has to be. All I want to do is tie you to one of those trees and leave you there while I put some distance between us. You'll eventually be able to free yourself, and then you can head back to San Luis and hook up with Doc again. Hell, I'll even leave you that nasty-tempered paint of yours, so you don't have to walk."

"And I suppose you expect me to thank you for your consideration?" she retorted as she tried to wriggle out from beneath his weight.

Abruptly, Nick realized the dangerous position in which he'd put himself, but by then it was too late. Her breasts were pressed in a tantalizing fashion against his own chest, while her bound hands were molded squarely to his crotch. Now, as she moved beneath him, her struggles only intensified those sensations, so that he felt his loins tighten in swift response.

It took Jess a moment longer to realize what was happening, and then she went still, her dark gaze wary as she stared up at him. Her own hat had fallen off in their earlier struggle, and her hair had tumbled from its pins, so that the dark locks now spread in an inviting sable tangle beneath her head. He raised a cautious hand to her face and brushed back a stray strand that lay across her cheek.

She trembled slightly at his touch . . . from fear, perhaps, or maybe from something else. The reaction sent an answering surge of heat through him, and he swallowed back a groan of pure need. "Damn it, Jess," he muttered again, and then brushed his lips against hers.

She gave a soft gasp but did not pull away, so he kissed her once more. This time her lashes flickered shut and she kissed him back, a tentative touch that made him shudder in response. He eagerly pressed his mouth to hers again, thrusting his tongue past her parted lips in an urgent need to taste her sweetness. She moaned and returned his caress with untutored eagerness, her body straining against his as she moved beneath him.

A surge of purely masculine satisfaction swept him, and he eased himself up enough so that he could reach a hand between them to fumble with her shirtwaist. This was how it should have been last night, he told himself as he unfastened the first pearly button and started on the next. He should have followed his first impulse and awakened her, so that they could have satisfied both their needs in the relative comfort of that bed.

Instead, they were reduced to rolling about in the dirt and rock like a pair of hounds, fully clothed and unfastening only what garments were necessary to get the job done. Not that he particularly cared about the niceties at this moment, he told himself as he slid his hand into her open shirtwaist and eagerly cupped her breast.

Christ, what in the hell are you doing?

The accusation abruptly rang in his mind, breaking through the burgeoning wave of pure desire that threatened to engulf him. He groaned again, but this time the sound was one of frustrated despair. With an effort, he rolled off her and got to his feet, then pulled her upright as well.

She gasped as he steadied her, and he knew that the stunned play of emotions washing over her face must reflect his own uncertainty. With an effort, he resumed the cool facade he'd used with her so many times. "Nice try, Jess, but it didn't work. I'm still leaving you behind."

Ignoring her outraged sputter of denial and his own still-throbbing loins, he dragged her over to the sturdiest of the trees and swiftly looped the rope over an overhanging branch twice, then tied it off around the tree's slim trunk. When he was finished, Jess stood beneath that tree with her bound hands raised head high before her. If looks could kill, Nick grimly told himself, a preacher would be saying words over his grave right about now.

"Damn you, Nick, you can't leave me like this!" She rushed toward him, only to be jerked short by the rope before she could take more than two steps. "Damn you, Nick," she repeated. "Untie me . . . now!"

He took a few prudent steps back, in case she decided to spit in his face or kick sand in his eyes . . . neither of which actions would he blame her for trying. He watched while she tugged fruitlessly at her bonds for a moment, only to subside with a gasp when her struggles merely tightened the knots. Tied as she was, with her shirtwaist half unbuttoned and her dark hair spilling in a tangle over her shoulders, she looked like a prisoner ready for the lash. One corner of his mind—the portion that was not now wracked by guilt—found the sight undeniably titillating. Steeling his body against further lapses of judgment, he moved toward her again.

"Don't worry, Jess," he told her as he brushed the hair back from her face and began refastening her blouse. "The knots are tight, but you can use your teeth to undo them. It shouldn't take you more than an hour or so, and then you can be on your way. But, for God's sake, just don't try to follow me when you finally do. Without a map, you'll only get yourself lost."

His fingers paused on the last button and met her silent glare. Chances were good that he'd never see her again, he realized, trying and failing to convince himself that this was no different from the countless other such partings he'd experienced over the years.

Impulsively, he tilted up her chin and kissed her again, grimly aware that she did not return his caress this time. His lips lingered on hers a moment longer until, with a sigh of regret, he released her and took a step back . . . but not soon enough to avoid her booted foot before it connected with his shin.

He choked back a curse and promptly hobbled out of range. "All right, you owed me that one," he said, wincing as he rubbed the bruise, "but that's the only free shot I'll give you. Now try to conserve your strength. You'll need it for the ropes."

So saying, he snatched up his hat from where it earlier had fallen and slapped it against his thigh, so that the dust billowed from it. Clamping the Stetson back on his head, he limped over to his mount and swung himself into the saddle, then turned toward the trail. "Good-bye, Jess," he softly called back to her. "And remember, don't try to follow me."

He dug his heels into the roan's side and started down the trail at a fast clip, the black hound trailing after him, as always. As he rode off, a spot squarely between his shoulder blades tingled as he felt Jess's angry gaze follow him. He'd done what he had to do, he reminded himself as the mare's swift hooves steadily increased the distance between them. And later, when she was back in Brimstone, with her aunt safely returned to her, Jess would realize that he'd done the right thing, too.

The right thing.

The professional thing.

So why, then, did he feel like he'd just been kicked in the gut?

Chapter Nineteen

Tears of angry frustration welling in her eyes, Jess watched as Nick disappeared into the distance, the black hound trailing after him. ‘‘Blast it all!’’ she muttered, blinking away that dampness as she debated with whom she was more furious . . . him or herself.

I guess I've been foolish, thinking that I couldn't trust you.

She heard her own guileless words echo in her mind, and heat flamed in her face. She'd been foolish, all right, but only because she hadn't listened to her instincts. It didn't matter if he were a bank examiner or a Pinkerton detective, or neither of the two. The man had lied to her from the very start . . . and now he had the map that would have led her to Maude, while she was left tied to a tree. But that was not the worst of it.

The worst was that she had let him kiss her . . . and that she'd kissed him back.

It never would have happened, she miserably told herself, if not for last night. The fact that they had practically shared both a bath and a bed had sent her thoughts spinning in unexpected directions. Then came the way he had rescued her from what doubtless would have been a most unpleasant fate, and had done so in the most dramatic fashion possible. Even now, she couldn't forget the sight of him bursting into the room, bare-chested and coolly wielding a rifle. The remembered image was enough to set the heart of any woman with a pulse beating faster.

But what had undone her, for all practical purposes, had been the dream.

Even the memory of it sent a most unsettling heat flaring low in her belly. The dream had started with her falling asleep in the same bed with Nick, just as she actually had done. But rather than slumbering peacefully through the night, she had wakened to find herself wrapped in his embrace. So natural had it felt that she'd idly begun to trace the lines of his half-naked form, feeling the soft rasp of his chest hair beneath her fingers as she ran her hands down his torso.

And then she had felt his hands begin to explore her body in a most intimate fashion, so that she had shivered with pleasure at his touch. Emboldened, she had let her fingers drift lower still, until she cupped the hot bulge of his erection. This evidence of his desire had sent an answering heat flooding through her veins, a heat so intense that she did not stop to wonder at the consequences. Instead, she had eagerly given herself to him, welcoming him into her body . . . letting him fill an emptiness within her that she'd not realized existed. In her dream she had found for the first time the sort of soul-searing release that could make even a practical woman such as she long to experience that bliss on a regular basis.

So real had the dream been that she'd been almost surprised to awaken at dawn, alone in the bed and still dressed in her undergarments. And then, seeing Nick stretched out on the floor, she'd been swept by momentary mortification. What if, caught up in her dream, she'd squirmed about in her sleep in a most unseemly manner, and so had driven him to sleep elsewhere?

To her relief, his defection from the bed had not been her fault. Even so, she had avoided his gaze for fear that he might read in her eyes the odd sense of loss she felt for the fact that it had been a dream, after all. It wasn't until they had bid Doc farewell and ridden out of San Luis that she had taken her first good look of the morning at him.

What she'd seen had proved unsettling, and in more ways than one.

Perhaps knowing that she no longer thought he was Jake Hancock, bank examiner, he had decided to discard the wardrobe with the persona. Or maybe he had found his city clothes to be a disadvantage on the trail, and had decided to exchange them for something more practical. Whatever his reasons, by the simple expedient of procuring a new wardrobe, he had transformed himself into a virtual stranger . . . just as handsome as Hancock, but far more dangerous.

So distracted had she been by this transformation that she had thoughtlessly given him the map, spurred on by the lingering inner warmth from the previous night's dream. Thus, it had been like a chill dash of water to her face when he had pulled the pistol on her and ordered her to dismount. But later, when she had been lying beneath him, and he kissed her, that remembered heat had filled her again, so that she had returned his caresses with an eagerness that now made her blush.

More mortifying was the fact that she was not an innocent girl, untutored in the secrets of lovemaking and, thus, easy to lead astray. She had been a wife, after all, and was more than familiar with what went on in the marriage bed. But lovemaking with Arbin had been, at its best, a pleasant duty. With him, she had never experienced anything approaching the shattering climax that had swept her in her dreams of Nick. But doubtless their kiss had been but a forgettable interlude to Nick, a momentary distraction he'd used to stun her into silence so he could regain control of the situation.

Why else had he ended the kiss the moment she had begun to respond?

Yet even as she'd felt, in turns, frightened by and unwillingly attracted to this dangerous stranger, she had been struck again by the same feeling she'd had the day she first met him: that she knew this man from somewhere else. Even now the feeling persisted, though the overwhelming emotion that currently spurred her was pure feminine rage . . . partly for tying her like a stray mare, and mostly for arousing in her a heated need that she had never expected to feel for any man.

Forget him for now. Concentrate on getting loose, her inner voice chided her. Nick had suggested that she chew her way to freedom, she reminded herself, frowning now at the cluster of knots that bound her wrists. And while it might not be the most dignified way to go about matters, using her teeth did seem to be about the only means left her.

She spared a sour look for Old Pete, placidly nibbling on a few stray stems of grass nearby. The paint rolled an eye in her direction, and she read in his expression a bit of equine pleasure at the fact that, for once, she was tied and he wasn't. At least he hadn't abandoned her, like Nick and the black hound, but he would not be of help in her current situation.

Gingerly, she drew her bound wrists closer and sank her teeth into the first knot, grimacing at the strong taste of hemp. After a few moments' struggle she managed to tug that knot loose. Cheered by her success, she started on the next knot, which was smaller and pulled even more tightly than the first.

By the time she managed the third knot, her jaws were sore and her arms were growing numb. Moreover, chewing on the rope had dried her mouth, so that she stared longingly at her canteen, draped from Old Pete's saddle. The least Nick could have done was leave the canteen hanging, as well, she thought in no little pique. The way things were going, she might well swoon from thirst before she made it through the entire series of knots.

Damned if I'll give him the satisfaction.

Spurred on by that renewed surge of anger, she tackled the next knot. A few minutes later, she had tugged free the last knot that bound her wrists together. Her moment of triumph was short-lived, however, as she discovered that she'd only freed one hand. Her right wrist was still snared in the original loop, which was held together by yet another series of complicated twists.

For a moment she was tempted to weep in frustration, until it occurred to her that that was probably what he expected her to do. The thought renewed her determination. She waited a moment, until the blood had begun circulating again in her free arm, and then began battling the next series of knots.

Perhaps an hour had passed from the time Nick left to the moment she tugged apart the final knot and sagged in an exhausted heap onto the ground. Her right wrist, especially, was chaffed raw, and both arms ached from being tied at such an uncomfortable angle. Her lips and jaw were sore, as well, and she gracelessly if fruitlessly tried to spit out a few stray rope fibers that had caught in her teeth.

Water, she thought with an inner groan and gazed about for Old Pete. The paint had strayed a few yards farther, his reins dangling to his hooves. "Come here, fellow," she called . . . or tried to call, for her mouth was so dry that the words seemed to stick to her tongue. Scrambling to her feet, she raked a few stray locks from her face and started toward him, her hand held out as she crooned soft endearments to the beast.

Old Pete looked up lazily and waited as she reached for the reins, then neatly gamboled out of reach. "Damnable creature," she muttered through clenched teeth as she feigned a nonthreatening smile and started toward him again. This time her fingers brushed leather before the paint abruptly pulled back and circled around her.

They repeated this horse-and-human dance twice more, with Old Pete avoiding capture each time. By now Jess was seriously contemplating taking out her pistol and blasting the stubborn steed, and only refrained from doing so when she recalled that she needed the horse to ride out of there. "Besides, if you can't outsmart a mere horse," she muttered to herself, "how can you expect to outsmart a gang of outlaws?"

This time she did not chase after him again; rather, she gave an exaggerated sigh and sank to her knees, head bowed and back to the paint. A moment later, she heard the soft jingle and creak of tack, accompanied by the plop of hooves as the gelding cautiously made its way toward her. She remained patiently in that pose while the paint moved still closer, his curiosity over this new game apparently outweighing his caution. Soon she heard his soft nicker directly behind her.

Willing herself to remain calm, she waited until she could see the trailing reins from the corner of her eye as the paint dropped his head to snuffle at her shoulder. Then, quite calmly, she caught hold of the reins and scrambled to her feet. Old Pete gave a snort of surprise and tried to pull back, but she held his head steady until, sulking, he stood still again.

"Nice try, fellow," she said with a grin of triumph. She led him back to the trees and, using the same rope with which Nick had bound her, tied the paint securely to one of them. Then, snatching the canteen from his back, she settled beside a nearby boulder and let the cool water splash over her raw lips.

A few moments later, her thirst quenched, she sagged back against the boulder. *What now?* she wondered with a small sigh, her earlier moment of triumph long since spent. Nick had put little more than an hour's distance between them, but he had both the map and the compass now, and she had neither. And though she could make her way as far as Las Tres Cabezas without any problem, from there she would be relying on memory. Once in the mountains, the going would be far more uncertain and the trail less easy to cling to, so that she could easily become lost.

So why not simply do as Nick had said . . . return to San Luis and let him take care of tracking down the Black Horse Gang and rescuing Maude? For, despite the fact that she no longer trusted him, she had no doubt that he was a professional at being a detective . . . or whatever it was that he actually did.

For several long moments she considered that option. Undoubtedly, Nick was right. Tracking outlaws *was* a job best left to professionals, and her presence could easily do her aunt as much harm as good. Guilty as she already felt over Arbin's murder, how much more distraught would she be if her unwitting interference caused the Black Horse Gang to shoot Maude before she could be rescued?

And what about her father? What would happen to him, should she somehow manage to get herself killed? Ill as Harvey was, he could not manage without her and Maude, both. Even now, he undoubtedly was sick with worry over them, since he would have heard nothing of the situation since Jess left Tombstone. True, Ted Markham probably had showed him the telegram from Marshal Chapel, so he would know that his daughter, at least, was still alive . . . but even that small bit of news would not be sufficient to relieve his concerns. Had he any say in the matter, Harvey would want his daughter home, and now.

It occurred to her, too, that even if she turned back now, she still would have done more to rescue Maude than all of Brimstone put together. With the map she had uncovered, Nick stood a better chance of finding the gang than if he'd had to rely on his tracking skills alone. Indeed, the old miner's parchment might make the difference between finding Maude alive, and finding her dead. Truly, then, she could say that she had done her part, so no one could think the less of her.

Except for herself.

Grimly, Jess got to her feet and started toward Old Pete, confident that the reasons for continuing on outweighed the excuses to turn back. She hadn't come this far just to give up when she'd almost reached her goal. Dead Squaw Canyon was no more than a day's ride farther, she was certain, and surely Maude was waiting there to be rescued. And while she trusted Nick just about as much as she trusted the black hound, that did not preclude her from being able to work with him. As a banker, she dealt often enough with unpleasant people to be confident of her ability to handle him in a professional manner.

And someone needed to ensure that he would not be so distracted by trying to capture the entire gang, single-handedly, that he would sacrifice Maude in the process.

She grabbed up her fallen hat and untied the paint, then mounted up. If she recalled correctly, Las Tres Cabezas was just over the next rise. From there, she would head south through the foothills, and hope she could either pick up Nick's trail or else be lucky enough to stumble across the arroyo on her own. Either way, she would push on. She might have failed Arbin, but she was not going to fail her aunt.

Once she reached the crossroads with the three head-shaped boulders, her initial heated rush of enthusiasm had cooled to quiet determination. She flinched only a little as she bypassed the spot where they'd found the dead outlaw the day before. A single buzzard was perched on the ravaged corpse. Jess knew that, before much longer, the desert's other scavengers would have scattered what little was left of hair and flesh and bone, so that the man's final resting place would never again be found. She wouldn't let that happen to Maude . . . no matter what.

The trail heading south proved little more than a faint depression in the rocky soil; still, at that jumping-off point, Jess spotted what appeared to be the fresh tracks of a single rider and another, pawed creature. Nick and the black hound, she thought in satisfaction. But those tracks were the last she spotted as the trail began leading into the foothills.

By the time the sun had risen to its peak, the trail had dwindled to the occasional bare spot amid the rocks and high desert vegetation. Once, she completely rode off the narrow track and had to circle for some moments before she found it again. Worse, none of the landmarks seemed to match anything that she recalled from the map, so that she was reduced to using the angle of the sun as a guide whenever the trail began to blur. But now that she was in the foothills, even that celestial landmark was hard to keep in sight as the afternoon progressed, and the sun started to sink behind a wall of peaks and rises.

The second time she veered off the trail, she rode in circles for a good half an hour trying to find it again. And, though she tried to reassure herself otherwise, a frantic sense of worry gripped her as she realized that she truly had no idea if she was headed in the right direction. Finally, she conceded defeat and reined in Old Pete, then dismounted and perched on a rock to gather her splintered composure.

The trail had to be somewhere nearby, she was certain. The

problem was that she had no convenient landmark to guide her, nor could she see for miles, as she had when they'd been traveling in the flatlands. Here, it was all peaks and rocks, with each looking like the next. Even if she could manage to keep in a southerly direction, the likelihood now was slim, indeed, that she ever could find Dead Squaw Canyon. As for making her way back to San Luis, her odds of that were equally remote.

Lost.

Jess silently tried out the word, bracing herself against an answering inner shriek of panic that, to her relief, did not come. Emboldened, she said it aloud. "Lost."

The breathless syllable echoed in the silence about her and then was swallowed up by the hills. Save for Old Pete's restless shuffling, the only other sounds she could hear were a whisper of breeze and her pulse beating in her ears. Above her, the sky was a brilliant blue but utterly empty, with not even the lazy black drift of an errant vulture to mar its azure surface. Not only was she lost, she was alone.

The enormity of her predicament slowly began to envelop her. She had food and water for another day . . . perhaps two, if she was sparing with it. And while the high desert was not without water, finding it would be her problem. In the meantime, Nick would assume she had gone back to San Luis, while Doc would not know to expect her and, so, would not be concerned when she did not arrive. It could be days, or even weeks, before anyone realized she was missing.

She shivered at the unsettling vision of her own body being set upon by vultures. With the same mental clarity, she saw her stripped bones being scattered about by coyotes and other scavengers so that, even if they were found, no one could guess to whom they belonged. Just like the dead outlaw at Las Tres Cabezas, her final resting place might well become another of the desert's well-guarded secrets.

"Stop that," she murmured with a sharp mental shake to dispel that disturbing scenario. She might be lost, but she was a long way from being dead. She just needed a few minutes to think over the situation and decide how best to proceed. If only she'd thought to make an extra copy of the map.

The map. She frowned, thinking back to those few moments when Nick had looked over the parchment before permanently seizing it. He'd had another page of his own with which he'd compared it and, though she had thought it odd at the time, she'd had no chance to question him regarding it.

Another map? Perhaps . . . but then, why would he have needed hers? As she puzzled over the question, a sudden rustling in the nearby brush made her straighten and set her heart to beating even faster.

Not alone, after all, she thought with a shiver, unsettled by the very realization that should have cheered her. Maybe because she sensed something stealthy about the sound, as if someone or something was deliberately remaining concealed. Whether it was man or beast that lurked nearby, however, she could not guess. More unnerved than she cared to admit, even to herself, she reached for the pistol in her boot and summoned a casual air as she glanced around.

If the intruder fell into the category of beast, it could be any of a number of different creatures, some less benevolent than others. Wolves and mountain lions roamed the territory, she knew, though she'd always thought them to be nocturnal in habit. But the sound had been too loud for a hare or a bird.

And what if it was a man?

The rustling sound repeated itself, and Jess suppressed another shudder. It had not been that long ago that the Apache Indians roamed this territory, and some might still remain who would resent interlopers in what once was their mountain stronghold. As for outlaw bands, the Black Horse Gang surely was not the only one to seek refuge here. True, the intruder could be an innocent miner or cowboy who had wandered onto her, but why would he not step forth and announce himself?

Willing her trembling legs to hold her, she rose from her perch and took a few steps forward. "Who's there?" she called and raised her pistol with both hands. "I have a gun, and I won't hesitate to use it."

The rustling ceased again, and Jess froze. Whoever—or whatever—it was, it had heard her. If she was right, the sound had come . . . from right . . . behind her.

She swung about with a gasp as a nearby shrub erupted with a crash, and a flash of black headed straight for her. In the space of a heartbeat she had pulled back the hammer and leveled the derringer to fire, when the black blur abruptly halted just a few feet before her.

"You!" she gasped out and lowered the pistol.

The black hound gave a short bark and stared up at Jess, his red tongue lolling from his open jaws. On any other dog, the gesture would appear to be a friendly greeting. With the black hound, it looked faintly menacing; still, she gave the beast the benefit of the doubt and held out a tentative hand.

The hound did not deign to respond to her overture. Instead, he rose and trotted a few steps away, then sat again and uttered another sharp bark.

Jess stared back, a thin tendril of hope uncurling in her breast. The last she'd seen of the beast, it had been following Nick . . . which either meant that Nick was nearby, or that the hound had come looking for her with the intention of leading her to him. Or perhaps the dog was as lost as she, and now they could be lost together. Either way, she found herself quite vastly cheered.

"Good fellow," she breathed in relief, mentally promising the beast a fine steak from Chan's if they ever made it back to Brimstone again.

Tucking away the derringer, she hurried over to Old Pete, who appeared singularly unimpressed by this canine show of intelligence. By the time she had swung into the saddle, the black hound already was loping back in the direction from which she'd most recently come. Jess put her heels to the paint's side and followed after him.

After a few minutes, the black hound halted at a familiar looking rut that led in a southerly direction. He waited for Jess to catch up to him, then put his nose to the ground for a few seconds of deliberate sniffing. Then, with a triumphant bay, the hound began trotting down the trail.

Two steaks, she mentally amended, and urged Old Pete in the same direction. But even as she concentrated on the trail ahead, she spared a concerned look for the sky above. Purple shadows had begun to creep down the mountains, while fingers of pink and orange now thrust their flamboyant way into the sky's virgin blue. Night came early and swiftly in the mountains, she knew. In another hour or so, true darkness would fall. If she hadn't found Nick by then, she would have to make camp and wait for first light to continue on . . . that was, if she could convince the black hound to wait, as well.

Daylight steadily faded as they traveled on. More than once, Jess temporarily lost the black hound when his dark fur blended into the dusk. Each time her breath caught in her throat for what seemed like hours until she spotted his sleek form again, trotting confidently before her. But while he moved with ease through the deepening shadows, Old Pete did not fare so well in the darkness that was cloaking the steep and rocky terrain. Soon Jess was forced to slow him to a walk, lest he stumble and send her tumbling, or else break a leg.

But darkness was not the only problem that plagued her. As dusk had approached, the temperature had begun to drop. The cool mountain breeze that had been so pleasant earlier in the day was now distinctly brisk. Had she dared take her eyes from the hound, she might have halted long enough to pull a blanket from her bedroll and wrap up in it. As it was, she scrunched as low as she could against the paint, burying her fingers in his shaggy mane and hugging his broad neck for warmth.

But barely had she thawed her chilled flesh just a little than she halted Old Pete and sat up again. The black hound, which had vanished several minutes ago, still had not reappeared. A frisson of worry swept her as she glanced about the dark mountain trail. What if the beast had fallen into a ravine, or been snatched up by a passing mountain lion? Or what if he'd simply grown bored with the game and decided to continue without her?

Yet even as she debated halting or continuing onward, a whiff of wood smoke drifted to her. *A campfire,* she thought in excitement, *but whose?*

She urged Old Pete forward a few steps, winced as his hooves crunched far too loudly on the rock, and then reined him in again. Given that she might find herself stumbling into a stranger's camp, or even that of the Black Horse Gang, she did not care to announce her approach until she was certain of her reception. Perhaps it would be quieter if she led the paint down the trail . . . but that would mean she would be trudging on foot. What if she stepped on a rattlesnake, or a tarantula, or another unpleasant creature enjoying the night?

Longingly, Jess thought of her snug, whitewashed bank with its gleaming counters and polished wooden floors. If ever this adventure ended, she vowed, she would never again venture into the wilderness, and certainly not at night.

She gritted her teeth and climbed down from Old Pete, then wrapped the reins securely around one hand and gingerly led him on. After slipping a time or two, she found herself envying the paint's four hooves, which certainly had better purchase on the uneven trail than did her two feet. The smell of wood smoke had grown stronger, though she had not yet glimpsed any telltale flicker of light that would guide her to the fire from which it originated. Neither did she hear the nicker of horses or the murmur of voices that would mean someone occupied that unseen spot.

A few yards farther along, the trail abruptly dipped. Jess skittered for a few unplanned steps before she regained her balance and halted. Now, she could see a pinprick of light ahead, signaling that she had reached her destination,

Please let it be Nick, was the silent prayer she offered the night as she tied Old Pete to a tree and began creeping down the trail. The moon was just now rising over the mountain peaks, so that a faint silver glow helped her progress through the shadows. A few minutes later, she could see that the camp in question lay in a small clearing several yards from the trail, and nestled alongside several fallen boulders. On stealthy feet, she made her way still closer, watching for some sign of movement, some sound.

By the time she reached the edge of the clearing it was apparent that the camp was empty. How long ago it had been abandoned, she wasn't certain. A few tiny tongues of flame still flickered in a ring of rocks; otherwise, she saw no sign that anyone had been there. No blankets were spread by the fire, no coffeepot boiled on the coals, no horse was tied to a nearby tree.

She watched the empty camp for several minutes, debating whether to move quietly back to where she'd left Old Pete, or boldly walk up to the fire and claim the site for her own. Another breeze scattered a few fallen leaves at her feet and sent a chill through her. A fire would be nice, came the longing thought.

And then she heard a twig snap behind her.

Too frightened to gasp, she reflexively swung about. She saw a glint of steel in the moonlight and heard the sharp, metallic click of a hammer being cocked just before a dark figure loomed from the shadows and shoved a pistol squarely in her face. In the space of a heartbeat, she pictured what would come next. A deafening roar . . . an explosion of pain . . . and then she would be lying dead, just like Arbin.

But even as she braced herself for these last fearful seconds, she heard an incredulous voice saying, "You!"

Chapter Twenty

"Me," Jess breathed in agreement as she felt Nick's strong arms wrap around her and draw her to him.

For several glorious moments, she sagged against him, letting the warmth of his body wash over her. She was shivering as much from delayed reaction as from the cold, she realized, and his embrace worked upon her like a drug, dulling her frightened senses and leaching the strength from her. In another moment, she'd be quite incapable of movement, but she didn't care . . . not now.

And then she felt his hands grip her shoulders with bruising pressure as he shoved her from him and gave her a sharp shake. "Damn it to hell, Jess! I nearly shot you just now! What in the hell are you doing here, anyway? You're supposed to be back in San Luis!"

The brusque greeting reminded her of the fact that she no longer liked or trusted the man . . . that, indeed, she was quite furious with him. "Blast it all, Nick!" she sputtered back at him. "Quit shaking me and I'll tell you."

Abruptly, he released her, and she drew a deep breath. Her intent was to lecture him on the dangers of hastily drawing one's pistol without first ascertaining at whom one was pointing it. Then, she would berate him for tying her and leaving her behind, and demand an apology for all she'd endured this day. But the intended tirade never reached her lips, instead melting into an odd buzzing in her head as she felt herself begin to sway.

It's nothing . . . I never swoon, she assured herself just before she hit the ground with a graceless thud.

"Christ," she heard Nick mutter, before the buzzing blocked out all sound.

The next few moments were an unsettling but not entirely unpleasant blur. She was aware of Nick scooping her up in his arms and carrying her to the fire, then setting her down before it and wrapping her in a blanket. She huddled there quite contentedly while he added a few sticks to the flickering coals and prodded them into a full-fledged blaze. What she could see of his expression through the shadows was a look of hard-edged grimness, but for now she didn't care that he was angry with her. All that mattered was that she wasn't alone and lost in the mountains in the dark.

He paused before her, and she heard the repressed irritation in his voice. "I'm going to bring in the paint. I presume you tied him somewhere up the trail?"

When she managed a nod, he went on. "I'll be back in a few minutes. Don't move away from this fire, understand?" With that curt command, he strode back into the shadows. She noticed that *his* boots made almost no sound on the rocky ground . . . though, light-headed as she currently felt, she could probably drift along the trail quite silently now, herself.

As the chill eased from her body, however, she began to feel much like herself again. Now, embarrassment swept her as she realized that she *had* swooned, if only for a moment. And though she perhaps had any number of acceptable excuses—weariness; cold; the shock of finding a pistol shoved into her face—her display of what Nick surely would dismiss as feminine weakness likely had strengthened his conviction that she would be a liability to him. Chances were that *he* had never collapsed like that, just because he'd spent a few hours lost out in the wilds.

By the time Nick reappeared a few minutes later, leading both Old Pete and the roan, she had settled the blanket more comfortably about herself and had begun to reflect on what might happen next. For tonight, at least, he'd be stuck with her, but tomorrow loomed rather more uncertainly. Between now and then, she would have to convince him that he needed her help; otherwise, morning might find her tied to another tree.

While she was frowning over that last image, Nick had settled the horses and piled both her gear and his near the fire. Now, the explanation for the empty camp occurred to her. He must have heard the sound of her footsteps coming down the trail. Thus forewarned, he had stashed everything from horse to bedroll behind the nearby rocks before slipping away to ambush whoever was approaching.

Luckily, he'd not misplaced the familiar, battered coffeepot in the process, she thought with relief as he pulled it from the jumble. Since she did not have Doc's whiskey as a restorative, coffee—hot and black—would be the next best tonic. She watched impatiently as he added water and a handful of grounds, then set the pot to heating in the coals. But the domestic tranquillity of the scene was abruptly shattered when he hunkered down beside the fire and fixed her with a chilly look.

"All right, Jess; let's hear it. Why aren't you in San Luis?"

"Because I couldn't abandon my aunt . . . not that you'd understand such loyalty."

Something flickered in his azure gaze but was gone before she could read it. "I do understand, Jess, and better than you might think . . . but it doesn't change the fact that you're more likely to be a liability than a help in rescuing her. I thought we had an agreement that you'd turn back."

"*You* had an agreement. *I* was the one tied to the tree. I might have gotten gangrene if I'd hung there much longer."

"I doubt that," was his dry response. He caught up the coffeepot, which had begun to steam, and poured out two tin cups of the muddy liquid. "Here. Drink up, and then tell me how you managed to find me."

She grabbed up her cup and took a tentative sip of the hot, bitter liquid, wondering if she should regale him with an impossible tale that featured her keen tracking ability—the equal of any Pinkerton's—or give him the truth, which was equally fantastic. In the end, she settled on the truth . . . though leaving out the embarrassing details of her struggle with Old Pete once she'd untied herself.

"Then I rode back to Las Tres Cabezas and started south," she continued. "I lost the trail after a couple of hours, and while I was trying to decide what to do, the black hound came back for me."

She paused as he raised a brow in disbelief. "Don't look so skeptical. At least the dog showed a modicum of concern for my well-being, even if no one else cared. Anyhow, he barked at me to follow him, and I did, presuming that you must be nearby."

"Interesting," Nick murmured, and now she saw a flicker of amusement in his eyes. "Do go on."

"The hound led me back to the trail, and then up the mountain for almost an hour, before he disappeared again. While I was looking for him, I smelled your campfire and followed the smoke. I believe that you know the rest."

"Right. From the sound of things, I thought I was being set upon by an army of outlaws, not by one woman. You're damned lucky I didn't blow your head off first, and ask questions later." While she huffed a little at that insult, Nick gave a thoughtful frown. "Not bad detective work, for a dog. I wonder where that ugly black cur is now."

"Probably out capturing the Black Horse Gang, on his own," she muttered, piqued that the black hound now had proved his value to the expedition, when she had yet to do so. Next thing she knew, he'd be canonizing Old Pete.

To hide her irritation, she took another drink of the strong coffee. This time, however, the hot brew scalded her chafed lips, and she winced.

The reaction did not go unnoticed. "If you're going to complain about how I make coffee—"

"I wasn't." She cut him short. "It's just that my lips are scraped from chewing on those blasted knots you tied. The coffee burns them, that's all."

"Really? Let me take a look."

He set down his own cup and moved closer to her, then lightly caught her chin in his hand and tilted her toward the firelight. So close was he that she could breathe in the faint scent of leather and male sweat that clung to him, an aroma as enticing as any exotic perfume. The strain of the past days had taken their toll on him, as well; she could see lines beneath his eyes that had not been there two days earlier, and the hollows in his cheeks beneath several days' growth of whiskers. She resisted the urge to reach out her own hand and brush the dark stubble that contrasted with his pale eyes and made him look both dashing and dangerous.

His gaze abruptly clashed with hers, and she saw those blue eyes darken. For a breathless instant she feared that he had read her thoughts, that he knew all about that erotic dream of hers that had so prominently featured him. If so, he must guess that another kiss from him would be her undoing. If he kissed her now, she faintly thought, she might promise him whatever he wanted, might even agree to turn back tomorrow instead of accompanying him to Dead Squaw Canyon.

Just as swiftly, the chill returned to his eyes and he released her. "You'll live," was the curt diagnosis, before he returned his attention to his coffee.

Jess turned away and took another swift drink from her own cup, uncertain whether to be disappointed or relieved. Not that she cared to be pawed at and pursued by a man who was likely as dangerous to her as any outlaw might be . . . her long-suppressed female vanity just wanted him to *want* to do those things. Yet here they were, miles from civilization, and it seemed he wasn't even tempted to take any liberties with her. Which was, when one thought about it, rather insulting.

Hiding her pique beneath an elaborate cloak of dignity, she

got to her feet and retrieved her gear. Inside one saddlebag were the remnants of Mrs. Meeks's jailhouse supper, which the older woman had thoughtfully wrapped for their journey. Putting aside a portion for herself, she handed Nick the remainder of the paper-wrapped victuals.

"Supper," she succinctly explained, "unless the black hound already has seen to that, as well?"

Her words drew a swift, weary grin from him that suddenly made him look quite less dangerous than before, if no less dashing. "I'm sure he's out scavenging his own meal, and the rest of us be damned."

Truce lines drawn, they ate in a companionable sort of quiet broken only by the soft popping of the dying fire. By now, reaction from the day's events was taking its toll on Jess, so that she could think of nothing better than to crawl into her bedroll, no matter how rocky the ground beneath her. But the question of what would happen tomorrow, when they finally confronted the outlaws—if, indeed, they truly were at Dead Squaw Canyon—had to be settled, first.

"Do you know how far we still are from the Black Horse Gang's hideout?" she ventured.

He nodded. "The entrance to the canyon is about a mile from here. Even with that map of yours, though, I had a hell of a time finding it. Until you get right up to it, the opening looks like a solid wall of rock, if you look at it straight on."

He set down his coffee and, with one forefinger, traced a few crude marks in the loose earth between them. "The trail ends here"—he pointed to one ragged line—"and the way inside is here"—he paused and stabbed at another mark—"behind a pile of fallen boulders. I could see signs that about a dozen riders had gone through there within the past day or so. The passage itself is wide enough for one, maybe two men to ride abreast. It angles off in a straight line for about a dozen yards, then opens into a section of the arroyo about as wide and half as long as Brimstone's main street."

"You went into the canyon, then?" A sudden rush of excitement quickened her words, and she leaned closer to the crude diagram in the dirt, as if it might reveal more secrets. "Did anyone see you?"

"I don't think so . . . but then, I didn't see anyone standing guard, either, so they were probably posted somewhere inside the canyon. I didn't take any chances, though. I left the roan back down the trail and made my way to the entrance on foot. All I did was poke my head out long enough to tell that the arroyo makes a blind angle back into the mountain."

"So you don't know if my aunt was with them," she said in disappointment. "Did you learn anything of value, then?"

"I learned that the tunnel is a hell of a spot for an ambush. All it would take would be two gunmen—one at the entry and one at the entrance—to trap a whole posse inside. Tomorrow morning, as soon as it's light, I'm going to do a little more scouting around, see if there's any way up the side of the canyon, instead."

Jess absently nodded her agreement with that plan, even as she contemplated the wisdom of her next words. Still, better to get all this out in the open now, rather than wait until morning to debate it. "Nick, you do realize that I intend to go with you tomorrow, don't you?" she said, setting aside her cup and girding herself for an argument.

She was not disappointed. Nick gave a faint sigh of exasperation as he set down his coffee and turned toward her. "We've already had this discussion once before. It's too dangerous. You can't go with me, Jess, and that's final."

"But you can't stop me from—"

"I've already stopped you once, if you'll recall," he coolly pointed out. "If it wasn't for that damned dog, you'd never have made it this far on your own. So, unless you enjoy being tied to trees, I suggest you rid yourself of that idea right now."

Jess heaved an impatient sigh of her own. "Really, Nick, you are being quite unreasonable . . . and if you truly believe you can capture the entire gang by yourself, you're being foolish, as well. At the very least, you will need someone to watch your back when you confront them, and it shouldn't matter if that person is a female. I dare say that, if Doc was here, you wouldn't refuse his offer of help."

"Damn right I wouldn't. Doc Holliday is a professional shootist, and you're a lady banker. There's a hell of a difference between the two of you, and it has nothing to do with the fact that you wear a skirt instead of trousers."

In the light of the dying campfire his features looked harder than she'd ever seen them, but the sight only stiffened her own resolve. Still, she'd learned by now that no amount of arguing would make Nick change his mind once he'd come to a decision. Her best course would be to let him think he'd won the battle, until she could come up with a satisfactory counter-strategy.

For now, she merely nodded. "I suppose you are right. I wouldn't do you or Maude much good if I managed to get myself shot. I'll just wait for you here."

"That's a sensible enough solution, as far as it goes . . . but suppose something happens to me and I don't make it back?"

The question was a legitimate one, but she heard a note of irony in his voice that set her teeth on edge. She managed a guileless tone, however, as she replied, "Why, Nick, I have every confidence you'll succeed. You are a professional, after all. But if the worst happens, I'm sure the black hound can lead me back as far as San Luis."

"Forget the damned dog. I'll leave you the compass and the map." He dashed the remains of his coffee into the fire, then got to his feet. "Give me until noon tomorrow. If I'm not back by then, it means something went wrong, and you should head back to San Luis to see if our good friend, Marshal Chapel, will give it another try."

"Very well," she agreed, finishing up her own coffee and rising, as well.

With less success did she push aside the quite frightening realization that, accompany him or not, the situation might well end with Nick's death. Suddenly the possibility that she might never again see him after tomorrow morning loomed before her, so that she had to bite back a reflexive cry of denial. She might not trust the man—might not even like him—but she certainly was not indifferent to his fate.

Blast it all, she would just have to hit upon a way to convince him that he needed her . . . and she'd have to do it before too many more hours passed.

The Black Horse Gang had reached their arroyo hideout just after noon, thundering into that small canyon through a gap in the mountain barely wide enough for two horses and riders traveling abreast. The entry would have been almost impossible to spot had one not known its exact location, Maude had realized as Len led her through the tunnel-like expanse of rock and into a narrow gorge that snaked its way through the belly of the mountain. She had understood then why the gang had taken such pains to flee there . . . and wondered just how safe she would remain now that they had reached their destination. Surely it must soon occur to the outlaws that her knowing the location of their hideout made her a threat.

But to her relief, the men had all but ignored her presence as they went about the business of putting the camp to order. With a curt warning—"You can stretch your legs a bit, but there's two men posted just inside the canyon entrance, so don't give no thought to wanderin' off"—Len had left her to her own devices. Keeping to a spot behind the crumbled remains of a wall, she reveled awhile simply in sitting without simultaneously bouncing about on a saddle. When that novelty had worn off, she gave herself over to studying her surroundings.

The narrow channel into which they'd first ridden had angled off into a boxlike expanse the size of a city block. Long before the Black Horse Gang had ever found the place, someone else had used this portion of the canyon as a secluded stronghold. Three crude wooden shacks, their doors dangling off rotting leather hinges, formed a row along the farthermost wall of granite. A collection of barrels and crates—some broken and tumbled in a heap, others neatly stacked—filled the gaps between them.

In front of those buildings was a corral into which the gang already had herded their coal black mounts . . . .hers, included. Several yards from that was a covered ring of rock that she learned housed a meager well. Not far from where she watched was a large oval of stone in which one of the bandits had built a fire. There, a dozen or more large rocks were arranged like chairs in a parlor, forming a public area of sorts.

''Rory gets one shack,'' Len had explained to her earlier, ''and the other two hold all our supplies and stores. The rest of us spread out near the fire, 'cept when it rains. Then we move up there.''

He pointed to a wide if shallow hollow perhaps twenty feet off the canyon floor along the nearest rock wall. A well-worn series of handholds chiseled in the granite formed a crude ladder reaching up to it. It would have been a simple enough climb, she determined, save for the cluster of sharp-edged boulders scattered at the base of that wall that added an unexpected element of danger. A fall from even that short a height could well prove deadly, given that the unlucky climber would land squarely atop that ragged outcropping of granite.

She only had nodded, however, for she was familiar with tales of the occasional flash floods that swept the mountain gorges. In such circumstances, the risk of the climb would be far outweighed by the danger of remaining below. Then, giving voice to another cause for curiosity, she said, ''I heard someone call this place Dead Squaw Canyon. How did it get such a morbid name?''

''All I know is what some of the other fellas have told me, and who knows how much of that is true? They say a band of Confederate soldiers made their way to Arizona Territory durin' the war, lookin' for gold to help pay for the Cause. Legend had it that a big box of coins and gold cups and such had been buried somewhere near here by a bunch of Spanish friars.''

He'd paused and given her a boyish grin, looking pleased that she'd asked. No doubt, like most men, he enjoyed repeating a sensational tale. ''Anyhow, one of them had some sort of map that came from someone whose granddaddy was a Spanish soldier back then. Problem was, the Apaches didn't take kindly to a bunch of white men running around their mountains, and they killed off about half the soldiers. The ones that were left managed to get hold of an Apache girl. They used her as a hostage while they searched for the gold."

He hesitated again, his grin fading a bit, and Maude wondered if perhaps he was uncomfortable with the parallel between her situation and the fictional Indian girl's. Given that the arroyo was called Dead Squaw Canyon, it took little imagination to guess that the story did not end happily. Determined not to be morbid, herself, she asked, "And did they find the gold?"

He shrugged. "Some folks swear they found it and brought it back to General Lee, himself. Other people say they never found a thing, and either were killed by Indians or else went back home in disgrace. But all the stories tell how the Apache girl managed to escape and climb up the ledge of this here arroyo. When the soldiers tried to capture her again, she fell . . . or maybe jumped on purpose, I don't know." He dropped his gaze to his boot toes, then finished in a mumble, "Anyhow, that's how the place got its name."

Oddly enough, the tragic little tale did not depress Maude quite as much as it seemed to upset Len. Perhaps it was because the young woman had taken her fate into her own hands, rather than let herself simply be swept about by events. The fact that she had chosen death over captivity was secondary.

It was then that he'd given her his brusque warning before rejoining the other outlaws. The place where he had left both her and their gear was far enough removed from the other men that the worst of her misgivings were relieved. Now, however, with darkness upon them, Maude stared longingly at the flickering fire some distance from her.

What she wouldn't give to warm her chilled feet and hands at that cheerful blaze, she thought, even as she realized the danger that such an indulgence would bring with it. For, with the camp in order and the evening's meal finished, the outlaws had settled down to the serious business of drinking the cache of whiskey left there from previous times, and with dividing the loot from the robbery.

Even split among that many men, the combined take was substantial. This much Maude could judge both from what she, herself, had witnessed, and from the eager voices that now drifted to her. The clink of coin and bottle mingled with the sounds of crude merriment that grew louder as the minutes passed. Would Len regret giving up his share of the money? she wondered with a sudden shiver that had nothing to do with the cold. Maybe he'd reconsidered his decision and, even now, was thinking of giving her back to the group in return for his portion.

Nervously, she searched the raucous group until she spotted him perched some distance apart from them. To her relief, he appeared content merely watching his companions. He even glanced her way a time or two with a look of concern, though surely he could not see her for the shadows. Even so, the gesture was enough to warm her, so that she no longer missed the fire.

As the minutes ticked on, however, and the sounds of celebration grew louder, she realized her attention still was fastened on Len's youthful features. Abruptly, she tore her gaze from him and focused instead on the flickering light of the campfire, all too aware that her thoughts were wandering dangerously close to where they had strayed the night before. Once again, she was finding herself looking on him with feelings far less benevolent than merely maternal.

Indeed, were she forced to be totally truthful, she would have to confess that what she'd been feeling for him since last night was unadulterated lust.

"Oh, dear Lord," she choked out.

The shock of the realization sent her running into the shadows . . . running from herself, this time, she realized miserably. It was laughable—no, almost obscene—that a woman her age felt that way toward a man so many years her junior. And why, after so many years of chosen celibacy, should she suddenly find herself mooning after a man who was not only younger, but also was a vicious outlaw? It made no sense. Truly, she must being going mad!

Madness.

That was the answer, she thought with an odd sense of relief. The stress of being kidnapped must have worked upon her mind in some insidious fashion, so that she was acting nothing at all like her usual proper self. And while the notion of madness frightened her—indeed, almost as much as the feelings that now gripped her—surely it was better to account herself insane than to think she was indulging in such fantasies while in her right mind.

But even as she reconciled herself to her unbalanced state, she heard a footstep behind her and gave a guilty start. A long shadow spilled onto the rock wall before her, and she realized that Len must have noticed she'd abandoned her post. Composing herself, she turned and managed a tremulous smile. Whether he was angry or concerned she did not care, so long as he did not guess her shameful secret.

"I'm sorry, Len," she said in a breathless voice she barely noticed as her own. "I promise, I wasn't wandering off. I just was a bit restless, was all."

"Restless . . . are ya?"

A guttural laugh that was not Len's issued from the shadows. Maude bit back a disbelieving gasp as she belatedly recognized the speaker's voice. A moment later a stout, curly-haired man stumbled toward her, an evil leer on his face and a half-empty whiskey bottle in his hand. Even without that last evidence, she could tell by his ragged voice and the alcohol fumes wafting from him that he already had drunk his share of the whiskey.

"Well, now," Carson went on, "I've got somethin' . . . to calm ya right down . . . if ya know what I mean." With another guttural laugh, he tossed aside the bottle and reached for her.

Chapter Twenty-one

Maude gasped again and jerked away, so that Carson's groping fingers closed on air. Though the action kept her out of his reach, she was backed against the rock facing . . . a far more dangerous situation, she realized, than she'd been in only a moment ago. Drunk or not, he easily could pin her against that sheer wall if she was not careful. Her only chance would be to distract him with a few well-chosen words and then rush past him before he realized what she was doing.

"Now, Mr. Carson," she replied, in as stern a voice as she could muster, "you know that Len would be very upset to find you bothering me. Why don't you go rejoin the other gentlemen, and I promise I'll mention nothing to him about this incident."

"Ya ain't gonna mention nothing . . . that's fer damn sure," he countered in an uneven voice, his foul breath washing over her in a nauseating wave. "This'll be . . . our lil' secret. Ya say anythin' t' Len . . . an' I'll kill ya both."

The threat was not an idle one, she knew, just as she knew with chill despair that she could not risk putting Len's life in jeopardy. While she was certain that Len could easily best the other man in a fair fight, she also felt sure that he would never face the younger man head on. With a drunken bully like Carson, it would be a bullet in the back or a knife in the dark when Len least expected it. And letting Carson brutalize her this once would be a small price to pay to ensure Len's safety. Unless . . .

The germ of an idea niggled at her, and she took a deep breath. If she was very clever—and very careful—perhaps she could somehow put an end to it all now. It was a gamble, and a dangerous one, but a gamble that she had no choice but to take.

"I won't tell," she softly agreed. "In fact, I'm already tired of Len. He's not quite the man he pretends to be."

"I knew it," Carson chortled, moving closer to her. "Now, how's about I show ya . . . what a real man can do."

"Of course, but not here, where someone might find us."

Steeling herself, she summoned a smile and lightly touched his arm, willing herself not to squirm in revulsion as she did so. "If we go up there"—she nodded up at the hollow in the wall above them—"we'll have a bit more privacy. I'm sure you wouldn't want anyone interrupting us, would you?"

She could feel her smile stiffen as she waited for what seemed an eternity for his answer. If he grew suspicious, if he didn't take her bait now, it would be too late for her to escape him. *Please, just say yes,* she frantically prayed.

A moment later he leered again and gave an approving grunt. "Yer right. One of them other boys . . . might decide t' join in. C'mon, then."

Maude bit back the relieved sigh that threatened to escape her and silently moved through the waist-high boulders, a staggering Carson at her heels. The moon had risen above the walls of the arroyo by now, so that the handholds she earlier had seen formed a dark pattern along the face of the rock wall. She reached for the first hollow, and a shiver ran through her. She'd never had a head for heights, and she had never before attempted such a climb. Perhaps she should forget this wild scheme and just let Carson do what he would with her.

But the Apache girl didn't give up, her inner voice reminded her. And if Jess was here, surely she would make the climb without sniveling about it.

Gritting her teeth, Maude pulled herself up the first step, and then the second. Though the sharp rock cut into her soft hands, she found that each hollow had a lip of sorts that gave her better purchase on the slick surface. And because it was night, the cruelly-edged boulders below were hidden in shadows.

To her surprise, her progress up the wall proved far more easy than she'd hoped. Carson was faring less well, for she could hear his panting and muttered curses as he inched his way after her. A few moments later she was awkwardly pulling herself up over the edge and into the shallow cavern.

For the space of several heartbeats she simply lay facedown on the cool, windswept floor, consumed with relief that she had made it to the top without incident. Then, remembering the reason for her climb, she eased herself into a sitting position and gingerly peered back down again. Carson was a little more than halfway up now, she saw, aware now that her hands were cold and damp with sweat. In another few moments he'd be climbing over the edge to join her.

And when he did, that would be when she would shove him off the ledge and onto the rocks below.

It would be murder, pure and simple, she faintly realized, but what other choice did she have? If she left Carson to his own devices, he would brutalize her tonight . . . and the next night, and the next. Even if she kept silent about the rapes for Len's sake, he still might decide to kill the younger man. And surely, when he tired of the sport, he would kill her, too. Stopping Carson now was little more than self-defense . . . a bit before the fact, perhaps, but self-defense, nonetheless.

But even as the man's leering face appeared at the cavern's mouth, Maude's nerve failed her. She might wish for his death, might cheer to see him breathe his last, but she could not kill him, herself. All she could do now was pray that he slipped from the ledge of his own accord.

But he didn't slip.

Maude almost wept with defeat as he dragged himself over

the edge and then staggered to his feet. He blinked drunkenly against the shadows for a few moments. Then, spotting her huddled a short distance from him, he gave another chortle of laughter and started toward her.

"All right, lil' lady," he slurred as she scurried backwards, "we got ourselves . . . some privacy. So how's about doin' for me . . . what ya done for Len."

"And just what the hell would that be, Carson?" a low voice rumbled behind him.

The question stopped Carson in his tracks. Unsteadily, he turned back to the mouth of the cavern, his bleary gaze fixed on the tall silhouette of the third person to have made the climb that night.

"Shee-it," he gurgled, the bluster dropping from him like a fallen coat as he shuffled back a few steps.

Len moved on silent feet toward him, a stray beam of moonlight turning his blond hair silver while washing his broad form in shadow. Her avenging angel, Maude faintly thought, save that this vision brandished a six-shooter instead of a flaming sword. She scrambled to her feet and moved to one side, guessing that the drunken Carson would not readily be driven from this figurative garden.

He promptly proved her right. "There ain't no cause for ya to be pointin' that gun at me," he snarled, raising his hands in a mock gesture of surrender, "lessen ya want to shoot an unarmed man. Ya can see I ain't heeled. An' besides, the lady asked me up here, so why don't ya just wait yer turn?"

"All right, Carson, I'm gonna tell you this just one time," the younger man replied, holstering his pistol. "I want you to climb back down now and sleep off your drunk . . . and then, tomorrow, I want you outta here. If you ain't gone by first light, I'll stake your ugly carcass out for coyote bait. Am I makin' myself clear?"

"Hell, boy, who do ya think ya are, tellin' me what t' do? Don't be stickin' yer nose where ya got no business."

With those words, the outlaw abruptly staggered toward Len and threw an awkward punch. Len easily sidestepped the wild swing, while Carson tumbled to one knee, missing the cavern's edge by inches. Shards of crumbled granite skittered off into the darkness, lightly raining onto the rocks below.

"This ain't gonna end pretty, Carson," Len warned as the other man dragged himself to his feet again. "Why don't you quit while you're ahead?"

"I ain't quittin' for shit!"

The outlaw shook himself like an angry, puzzled dog; then, with a wordless snarl, he launched himself at the younger man once again.

Again Len stepped aside, once more avoiding the blow even as the force of the swing sent the outlaw overbalancing. This time, however, Carson had fatally misjudged his distance from the edge.

Maude watched, wide-eyed, as Carson teetered wildly on the cavern's narrow lip, hands scrabbling wildly at the air as he sought a handhold that was not there. Then, with a despairing little gurgle, he plunged into the darkness. A few seconds later she heard a soft thud as Carson's body landed on the ragged rocks below.

The silence that followed was broken only by the faint sounds of the other outlaws celebrating below, oblivious to the fate that had befallen one of their fellows. Maude briefly shut her eyes, relief that the man would never again harm her mingled with a sick feeling over the manner of his death. When she opened her eyes again, Len was still standing at the cavern's edge, looking out into the darkness.

As if feeling her gaze on him, he slowly turned and started toward her. He halted an arm's length from her, then simply asked, "Are you all right, Maude?"

"I-I'm fine," came her halting reply. "He-he never touched me, if that's what you want to know."

"That's good," he said with a nod, " 'cause I'd hate to want to kill a dead man. Do you want to tell me what happened?"

"He took me by surprise. He intended to rape me, and he said he'd kill you if I told. All I could think was that I had to stop him, somehow. I-I thought if I could get him up here, then I could push him off. He'd be dead, and that would end it."

She hesitated and drew a ragged breath, feeling as if a cruel, cold hand had clamped over her heart. "But I couldn't do it," she finished in a miserable rush. "I couldn't kill him, not even to save you. I-I'm so sorry."

The tears that she'd been holding back for days abruptly tumbled down her cheeks in a hot torrent that made her despise herself, even as she knew she was powerless to stop the storm. And then Len's arms were around her, pulling her to him as he softly whispered, "Don't be sorry, Maude, honey. That's why I love you, because you're so kind and gentle and good."

For a long moment she was certain she had imagined his words. Then a flicker of hope ignited within her, so that the icy hand around her heart began to melt away. Carefully, she pulled back from him so that she could see his face.

"Did you say that you love me?" she asked in a soft voice, the words tinged with a mingling of fear and hope.

He slowly nodded and dropped his gaze. "I know I'm a fool, thinkin' a fine lady like you could care for me. Hell, I'm an outlaw, not one of them fancy city fellas. I can barely read an' write, I rob banks for a livin', an' I've killed two men—three, if you count Carson. You'd be crazy to give me a second look."

Maude softly smiled. "Then I suppose I must be crazy. And I must be a fool, as well, thinking that a rugged and handsome young man like you could care for me. I'm almost old enough to be your mother, I've got wrinkles on my face and gray in my hair . . . and I can't ride a horse worth a darn."

A long moment of silence held between them. Finally, Len raised his head again, and a faint smile touched his lips.

"I can teach you how to ride a horse, Maude, honey . . . an' I promise you, I ain't never kissed my mother like this."

Sometime later, as they lay naked and exhausted in each others' arms, Maude wholeheartedly agreed that she could never mistake his kisses for those of a son.

* * *

Jess knew what was about to happen . . . but, as always, she was powerless to stop it. Once more, her screams of warning went unheard, as if she were encased in glass, a spectator to events but somehow not a part of them. And when she tried to rush to him—to stop him—that same invisible barrier held her firm, so that she struggled in vain to break free.

The same events began slowly to unfold. Even at a distance, she could see Arbin slide open the drawer where the derringer lay. He hesitated, flicking a questioning glance in her direction, before giving himself a silent nod. Then, as she watched in horror, he raised the tiny pistol in the direction of the bank robber.

The outlaw was smiling, Jess knew, though a filthy red handkerchief covered his face from nose to chin and hid that look of amusement. His blue eyes, glittering with anticipation, locked on Jess's horrified gaze for a heart-stopping instant. Then he turned his attention to Arbin and raised his own oversized revolver.

Say your prayers, partner. It's over now, 'cept for the burying part.

Two pistols erupted simultaneously, one emitting an ineffective little pop, while the other loosed an ear-shattering roar. A look of utter surprise crossed Arbin's mild face as the outlaw's bullet ripped through his chest. An instant later a gruesome blossom of red appeared on his white shirt front, and then he slumped to the ground.

And then Jess was beside him, cradling his head on her lap while his dark blood bubbled in an unstaunchable stream onto the floor. He gazed up at her, his puzzled expression dulling, and she gave a despairing cry as he softly whispered, *Jess. Jess.*

"Jess. Jess."

She was aware of someone shaking her, of a familiar voice calling her name from what seemed a long distance. She moaned and kept her eyes shut, not wanting to face the sober gathering of mourners that would be there at the cemetery this day . . . not wanting to face her own guilt in the mirror over her washstand. Why couldn't they all just leave her alone, and let her wallow in her feelings of anger and self-pity a little while longer?

"Damn it, Jess, wake up," came the same curt voice directly in her ear now. "You're having a bad dream."

And then she was truly awake, staring up into the stark desert night, with Nick's grim face looming over her. Arbin was long dead and buried, and she was somewhere in the chilly foothills of the Huachuca Mountains, searching for his killer and sleeping alongside a man who might or might not be a Pinkerton detective.

"You can stop shouting now. I'm awake," she murmured, and wearily dragged herself into a sitting position. She was shaking with reaction, as she usually was after one of these dreams, and she huddled in her blanket for comfort. A moon hung high above her, spilling silvery light across the camp and throwing every tree and rock into sharp relief.

A moment later Nick was leaning over her again, thrusting a cup of something blissfully hot into her limp hands. "Here, drink this. And I wasn't shouting . . . you were. I had to wake you before they heard you all the way up at Dead Squaw Canyon."

His ironic tone set her teeth on edge, but she duly took a sip from the cup, only to choke in surprise. It was coffee, but liberally laced with whiskey. Still, its swift warmth banished the worst of her dream, so that she could face Nick now with equanimity. "Thanks. I'm sorry I woke you. Is it almost morning yet?"

"It's just a little after midnight. And don't worry; I wasn't asleep."

Jess stared back at him, surprised by a sudden rush of concern for him. The fire had long since died to coals, and the faint red light threw his features into harsh relief. He must be worried about tomorrow, she realized, despite his claim that he could handle the situation on his own.

She took another drink of the potent coffee and debated whether or not to offer any words of reassurance. Likely, he'd either resent her impertinence or else laugh off her concern, neither of which responses would set favorably with her. In the end, she simply sipped her coffee and let the pop and gleam of the red coals lull her into comfortable numbness.

Nick settled beside her, nursing his own cup as he, too, fixed his gaze on the glowing bed of embers before them. He was the first to break the silence again when, a few minutes later, he softly asked, "What were you dreaming about, Jess?"

It was no idle question, and she opened her mouth to tell him in no uncertain terms that her dreams were none of his business. Instead, she suddenly found herself telling him about the nightmare that had dogged her ever since Arbin's murder.

"And it always ends the same way," she finished in a shaky tone, "blood everywhere . . . and then I wake up wondering why I wasn't able to stop him. Blast it all, I never told *him* to stand up to the Black Horse Gang. The only thing I ever said was that *someone* should."

"And he decided he should be that someone."

Nick set down his coffee, his blue eyes unreadable in the shadows. "Remember how I told you earlier that I wouldn't let you go with me to Dead Squaw Canyon, that it was too dangerous for you? Just suppose you went anyhow, and got yourself killed. Don't you think I'd be having the same sort of dreams about you that you have about your husband?"

"But why?" she protested. "It wouldn't be your fault I was dead, Nick . . . it would be mine."

"And it was your husband's fault that he got killed . . . not yours. He picked up the gun, not you. He made the choice, and he paid for it. So why do you feel so guilty?"

"Because I—"

She broke off and shook her head, all too aware of his gaze fixed upon her. "I don't know why," she finally admitted. "Maybe it's because I didn't love him enough, to start with

. . . because I thought he was someone he wasn't, and I married him for all the wrong reasons. And then, when he died, I wasn't prostrate with grief like everyone seemed to think I should be.''

She hesitated, trying to explain—to herself as much as to him—just how she had felt. ''I was terribly sorry, of course, and sad . . . but sad in the same way I'd be for a friend I hadn't seen in a long time. He and I were friends once, before everything went wrong between us. And he had many fine traits . . . he wasn't a bad person, at all.'' She paused, and then met Nick's gaze again. ''It's just that he wasn't the right husband for me, and I wasn't the right wife for him.''

''And that doesn't make you a bad person, either, Jess. You can't make yourself love someone, just because you think you should . . . and you can't always turn your back on someone, just because they don't deserve your love.''

His gaze drifted back to the fire, and silence fell between them again. Jess took another sip of her coffee, puzzling over his last words. Somehow, it seemed as if he'd been talking about himself then, and not her, though what it all meant she could not venture a guess.

But, oddly enough, telling him about her dream *had* eased a bit of the guilt she'd harbored ever since Arbin's death. Once they'd found Maude and brought her safely home again, perhaps she could begin to move on with her life, without her late husband's disapproving ghost clinging to her.

Feeling far more cheerful than she had but a moment ago, she set down her cup and lightly touched Nick's arm. ''Thank you,'' she murmured as he turned toward her again. ''I'll remember what you told me.''

''You do that, Jess,'' he softly replied and caught her fingers in his. ''Now, do you think you can get some sleep?''

His unexpected touch sent a shiver through her and left her at a momentary loss for a reply. *Not while you're holding my hand like that,* a small, wanton corner of her mind spoke up.

Just tell him yes, her rational voice hurriedly broke in. But when she finally recovered her powers of speech, what she said in an oddly breathless voice was, "I-I'm not certain. My wrist still hurts from where you tied me."

"Let me have another look at it, then."

His fingers were warm against her chilled flesh and, suddenly, it was all she could do not to fling herself into his arms. She must have made some sort of soft sound, however, for he glanced back up at her again. "I didn't mean to hurt you, Jess . . . not now, and not before. You do believe me, don't you?"

"Yes."

The word was little more than a murmur of affirmation, but it was all she could manage for the moment. It was enough for him, as well, for he raised her left wrist to his lips and lightly kissed the chafed flesh. "Better?" he softly asked.

It was much better than better, she thought with a sensuous little shudder. She nodded, and he gave her a slow smile that worked on her much the same way as his kiss had just done. "Then I should take a look at the other one, don't you think?" he said and reached for her right hand.

Rather than simply kissing the bruised flesh, however, he lightly ran his tongue along her wrist. This time the sensation sent a shiver clear down to her toes, and she bit back a moan of pure pleasure. All too soon, he raised his gaze to meet hers again, his blue eyes almost black in the shadows.

"What else, Jess?" he urged in the same low tones. "What else hurts?"

"My lips," she managed to reply, just before his mouth found hers.

His kiss was nothing like the light caresses to her flesh, nothing like the chaste brushing of lips that she had known with Arbin. His mouth was hot and demanding, almost bruising in its urgency, yet she found herself responding with equal abandon as he tumbled her onto her sprawl of blankets beside the dying fire.

Then his mouth was tracing the soft lines of her throat while his fingers fumbled at the buttons of her shirtwaist. A moment later he had divested her of that garment and her camisole, as well, baring her breasts to the night air. Her nipples tightened into hard little buds, and she shivered, but not with the cold. Not cold, at all, she thought with a mindless little moan, for now his warm hands were cupping her soft flesh, almost burning her with their touch. Yet even as she reveled in this sensation, his mouth moved lower still, until he was lightly tonguing first one stiffened nipple, and then the other.

"Oh, Nick," she softly cried and clutched his shoulders, arching against him with wanton abandon.

Then he raised up again, his dark gaze burning into hers. "If you want me to stop, Jess," he said in a ragged voice, "for God's sake tell me now. Otherwise, there won't be any turning back."

He was as aroused as she, Jess knew, for she could feel the hot bulge of his erection beneath his trousers as he pressed himself between her parted thighs. The sensation sent a wave of feminine satisfaction washing through her. She slid her hands down his back until she was cupping his muscled buttocks, molding him more tightly to her.

"If you stop now," she breathlessly told him, "I shall never forgive you."

Chapter Twenty-two

Nick groaned by way of answer and captured her mouth with his again. Jess shuddered with satisfaction and opened her lips to him, parrying every thrust of his tongue with an eager touch of her own. By now he had tugged his shirt free of his trousers and was swiftly unbuttoning it, so that a moment later her breasts were rubbing against his bare chest.

The coarse texture of his chest hair against her delicate flesh only intensified the sensations that were sweeping over her. Eagerly, she slid her fingers along his back, tracing the muscled lines of his shoulders and moving down to his ribs. By now his searching hands had found the hooks of her skirt. Before she realized what was happening, he was sliding that garment off her hips, until all that was left to her were her pantalets. A moment later those were gone, too.

For a moment she was suffused with keen mortification at the thought of being completely naked before a man . . . especially one who was not her husband. Whenever she and Arbin had made love, it had been in the dark beneath the bedcovers, with both of them partially clothed. Never had they indulged in such wanton behavior, nor had it ever occurred to Jess until tonight that such an intimate act could be performed out of doors.

As if sensing her dismay, Nick brushed a kiss against her forehead and murmured, "Don't worry, Jess. I won't do anything to hurt or embarrass you, I promise you."

"It's all right," she whispered back. "I trust you."

He eased off of her then, and slid one hand down her belly, until he reached the apex of her thighs. His fingers brushed the soft nest of curls there, before moving lower still. Dear Lord, what was he doing? she faintly wondered, certain she should protest this liberty but not quite sure why. And then he touched her there, in a place where no man had ever touched her before.

"Oh, Nick!"

"What's wrong, Jess?" he murmured, and she could hear a wicked note of amusement in his words as he stroked her again. "Should I stop?"

"No . . . oh, no," she gasped out, her thighs parting wantonly. "It's just that I never . . . that is, no one ever . . ."

She gave up trying to explain and let sensation sweep her. Whatever he was doing, it was sheer bliss, no matter that it seemed she might swoon from it all. This was how she had felt in her dream, she realized, gripped by a sweet, shuddering need that seemed to build with every touch of his hand. But even as she was certain that she would die from sheer pleasure, he slid a finger deep inside her.

She gave a sharp, shuddering gasp and shut her eyes. "Oh, Nick," she cried out again, "I don't think I can bear this . . . but please don't stop."

"I'm not stopping anything, sweetheart."

And, indeed, he was stroking his finger in and out of her now, so that she fairly writhed beneath his touch. She could barely believe this was happening to her, even as she prayed it would never end. If this was what she had been missing all this time, she faintly told herself, she might have considered taking off her clothes in front of Arbin.

Yet, too soon, Nick's hand slid away, and she gave a soft

moan of protest. ''Don't worry,'' she heard him say in a ragged voice. ''We're not finished yet, not by a long shot.''

She opened her eyes again to see him on his knees now, fumbling with his trouser buttons. She sat up, her hair tumbling in disarray around her shoulders and the warm place between her thighs fairly aching with unfulfilled need. That sensation only intensified as she watched with wanton interest while he freed his engorged organ from the confines of his drawers. Her eyes widened at the size of him, and she felt herself blush. She had once glimpsed Arbin in an aroused state before he had crawled beneath the bedclothes, but he had looked nothing like that.

''Oh, my,'' she murmured with no little concern as he stood and slid his trousers down over his hips, giving her an unobstructed view of his erection. Why, the man was a danger to women everywhere, she faintly thought, and in more ways than one.

''Like what you see, Jess?'' he asked with a slow grin that seemed to melt her from the inside out.

Embarrassed to have been caught staring, she could only nod as he knelt before her. ''Then touch me, if you like,'' he murmured as he pulled her to him for another kiss.

For a moment she was lost in the taste of his lips and the feel of his mouth on hers, and the way his strong fingers cupped her buttocks. Soon, though, she was aware of the insistent throbbing of his erection against her belly, the heated flesh between them demanding her attention.

Curious, now, she let her hands drift from his shoulders and down his ribs, pausing finally at his hips. This, too, was something she had never before tried, and she hesitated. But perhaps he would forgive her inexperience, after all, she told herself as she slid her hands between them.

Almost immediately, her searching hands found his throbbing rod, far harder and hotter than she'd ever imagined it might be. Lightly, she moved her fingers along the length of him, marveling at how something so rigid could feel so silken, like a knife in a velvet sheath. But barely had her fingers closed upon him again than Nick shuddered and broke free of their kiss.

"I'm sorry; did I hurt you?" she whispered in dismay, silently berating herself for her clumsiness in such matters. She started to loosen her hold on him, but before she could he had laced his fingers over hers.

"You didn't hurt me . . . not in the way you're thinking," he replied, his tone somewhere between a laugh and a groan. "But just keep touching me the way you're doing now, and things will be over with sooner than I'd hoped."

"Oh, my," she murmured, suppressing her own little smile. "We can't have that, can we?"

Or could they? After all, she wryly thought, hadn't he just made her gasp and shudder with abandon? He'd seemed more than eager to subject her to the most exquisite torture *she'd* ever known. How could she do anything less than the same for him?

Slowly, she began moving her hands up and down the length of him again. With a groan of surrender, he let her have her way, clutching her shoulders as she commenced her own sly brand of torture.

He'd grown even harder, if that were possible, and she could now feel the small drops of moisture that pearled at the blunt tip of him. Lightly, she brushed her fingertips over that delicate skin, feeling a surge of feminine satisfaction as he shuddered again and clutched her more tightly. Then she slid her hands down again, until she cupped the heavy twin sacks at the base of his erection.

"Damn it, Jess," he choked out as she lightly squeezed him, "I can't take much more of this."

"I don't recall your showing me any mercy," she replied with a smile, somewhat breathless now, herself.

The heat between her thighs had erupted into a full-fledged flame, while her breasts seemed swollen to twice their modest size, their nipples almost painfully hard. Truth be told, she couldn't take much more of that, either. But perhaps she should torment him just a moment longer, she told herself as she gently squeezed him again.

Suddenly she was on her back beneath him, her thighs spread wide as he knelt between them. At her cry of surprise, he gave her a ragged grin.

"I tried to warn you, Jess, but now it's your turn to beg for mercy," he said, and slowly eased himself into her waiting warmth.

Her first reaction was a gasp at the sudden, insistent pressure. Then he pressed deeper into her, and she slowly felt her sheath stretch to accommodate the hard, hot length of him. He seemed to fill every inch of her now, and the sensation was something she had never before experienced . . . much to her belated regret and quite happy anticipation.

"You're so warm, so tight," he murmured, slowly easing himself halfway out of her again. "Wrap your legs around me, sweetheart, and I'll let you beg for that mercy now."

"I never beg," she started to inform him in a lofty tone, only to break off with a gasp of pleasure as he thrust into her again. "Oh, Nick."

He began moving within her . . . slowly, at first, and then with a more rapid rhythm that triggered a heated rhythm of her own as she clung to him. The same shuddering need that she earlier had felt began to build within her again, coiling more tightly upon itself until she was aware of nothing save a heated tingling all through her body and the sound of Nick's harsh breathing as he moved with her.

From some distant place within her came the realization that she would beg now, if she could, save for the fact that she was far beyond speech. By now, pain and pleasure twisted into a single, almost unbearable need that she feared would never be satisfied . . . and then the tight coil abruptly exploded into a climax of sensation that made her cry out in pure delight.

While shudder after shudder wracked her, she felt Nick reach his own release. He thrust into her a final convulsive time, spilling his seed deep within her, before subsiding with a muffled groan.

They lay entwined for several moments longer . . . long enough for Jess to hear Nick's heartbeat slow to a regular pulse. Finally he eased off of her and settled alongside her, pulling one of the scattered blankets over them and drawing her into his embrace. She cuddled contentedly against him, wondering how she ever could have doubted him before. True, he might yet harbor a few secrets, but she knew the important ones. The rest, he surely would tell her afterwards . . . if, indeed, there would be an afterwards for them.

A small wave of foreboding lapped at her contentment, melting away the sugary illusion of happiness that had coated her for a few brief minutes. What was left behind now was a sense of uncertainty, tinged by more than a little fear. Nick would be walking into grave danger tomorrow, a fact that he must know quite as well as did she. Given that, how could she possibly let him go after the Black Horse Gang?

But then, again, how could she not? she miserably asked herself. After all, Maude's life still hung in the balance, and Arbin's killer had not yet paid for his crime. And with no posse in sight, who else but Nick could possibly right these wrongs?

He must have sensed her restlessness, for he tightened his arms around her and lightly brushed his lips against her tangled hair. "Don't think about it now, Jess," he murmured. "Nothing's going to change before morning, so you might as well get some sleep."

"I'll try," she whispered back, shutting her eyes as she nestled against his shoulder. Perhaps the best plan for now was simply no plan at all. With luck, by dawn he would realize that he could not face those killers single-handedly.

And if he didn't?

If he didn't, she firmly told herself, she would just have to follow after him.

"I-I'm not sure I can do this," Maude thinly protested, aware that her voice held an unseemly note of desperation in the chill pewter dawn.

Len gave her an encouraging smile. ''Sure, you can do it, honey. I've done it a hundred times. You did it last night, didn't you?''

''But that was different. It was dark and I . . . I had to.''

''And you have to now. But don't worry; it'll be over before you know it. Now relax, and take it real easy.''

She took a deep breath and nodded, though her deathlike grip on Len's hands belied that pretense of relaxation as he lowered her over the cavern's edge. Swiftly, she scrabbled with her booted toes to find purchase in the rock wall, reminding herself that there were any number of hollows to which she might cling. For a frantic moment, however, she thought she never would find any of them . . . that she simply would hang off the edge of this cliff until Len tired of holding her and she plunged to her death on the ragged boulders below.

Maybe they'd rename the place Dead Maude Canyon, she told herself, a hysterical little laugh bubbling in her chest at the morbid notion.

Then—quite miraculously, she thought—her feet slid into a pair of rough grooves. ''All right,'' she faintly told him. ''I've got it. Now w-what?''

''Now I'm goin' to let go of your right hand, and I want you to reach for that handhold right in front of your nose. Can you do that?''

She nodded, not trusting herself to speak as he gently disentangled his fingers from hers and she swiftly grabbed at that narrow lip.

''You're doin' just fine,'' he told her. ''Now I'm gonna let go of your other hand, real slow, and I want you to grab onto another spot. Are you ready?''

''No . . . yes,'' she whispered, biting her lip as she felt his strong grip on her wrist loosen. For the space of a heartbeat she felt her head spin, and then she seized the handhold before her.

''All right, you're set.'' Len gave her an approving grin. ''Now just keep your eyes on the wall in front of you, and you'll be fine. It's just like climbing a ladder—foot, hand, foot, hand—all the way down. Go as slow as you need to, and I'll tell you how you're doin'."

She nodded again, afraid that if she tried to speak, she would simply babble in terror. Even before Len had lowered her over the edge, she'd caught a glimpse of Carson's mangled body on the rocks below, a grim warning in the silent dawn. One tiny misstep, and she'd be there with him . . . and no doubt the two of them would haunt the gorge ever after.

Maude gritted her teeth, her resolve stiffening. No way would she spend eternity with that sorry excuse for a man, even if it were as a ghost.

"Foot, hand, foot, hand," she whispered to herself as she took the first shaky step down, and then the second. "Just like a ladder."

"You're doin' fine, Maude, honey," she heard Len say again. "Just keep goin' like you are."

Foot, hand, foot, hand. The granite rubbed her hands raw, but the steady rhythm kept her on an even keel. "Halfway there," she heard Len softly call, and then, "Just a few more steps."

And, far sooner than she had believed possible, both feet were indeed on solid ground once more. She gave a soft cry of triumph and gazed back up at the cavern, where Len was grinning down at her. He promptly lowered himself over the edge and with catlike grace began making his own descent.

A few moments later he had swooped her up in his arms and given her a resounding kiss. "I'm real proud of you, Maude, honey," he said with another grin once he had released her. "You climbed down better'n most folks would have their first time. I bet you didn't know you were such a brave lady, did you?"

"No, I guess I didn't," she said with a dawning sense of wonder.

Of course, she had always considered herself resourceful, but strictly in social and household matters. She could entertain unexpected guests with a smile, smooth ruffled social feathers with a few choice words, undertake charitable causes with aplomb. But never in her wildest fantasies would she have pictured the soft-spoken and demure Maude McCray surviving a bank robbery and kidnapping, a brutal cross-country ride, two brutal assaults, and, now, a dangerous climb down a cliff.

But she *had* survived it all . . . and she intended to survive whatever else happened, as well.

Her moment of euphoria faded a bit, however, as she caught another glimpse of Carson's broken body. Already, she could smell the faint odor of decay about him, and she shivered. "What shall we do about him?"

Len's expression grew grim as he glanced over at the dead man. "I'll see to him. I don't think Rory will much care, 'cept to take back Carson's share of the loot. But there's something else we need to talk about—"

He broke off, his attention drawn by the sounds of men stirring around the camp. Maude followed his gaze, watching as the outlaws, one by one, began rolling from their blankets and staggering in the direction of the fire. Now the silence was broken by horses wickering and men muttering, those sounds punctuated by a pungent curse and the sound of an empty whiskey bottle shattering against rock.

"Guess I'd best be joining them," he said with a wry shake of his head as he walked her back over to where they had left their gear the night before. "I'll square things with Rory about Carson, and then I'll bring you some grub."

"And then we'll talk?" she tentatively asked, uncertain whether to be cheered or depressed by the prospect.

He had given no sign that he regretted what had happened between them last night, but maybe that was because they had made love once again that morning, as the first few stray rays of dawn had lit the shallow cavern. He'd been cheerfully solicitous of her afterwards, and while she was making that terrifying climb down the cliff. But once he was back among his fellow outlaws again, he might reconsider the situation. Maybe he would decide that what he'd thought he felt for her was not love, after all, but momentary loneliness and lust. With both emotions temporarily slaked, he might decide he no longer had a need for her, either.

What he was thinking, however, she could not guess, for his youthful features had hardened into the same outlaw mask he had worn at the first. "We'll talk," he curtly agreed, not looking back at her as he strode over to the fire.

She huddled uncertainly where he had left her, gnawing at her lip as she watched and waited for Devilbiss to appear. A long while later he staggered, half-dressed, from his shack and made his own way over to the fire. Len got up from his spot and joined the outlaw. They talked for several minutes, Devilbiss gesturing a time or two in her direction. Abruptly, Len stood again and started back toward her.

He handed her the plate of food he was carrying, then settled himself a short distance from her. Not looking her way, he said in a low tone, "I squared things with Rory. I told him I was the one Carson was after, that he still held a grudge from the other night. A couple of the boys and I will take his body out of here in a little bit. Then I gotta decide what to do with you."

An air of finality tinged his words, so that a chill ran through her. Dear Lord, he *had* changed his mind! The disquieting image of her dead body dumped alongside Carson's in the desert flashed through her mind, and she bit back a cry.

Then he turned toward her, and his grim expression softened. "If I could, Maude, I'd take you out of here today." The poignant words dashed away her morbid imaginings, so that she heaved a small sigh of relief. "But it wouldn't sit well with Rory, not after what happened with the last Brimstone bank robbery."

He shook his head. "One of the boys—Whitey Kilroy, was his name—pulled a double-cross on us. He was the one we always let hang on to the money, 'cause Rory said he could be trusted. Well, old Whitey had had enough of bein' trustworthy, I guess, on account of he ran off with all the loot after we got back here to the hideout."

"But it was so much money," Maude exclaimed, recalling the figure that Jess had told her. "Didn't you go after him?"

"We all went out lookin' for him," he went on, "but all we found was his horse, with a couple of legs broke and shot through the head. We never did find Whitey or the money. Either he hid it and then died somewhere in the desert, or else he got plumb away, money and all." He frowned again. "I ain't never seen Rory so furious before. I think he would've killed Whitey with his bare hands if we'd found him."

"So if we leave now, he'll think you're trying to double-cross him, too?"

Len shrugged. "You never know with Rory. He's my friend and all, but sometimes I think he's not quite right in the head. And he won't like me taking you with me. You know where the hideout is now, so you'd be a danger to him. I don't think he'll want you to leave . . . ever."

Those last words seemed to echo in her mind, and Maude shut her eyes. Surely she had expected as much, she tried to tell herself, but hearing it spoken aloud lent a chill sense of truth to her fears. Dear Lord, would she truly end her days with these brutal outlaws, after all?

"Don't worry, Maude, honey," she heard Len softly say as she opened her eyes again to see him turn a wry smile in her direction. "I'll get you out of here, I promise, and then we'll go anywhere you want. You just have to be patient a little while longer."

"I will." She lifted her head and summoned a smile in return. "Tell me, Len, where would you like to go, if you had the choice?"

"I did always want to see San Francisco," he said, and she heard a boyish, wistful note in his voice. "Fact is, that's where I was headed when I met up with Rory. It seemed like a right excitin' place, with all the ships and people and fancy houses. I thought maybe I could get me a job on the docks, maybe even be a sailor. Or I could stay put and open a livery. Folks is always needin' a place to keep their horses . . . "

He trailed off rather sheepishly, and Maude gave him a warm smile. "You're right; they do. And I've often wished to visit San Francisco, myself, but I was always a little frightened at the idea of making the trip all alone. If we went together, I wouldn't be frightened at all."

"It sounds like we've got us a plan," he agreed, his earlier smile broadening into a grin. Then he sobered. "There's one last thing I need to tell you, and then I'd best be seein' to Carson."

"What is it, Len?"

"You know we have to be real careful now, especially after last night." She nodded, and he went on. "Until we get out of here, I can't treat you like I should, or else Rory will get suspicious. So if I say or do somethin' hurtful to you, it's only to keep you safe. Do you understand that?"

"I do understand," she softly answered. "And no matter what happens, I'll never forget how you've taken care of me, how you've made me feel so special. I promise you that, Len."

He shot her a careless grin, and her heart clenched a little as she watched him standing there in the morning sun, looking so young and so fearless.

"Now, Maude, honey," he said with a shake of his blond head as he started to walk away, "with all that talk of promises and not forgettin', it sounds like you think I'm fixin' to die."

Chapter Twenty-three

"This is where we are right now"—Nick made an *X* on the map with a stub of pencil he'd pulled from his saddlebags—"and this is Dead Squaw Canyon. And this is how you get to San Luis."

As Jess peered over his shoulder, he penciled in a new trail from Las Tres Cabezas to a spot to the east of it. He added a few coordinates, then handed her both the parchment and the compass.

"The trail is pretty well marked," he reminded her, "so you should do just fine following the map. But just in case you manage to lose your way again, do you know how to use one of these things?"

When Jess ruefully shook her head—contrary to what he might believe, she didn't make a habit of getting lost, so that she needed a compass—he gave her a wry grin. "Well, sweetheart, you're about to learn now."

She tried to focus on him as he swiftly explained the difference between directions and coordinates, and then showed her how to walk her way across camp using that information. But despite her best efforts, the greatest portion of her attention was fixed on the sky. Jagged fingers of blue and pink had thrust their way past the surrounding peaks, still cloaked in shadow, and lightened the sky from black to dull gray. Soon dawn would arrive in earnest, and Nick would be making his way toward Dead Squaw Canyon. Alone.

"But the simplest way," he now was telling her, "is to sight in your coordinate and then pick out a landmark that falls along that same line—a large tree, a peak, anything you can keep in your line of vision. Once you reach that landmark, you take another reading, find yourself another landmark, and so on. Now, can you remember all this?"

"Yes," she absently agreed, though in truth she had heard little of it.

She had awakened well before first light to the dual realizations that she'd had no blaze of insight in the few hours that she had slept and that she was still comfortably wrapped in Nick's embrace. She managed to put aside the first concern for the second, since by then Nick was also stirring, and in all senses of the word.

For several quite glorious minutes she had thought of nothing at all save the way his touch could bring her to the very heights of sensation. But afterward, as she had lain sated in his arms again, worry had begun to gnaw at her once more. She had made a hasty toilette and dressed, then began packing up their gear while Nick silently checked over his weapons. As the light began to build, he had pulled out the map and given her those final instructions.

"Jess, look at me," she heard him softly say now, and she dragged her anxious gaze to his. "We both know that if we wait around for another posse to show up, it might be too late for your aunt. I'm going to do what I can to get her back safely, but there are no guarantees that both she and I will make it."

"Then let me go with you," she urged one last, desperate time, grasping his hand. "Even one extra gun against the Black Horse Gang will help."

"I can't let you do that, Jess." He brushed his free hand along her face, the heat of his fingers seeming to sear her skin.

"I don't doubt your bravery, and I know you're used to doing things your own way, but the best help you can give me is to stay here, so I don't have to worry about you."

"And what if you don't come back?"

He gave her a faint smile. "Then you ride home to Brimstone, back to your father and all your friends and that bank of yours, and you carry on with your life . . . just like you did after your husband was killed."

"But-but I don't know if I can do that again."

To her horror, the words trembled dangerously on the verge of tears. And it was true, she realized. Coping with the aftermath of Arbin's death had been painful enough, simply for the fact of her own guilt and the knowledge that so much had remained unsettled between them. The very idea of losing Nick, however, slashed at her heart with an intensity she had never expected.

But then, she had never loved Arbin the way she loved Nick.

For love him she did, she realized now with mingled pain and joy. For a heart-stopping moment she was tempted to fling herself at his feet and beg him not to leave. But if he stayed, he would not be the same Nick she had fallen in love with, and if he went, the memory of her wailing at his knees might well distract him long enough to get him killed.

"Christ, Jess," he murmured, "I'd rather listen to you yell at me than watch you cry."

"I'm not crying," she protested, swiping the telltale tear away and lifting her chin. "That was merely a reaction from being overly exhausted these past few days."

He chuckled softly and drew her into his embrace. "Don't worry, sweetheart. I have every reason to want to make it back to you . . . and that's something that I've never said to any other woman."

He brushed his lips across hers and then glanced up at the sky. "Time to go," he said, and a cool mask seemed to settle over his features. He caught up his Winchester and his hat and headed for the roan. "Remember what I told you . . . wait until noon, and if I'm not back, head for San Luis."

"All right, I will." She settled herself at the fire and calmly reached for the coffeepot, vowing that she'd not give way to any further show of emotion . . . at least, not until he was gone. "Be careful, Nick, and good luck."

"Don't worry, Jess." He paused alongside the roan and turned to give her a slow grin, the same grin that always transformed her insides to jelly. "It's all over now, except for the burying part."

The coffeepot dropped from her suddenly nerveless fingers, clattering onto the ring of rock. Barely noticing the hot liquid that sloshed over her boots, she stared up at him. "What did you say?"

"I said, don't worry."

She shook her head. "No, after that."

"And then I said, it's all over, except for the burying part."

By now his grin had faded to a frown. Hanging his hat off the saddle horn, he started back toward her.

"Jess, there's coffee spilling all over your feet." He set down his rifle and snatched up the pot, propping it back in the fire again. "And you look white as that shirt of yours. Is something else wrong, something I said?"

"No, nothing it all," she lied in a shaken voice. "I-I just burned my fingers on the coffeepot, is all."

It's all over, except for the burying part.

She'd heard that same phrase dozens of times in her dreams, had heard it that day in the bank, just before one of the Black Horse Gang had shot Arbin down in cold blood. Slowly, she met Nick's cool gaze . . . those blue eyes, so familiar, even from the very first moment they had met. She thought she had known him from somewhere else, that day when he stepped into her bank, calling himself Jake Hancock. But, try as she might, she'd not been able to place his face, his voice.

Until now.

No, no, a despairing little voice inside her head wailed. It had to be a terrible coincidence, that he'd spoken those same odd words. She couldn't have made love to the very man who had killed her husband.

She took a shuddering breath, while the questions flashed

through her mind in the space of a heartbeat. If he was a member of the gang, why would he be trailing after them, instead of with them? Why would he have needed a map to find the way, when surely he had been to Dead Squaw Canyon before? Why play the role of bank examiner when he hadn't even been there during the second robbery?

And why had he let her ride with him . . . and why, dear God, why had he made love to her?

Maybe it had all been a cruel ruse, a different inner voice—this one cool and rational—answered just as swiftly. Maybe his job had been to act as decoy for the gang, to make certain that no posse followed after them. It would have been easier to let her travel with him, so that he could keep an eye on her, rather than risk her gathering up other riders to continue the pursuit.

Indeed, the voice reminded her, he'd not seemed unduly distressed to learn that Sheriff Behan had no men to send after the outlaws. Neither had he protested when Marshal Chapel declined to offer his services, as well. And when Jess had discovered he wasn't really Hancock, he'd simply chosen another lie with which to lull her, making her think that the law truly was in pursuit of the gang.

And, had the situation come down to it, she surely would have served as his hostage, just as Maude was hostage to the rest of the outlaws. The fact that she had so willingly made love to him, he must have seen as an amusing bonus for his hard work. But no longer needing her, he was leaving her behind . . . or was he? For, now that she knew the location of the Black Horse Gang's hideout, she was a danger to them all. Doubtless, once Nick had ridden off, the other outlaws would swoop down on her and murder her.

In the space of a few more heartbeats, she knew what she must do.

"Really, I'm quite fine," she said aloud now. "But would you do a favor for me before you leave? Could you bring my saddlebags closer to the fire?"

"Sure," he said with a small frown, "if you're certain you're all right."

He rose and headed toward where her gear was neatly piled. Jess waited until he was well out of reach, then silently took up the rifle he had left behind. Then, rising softly to her feet, she lifted the Winchester to her shoulder and pointed it squarely at his back.

"Oh, and Nick—or whatever your name *really* is—I do have one more favor," she added in a voice that shook only slightly. "Would you mind throwing up your hands and turning around . . . slowly."

He halted and turned around. His blue eyes—those same eyes that had once stared at her from over a dirty red bandanna—now narrowed in disbelief. "Christ, Jess," he said softly, "what the hell do you think you're—"

"Your hands, Nick; raise them. If you don't do it now, I swear I'll shoot you where you stand."

"All right," he agreed, and raised his palms to head level. "Now, why don't you tell me what's going on?"

"I'm bringing my husband's killer to justice, Nick, that's what is going on."

She took a few careful steps closer to him, though staying far enough away so that he couldn't reach out and wrest the rifle from her grasp. "I want you to use just two fingers and, very slowly, pull your pistol out of your holster." When he'd complied, she nodded. "Now, toss it over in the direction of my bedroll."

"This is ridiculous. Why don't you put that rifle down, and we'll talk."

"It's too late for talking, Nick. You see, I recognized you the first moment I saw you in the bank, though I just didn't realize it at the time. And even after we'd been traveling together for a while, I kept having the odd feeling that we had met before. But I probably would never have put it all together if you hadn't said what you did just now."

"Damn it, Jess, you're not making any sense." His words had taken on a hard edge now . . . the steely sound of a man used to confrontation at the point of a gun. "What in the hell did I say that set you off like this?"

"It's all over, except for the burying part," she softly repeated. "That's what you said before you killed Arbin."

He shook his head and gave a disgusted snort. "Christ, that's something my father always used to say. It doesn't mean a damned thing . . . and it damn sure doesn't mean I killed your husband."

"That's not all."

The rifle was shaking in her hands now, but she willed herself to remain steady, just for a few moments more. "That day you killed Arbin, you looked at me before you pulled the trigger, and I saw your eyes. They were blue and cold, like ice on a river. I knew at that moment that I would never forget your eyes, and I didn't."

"You're wrong," he told her in a soft voice. "I didn't kill him. I swear it."

For a single, desperate instant, she believed him . . . and then she shook her head. "You've lied to me too many times, Nick. I'm sorry, but I just can't trust you anymore. Now put your hands on top of your head and turn around again, slowly."

She heard his muttered curse, but he did as she asked. "All right, what now? Are you going to shoot me in the back?"

"Only if you try to run. Now kneel down."

For a terrible moment she thought he would refuse her order, so that she *would* have to shoot him, after all. Then, with another curse he didn't bother to muffle, he complied. She slowly advanced on him, not daring to lower the rifle . . . not yet. When she stood but an arm's length behind him, she paused.

"All right, Jess," Nick began again in the reasonable tone of someone dealing with a madwoman, "I did lie to you—and about more things than you know—but killing Arbin wasn't one of them. If you'll just give me a few minutes to explain, you'll understand I've been trying to help you all along."

"You should have explained everything back in Brimstone, before we went riding all over the territory together . . . before I—"

Before I fell in love with you, the despairing little voice in her head whispered. With a swift, mental shake, she dispelled that voice and finished aloud, "—before I found out the truth on my own."

Slowly, she lowered the Winchester and quietly twisted it about so that she now clutched it by the barrel. It had worked for Nick at the Silver Mule, so why not here for her? she told herself, focusing on the back of his head. For a moment, however, she found herself distracted by the boyish way his dark hair curled against his collar. In his guise as Hancock, he'd slicked down his hair with pomade, so that she had never noticed its unruly tendencies.

With an effort, she shook off that frivolous train of thought and moved a step closer. "Go ahead and lower your hands, but don't turn around."

"Damn it all, Jess," he said, exasperation edging that steel now, "you're making one hell of a mistake—"

He broke off quite abruptly as the rifle butt connected with his skull with a sharp little crack. For a long moment he remained kneeling, and she feared she had done no damage, after all. Then, with a groan, he hit the ground like a sack of wet feed and lay still.

Jess dropped the Winchester with a clatter. Dear Lord, what if she had killed him, without even meaning to?

Stifling a cry, she knelt beside him and lightly touched the side of his head where she had hit him. A lump was already rising behind his ear, and when she pulled her fingers away, they were tacky with blood. But he was still breathing, she saw with relief, so likely he would live a bit longer.

Scrambling to her feet, she hurried over to grab up his discarded pistol, which she tucked in the waistband of her skirt. Next, she headed for her saddlebags and pulled out the long coil of rope Nick had used to tie her the day before. Another moment's search brought forth an extra white handkerchief. Clutching both items, she hurried back to where Nick lay.

She puzzled a moment as to how best to tie him. He would have to ride, and if his hands were behind him, he couldn't climb into the saddle . . . certainly, not without her help. And after seeing how he'd handled Slaton at the Silver Mule, she suspected that, even tied, he still might get the better of her if she moved too close to him. So she would bind his hands in front of him, but make certain he had limited use of them.

With more difficulty than she expected, she managed to roll him onto his back. Picking up one end of the rope, she swiftly began tying his wrists together, doing her best to duplicate the same complicated knots that he'd used on her the day before.

The task should have taken but a few moments. Instead, she found herself pausing halfway through to gaze down at his still features. Now that his cool blue gaze was no longer fixed on her, she found it harder to believe he truly was the man against whom she had sought vengeance these past long months. The handsome if harsh planes of his face were softer in repose, and certainly not the cruelly twisted features of a cold-blooded killer. Dear Lord, the despairing voice spoke up again, what if she *had* made one hell of a mistake, as Nick had tried to claim?

No mistake, her rational voice insisted. Too many oddities, too many lies tipped the balance against him. She had the right man, no doubt about it.

She finished tying his wrists, leaving a short end hanging to one side and perhaps another ten feet of rope still coiled beside him. The former end she knotted to his belt, so that he could raise his bound hands only a few inches above his waist. The handkerchief she turned into a makeshift gag, which she knotted over his mouth. That accomplished, she picked up the coil of rope and looped its free end around Old Pete's saddle horn.

Then, with a mingled sigh of regret and satisfaction, she settled with the rifle across her lap a short distance away and waited for him to regain his senses.

Chapter Twenty-four

Someone was licking his ear . . . slowly teasing his lobe with a tongue that was warm and soft and wet.

Nick struggled to open his eyes, so that he might see who was responsible for the sensations that were resulting from such treatment, but the effort proved too great. Instead, he subsided with a groan and tried to recall what he'd been doing to end up in this most interesting situation.

The most likely explanation he could conjure was that he'd wound up in bed with some female or another after a night of uncharacteristic hard drinking. That would explain why his head was pounding to the point where even the simple act of thinking brought on excruciating pain. But he hadn't made it back to town yet, he was almost certain . . . so that scenario couldn't be right. In fact, the only thing he knew with any certainty was that he was lying on his back.

Slowly, the fog that had enveloped his brain began to lift, and events began to settle back into place. The last memory he had was that of arguing with Jess over something, though what that something had been, he couldn't say for the moment.

Yet it couldn't have been too serious a disagreement, since it had to be she who now was toying with him.

He tried to say her name, but the word came out oddly muffled, as if his mouth was stuffed with cotton. And he was having a hard time moving, as well. He tried to reach for her, only to feel as if his arms were weighted, so that he could lift them but a few inches. Indeed, something was very wrong, he decided, as he gave it another try and slowly opened his eyes.

Two wide brown eyes stared back at him, mere inches from his face. He blinked, and those eyes abruptly drew back, giving him an unimpeded view of a long black snout from which lolled an equally long pink tongue.

The black hound, he said in disgust . . . or tried to. A strip of cloth was wedged between his teeth, so that all he could manage was an unintelligible mumble. He'd been gagged, he abruptly realized. With a muffled sound of outrage, he reached up to yank off the offending cloth, only to be stopped short by the rope that bound both hands to his waist.

Tied, too.

His anger swiftly cooled as it dawned on him that he was someone's prisoner. And if someone had overpowered him, came the chilling realization, then perhaps they had captured Jess, too. But he didn't remember riding into Dead Squaw Canyon, nor did he recall a raid upon their campsite. And, oddly enough, the view above him was the same he recalled from last night, save that dawn had lightened the sky to pale blue.

Aw, shit, he thought in mingled fury and disbelief as memory finally returned in its unpleasant entirety. The view looked familiar because he'd never left camp. He dragged himself into a seated position alongside the black hound and, squinting against the pain in his head, gazed about for some sign of his captor.

"He came back while you were unconscious," he heard Jess's voice from somewhere behind him. "He might only be a dog, but at least he's trustworthy."

He heard the soft sound of footsteps, and then she was

standing in front of him, his Colt shoved in the waistband of her skirt and his Winchester cradled in her arms. *His* Colt. *His* Winchester. She'd ambushed him with his own weapons, practically the most mortifying thing that could happen to a man. It was a damned good thing he was tied, he told himself, or he'd likely be throttling her at this very moment.

She seemed to guess as much, for she kept a prudent distance from him. Her dark eyes held the same determined expression he'd first seen in them when they had ridden out of Brimstone together, while her full lips were thinned into bleak if controlled lines. It was obvious that she was not enjoying her role as captor . . . and equally clear that she intended to carry that role to whatever lengths she deemed necessary.

Damn it all, she really did believe *he* was the one who had killed her husband.

The realization ripped at his gut like a cold and jagged knife. How in the hell could she think that, after last night? To his mind, at least, what had happened between them had gone beyond simply satisfying a mutual need. He hadn't intended things to go that far between them—hell, he'd learned his lesson the night before in San Luis—but then he had kissed her, and things had progressed quite satisfactorily from there.

Memories of their lovemaking crowded in on him, and for the space of a few heartbeats he relived them . . . the sweet taste of her lips, the softness of her breasts, the eager way she had welcomed him into the tight warmth of her body. He'd been with many other women before, but never with one who had given of herself in quite the same way. If he'd had the choice, he would have been content to forget the Black Horse Gang—his own brother included—and simply lie in her arms for the next forty years or so.

But he did not have that choice . . . not then and, obviously, not now.

"I suppose you're wondering what I'm planning to do with you," he heard Jess say, her cool tone returning him to the present. "I'd bring you back to Tombstone for trial, but there's my aunt to think about, first, so I've decided I'll have to forego the pleasure of seeing you hang for your crimes. Instead, I intend to use you as my bargaining chip with the Black Horse Gang. I'm going to trade you for Maude.''

Trade him for her aunt?

Nick shook his head in disbelief, wincing a little at the pain. Christ, all she was going to accomplish was getting all three of them killed. If she'd only given him the chance to explain the situation, instead of jumping to conclusions and bashing him over the head like she had, he could have told her as much. Somehow, he had to stop her before she rode into Dead Squaw Canyon, right into the barrel of Rory's six-shooter.

''I see no point in postponing this any longer,'' she said with a small sigh, moving toward her paint, tied a few feet from them. ''Just so you know, I made a copy of my map the morning we left Tombstone and had it delivered to Sheriff Behan. With any luck, the Earp brothers are already headed in our direction, so that they will recapture you after my aunt and I are safely away.''

So that was one thing that had gone right, then. In his own arrogant quest to somehow rescue his brother from the hangman's noose, he'd convinced himself that he could capture the whole gang single-handedly. But given that he'd been outsmarted by an amateur like Jess, it seemed he needed all the help he could get. With luck, the Earps would stumble upon them in time . . . if not to rescue them, then to bring their bodies back for a decent burial.

Her gaze still fixed on him, she mounted up. He noticed that the other end of the rope that bound his wrists had been looped about her saddle horn.

''Now, I'm giving you a choice, Nick. You can either cooperate, and I'll let you ride with me, or you can make things difficult . . . in which case I'll be forced to drag you along behind me. So, what will it be?''

He gave the question swift consideration. Had she simply been holding the other end of the rope, he would have used the weight of his body to yank her from the saddle, and then used his legs to kick his weapons from her grasp and overpower her. Afterwards, it would have been a matter of contorting himself sufficiently to wrestle his knife from his boot so he could saw apart his bonds.

Unfortunately, she had been clever enough to keep clear of the rope by tying it to her saddle. Now, if he rushed her, she could simply tap her heels into the paint's side and knock him off balance. And if he tried to stymie her by refusing to move, she could use that same tactic with equal success . . . that, or she could shoot him with his own rifle.

He allowed himself a grim inner smile. Though her overall plan to launch a one-woman assault on Dead Squaw Canyon verged on outright madness, he had to admit that she'd done an admirable job on the preliminary details. Given her obvious aptitude for such work, perhaps he should have taken her up on her original offer to act as his backup. In the meantime, however, he would be damned if he would let her drag him all over creation at the end of a rope.

With as much dignity as he could muster, Nick marched over to the roan and climbed into his saddle. Barely had he settled himself than she nudged the paint forward, so that he had to grab at the horn or be pulled right out of his seat. He muttered a curse through the strip of cotton that was biting into his face and swiftly urged his own mount forward. The black hound, as always, dragged itself to its feet and followed after them.

Dawn had given way to true daylight by now, so that the sky above them was a faded blue and a yellow disc of sun was visible through the mountain peaks. Nick paid no heed to the surrounding beauty, however, more caught up in the passage of time than he was in the day's eventual burst into full-fledged glory. Rory and his cohorts should be rising by now, so that the element of surprise would be lost long before they reached the canyon. From what he'd learned from Whitey, he could almost be assured that those guards he'd not seen yesterday were posted somewhere not far from the entry. Unfortunately, he had no idea if their instructions were limited to the simplest policy possible—kill all intruders, no questions asked—or if they took prisoners and left the decision up to Rory.

The second scenario, Nick knew, would strictly be a postponement of the inevitable . . . in his own case, at least. The minute Rory learned his estranged brother had come calling, he likely would finish the job he'd tried to start two years earlier. Jess would last a while longer, until the men had had their fill of her, which could be weeks, or days, or only hours. One way or the other, she and her aunt eventually would vanish into the desert foothills, along with the elder of the two Devilbiss brothers.

Christ, he had to stop her before they reached Dead Squaw Canyon. The question was, how?

Even moving at the necessarily slow pace that the steep trail enforced upon them, they would reach the canyon's entrance within a half hour, so time was of the essence. He gave an experimental tug on his bonds, finding them tight, but not impossibly so. Then he turned his attention to Jess.

She rode just ahead of him, her gaze constantly flickering from the trail to him, and then back again. She couldn't watch him every instant, and if he appeared cooperative, even helpless, she would likely relax her vigilance.

He sagged a little in his saddle, as if the blow to his head had weakened him. If he could just untie the end of the rope that was knotted to his belt, he'd have enough freedom of movement to try something, anything. And though she had relieved him of both pistol and rifle, she had not found the knife he kept in his boot.

His gaze fixed on Jess, he worked at those knots by feel, making his way through them in rapid succession. A few minutes later his wrists were no longer secured to his belt, though untying the rope that bound them together was going to prove more problematic. He probably could pick apart those knots with his teeth, except for the fact that he was gagged, and she would likely notice if he tugged that handkerchief from his mouth. He could try to pull the knife from his boot and try to saw the bonds apart, but such a plan would require a fair amount of bodily contortion on his part that she couldn't fail to notice, either.

Perhaps his best bet would be to try to fling himself off the roan and onto the back of her paint. If he could manage that fancy bit of horsemanship, he'd have the situation back under control again. Of course, if he failed in that attempt, he'd end up trampled, dragged, or both.

Shit, he succinctly assessed the risk. Still, it was one he'd have to take, since the end of the trail was fast approaching. Once inside the canyon, he'd be like an empty whiskey bottle on a fence post . . . an easy target for any shooter. If he didn't try something now, he'd not get a second chance.

Stealthily, he urged the roan a bit closer and eased his feet from his stirrups, experimentally shifting his weight off the saddle and onto his hands, which were gripping the saddle horn. He would first have to vault into a crouching position atop his saddle and then make the leap from the mare to the gelding. Timing would be crucial, but surprise would be on his side and would gain him a few seconds before she could react to the attempt. And the best place to make that attempt, he decided, would be at the level spot where the trail dead-ended into the canyon's outer wall.

As the canyon wall loomed closer, Jess continued to glance in his direction every few moments. He willed himself to appear relaxed under her scrutiny, even though the muscles of his arms and legs fairly thrummed with anticipation. Finally the trail dribbled off. Jess slowed her paint, her gaze fixed at a more distant point down the expanse of sheer wall before them. He heard her softly mutter, "The opening should be somewhere near here."

He let the roan settle in behind her so that she'd have to turn to see him. With a minimum of movement, he reached up and tugged his gag down over his chin, letting the loop of cloth dangle around his throat. Working his bruised jaw, he grabbed for the saddle horn and took a firm grip on it.

Now, his inner voice commanded.

With a single fluid movement, he was crouched atop the roan . . . and then he sprang.

He landed neatly on the saddle behind Jess. Her gelding gave a protesting snort and hop at this unexpected addition of weight but skittered only a few steps from the roan before subsiding. As for Jess, she had time for only a cry of surprise before he slid his arms over her and effectively locked her in his embrace.

"Got you," he muttered triumphantly in her ear, pinning her elbows to her side so that she could not draw his revolver from her waistband. The Winchester had already tumbled from her lap onto the ground, so she lacked that weapon, as well. He would relieve her of her derringer once he'd managed to untie the rope from the saddle horn and then free his wrists.

He managed the first with relative ease. The second, he swiftly determined, would require Jess's help . . . though gaining her cooperation might take some doing.

"All right, Jess," he told her, "let me explain to you how this is going to work. First, you're going to untie my hands, and then we're going to head back to camp together and discuss the situation. You can cooperate or not—the choice is yours—but let me assure you that you'll find cooperation to be a hell of a lot more pleasant experience than trying to fight me. So, what's your answer?"

After her first gasp of shock, she had subsided into stillness, though he could feel the rapid beat of her heart against her ribs that belied her pretense of calm. He felt her hesitation, as well, and knew she was weighing the possible consequences. "Don't take too long to decide, Jess," he warned her softly, "or I'll make the choice for you."

The implied threat spurred her to a response. "Very well, I'll cooperate," she agreed in a stiff little voice. "But you're going to have to release my arms if you want me to untie you."

"I will . . . but for God's sake, don't try for that pistol. One of us will end up shot, and it won't be me." She gave a grudging nod of acknowledgment, and he eased the pressure on her arms so that she could slide them free. "And try to hurry. We're too damn close to the canyon entrance for comfort."

Whether it was that reminder or her own wish to be free of him as swiftly as possible, she began plucking at the knots. Unfortunately, she'd done a tolerable job of tying him in the first place, so the process took longer than he had hoped. He controlled his impatience with an effort, knowing that his literally breathing down her neck would only distract her. Hell, he was feeling pretty distracted, himself.

For, despite his need to remain vigilant to their surroundings, he found himself focusing on his reactions to her. He was holding her quite as closely as he had held her a little more than an hour earlier, when they had made love in the chill darkness of predawn. Seated as she practically was in his lap, her trim rear end molded to his inner thighs, she rocked back against him in a most intimate fashion with the gelding's every impatient stomp.

Somehow, he'd also managed to angle his arms directly under her breasts as she worked at the knots at his wrists. Deliberately, he shifted his position so that their soft warmth pressed against him. She gave a little gasp at this intimacy, her fingers pausing over the ropes for an instant before she hastily resumed tugging at the strands.

He allowed himself a cool smile at her reaction. Her mind and her heart might be clamoring that they hated him, but he could almost guarantee that her body would sing quite a different song if given the chance. Hell, the fact that *he* was furious with *her* for this little stunt of hers didn't stop his loins from pleasurably tightening as she wriggled against him . . . which was why he let a few too many moments slip past before he recognized the import of the low rumble emanating from the nearby rock.

''Shit,'' he choked out, ''someone's headed out of the tunnel.''

At that moment, he felt the last knot give way. He swiftly shook off the rope from around his wrists, then snatched for the reins and whirled Old Pete around. It was too late now to retrieve either his rifle or the roan. The best they could hope for was that the abandoned horse and weapon would distract the approaching rider long enough to give them a head start back down the trail.

But even as he put his heels to the paint's ribs, three men on coal black steeds—one of whom was leading a fourth horse—burst from the tunnel opening. The trio pulled up short with shouts of surprise; then, drawing their pistols, they squeezed off a few shots and promptly started in pursuit.

Nick's free hand closed over his pistol, still tucked into Jess's waistband, but he didn't draw it. The outlaws' mounts had already outpaced the overburdened gelding on the uneven ground. If he tried to shoot back now, he'd only succeed in getting both Jess and himself killed. With a pungent oath, he instead jerked the paint to a halt.

For God's sake, Jess, let me do the talking, came Nick's fervent prayer as one of the outlaws caught hold of the paint's bridle, while the other two raised their pistols and looked menacing.

Casually, he let his arms drape around Jess's waist, hoping the gesture effectively hid the pistol butt. Aloud, he said in a cool tone, "Howdy, boys. Hope we're not disturbing anything. The lady and I were just out for a ride and decided to rest the horses for a minute. We didn't realize anyone was up here."

"Listen to that, Len. These folks ain't realized no one was up here."

The speaker, a red-haired youth whose green eyes appeared affixed in a permanent squint, was the same one who had caught hold of the paint. He gave a high-pitched chortle and raised his own pistol. "Now, don't that beat all? I guess we could just allow as how they made a mistake, but I say we should just kill 'em."

Chapter Twenty-five

"Now, boys, there's no cause to be shooting anyone," Nick countered in the same cool voice. "Why don't you just let us ride out, and we'll forget we ever saw you?"

Jess listened to this exchange with fearful confusion. It seemed as if these outlaws didn't know Nick, while he certainly was acting as if he didn't know them. She would have expected them to welcome him with open arms, perhaps cheer him for bringing them another hostage. Was this some bizarre charade being played out for her benefit . . . or had she truly made, as Nick had claimed, one hell of a mistake?

At the possibility, she felt her insides twist into an icy little knot of fear. Already, she'd been berating herself for the lapse of attention that had allowed Nick to overpower her and turn the situation to his advantage. Now, in her impulsive leap to condemn Nick for Arbin's murder, it seemed she unwittingly had put an end to any chance of rescuing Maude. There would be no exchange of Nick for her aunt, for he was not one of the Black Horse Gang.

Even as these thoughts flashed through her mind, the outlaw she presumed to be Len slowly was shaking his shaggy blond head. "Sorry, partner, we can't just let you go." He turned to the youth and added, "But there ain't gonna be no killin', Matthew, not unless Rory says so."

Rory.

He must mean Rory Devilbiss, leader of the Black Horse Gang, Jess thought with an inner shiver. At least, she had succeeded in her goal of finding their hideout, though the knowledge gave her scant satisfaction at this particular moment.

Len's youthful features set into hard lines beneath the brim of his hat as his pale gaze flicked from Nick to Jess, and then back to the red-haired youth. "Matthew, go ahead an' finish up with Carson. Bobby an' I'll take care of things."

"But, Len, I don't wanna—"

"You'll do as you're told, or Rory will hear about it."

With a muttered curse, Matthew released his hold on Old Pete's bridle and roughly pulled his black gelding around. It was then that Jess noticed the fourth, riderless horse was not quite riderless, after all. A long, blanket-wrapped bundle was draped over its saddle. From one end protruded a pair of scuffed brown boots, the late owner of which doubtless was the luckless Carson.

Another belated victim of the Brimstone shoot-out, she faintly wondered, or someone who had tried and failed to bring these brutal outlaws to justice?

While Len and Matthew had debated the issue of cold-blooded killing, the third outlaw had remained silent. Now, as Matthew rode off to dispose of Carson, that man's pockmarked face lit up with a sudden leer of comprehension.

"Hellfire, Len, I knew this fella looked familiar, an' I think I know why." He gave a dry chuckle. "I cain't wait t' see Rory's face when these two set eyes on each other."

Len gave Nick a long, searching look, and then nodded. "Yeah, you might be right . . . and I guess it'll be interestin'." Turning his attention back to Nick, he gestured with his pistol. "That your Winchester I saw lyin' on the trail?"

"It is. Guess I must have lost track of it in all the excitement," he answered with a shrug.

Len frowned at this show of unconcern. "An' what about that holster of yours? It looks mighty empty."

"I lost my pistol, too. I'm not real good with guns."

Bobby gave a disgusted snort. "Yeah, I'll just bet you ain't. Now throw up yer hands, so we can see 'em, an' lean back, so we can see if you got anything stashed in yer belt."

Slowly, Nick complied. As his arm drew away from her waist, Jess casually crossed her arms over the pistol butt still protruding from her waistband. Thank God she had his pistol, rather than he. With luck, they would assume a woman would not be armed, and wouldn't think to search her.

"Okay, Len," the other outlaw said, "looks like he's not heeled."

"Then let's get moving. Just keep that paint right between me an' Bobby, an' no one's gonna get hurt."

At least, not yet, Jess silently amended for him, hoping her terror didn't show on her face. These two might not know Nick, themselves, but they seemed to think that the outlaw leader did. Maybe Nick truly was the Pinkerton agent he had claimed to be, and he had confronted Devilbiss once before. That might explain, in part, why Nick had set out after him by himself.

But now did not seem quite the time to pepper Nick with questions. Instead, she took a bit of comfort from the fact that his arms were wrapped about her in a most protective fashion as he handled the reins. Thank God, as well, that she had untied him before the outlaws had swooped down upon them. Given that he'd already demonstrated his ingenuity in resolving threatening situations, perhaps he would manage some way of extricating them from this fiasco. And if they found his pistol on her . . . well, she still had her derringer stashed in her boot that one or the other of them might use.

But that possibility did little to ease the cold knot that had settled beneath her ribs. She bit her lip and willed herself to remain calm, knowing that if she gave way to her fear, she would only hasten the end. Then she heard Nick's voice low in her ear, the ironic murmur meant only for her.

"So, do you believe me now, Jess?"

She gave a little nod, torn between hysterical laughter and wailing despair. She settled, instead, for a whispered apology—"I'm sorry, Nick"—that she knew to be woefully inadequate, for all that it was sincere.

"No talkin'," Len decreed . . . quite unnecessarily, for she could think of nothing more to say.

They paused, at one point, just long enough for Len to grab up Nick's fallen Winchester, and then continued along the base of the sheer rock wall. A few moments later, they had reached what Jess assumed from Nick's previous description to be the entrance to Dead Squaw Canyon. Bobby and his black led the way inside while Len, atop his charcoal steed, followed closely behind.

The tunnel-like fissure stretched the height of the canyon walls, so that Jess could see a ribbon of blue sky above them. Immediately, she understood what Nick had meant when he described the passage as a good place for an ambush. Once inside, an intruder could readily be trapped, for a horse could turn about in the narrow pass only with great difficulty . . . and a stubborn steed like Old Pete, likely not at all. And though the passage was open at the top, its walls were too steep for anything other than a lizard to crawl up.

Sooner than she expected, they trotted out into the bright light of the open canyon. Jess stared about, wide-eyed, mentally comparing the reality with the inked representation she had studied these past days. The actual canyon was far larger and bleaker, all in shades of brown and tan, and stretching deeper into the mountain than she would have guessed. For the moment she saw no sign of life other than the four of them . . . and then a pair of rifle-wielding riders on coal black steeds thundered out from a nearby outcropping of rocks.

"Don't worry, boys," Len assured the newcomers as they reined to a halt in a cloud of dust and with a dramatic clatter of hooves. "These here folks are just a couple of intruders we found wandering nearby. Bobby 'n I got this under control."

"Sure, Len," one of them replied, while the other simply

nodded and spit a stream of brown tobacco juice into the pale dirt.

Leaving the pair to their post, the two outlaws urged Jess and Nick forward again. Jess tightened her arms over her waist, reassured by the feel of the pistol and the pressure of Nick's chest against her shoulders, even as she felt her breath coming now in shallow little puffs. *Stay calm,* she told herself. Soon enough she would know if her aunt was here with the outlaws . . . and, soon enough, she would know just how long the three of them had left before Rory Devilbiss passed sentence on them.

They rounded the point where the canyon abruptly angled into the belly of the mountain, revealing the Black Horse Gang's camp. Half a dozen of the namesake black steeds were corralled in a crude ring of rock and split timber, while the outlaws themselves were gathered around the campfire just beyond it. At the sound of the approaching horses, they rose from where they sat or crouched.

''Hey, Rory,'' Bobby called when they were within hailing distance, ''we done brung you a visitor.''

Climbing from their horses, he and Len kept their pistols at the ready while gesturing her and Nick to dismount, as well. Nick slid from the saddle first, then reached up to help her. His hands encircled her waist for a moment as he lightly swung her down, and then steadied her before him.

''Are you all right?'' he murmured.

She looked up at him and nodded, trying to read what she could in his eyes—anger, determination, forgiveness, promise—but his blue gaze was shuttered, revealing nothing. In a gesture that should have been tender but somehow was not, he brushed one hand against her cheek . . . and, with the other, he slid the pistol from her waistband and tucked it beneath his vest.

''C'mon,'' Bobby urged, abruptly grasping Jess by the shoulder and shoving her in the direction of the gathered men. Len prodded Nick with his pistol barrel, urging him forward, as well.

By now, one of the men had broken from the others and was moving toward them with easy grace. He was dressed like the others in dusty brown trousers and vest, with a white shirt whose sleeves he'd rolled back to expose his tanned forearms. His broad hat shadowed his face, so that all she could tell was that he was tall and well-built. He had a distinct air of command about him, however, so that Jess was certain he must be Devilbiss.

The outlaw leader halted a few feet from where she and Nick now waited, flanked by the two men. He stood in silence for a few moments, arms crossed over his chest as he studied them. Then, lazily, he tipped up the brim of his hat so that his face was clearly visible beneath an unruly shock of dark hair.

The first thing Jess noticed were his eyes, cold and blue and frighteningly familiar. The rest of his handsome features were familiar, too . . . sharper and crueler, perhaps, but familiar, nonetheless. A smile twisted his well-formed lips but never reached those cold eyes as he murmured, "Well, I'll be damned, if it isn't my loving older brother, come to visit me."

Brother.

The word echoed painfully in Jess's mind, and she briefly shut her eyes, willing herself not to swoon or shriek. Dear Lord, this explained it all. Rory was the one who had killed Arbin. Nick was searching for not a gang of outlaws, but his brother. But why hadn't he explained this all to her from the first?

"Hello, Rory," she heard Nick answer in an equally chill tone, so that she opened her eyes again. "It's been a long time."

"Two years."

Casually, the younger man drew the pistol on his hip and raised it so that the muzzle pointed at Nick's face. Then he glanced about at the other gang members, who were slowly gathering about them, and smiled again.

"Boys, I've got a deep dark confession to make. You see,

not only do I have an older brother who I hate with all my soul—that is, if I had a soul to hate with—but that brother just happens to be a fucking Pinkerton. So I guess he's not just here for a friendly visit, after all.''

A rumble of mingled anger and crude amusement rose from the other outlaws, the threatening sound sending a shiver through Jess. Nick merely shook his head.

''Damn it, Rory, I'm not here in an official capacity. I want to help you, not bring you back in.''

''Help me? When the hell did you ever want to help me, big brother?''

The earlier cold amusement fled his face, and Jess saw his grip on the revolver tighten. ''Two years,'' he softly repeated, ''and every single day of those two years, I swore I would kill you if I ever saw you again. Looks like I finally got my wish, didn't I?''

''You may have, but I'll lay odds you botch the job this time, too.''

With those cool words, Nick moved a few steps closer and slowly began raising his hands. ''Here, Rory, why don't you let me turn my back, and give you an easy shot . . . or are you as bad with a pistol as you were with a knife?''

An angry spasm contorted the other man's face. ''Damn you to hell, Nick. You think you're so damn smart, but you're not. The only reason I didn't kill you that night was because your friend, Holliday, interfered. Otherwise, you'd be nothing but bones and dust by now.''

''Well, Doc's not here, so why don't you give it another try?''

What happened next occurred in the space of a few heartbeats so that, had Jess blinked, she might not have seen it. As Nick began to circle, his hand slid beneath his vest. In a flash, he had drawn the pistol and spun about to face his brother again, the weapon squarely pointed at the younger man's chest.

The click of the hammer falling back was promptly echoed by Jess's warning cry and the sound of a half-dozen or more other revolvers being cocked. The rest of the Black Horse Gang had moved in, responding to the threat. Rory, meanwhile, shot Len and Bobby a furious look.

''Damn it to hell, didn't you think he'd be carrying a fucking gun on him? Why the hell didn't you search him?''

''I swear, Rory, we did,'' Bobby sputtered, his own pistol wavering in the face of the outlaw leader's outrage. ''We found his rifle, but we didn't see no pistol. He must've had it hidden somewheres.''

''Call them off, Rory,'' Nick warned, taking a step closer to his brother.

Rory turned his attention back to him and sneered. ''Hell, big brother, can't you count? There's more of us than there are of you. Pull that trigger and you're dead.''

''Yeah, but as long as I take you with me, it won't much matter.''

Jess saw the uncertainty flicker over the other man's face for a moment as he considered that proposition, and she shivered. Dear Lord, what if Rory hated his brother so much that he was willing to die if it meant that Nick died, too? But, to her relief, he finally shrugged.

''Put 'em away, boys. This fight's between me and my big brother.''

Amid muttering and shuffling, the rest of the gang did as ordered, until only Nick and Rory stood facing each other, pistols still at the ready. A Mexican stand off, she had heard such situations crudely called. Both were armed and ready, with neither having the advantage. But even as she wondered what could break that impasse, Jess heard a tearful voice from near the makeshift corral.

''Jessamine? Dear God, Jessamine, is that you?''

A waiflike figure dressed in outsized men's clothing hurried toward her, the sun glinting on the girlish braid bouncing about her shoulder. For a moment, Jess didn't recognize her. With a surprised gasp, she replied, ''A-Aunt Maude?''

''It's I,'' the woman agreed with a tearful laugh as the two embraced.

Her aunt's slight frame felt far thinner than it had just a few days before. To Jess's relief, however, the older woman appeared to have survived her physical ordeal relatively unscathed. Whether she survived it emotionally would be another question . . . but one to which a grateful Jess swiftly had her answer.

Though Maude appeared quite sensibly frightened by her situation, her light brown eyes did not reflect the cowed despair of a hostage barely clinging to sanity. Instead, her gaze was the determined look of a woman who had endured as best she could, and who had no intention of giving up now.

"Well, ain't that touching," Rory's chilly voice interrupted them. "Looks like we got us another family reunion on our hands. Too bad it's gonna be a real short one."

"Those women are riding out of here, Rory, and I'm going with them. You can keep the bank's money, and we'll call it even . . . and no one has to get hurt."

"But I want to hurt you, Nick, or are you just too damn stupid to understand that?" He gave a brittle little laugh. "I want to kill you, of course, but I want to make you suffer awhile first. So, hell, maybe I should just let you watch me shoot one of those lady friends of yours."

Abruptly, he swung his pistol about so that it was pointing directly at Jess. She froze where she stood, her hand tightly clenching Maude's as she looked into Rory's cold blue eyes.

Memories of that terrible day flashed through her mind. *Arbin, reaching for his derringer. Her unheeded cry of warning. A masked man with cold blue eyes gazing at her, smiling as he pulled the trigger.* But now, after all this time, she finally knew that killer's true identity.

Recognition hit him at the same time, and he broke into a grin. "Well, I'll be damned," he softly said, "we've done this before, ain't we?"

She nodded. "It was in Brimstone," she managed in a choked little voice. "You robbed my bank, and you murdered my husband in cold blood."

"You were married to that spindly-lookin' fellow? Shit,

guess there ain't no accountin' for taste.'' He shook his head and deliberately cocked his pistol. ''Looks like you'll be seein' him again, real soon. Say your prayers, lady. It's all over, 'cept for the buryin' part.''

Chapter Twenty-six

"All right, Rory, you win."

With those swift words, Nick let the hammer of his pistol fall back into place and lowered the weapon, praying that he didn't sound as desperate as he was. Christ, but he'd made an arrogant, terrible mistake in thinking he could somehow redeem his brother. No matter how persuasive Nick might be, Rory would never agree to emigrate, would never let Nick bargain for amnesty for him. Unwillingly, he recalled Doc's comments to him that night in Tombstone.

You're like two dark angels . . . one long since fallen from heaven and happily carving out his new niche in hell, and the other still clinging to those pearly gates, too stubborn to admit that the Almighty has booted him out of Paradise.

Doc was right. Rory had carved out his niche in hell, and he was enjoying his stay. The only question remaining, then, was how to get himself and the two women out of Dead Squaw Canyon alive.

He crouched and set his Colt on the ground, then raised his hands and moved a few steps from it. "You don't need to shoot her,'' he went on in a reasonable tone. ''You've got me . . . and that's what you really want, isn't it?''

''Hell, I don't know, Nick.''

He walked over to Jess and abruptly seized her by the arm, dragging her into his embrace. Lightly, he brushed the pistol along her cheek, then turned his gaze from her back to him. ''I ain't never shot a husband and wife before. It'd do wonders for my reputation . . . and it would be worth it, just to see the look on your face.''

''Shoot her, then, if you must. It's no skin off my nose.''

He lowered his hands and crossed his arms over his chest. His outer air was one of supreme unconcern, camouflaging the inner terror that clawed at his gut at the sight of that gun pressed to Jess's face.

''But just remember, Rory, she's not the one you hate. She's not the example you could never live up to . . . the one who was always better than you. That was me, Nick.'' He paused and gave his brother a cool, deliberate smile. ''And while I'm still breathing, you'll always be second best.''

Another spasm of rage flickered over his brother's face and, for a heart-stopping instant, Nick feared he had pushed him too far. Then, with a pungent oath, Rory uncocked his pistol and shoved Jess away, then strode toward him.

''You're fucking wrong, Nick. I'm not second best. You are,'' he said, and slammed the revolver against the side of Nick's face.

It was the second time in one morning that he'd suffered such a blow. This time, however, he'd been expecting it and turned his head, so that he'd not suffered the full force of the impact. Even so, it dropped him to his knees, and he felt warm blood pour from his nose. *Let him do it,* he told himself as he tried desperately not to be swallowed by the pain and the blackness that gripped him. *Don't fight him—not yet.*

But barely had he regained his feet when Rory landed a second blow . . . this one a kick squarely to his gut. He dropped to his knees again, gasping for air and clutching his burning ribs, willing himself to remain where he was. Had the fight been with anyone else, he would have rolled out of reach at the very first blow and then responded in kind.

But Rory was out for blood, for pain . . . and until he got that satisfaction, there'd be no dealing with him. With the odds stacked against Nick and the two women the way they were, dealing was the only way out of this situation. And if it took getting beaten to a pulp to reach that point, then he'd just have to let Rory do his worst.

He could hear Rory laughing now, and he braced himself for yet another blow. He wasn't disappointed. "What's the matter, big brother, not feeling too well?" Nick heard him say, just before the younger man kicked him again, and then again.

That last impact knocked him flat, while the fire in his ribs erupted into a blaze that shot down his entire side. Vaguely, he was aware that he was rolling on the ground, clutching his gut and trying not to retch with the pain. But so long as Rory's attention was fixed on him, Jess and Maude were safe. For the moment that was all that mattered.

"Hell, don't just let him lie there," he heard Rory shout. "Stand him up, so I can hit him again!"

A pair of arms on either side of him abruptly dragged him upright. Still gasping for breath, he squinted through the eye that hadn't begun to swell shut yet, trying to focus on his brother's face. The familiar features, so like his own, were twisted into an almost unrecognizable mask of fury. *Two dark angels.*

But Rory was a brutal killer. Nick's job was to uphold the law, though how he accomplished that task was up to him. And while he had bent the rules, had cheated and lied with nary a qualm of conscience, he had killed only twice in his life . . . and, both times, in self-defense. Doc was wrong. He wasn't like Rory, a soulless murderer.

But when the time was right, he could summon that same sort of rage, and use it against his brother.

And now was the right time, Nick judged. As Rory lunged at him again, he gathered his strength and lashed out with a booted foot, catching Rory squarely in the chest. The blow knocked the younger man backwards, this small triumph gaining Nick another few seconds of respite and giving him a renewed surge of strength.

But, all too quickly, Rory shook off the blow. "Bastard," he choked out as he staggered toward Nick again. Nick kicked him a second time, this time connecting with his chin. Rory's head snapped back, and he went sprawling.

"All right, that's enough!"

The booming voice came from the blond outlaw, Len. "Let 'im go," he commanded the pair who held Nick pinned between them. The two abruptly complied, and Nick toppled face down into the dirt. Through the roaring in his ears, he could hear Rory cursing and Len arguing. Finally, he was aware of being carried . . . and, after that, nothing for a long while.

When he opened his eyes again, the roaring in his head had dulled to an irritating ringing, and Jess's pale face was floating above him. He blinked a few times, and the image sharpened as much as it could, given that one eye was swollen shut. Now he could see that Jess was kneeling beside him, rather than drifting about like some spectral creature.

"Thank God you're awake," she breathed, sitting back with a sigh. She dampened a cloth in a basin of water, folded it, and then laid it across one side of his face. "How do you feel now?"

"Like that damn paint of yours kicked me."

Still, the cool cloth brought a few moments' relief to the tight, swollen flesh where Rory's pistol had connected, while the feather-light brush of Jess's fingers against his forehead assured him that her concern for his well-being had been genuine . . . as well it should be. If he was going to get himself beaten half to death for a woman, she better damn well appreciate his efforts.

Aloud, however, he merely asked, "How long have I been out?"

"Maybe a quarter of an hour. Len had a couple of the men bring you over here, and he and your brother have been arguing ever since."

Over here proved to be at the base of the outermost cliff, a short distance away from the main camp. Nick dragged himself into a sitting position, noting that the front of his white shirt was liberally spotted with his own blood. The minor effort of moving, meanwhile, sent a renewed wave of pain through his head and ribs, though it was more bearable now than it had been before. Gingerly, he peeled off the damp compress and probed at his battered face, wincing as he brushed against the bruised skin.

"Bad?" he asked, already knowing the answer.

Jess bit her lip and nodded, handing him a tin cup of water. "You've got a black eye, one whole side of your face is swollen, and I think your nose is broken. And I wouldn't be surprised if you had a cracked rib or two, as well. Aunt Maude and I cleaned the worst of the blood and dirt off you, but you still look pretty frightful."

"Believe me, it hurts even worse than it looks."

He greedily drank down the water, savoring every drop of it like the finest wine. Then, with a sigh, he squinted in the direction of the main camp, trying for a glimpse of his brother. "So, what are Len and Rory arguing about . . . other than whether to kill all of us, or just me?"

"Actually, Mr. Hancock—or should I say, Mr. Devilbiss?—I think that is exactly what they are discussing."

The soft words came from Maude McCray, who had settled on the ground beside her niece. Dressed in men's clothes, with her braid of blond hair carelessly draped over one shoulder, she appeared almost as young as Jess now, so that he would hardly have recognized her as the same gracious matron who had served him supper that night in Brimstone.

He gave her a crooked smile. "You can call me Nick. And I'm very glad to see you alive and well, Miss McCray."

"Maude," she corrected with a fleeting smile of her own. "And thank you for what you did out there earlier. I truly fear your brother would have killed Jessamine, had you not turned his anger back on you. You bought us all a bit of time . . . but how much, I do not know."

"I guess we'll soon find out."

He now saw that Rory and Len had risen from where they had been crouched around the fire. The former was doffing his shirt and striding off toward one of the shacks, while the latter was headed in their direction.

"What about this Len?" he asked with a nod toward that approaching figure. "He seems a reasonable enough fellow. Do you think we can trust him?"

"Oh, yes!" A flush rose in her pale cheeks, and she added, "That is, I am certain that you can. He is the one who kept me safe from . . . from the other men, and he has already told me that he would help me escape."

"Then I'm sure you're right."

Privately, however, he was prepared to withhold judgment awhile longer. From what Maude had said—as well as what she hadn't—he suspected that her assessment of the man's character might be clouded by gratitude . . . or, worse, infatuation. It was a situation he had stumbled across before, the enforced proximity of a man and a woman in a stressful situation generating emotions that might or might not prove to be genuine.

So what about you and Jess? his inner voice wanted to know. *Were last night's strong emotions merely a result of too much time spent together too quickly?*

He had no time to speculate on those uncomfortable questions, however, for Len had reached them. The blond outlaw hunkered down beside them, his expression grim as he focused on Nick.

"So you're Rory's brother," he said without preamble. "Can't say as I'm pleased to meet you, under the circumstances."

"I'm not too thrilled with the situation, either," Nick wryly admitted, "but thanks for putting a stop to the fight."

"I only did it because you're his brother, an' I don't like seein' family fight like that. If you'd just been some lawman, or a bounty hunter, I would've let him do what he wanted with you."

Len paused and shook his head. "Hell, you were either plumb stupid or real smart, the way you just let him go at you. I've seen what Rory can do to a man when he gets all riled up, an' it ain't pretty. But if you'd fought him back too soon, all three of you would've been dead now."

"Believe me, I've battled it out with my brother a time or two over the years, and I know how he thinks . . . most of the time." Nick hesitated, then squarely met the other man's gaze. "I understand you were over there with Rory just now, helping to decide our fate. Do you mind telling us what the verdict was?"

"Rory and me, we cut a deal. Maude and her niece can go. You can't."

"No!" Jess protested, grasping at Nick's hand. "We're not leaving him behind. His brother will kill him if we do."

"Better just him than all three of you. Sorry, ma'am, but that's the best I can do." With those words, Len rose, towering over all of them. "I'll get the horses an' gear together, an' then we'll head out. Rory said I could lead you as far as the main trail."

The outlaw glanced over at Maude, and Nick sensed an unspoken communication between them. Len would be going with Maude, he realized . . . not just as far as the trail, but wherever the two of them had already made plans to go. But surely Maude would insist that her niece be taken somewhere safe first. Perhaps San Luis, where certainly Jess could find an escort the remainder of the way back to Brimstone.

But as Len strode back to where the horses were corralled and Maude began gathering their gear, Jess edged closer, clutching his hand more tightly.

"I'm not leaving you behind, Nick," she said, and he saw the fear in her whiskey-dark eyes as she gazed up at him. "It's my fault things worked out this way. If I had just trusted you awhile longer, and let you go after him your way—"

"Jess, sweetheart, you're breaking my fingers," he said with a crooked smile, gently loosening her grip on him. "And it's not your fault, believe me. If I'd gone in on my own, chances are that things would have worked out the same way. At least, now, I'll know that you and Maude are safe, no matter what happens to me."

"Blast it all, Nick, don't you understand?" A single tear trickled down her cheek and she impatiently dashed it away. "I don't want you to die. I-I love you."

Her words sent a painful knife of regret into his heart. He sighed and drew her into his embrace, wincing just a little as she nestled into his bruised ribs. "I love you, too, sweetheart," he murmured against her hair, realizing in surprise and relief that it was true, "which is why there's no damn way I'm going to let you stay behind with me. You're riding out of here with Len and Maude, and that's final."

"But, Nick, I've still got my derringer in my boot. None of them thought to search me." She pulled back just a little, so that he could see the determined look on her pale face. "If we could just somehow take your brother unawares, maybe there's some way to bargain for your life, too."

When she had moved, he had felt the familiar crinkle of paper in his breast pocket . . . Whitey Kilroy's map. Now, he gave a thoughtful frown as he reminded himself just what was on that page. Hell, it was worth a try. The worst that could happen was that Rory wouldn't believe him, and he'd be as dead as if he hadn't made the attempt.

"Maybe you're right, Jess. I might be able to give Rory something that he wants even more than me."

He glanced up to see that his brother had left the shack he'd earlier retreated to, and was now stalking in their direction. "Quick, Jess," he muttered, "slide your derringer into my right boot, and then help me stand up."

By the time Rory reached them, Nick was on his feet again, with Jess supporting him on one side. Maude had finished with the gear and joined him on the other side, letting him rest one hand on her thin shoulder for balance.

As casually as he could, given his battered state, Nick met his brother's contemptuous gaze. "Back for another round?"

"You look like shit, big brother. What's the matter, lose a fight?"

"You don't look so great yourself, Rory," Nick returned, taking cool satisfaction in the younger man's split lip and the purple bruise along his jaw, as well as the fresh shirt he wore. The garment he previously had been wearing must have been bloodied in the course of their fight, just as Nick's own shirt had been. "Maybe next time you'll duck when someone tries to kick you in the face."

"There ain't gonna be no next time, big brother . . . not for you."

Rory's chill blue gaze flickered from him to Jess, and his cut lips twisted into the semblance of a smile. "You know, I'm kinda sorry I made that deal with Len. This little lady of yours is real fetchin'. She and me, we could have a real good time together after you're gone. Hell, she's gotta be a better lay than her lovin' old auntie."

Nick heard Maude's anguished little gasp and felt her stiffen beside him, so that he knew those words were not just a cruel jibe. A wave of cold anger washed over him, and it took every effort not to launch himself at the younger man again. *Later,* he grimly told himself. *Don't let him distract you.*

Jess's reaction, however, was immediate and to the point. "You lay a hand on me or my aunt," she lashed out, "and I swear I'll kill you."

"She's fiery, ain't she? Hell, big brother, you must've had a devil of a time keepin' her satisfied." He gave Jess a lewd wink, then turned his attention back to Nick. "But Len's my friend, and I made him a promise, so I guess I've got to let them go. But you're stayin' here so we can talk about old times."

"Let's cut to the chase, Rory," Nick countered. "You want me dead, and I'd just as soon stay alive, so why don't you and I make a bargain of our own. You let me walk out of here with Jess and Maude, and I'll tell you where to find the loot from the Brimstone bank robbery."

"Shit, did that little slap to the head make you plumb stupid? Me and the boys, we've already divvied up that loot."

"From the second robbery, maybe, but not from the first."

He watched in satisfaction as a heated look of angry confusion twisted his brother's features. "What the hell are you talking about?" he blustered. "We already took care of that—"

"You didn't take care of shit, Rory," Nick coolly cut him short. "Before you could divide it up, one of your gang members—a man by the name of Whitey Kilroy—ran off with all that money. You tried tracking him down, but you never did find him. All that effort—robbing the bank, shooting down an innocent man in cold blood—and you ended up with nothing to show for it . . . except for being wanted, dead or alive. That's always been your problem, little brother," he softly finished. "You're just no damn good with the details."

"Fuck the details . . . how the hell do you know all this?" Rory demanded with a sneer. "What, did Whitey's ghost pay you a visit?"

"Close. You see, I just happened to stumble across Whitey down in Texas, while I was looking for information about you.

"It seems Whitey had a bit of bad luck while he was fleeing with all that stolen money," he went on when Rory made a rude sound of disbelief. "His horse stumbled and broke a couple of legs, so Whitey was left on foot. And since all the money was too heavy for him to haul by himself, he ended up burying it in the desert, planning to come back for it later, when you would have figured he was long since dead."

Nick wryly shook his head. "Unfortunately for him, he contracted a case of lead poisoning in Dallas before he was able to do that. But, fortunately for me, I found him lying in an alley, his belly tied up in rags . . . and willing to trade me the location of the stolen money for a bottle of whiskey, just before he died."

Chapter Twenty-seven

Jess waited for what seemed an eternity before Rory gave a snort of disgust. "You're lyin', big brother," the younger man declared, though she heard a note of uncertainty in his voice. "Whitey didn't tell you shit."

"Believe what you want. Hell, if you don't want to deal, maybe Len or another of your boys might be interested in what I have to say," Nick replied in a casual tone.

But Jess knew with a pang the effort it must be costing him to maintain that easy air. He was leaning on her more heavily now than he had been just a few moments ago, and the palm resting on her shoulder was damp with sweat despite the coolness of the day. Surreptitiously, she reached her arm around his waist to steady him. Maude noted her action and followed suit.

Nick lightly squeezed Jess's shoulder, indicating his thanks, but his attention remained fixed on Rory. By now, the younger man was pacing angrily before them, cursing under his breath.

Finally, Rory halted and shot Nick a furious look. "So, let's say I do believe you. What's your deal?"

"It's simple. You and I'll ride out to where the money is buried. We'll dig it up, you'll keep it all, and I'll ride off."

"Simple," Rory agreed with another sneer, "but for all I know, this is just a trick to get me out in the desert alone, so you can try to kill me."

"You've got my pistol and my rifle," Nick pointed out, "and I'm a bit too stove up right now to be any good at fighting. If it turns out I'm lying, then you can kill me, just like you planned from the very start. Either way, we'll never have to see each other again . . . but my way, you'll wind up a hell of a lot richer."

Jess waited in an agony of suspense while the younger man considered the offer. Whether Nick truly knew the location of the stolen money she did not know, nor was it important. What mattered was that this might be his last chance to walk out of this situation alive.

Finally, Rory nodded, his blue eyes aglint with animal cunning. "We'll look for your buried loot, big brother, but it won't just be you and me. I'll take along Len and Bobby, and you can take these two ladies, just so the numbers will be even."

"All right," Nick agreed, "but I'll need a horse. Do you think one of your men can round up that roan of mine we left on the trail?"

Rory gave a disparaging laugh as he turned back toward the camp. "So you're the one who belongs to that plug Matthew brought back with him. Hell, we find that money, big brother, and maybe I'll give you a couple of dollars so you can buy yourself a real horse."

It wasn't until Rory was out of earshot that she heard Nick's own weary curse. "Shit," he softly groaned out, his grip on her shoulder abruptly tightening. "I thought he was never going to shut up."

"Sit down a minute," Maude urged, grasping his arm.

Jess, feeling him begin to sag against her, nodded her agreement and glanced over at her aunt. "I'll help him. You bring us some more water."

Nick needed no further coaxing but slid to his knees, leaning back against a convenient boulder and shutting his one good eye. Already, the bruises on his face had begun to darken, and guilt swept her as she reminded herself that she had contributed to his injuries. She brushed aside the dark hair that tumbled across his brow and lightly kissed him, knowing it was not apology enough for what she'd done, but praying he could forgive her that one thing.

By now, Maude had returned with Len's canteen and swiftly knelt beside them. Jess splashed a bit more water into the tin cup, then lightly shook Nick's arm. "Here, drink this," she told him, steadying his shaking hands as he swallowed it down.

Maude waited until he had sagged back against the boulder, then rose once more. "I'll see if Len needs any help," she softly said, "and you just keep an eye on your young man."

Her young man.

A bittersweet little pang pierced her heart as she gazed at his battered, bloodied features. Had it been just a few days ago that she had protested when Lily and Reba had referred to him as *her* Mr. Hancock? And now that she would give anything to make that claim, she was in danger of losing him.

Once Maude was out of earshot, however, she put aside that worry and asked the question that had been nagging at her. "Nick, I need to talk to you," she softly urged. "Do you truly know where the money is, or is this just a ploy, as Rory suspects?"

"I know where Whitey told me it was," he replied, opening his good eye and flashing her the faintest of grins. "Hell, he was delirious with fever from his bullet wound, so who knows if he was remembering correctly. But his map corresponds surprisingly well with yours, so I think there's a possibility the loot is really buried at that spot. I just wish Rory hadn't insisted on you and Maude riding along . . . though I think we might be able to count Len as one of ours."

"What do you mean?" she asked in some confusion.

He lifted a wry brow. "I mean that Len is sweet on your aunt, and he'll do whatever he can to help her. Don't look so surprised, Jess," he added as she gaped at him, not quite believing that her spinster aunt could have an outlaw beau. ''She's a handsome, charming woman, and a rough fellow like Len was bound to find her irresistible. Let's just be grateful that he did.''

''All right,'' she agreed faintly, doing her best to come to immediate terms with this surprising turn of events. After all, who was she to begrudge Maude whatever happiness she had found as a result of her ordeal? Then, pursuing the original subject again, she asked, ''How long it will take us to get to wherever the money is buried?''

''An hour, maybe two . . . depending on how many times I fall off that plug of mine.''

That last was said in an ironic tone, but Jess bit her lip, aware that he wasn't joking. He was in no shape to make such a ride, she was certain, but what other choice did they have? As if reading her thoughts, he added, ''Don't worry, sweetheart. I'll be fine. But it'll be to our advantage to let Rory think I'm worse off than I really am.''

It would be, of course, and she nodded her agreement. ''I'd better find Old Pete,'' she told him and reluctantly rose. ''Will you be all right here alone for a few minutes?''

''I told you not to worry about me,'' he said before he shut his good eye. ''Oh, and Jess . . .''

''Yes, Nick?'' she asked in concern.

His eyes still shut, he softly said, ''Just so you know, I happen to find you irresistible, too.''

The words warmed her more than any flowery declaration of love could have done. Just as suddenly, she saw the contrast between Nick's confrontation with Rory this day and Arbin's attempt to stand up to the gang that long-ago morning in the bank. Each man had made the choice to fight of his own free will, she knew. But now, it was all too clear that the reasons behind both choices were strikingly different.

Arbin had reached for his pistol out of a need to feel important. He had needed to prove—to the town, to the outlaws, to her—that he would not tolerate what he perceived as a threat to his livelihood. Nick, on the other hand, was risking his life to save her life, and Maude's.

With the realization, her guilt over Arbin's death seemed to slip from her shoulders, like a coat she had outgrown. To be sure, she would always regret the fact that he had died far too soon, but no longer would she feel that she had driven him to that end.

She hurried over to the makeshift corral, where Old Pete had wandered to visit with his fellow equines. The roan was tied there, as well, with the black hound sprawled as sentry at her hooves. He sat up at Jess's approach, his pink tongue lolling in greeting.

"Good boy," she whispered in the dog's direction as she untied the roan and then climbed atop her paint.

Leading the mare, she trotted back to where she had left Nick. Maude and the outlaws were waiting there atop four coal black steeds, and Jess saw that a pair of long shovels were lashed behind the saddle of one of those beasts.

By now, Nick had dragged himself to his feet again. He reached for the roan's reins, his breath catching once as he swung into the saddle. His battered Stetson still hung from the saddle horn. He settled the hat atop his head, brim tilted low over his forehead so that his eyes were shadowed. Rory wore his hat the same way, Jess noticed, wondering if he had always done so . . . and wondering if it was in deliberate or unconscious imitation of his older brother.

Rory, who had smirked as he watched Nick stiffly mount up, abruptly frowned. "Hell, we're not going anywhere yet," he declared. "Not until someone checks out those saddlebags. Bobby, Len, make sure they ain't got no weapons stashed. He's already pulled that trick on me once today."

A leering Bobby leaned over and reached for Jess's carpet-bag. "Let's see what kind of purty things you got in here," he said with a dry little chuckle as he opened its clasps and began pawing through it.

She managed not to cringe as he displayed her undergarments to a grinning Rory, and then began digging through her saddlebags. Len searched through Nick's gear with silent efficiently, pausing only once.

"What the hell," he muttered as Jess glimpsed what appeared to be an old photograph in his beefy hand.

Curious, she leaned closer. Barely had she made out the stiff, unsmiling figures of two young, dark-haired boys—one taller than the other, but both almost identical in appearance—than Rory had snatched the photograph from his grasp.

"It ain't nothing," he snarled and ripped the image from top to bottom, then flung it away. The two ragged bits of pasteboard fluttered on the light breeze for a short distance and then tumbled to the dirt. "Now, let's ride!"

With a clatter of hooves and a jingle of tack, they started back toward the canyon entrance. Jess caught a final glimpse of the torn photograph beneath Old Pete's hooves, and her heart ached for Nick's sake. Though she knew Rory Devilbiss only as a vicious killer, his older brother would surely remember him as a laughing, innocent boy. She could only guess the pain he felt, knowing Rory had brutalized and murdered countless people in his rage to prove himself the equal of his older brother.

They reached the tunnel entrance a few moments later. Rory halted them long enough to give a few terse instructions to the two sentries Jess recognized from earlier that morning. Then, with a whoop, he spurred his horse into that narrow passage.

The rest of them followed, pounding single file through the rocks at a pace far more furious than Jess ever would have dared on her own. She clung to the saddle horn and gave the paint his head, shutting her eyes as the sound of two dozen clashing hooves thundered around her like a steam engine run amuck. Yet, almost as swiftly as they had entered that twilit passage, they emerged on the other side.

Jess gasped in relief and grabbed the reins again, slowing Old Pete to a more rational pace. Rory, meanwhile, appeared revitalized by their suicidal ride. With another whoop and a grin, he turned to Nick. "All right, big brother, which way now?"

"Back down this short trail, and then west."

They rode two abreast again, Rory and Nick at the lead, with Len and Maude bringing up the rear. Beside her, Bobby leered and leaned a bit closer. "Hell, you got me all excited, lookin' at those lacy duds o' yours," he said in a mock whisper. "Mebbe later you can try 'em on for me."

Jess bit her lip against the cutting retort she longed to make and kept her attention firmly fixed on Nick's back ahead of her. Doubtless the wild ride through the rock passage had done little good for his battered head and ribs; still, he seemed to be riding without any obvious difficulty.

But by the time they negotiated the steep downward trail and had started off in a westerly direction, Nick had begun to slump in his saddle. Likely, it was just an act, she tried to reassure herself, recalling what he had said about letting Rory think he was worse off than he was. But what if it wasn't?

They traveled at a swift pace for more than an hour, stopping twice for Nick to compare his coordinates with the same sheet of paper that Jess recognized from the day before. Once, Rory commented on the black hound, which silently was keeping apace of them, while still remaining a safe distance from these unknown riders.

"Hell, big brother, that's the meanest lookin' dog I've ever seen," he observed with interest. "Is he yours?"

"He belongs to the roan," was Nick's curt reply, drawing a chuckle from Rory and an answering dry laugh from Bobby.

"Well, if that don't beat all," the latter exclaimed. "I ain't never seen a horse that had its very own dog."

Soon after, they were out of the foothills and back in the high desert again, the greenery once more giving way to tan scrub. It was almost noon when Nick finally called a halt near a small wash where four man-sized boulders were arranged, sentinel-like, in pairs on either side of it.

"The loot is buried there," he said as he reined in the roan and pointed to a spot beyond the closest pair of boulders. "If you want it, help yourself."

"Hell, no, that's your job." Rory glanced back at Bobby

and gave him a chill grin. "Untie one of those shovels and give it to Nick. He's got some diggin' to do."

Nick grimly shook his head. "Forget it, Rory. Our deal was that I take you to where Whitey left the loot. I didn't say anything about digging it up for you."

"Shit, big brother, just how stupid do you think I am? You think I'm gonna let you point me to a spot and then just let you ride off?" Casually, he drew his pistol and crossed his arms over his saddle horn, the weapon dangling from his fingers. "Our deal says you don't leave until we find the loot. I don't know about you, but I can wait all day."

"Well, I damn sure can't."

The disgusted words came from Len, who had dismounted and was yanking the shovel from Bobby's grip. "I ain't gonna stand around while you two squabble like a pair of pups. Let's dig up the damn money and be done with it."

Shovel in hand, he stalked off in the direction of the wash. With a muttered oath, Nick stiffly dismounted and grabbed up the second shovel, then headed in the same direction.

Rory chuckled softly and flashed an amused look in Jess and Maude's direction. "I don't know about you ladies, but I'm gonna find myself a shady spot and watch the fun. C'mon, Bobby."

Reholstering his pistol, he reached into his saddlebag and drew out a half-full whiskey bottle. Tucking it under one arm, he swung from his saddle with lazy grace and settled himself in the shadow of the closest of the four boulders. A grinning Bobby followed suit, hunkering beside him and tilting down the brim of his greasy hat, as if in preparation for an extended nap.

Maude pursed her lips, and then sighed. "We may as well get comfortable, too," she murmured and dismounted, as well.

Jess nodded, though comfort was the last thing on her mind. She climbed from her own saddle, then led Old Pete and the roan to a spot not far from the two men, keeping both sets of reins firmly in her grasp. She had no idea what Nick planned to do but, whatever it was, she intended to be ready for it.

Nick and Len had begun digging in the tan ground at a spot midway between the first two boulders, their labor producing a rhythmic clink of metal upon stone. She saw with dismay that, after they had dislodged a first few easy shovelfuls of sand, they had barely made a dent in the rocky soil below. However had the infamous Whitey managed? Had he scrabbled in the dirt for hours, with nothing but desperation and his bare hands to move the earth, or had he had the foresight to bring a shovel of his own?

Or had he perhaps found a discarded tool—a shovel, or maybe a pickax—from someone who had been there before him, someone who'd been in search of Spanish gold?

Tantalizing as that last possibility was, she mentally stored it away to be examined later and kept a careful watch on the two men. By now, the sun was high overhead, and a dry heat had long since replaced the morning's chill. Len, who had already discarded his hat, now paused to strip off his vest and shirt before resuming his labors once more. His muscular physique, hairless and tanned, was impressive enough that Jess allowed herself a rather guilty if appreciative look before glancing over at her aunt.

Maude was doing a fair share of appreciating, herself, Jess noticed in chagrin. Doubtless, Nick had been right in his assessment of the situation between the unlikely pair. She could only hope for Maude's sake that the man had plans to reform his outlaw life; otherwise, there could be no hope for anything more lasting between them.

But her own concern, for the moment, was with Nick. By now, the pair of them had managed a hole knee-deep and several feet in diameter. He paused to follow suit with Len, stripping down to boots and trousers. Though leaner than the younger man, he was equally muscular; even so, Jess could tell that his injuries had taken a toll on his stamina.

His flesh was pale beneath his bruises, and the ragged red scar running down his right shoulder blade gleamed dully. Worse, he was sweating far more profusely than could be attributable to the dry heat. When he paused a second time to dash the sweat from his eyes, she handed over the reins to Maude and unsnagged his canteen from his saddle horn, then carried it over to him.

He wordlessly took it and downed several swallows, then handed it over to Len. The blond outlaw, with a murmured, "Thank you, ma'am," took a drink before passing the container back to Nick. The latter restoppered the canteen, then tossed it to her with a weary hint of a smile. "Thanks, sweetheart," he murmured, then added even more softly, "and be ready for anything."

She merely nodded by way of reply, all too aware that Rory was watching them. Indeed, as she started back toward Maude, the outlaw waved his bottle—which was far emptier than it earlier had been—and called out to her in a jeering tone, "Hey, little lady, why don't you come sit over here with me? I'm a hell of a lot better company than my big brother."

She ignored the taunt and made her way back to where Maude and the horses were waiting. Less easily, however, could she ignore his next words.

"Hey, Jess-a-mine," he called, parodying her aunt's soft drawling of her name, "I bet you always wondered about that big ol' scar on Nick's shoulder. I bet he never told you that I tried one time to kill him. I would've done it, too, 'cept for that damn interfering dentist."

"My God," Maude murmured in a trembling voice beside her, "I was right. He truly is evil, through and through."

"It's only words, now," Jess softly replied, though the callous sentiment had sent an unsettling shiver through her, as well. "Maybe if we're lucky, he'll drink himself into a stupor."

But the combination of the whiskey and his own tortured thoughts seemed only to agitate the outlaw. Taking another swallow from the bottle, he got to his feet and began making his unsteady way toward them.

"C'mon, Jess-a-mine," he crooned with a leer. "Let's you an' me go have some fun, while big brother digs up my money for me. Hell, if you're good enough, I might even buy you something nice with all my newfound wealth."

"Stay away from her, Rory."

The warning came from Nick, who had planted his shovel into the mound of newly dug sand and rock to fix his brother with a cold look. Len halted in mid-shovel and straightened, as well, a frown darkening his broad face. Rory glanced from one man to the other, and then grinned.

"Shit, big brother," he replied, plucking his pistol from its holster again and waving it, "just how the hell do you think you're gonna stop me? I've got this, an' all you got is that big mouth of yours."

"There ain't no call for this, Rory," Len spoke up. "A deal's a deal, an' she wasn't no part of it." He dropped his own shovel and took a step forward.

The other outlaw's grin faded. "Damn it, Len, you're startin' to piss me off. Hell, I'm startin' to think you're on their side, instead of mine," he choked out, leveling his pistol and moving closer.

Len shook his shaggy head. "Rory, we've been friends for two years. I ain't turnin' against you . . . I just think you're wrong about this."

"Wrong? I'll show you who the fuck is wrong," he snarled, and pulled the trigger.

Chapter Twenty-eight

The pistol boomed, the sound echoed by Maude's scream and Jess's ragged gasp. Len staggered, blood splashing down his side, and then tumbled forward.

Barely had he hit the ground than Rory fired again, that bullet raising a puff of sand inches from the prone man's head. Then, with a whoop, Rory spun in a drunken circle, the pistol swinging wildly with him.

"Don't move, anyone," he shouted, spittle flying from his lips as he finally staggered to a halt, "or I swear to God, I'll shoot every last one of you!"

After her first scream of fright, Maude had started blindly toward the fallen Len. Jess broke free of her own momentary paralysis and made a swift grab for her aunt, knowing with chill certainty that Rory wouldn't hesitate to shoot her, too. Maude made a soft sound of protest but promptly sagged in her grasp, her burst of fear-driven energy depleted. Jess clutched her more tightly, feeling the other woman shivering . . . and aware that she was shaking herself. Then, fearfully, she glanced over at Nick.

He had dropped to his knees beside the wounded man within

an instant of the shooting. For a terrifying instant she thought he had been hit, as well, until she realized it was Len's blood on his hands. He didn't look her way, however. An unreadable mask had slid over his battered face, and his gaze locked upon his brother.

Rory was the first to break that silent battle of wills, glancing wildly over his shoulder at Bobby. "What about you?" he demanded in the same frantic voice. "Are you turning against me, too?"

"Hell, no," the older man declared, his pockmarked face pale as he took a few steps back. "I ain't like Len. I'm with you, Rory, same as always."

"Then get over there and start diggin'. I want my fuckin' money, damn it!"

Bobby scrambled to comply, grabbing up Len's dropped shovel and frantically spraying dirt. Rory promptly seemed to forget him, however, as he wiped his mouth on the back of one hand and took a shuddering breath. For her part, Jess didn't dare to breathe as she huddled with her aunt and prayed he would forget their presence.

After a moment he shook his head, like a man waking from a bad dream. He gazed down at Len, who remained unmoving, and gave a strange little laugh. "Hell, look what you made me do," he choked out. "I didn't want to shoot you, but you just plumb pissed me off."

Then he focused his gaze on Nick, who slowly stood again. "That should have been you, big brother," he said in the same strangled voice. "Maybe it will be, if you don't hurry and find my money."

"I'll find your money," Nick assured him in a deadly soft voice. "But why don't you let me move Len out of the way, first."

Before Rory could reply, however, Bobby's shovel thudded against something that did not clang like rock. "Hell, Rory," the outlaw spoke up in amazement, "I think I done found it."

"Well, hellfire, don't stop now. Keep diggin'!"

Bobby tossed aside the shovel and started digging with his

hands, while Rory squatted beside the hole and urged him on. Nick, meanwhile, had rolled Len onto his back and dragged him to one side. He grabbed up his own already bloodied shirt to staunch the blood that still was dripping from Len's side.

"Let me go to him," Maude whispered in a broken voice.

She pulled free of Jess's grasp and rushed over to the wounded man. Nick moved aside for her, then shot Jess a grim look over the top of Maude's bowed head. *Not good,* he mouthed, and Jess felt her heart clench in remembered pain. Her aunt had been there for her, on that terrible day when Arbin had died. She would be there in the same way for Maude now, if need be . . . but, for Maude's sake, she prayed that need would not come to pass.

Then a whoop from Rory pulled her attention from her aunt. "Hell . . . fire! My big brother was right for once in his damn life!"

With those shouted words, the outlaw shoved his pistol back into his holster and grabbed one end of the filthy saddlebag that Bobby had uncovered. Still kneeling, he fumbled with the buckles and straps that held its flap, cursing in his haste. With a final yank, he pulled the flap free and dug out a fist full of green cash.

"We did it!" he exclaimed, flinging the money heavenward. "Hell, and there's plenty more where this came—"

He broke off abruptly as Nick, who had slipped up behind him, pressed the derringer to his ear and cocked the hammer. "Now, big brother," he said with an uncertain laugh as Nick reached with his free hand for the younger man's pistol, "what the hell are you doin'? We-we had us a deal."

"The deal's off, Rory."

With those cool words, Nick trained his brother's pistol on its owner. He never took his eyes from the younger man as he nodded to Jess, who had watched the entire drama in an agony of suspense. Now she hurried to his side, her hands shaking only a little as she retrieved the derringer that she had lent him.

With a murmured, "Keep it handy, sweetheart," he eased

the two of them a few steps back, then addressed his brother again.

"I'm bringing you in on charges of murder, attempted murder, kidnapping, bank robbery . . . and whatever the hell else anyone can think of. So why don't you drop the saddlebag and turn around, with your hands in the air?"

The younger man spat a few pungent oaths but complied, his face twisted in fury. "Goddamn it, Bobby!" he shouted to the other outlaw, who was crouched in the hole and staring up at him in bemusement. "I told you to search their saddlebags. Where in the hell did he get that pepperbox?"

"Details, little brother," Nick softly said, a humorless smile twisting his bruised mouth. "You just never were any damn good with details, were you? Jess had the derringer in her boot all along."

What Rory would have replied, Jess never heard, for the sudden rumble of approaching riders stopped him short. His blue eyes glinted in chilly amusement as his gaze flickered from Nick to the horizon behind him. "Someone's comin', big brother," he announced. "Question is, are they your boys, or mine?"

"Who is it, Jess?" Nick asked softly, not turning.

Jess glanced nervously behind her to see half a dozen silhouetted riders swiftly moving across the uneven terrain. "I-I can't tell . . . not yet."

Indeed, from that distance she could not even distinguish if they rode the trademark black steeds of Rory's men. If so, then it could be the rest of the Black Horse Gang, she thought, clutching her derringer more tightly. But then again, it might also be the long-awaited posse from Tombstone.

The seconds seemed to drag out intolerably as she strained to catch some more telling glimpse that might identify these unknown men. Then, as the riders negotiated the next rise, sunlight glinted off a shiny object pinned to one man's vest.

"A badge," she gasped out. "Nick, I think it's a posse."

Now she could make out a bay and a gray among the horses. The man riding the latter steed was hatless, and the only one of the riders not dressed in black. His pale hair shone as brightly as his mount's silver coat beneath the afternoon sun.

At the sight, an excited laugh bubbled in her throat. "My God, I think one of those riders is Doc," she exclaimed, glancing back at Nick.

His attention still fixed on Rory, he raised a wry brow. "If so, then I'll lay odds the other fellows with him are the Earps. Looks like you two boys are about to ride home with a passle of famous lawmen . . . so, Bobby, why don't you toss that pistol of yours out and climb up here with me and my brother."

"Hell, I ain't lettin' those murderin' Earps get near me!"

With greater fleetness than Jess would have guessed his stocky frame could possess, he scrambled from the shallow pit and barreled into Rory. The impact thrust the younger man into Nick's arms, their combined weight toppling them into Jess, as well. She hit the rocky ground with a graceless thud that knocked the breath from her and sent her derringer flying.

By the time she rolled into a sitting position and scrambled for the fallen weapon, Bobby already had grabbed hold of his mount and swung into his saddle. With a shout, he stabbed his heels into the stallion's side and took off at a gallop, so that he was out of her range long before she raised her derringer. But even as she debated going after him, two of the approaching riders immediately broke off from the others and started in pursuit of the fleeing outlaw.

Forgetting that man, she swung about to look for Nick. What she saw made her gasp in despair. The two men were rolling along the edge of the shallow wash, struggling for control of the pistol. She raised up to her knees and lifted her own pistol, desperately trying to focus on Rory. At this range, she knew, even an expert marksman would have difficulty hitting a target with such an inadequate weapon. As inexperienced a shot as *she* was, she could not possibly fire at Rory without risking hitting his brother.

Then she heard the sickening thud of a fist against flesh, and heard Nick groan. Rory broke free of their deadly embrace and struggled to his feet, the pistol in his grasp now as Nick clutched at his battered ribs. Panting, the younger man threw a desperate look at the approaching posse and then raised the Colt.

"They might get me, but not before I get you first," he choked out, cocking the hammer. "Say your prayers, big brother. It's all over now, 'cept for the burying part."

In the space of a heartbeat, Jess had pointed her derringer squarely at the outlaw, but even as she pulled back the hammer she knew that she was too late. She might hit Rory, even kill him . . . but Nick would already be dead.

Yet in the same instant as that anguished knowledge flashed through her mind, a baying black blur launched itself between Nick and Rory. The revolver discharged with a roar, and the baying broke off on a high-pitched whine that ended when the black hound landed with a thud at Rory's feet, then crawled off a few feet and lay still.

"Son of a bitch," she heard Rory say in amazement as he raised the pistol again, "that damned dog of yours tried to kill—"

Jess heard the deafening boom from behind her and saw Rory stagger, the pistol dropping from his hand. A splash of crimson exploded on his white shirt, and he clutched at his chest, a look of amazement on his face. Slowly, he sagged to his knees and then tumbled to his side.

"Rory," she heard Nick choke out as he dragged himself upright and started toward him. Never glancing Jess's way, he knelt beside his brother and gently lifted his head. The younger man's eyes were open, Jess could see, but blood bubbled in a bright stream from his lips.

"Damn it, Rory, it didn't have to end like this," Nick said softly, and the note of desperation in his voice tore at Jess's heart. Choking back a sob—though it was for Nick and not his brother that she wanted to weep—Jess sank back onto her heels and silently watched.

Rory struggled a moment to breathe, the wet sound of blood rasping through his lungs barely audible against the sound of approaching hooves. Then, with a final surge of strength, he grasped Nick's shirt with bloodied fingers and gave a burbling chuckle. "Go to . . . hell, big brother," he whispered. "I am."

Nick held his lifeless body for several minutes longer, not looking up even when the posse thundered up to the wash and six rifle-toting men dismounted, the luckless Bobby in tow. For herself, Jess stirred only when she heard booted footsteps beside her, and an elegant hand reached down to help her to her feet.

"Hello, Doc," she said, swiping away her tears and managing a smile as she looked up into his pale gaze. "Whatever are you doing here?"

"Well, my dear, that poker game with Big Al and Chinless Eddie turned a bit . . . unpleasant, shall we say," the gambler drawled in an ironic tone. "Someone mentioned something about cheating, and I fear there was a bit of gunplay."

At her dismayed gasp, he gave her a faint smile. "Oh, nothing fatal," he clarified, "but I decided it was in my best interest to leave San Luis. As I was headed back north, I ran into my friend Wyatt and his brothers. It seems that Sheriff Behan passed on the information you left him, and the boys were hot on the Black Horse Gang's trail. Do let me introduce you to them," he finished with a graceful gesture in the direction of the other riders.

Wyatt proved to be the tall and coldly handsome blond man with drooping mustaches who had left the group to station himself alongside Nick. With him was his older brother, Virgil. The latter was not so tall or handsome—and even more forbidding-looking, Jess privately thought—though it warmed her to see he had placed a comforting hand upon Nick's shoulder. The last Earp brother, Morgan—"though I believe there are still a couple more of their siblings wandering the countryside," Doc ironically observed—had a jolly look about him despite the gravity of the situation.

"And these other two fellows are Texas Jack and Frank Leslie," Doc finished the introductions, while those men murmured their greetings.

Jess acknowledged them with a polite nod, then turned back

to the gambler with a puzzled look. "But how did you know to find us here?"

"We had a conversation with a couple of fellows back at Dead Squaw Canyon," Morgan answered for him. "They were obliging enough to point us in the right direction, and when we heard shots, we figured we'd found the place."

"And in case you were worried," Doc smoothly added, "we left three very capable gentlemen behind to round up the rest of the gang. Our plan is to meet up again in San Luis by dusk, so we can avail ourselves of Marshal Chapel's jail cell for the night. I will, of course, make myself scarce for the night."

By now, Nick had risen, and the Earps were wrapping Rory's body in a blanket. "I'm afraid they will have to take him back to Tombstone," Doc murmured in her ear, "since he *was* wanted, dead or alive. However, I am certain he will receive a proper burial in that charming little acreage that the local wags refer to as Boot Hill."

Then, with a frown, he glanced about him and delicately asked, "Might I ask, what about your aunt . . ."

"Maude," she gasped out. Dear Lord, she had almost forgotten. "My aunt is just fine, but I'm afraid her friend may not be."

Jess swiftly made her way back to the spot where Maude was still kneeling beside Len's unmoving form. The older woman seemed oblivious to the fact of the posse's arrival, her attention fixed on the man before her. She still clung to his hand, stroking it, but Jess could tell from his still, slack face that the outlaw, Len, was dead.

With a sigh, Jess sank down beside her aunt and blinked back a few tears. Len, she could mourn, for he had seemed a man of courage despite his chosen life. And, if not for the way he had stepped in to protect her aunt, Maude might not now be alive.

"Do you know what the last thing that he said was?" she softly asked, and Jess shook her head. "He told me that he wasn't afraid to die, because then he would be with the angels, and they would all be me."

And then Jess truly cried . . . for Maude and for Len, for Arbin and for Nick, and even for Rory. So much happiness lost, so many lives gone astray, some lives cut far too short. As the tears continued to stream down her cheeks, she began to fear she might never stop crying.

And then a soft, warm tongue licked her face.

"The black hound," she gasped out, turning to see a familiar black muzzle peering at her. A slick patch of blood dampened the fur atop his head, but otherwise he appeared healthy enough.

Morgan Earp squatted beside her and grinned boyishly. "I found this fellow lying beneath a bush and thought he was dead," he explained. "When I went to pick him up, to give him a proper burial, he about took a bite outta me. I guess he must've been stunned by that bullet, but it looks like he's fine now."

"Thank you," Jess said with a tearful smile of her own. She wrapped her arms about the beast, and Morgan grinned even more broadly as he rose to rejoin the others.

"And, thank *you,*" she murmured in the hound's ear as she petted his silky black fur. For the dog had saved Nick's life, had taken the bullet meant for him . . . that she had seen with her own eyes. At least there had been one happy ending on this terrible day, she thought with a sigh.

She got to her feet and dropped a kiss atop Maude's bent head, then turned to the dog. "C'mon, boy," she softly said. "Let's go find Nick."

Chapter Twenty-nine

It was almost an hour later before the Earp posse prepared to ride off. The bodies of Len and Rory had been wrapped in blankets and tied across the saddles of their respective mounts. Bobby was lashed to his horse, as well, his expression one of bleak resignation. Chances were, Wyatt had informed her, the outlaw would be executed for his crimes, given that he also had shot a man in Phoenix six months earlier. The rest of the Black Horse Gang would receive varying sentences . . . some prison, some death by hanging.

As for the money stolen during the most recent robbery, Wyatt told her, his men had recovered the greatest portion of it as they raided Dead Squaw Canyon. The loot from the first holdup Morgan and one of the other posse members finished digging out, so that the remaining saddlebags were being loaded on the horses, as well. The fact that the loot from both robberies had been recovered would certainly please the Territorial Bankers Association, Jess thought with a sigh, although she no longer cared.

The riders had all mounted, Maude included. She had softly if firmly informed the Earps of her intention to accompany

Len's body back to Tombstone, where she herself would see to his proper burial. "I would take him back to Brimstone with me," she had explained to Jess, "but people there wouldn't understand. This will be . . . better. And I will be able to visit him sometimes."

To Jess's relief, the men had made no protest over Maude's riding with them on what would be a rugged and rather gruesome trip. No doubt they had been impressed by her obvious bravery in enduring what she had these past several days. That, Jess suspected, or else Doc had insisted she be allowed to accompany the posse.

"We'll meet you in Tombstone for the burials," Jess now told her as Maude bent from her black gelding for a final hug. "And make certain that Marshal Chapel has a telegram sent to Father just as soon as you reach San Luis."

"Don't worry, Jessamine," she replied with a determined smile. "I am quite capable of handling such matters. And do take good care of your Mr. Hancock . . . that is, Nick."

"I will," Jess assured her with equal determination, and then turned to Doc. "I don't quite know how to thank you for all your help."

"No thanks are necessary, my dear Jess," he drawled and kissed her hand in a courtly manner. "But I do have a small gift for you." He reached into his waistcoat and plucked forth two small pieces of pasteboard. "I found this photograph in Dead Squaw Canyon, while we were rounding up miscreants."

She realized with a gasp that what he held in either hand were the two halves of that long-ago image of the two Devilbiss brothers, the very image that Rory had destroyed and then tossed away. Save for the brutal tear down its center, however, the photograph seemed to have survived its subsequent treatment remarkably well.

With a shrug, the gambler fitted the pieces together, so that the two boys once again stood side by side, gazing out into the world with identical expressions of solemn dignity. "I believe the photograph could be restored with a little effort. Perhaps you might like to save it, and return it to Nick one day."

''I would.''

She carefully wrapped the pieces in her handkerchief, then gave the gambler an impulsive hug. His pale cheeks flushed, but he merely drawled in return, ''An unnecessarily extravagant gesture, my dear. A handshake would have sufficed.''

''Good-bye, Doc. I shall see you in Tombstone . . . and do try to keep well.''

With a final tearful smile and wave for her aunt, Jess waited with the black hound at her side while the posse rode off. She watched until they disappeared over the final rise before making her way back to Nick.

He was seated against the same boulder where Rory earlier had crouched, watching him and Len dig up the Brimstone loot. His hat was tilted low over his eyes, and the same whiskey bottle from which his brother had drunk now dangled from his own fingertips. The resemblance between the two was unsettling, and she suppressed a shiver as she settled down beside him.

''You should have gone with your aunt and the others,'' he told her, not bothering to glance her way. ''I won't be good company.''

''I know.''

The black hound curled up beside her, and she idly scratched his silky ears. The three of them sat silent for a long moment, so that the only sound was the soft skittering of sand from the hole that still gaped nearby. Morgan had not bothered to refill it for, as he had explained to Jess with a grin, someone else might come along who needed a place to bury his treasure.

Nick was the first to break the silence. He took a long swig from the bottle, then said with a sigh, ''I thought I could save him, Jess, but I couldn't.''

''I know that, too.'' The bleakness in his words sent a knife through her heart, for she knew too well the pain and guilt he was feeling. Carefully picking her words, she added, ''Some people don't want to be saved. I think Rory was one of those people.''

"Hell, maybe you're right." He took another drink, and then asked, "How was Maude doing when she left?"

"Holding her own. She intends to see that Len has a proper burial, so I told her we'd meet her back in Tombstone."

Silence stretched between them again, and for so long that Jess wondered if he had heard her. Finally, he said, "I'll take you that far, Jess, but I won't be staying. The first stage out, I'm headed back to Kansas City."

"I see."

But she didn't see . . . not at all. A cold, sick feeling swept her, and she bit her lip lest she cry out a protest. Hadn't he said he loved her? How could he just leave her, then, after all that had happened between them?

Aloud, however, she only said, "I'll get the horses ready. We'd better start out now, if we want to make camp before dark."

Nick spoke perhaps a dozen words to her from the moment they rode out until they stopped at dusk. They shared a silent supper, and when it was finished Nick merely stared into the fire. Once or twice Jess tried to begin a conversation with him, but when he answered only in monosyllables, or not at all, she finally lapsed into silence herself.

He's injured, and he's grieving, she reminded herself, trying not to give in to her own pain and loneliness as she finally curled up in her blankets, the black hound at her feet. And, lest she forget, he had made her no promises save that he would safely bring back her aunt, which he had done. While their lovemaking had been special, it had been an emotion of the moment . . . true for as long as it had lasted, but no more permanent than sand skipping across the desert. She should be glad of what she'd had, she sternly told herself, rather than cry for what could not be.

She woke during the night to feel a warm, heavy form curled up against her back, and for a joyful moment she thought Nick had settled down to sleep with her. Then she realized it was the black hound stretched out beside her, that Nick lay in his own blankets on the opposite side of the fire, and she forgot her own stern warning against weeping.

Nick slept well past dawn the next morning. Jess sipped at her coffee and was content to watch him sleep, reminding herself that he had suffered a beating to the body as well as to the soul, and that he needed time to heal. When he finally awoke, he seemed a bit more recovered physically, though the same bleakness clung to him as had the night before.

Another day passed, and another night . . . both little different from the day and night before. Once, Nick scooped up the black hound and draped him over the roan's neck, and the dog happily rode with him for the rest of that afternoon. And by noon of the third day, they were approaching Tombstone.

The familiar brash jumble of buildings scattered in the foothills should have proved a welcome sight. For Jess, however, it was a bleak reminder that her time with Nick almost was at an end.

The first stage out, he had said.

Out of her life forever, was what he had meant.

Their first stop was to check in with Sheriff Behan. The natty lawman listened with interest to their tale of the Black Horse Gang's capture, and he confirmed that the Earp posse had not yet returned.

"The logistics of transporting so many prisoners at a time," he had explained with a shrug. But from the terse message he had received from Marshal Chapel via the Silver Pass telegraph office, it seemed that Wyatt anticipated arriving that night.

With that established, Nick again procured them rooms in the Occidental . . . a single one for himself, and a larger suite that Jess would share with her aunt. Barely had he seen her safely to her room, however, than he departed to make arrangements for Rory's burial. Left to her own devices, Jess sent her father a wire confirming that she and Maude were both safe, and that they would be returning to Brimstone as soon as possible. That accomplished, she paid a visit to Old Pete and the black hound, safely ensconced in a stall at the O.K. Corral.

It was well after dusk when the Earp posse rode back into

town, their arrival heralded with shouts and cheers. By then, Nick had returned to the hotel, where Jess had been waiting ever since she had finished her own wanderings. He joined her and several other guests—some merely curious, others downright enthusiastic—who had gathered on the sidewalk outside the Occidental to view the posse's return.

The score of horses bearing the lawmen and their captives trotted past the gathered citizens like a cavalry unit at review, the rhythmic clomping of hooves rattling windows all along Allen Street. A few enterprising young men, caught up in the spectacle, even snatched up lanterns and rode before the group, lighting their way.

"Looks like a damned Fourth of July parade," Nick muttered with a shake of his head.

And, indeed, the spectacle did rival a holiday celebration, Jess silently agreed. By now the Earps had doffed their hats and were waving them . . . Morgan grinning wildly as he did so, while Virgil and Wyatt maintained a sober aspect. The Black Horse Gang, however, could make no such similar acknowledgment to the catcalls that followed them, tied as each man was to his saddle. Still, their identical black steeds added a look of precision to their motley ranks.

But the parade had a somber air about it, as well. Behind the riders rumbled a short wagon driven by Texas Jack and bearing a grim cargo . . . two plain pine coffins, securely lashed side by side to its bed. Beside that wagon, on her own black gelding, rode Maude, chin held high and blond hair rippling loose around her shoulders.

"Who's that pretty lady?"

The awed exclamation came from a curly-haired boy of nine or ten years standing next to Jess, and had been whispered to the younger girl beside him. That pigtailed miss wrinkled her brow, considering the question. Then her brow cleared, and she smiled triumphantly up at the youth.

"Don't you know, brother?" she replied in a clear, sweet voice. "Why, that's their guardian angel."

Just then, Maude glanced in their direction and caught sight of Jess. She gave her the faintest of sad smiles and then continued riding on as the posse made its slow way toward the jailhouse. The young siblings, meanwhile, exchanged delighted grins.

"The angel smiled at us," the boy declared with an important air to anyone nearby who would listen.

Of the fastidious gambler, Doc Holliday, Jess saw no sign.

For his part, Nick stood silently beside Jess, the dark bruises on his face barely visible in the shadow. His profile was stark, emotionless . . . his blue gaze shuttered. She knew that anyone else, seeing him, would think him untouched by the sight of his brother's coffin slowly wheeling past him . . . would think he had not heard the jeers that had greeted this symbol of violent death. But Jess had watched his hand clutch the post between them, his fingers biting into the wood, and she knew better.

Only when the posse finally turned the far street corner did he speak again. "Show's over," he declared in a flat voice. "I suppose we should collect Maude and make certain that all the arrangements are in place."

They followed the same route as the posse had taken, Nick purposefully striding through the clusters of onlookers who had begun to disperse. Jess followed at a more moderate pace, certain he would not notice even had she been on his heels. She sighed, wishing she dared take his hand in a show of comfort, even while knowing he would not appreciate the gesture.

It was outside the jailhouse, where Sheriff Behan and the Earps were dispositioning their prisoners, that Jess and Maude made their second tearful reunion. The other men were unloading the coffins, and Maude nodded sadly in that direction.

"It was your friend, Dr. Holliday, who persuaded a cartwright in San Luis to build them that same night," she told Jess, when Nick had stepped aside to speak with Wyatt and his brothers. "And he was so very kind to me the entire journey. Unfortunately, he had business in Charleston and could not continue on to Tombstone with us, but he asked me to send you his best regards.''

Jess smiled, recalling what Doc had told her about his reputation in Charleston. Doubtless the gambler had known that Maude would make his good deed known, and he had deemed it preferable to take himself off to less friendly climes, rather than own up to such a charitable gesture.

They made an early night of it, and the chill dawn found the three of them gathered on the stark slope of Tombstone Cemetery, Maude wearing a borrowed black gown. A mournful breeze skittered through the cluster of wooden markers, stirring the sandy soil and echoing the morning cries of a sleepy bird. There, amid the rock and cacti, a portly minister read a brief service, before two burly youths lowered both coffins into the twin graves dug the day before.

''Amen,'' Maude murmured as the minister closed his Bible. While he spared a few words of professional condolence for Nick, she turned to Jess.

''I hope Len will be happy here, in this lonely place, with only strangers for company,'' she said with a worried little frown. ''I didn't know where to find his family, or even if he had any left. Why, I didn't even know his full name to have put on the marker until I asked Marshal Earp.''

''Knowing you cared is what will make him happy,'' Jess replied, clasping her aunt's slim, gloved hand. ''And I suspect he would prefer to be buried out here, with the wind and the sand, rather than in some stuffy churchyard.''

''Ah, well, I'm sure you're right.''

She sighed a little, then glanced over at Nick, and Jess followed her gaze. He stood several paces from them, alone now that the minister had departed. He was dressed once again in his bank examiner's garb, the sober dark gray suit befitting the grim occasion. But Jess had noticed with a pang that he had neither bowed his head nor murmured a prayer during the impersonal little service. Instead, he had focused on the unadorned box that held his brother's body, his expression the same emotionless mask that he had worn ever since Rory's death.

Maude sighed again. "It must hurt you to see him grieve that way," she murmured, "holding it all inside him, and not allowing a single word of comfort. But I can feel his heart crying, Jess, though I don't know who he mourns the more deeply . . . his brother or himself."

Jess shook her head, thinking of the torn photograph, carefully wrapped and tucked into her saddlebag. Though the sepia image never would be quite the same, it could be made whole again. Another photograph, damaged differently, might never be fully restored. It was the same way with people, she knew . . . but only with time could one know who had been adequately mended.

She walked over to Nick and touched his arm. "Maude and I are going back to the hotel now," she softly told him. "Will you come back with us?"

"I think I'll stay here for a while longer," he replied, his words holding a familiar flat note as he stared at his brother's grave. Then he glanced over at her, a spark of warmth momentarily lit his cool gaze. "Thank you for being here, Jess. I know it was mostly for Maude's sake, but thank you, anyhow."

She bit her lip and nodded, not trusting herself to speak. But by then Nick had turned back to the half-filled grave, so that it didn't matter. She hesitated a moment longer, then rejoined Maude for the ride back into town.

Jess saw Nick one last time that day, as he was boarding the afternoon stage for Phoenix. She might have missed his departure had she not heard the loud rumble of wheels and the driver's shouts just outside the Occidental, and hurried from her room. Nick was standing beside the stage, handing up his gear to the man on top. He turned at her approach, and an emotion she could not quite identify momentarily breached his cool mask.

"I thought it might be better if I just left," he said without preamble as she halted before him.

She met his cool blue gaze with a heated look of her own. "Tell me the truth, Nick. Better, or simply easier?"

"All right, easier."

His jaw tightened on the blunt words, but before she could answer, he took her arm and led her a short distance from the stage.

"And here are some more truths, Jess. I didn't know what to say, or what you wanted to hear. For a while, back in those mountains, I thought I knew the answers, but now things have changed."

"Blast it all, Nick, things always change," she retorted, deliberately taking refuge in anger lest she give way to tears. "Sometimes it's for the better, and other times it's for the worse. But you can't use change as an excuse for turning your back on life."

"I'm not turning my back on you, Jess, not in the way that you think." He hesitated, and she saw him weighing his words. "You see, I've been thinking about what you said the day that Rory died, about how some people just don't want to be saved. But I think, with my brother, it was something more."

A flicker of pain dislodged his cool mask and darkened his eyes. "I think that Rory got lost somewhere . . . so lost that he couldn't find his way back. And I see that happening to myself, Jess. I'm getting lost, too."

"Oh, Nick," she said with a soft sigh, her anger crumbling about her. "If you're afraid that you'll turn out like your brother—"

"I'm more like him than you know, Jess." He shook his head in disgust. "Hell, I spend half my time tracking down criminals and the other half pretending to be one. And the line between pretending and being gets thinner all the time."

A shout from the stage driver abruptly cut him short. "Load up, folks! We're headin' out!" he called as the team began an impatient stomping.

Nick loosened his grip on her and took a step back. "It's easier this way, Jess . . . but it's better, too. Go back to Brimstone. You've got family and friends who need you."

But what about what I need? her heart cried out. Aloud, she simply said, "You're right, Nick. They need me, and you don't. Good-bye, then . . . and good luck."

He gave her a searching look, and for a moment she thought he might kiss her one last time. Instead, he turned and strode back toward the stage, climbing inside just as the driver was preparing to shut the door. With a sharp crack of reins and a clatter of hooves, the coach jerked forward and began rumbling down the dusty street.

"Life is heartbreaking, is it not?" a familiar voice drawled behind her.

Blinking back her tears, Jess turned to see Doc standing behind her. A faint smile played upon his pale lips as he turned his gaze from the departing stagecoach back to her. "Unfortunately, we seem to bring most of that heartbreak upon ourselves."

"Do you think I'll ever see him again, Doc?" she asked in a small voice.

Holliday raised a wry brow. "My dear Jess, I am the last person one should consult in matters of the heart. Of course, if you are asking me my professional opinion, as a gambler of some skill—"

"Blast it all, Doc, you are impossible," she muttered, though a small smile now tugged at her lips. "Very well, speaking as a betting man, what sort of odds would you give me?"

"Well, my dear, speaking as a betting man . . . I would say wager everything that you have."

Chapter Thirty

"Really, Jess, that black hound of yours is becoming quite impossible," Lily exclaimed as she shooed the beast in question out the bank door for the second time that afternoon. "He always manages to lie down right in the middle of where people are walking, and every time I make a cup of tea he stares at me until I pour him his own saucerful. And now that he's made friends with that stray brown puppy he found under the steps at the mercantile—"

"Now, Lily." Jess looked up from her ledger and favored the younger woman with a wry smile. "You know that Jake is entitled to special treatment."

For Lily was well familiar with the story of the black hound and how he had rescued Jess—lost in the Huachuca foothills—and then had intercepted the bullet from Rory's pistol that had been meant for Nick. The account she'd heard of what had happened in those days following the bank robbery had come directly from Jess. The rest of Brimstone's citizenry had learned the story from the pages of the *Brimstone Fire*.

BROTHER PURSUES BROTHER, one headline had exclaimed in Ted Markham's dramatic retelling of events. The story, which had spread to two pages, had been rife with the ironic fact that the vicious outlaw and the Pinkerton agent who had confronted him had, indeed, been brothers. Nick had been characterized as "the mild-mannered bank official turned dashing detective," whose brilliant undercover investigations had led to the Black Horse Gang's downfall. Jess was the determined lady banker who had vowed to see justice done, while Maude had been depicted as a valiant victim who had endured her trials like a true lady.

In true newsman style, Ted had made certain to tell the smaller stories, as well. Len, he had canonized as an outlaw-hero, who zealously had protected the kidnapped Maude's virtue and then selflessly given his life for her. Even the black hound, Jake, had received a figurative pat for his bravery in saving Nick's life. At Maude's insistence, however, the newspaper editor had refrained from simply demonizing the Black Horse Gang's leader. Instead, he had reminded his readers that Rory Devilbiss had once been a promising young man—just like many of their own friends and neighbors—who had embraced a violent lifestyle, with tragic results.

No one knew, not even Reba or Lily, what had happened between Jess and Nick that one wonderful night, though Jess suspected that both women were shrewd enough to surmise the truth of the matter.

Now the younger woman heaved a dramatic sigh. "Oh, yes, how could I forget that the dog is a hero? And tonight is his night for steak at Uncle Chan's, so we must close a few minutes early."

"Actually, I wanted to talk to you about that."

Checking the watch pinned to her shirtwaist, Jess closed her ledger and slipped it back under the counter with the others. "I meant to tell you, the citizens' board has a meeting this afternoon . . . in half an hour, to be exact. We're interviewing a candidate for the marshal's job."

The position had been open ever since Marshal Crenshaw's murder by the Black Horse Gang almost six weeks earlier. Deputy Bowser, still recovering from his own wound suffered in that shoot-out, had declined the promotion at the behest of Mrs. Bowser. Thus, Ted Markham had been appointed chairman of a five-person committee of local businesspeople, including Jess. Their job was to search out other potential candidates for the post, and then hire the best of them.

"From what Reba says, this man is far more qualified than the other two we already have interviewed," Jess explained. "All I know about him is that he should have arrived in town on the afternoon stage. With luck, perhaps we'll have a new marshal by tomorrow."

"That's wonderful," Lily exclaimed, even as her tiger-gold eyes narrowed in sudden suspicion. "But what does that have to do with Uncle Chan's?"

"Since I'll be tied up in that meeting for some time, I was rather hoping you might walk Jake over there for me."

"I was wrong, Jess. It's not the dog that's impossible, it's you!" Lily threw up her hands in mock defeat, a grin quivering on her lips. "Very well, go to your meeting, and Jake and I will have a pleasant supper together in the alley behind the restaurant."

Smiling as well, Jess left her behind the teller window and headed back to her office. A few small tasks still remained from that afternoon—among them, finishing the paperwork that authorized the procurement of a time lock for the bank vault—but she elected to put them off until morning. Instead, she picked up the most recent letter from Maude that had arrived just that day.

Within days of their return to Brimstone, her aunt had packed a small trunk and announced she would take the next stage to Phoenix, and then proceed on to California. "Some people might say I am running away," she had told Jess with a small smile, "but I'm not. I'm running *to* something . . . a future, a different sort of life. I may come back in a few weeks, or I may never return to Brimstone, but that doesn't mean I am abandoning you and my brother. I just need some time to myself."

Harvey, quite surprisingly, had been in favor of his sister's plans. "Hell, Jess," he privately had told her, "the woman has spent her life doing for everyone else . . . her mother, first, and then you, and now me. It's about damn time she gathered the gumption to leave us all on our own."

Now, with a smile, Jess opened the letter and reread its final few lines.

But although San Francisco is a beautiful city, alive and full of energy, some nights I find myself longing for the desert again. Strange; I never thought to say such a thing, but it is true. In those few days and nights I spent there, I learned more about myself than in all the many preceding years, so that I cannot regret living through that terrible ordeal. What I do regret is that Len is not here now to share my happiness. He was a good man, Jess, despite the violent life he led, and I truly think that he and I could have found contentment together. I wonder, have you heard from Nick yet?

Jess sighed, for she hadn't. At first she had clung to Doc Holliday's prediction that she would see Nick again, certain the gambler was right. But as the days turned to weeks, and no telegram or letter arrived, she began to have her doubts. Maybe Nick hadn't run away, as Maude would have put it, but wherever he was going, his destination did not seem to include Brimstone.

She picked up the letter once more.

I must close now, dear Jess, but I will write again soon. Send my love to Harvey. I am happy to hear that he is doing so much better. Perhaps the tea that Lily has been plying him with truly does have magical powers. And maybe someday soon, when he recovers more of his strength, the two of you might take a little holiday and come visit me here.

Love always,
Maude

Jess sighed again as she refolded the letter and tucked it back into its envelope. She understood the older woman's need to absent herself from the familiar for a while. Had she not had the bank to occupy herself, Jess might have been tempted to accompany Maude there. As it was, she would definitely consider that last invitation.

A tentative knock at her open door brought a halt to her musings. "Jess," she heard Lily say in an odd little voice, "there is a gentleman here to see you.'

"Don't you remember, Lily, I'm about to leave for my meeting. I'm afraid I'll have to speak with him another time." Jess wondered a little at the other woman's sudden timidity. Usually, when Jess was unavailable, Lily did not hesitate to inform a customer of that fact.

This time, however, Lily did hesitate, glancing over her shoulder at the unseen man before turning back to Jess. "He's quite insistent upon seeing you," she went on. "I really do believe you should speak with him."

"Blast it all," Jess murmured, glancing at her watch again to see that she still had a quarter hour remaining to her. The committee held its meetings in a back room of the Lucky Nugget, courtesy of Reba, who was one of the five. The walk to the saloon was a short one, so Jess was not yet late.

With a shake of her head, she conceded. "Very well, I can give this gentleman of yours exactly two minutes of my time, but that is all I can spare. Send him in."

Lily disappeared out the door again, and Jess got to her feet, brushing a wrinkle from the skirt of her sensible bottle-green poplin. She would conduct this meeting standing, so that it would be easier to urge the man out of her office again once his allotted two minutes were up. Then the sound of a footstep at the door made her glance up again, and she suddenly wished she had remained in her chair.

Nick Devilbiss was every bit as handsome as she remembered him . . . even more so, for the bruises on his face had disappeared in the intervening weeks. His nose boasted a new ridge to it, however, for its recent break had not healed cleanly. As if in compensation for that perceived flaw—though, in Jess's opinion, it only added character to his face—he now sported dashing mustaches that emphasized his well-formed lips.

Those lips were not smiling, though; rather, they were drawn in serious lines that befitted his sober city garb. He had exchanged his battered Stetson for a new one . . . black, this time, just like his suit. Balancing that hat in one hand, he merely said, "Hello, Jess. Do you mind if I sit down?"

"Please do."

To her relief, her tone sounded quite calm and businesslike. She resumed her own seat with rather more haste than she had intended, however, given that her legs seemed suddenly incapable of supporting her. With luck, he had not noticed that momentary weakness, nor the fact that her heart abruptly was ticking more loudly than the Regulator outside her door.

"This is something of a surprise," she went on in monumental understatement, maintaining her cool air with an effort. "Shall I assume you are here at the behest of Mr. Pinkerton and the Territorial Bankers Association? If so, you will be happy to know that I have drafted that letter to Mr. Sargent's company, and that our new time lock should be here in a matter of weeks."

"I'm glad to hear that, Jess . . . but I don't work for the Pinkerton Agency anymore." He gave a faint smile at her sound of surprise and went on. "I know you're too polite to ask so, no, they didn't fire me. I left of my own accord."

"I see." An odd little suspicion niggled at her, but she kept her tone even as she asked, "So what are you doing here, then?"

"I heard Brimstone was looking for a marshal. Since I needed a job, I decided to apply for the position."

"I see."

Vaguely, she was aware that she was repeating herself, and that her reply was anything but brilliant . . . but for the moment she was incapable of much more. *He came back,* one side of her brain proclaimed in wonderment.

He needs a job, the other half rationally countered. *Don't read anything more into it than that.*

She summoned a bland smile of her own and rose from her chair. "If that is the case, Nick, then we had both better make haste. You have an appointment to keep with the citizens' committee, and I just so happen to be one of those citizens. But don't worry; I promise to remain quite impartial when it comes to voting whether or not you get the job."

"I'm sure you will, Jess," he said and stood, as well. A hint of emotion flickered in his blue eyes now, but all he said was, "Perhaps we should make our way separately to the Lucky Nugget, just so no one reads any unintended favoritism into your actions."

"I quite agree. Do go on ahead, and I will follow in a few minutes."

She waited until she was quite certain that he had left the bank before she sank back against her chair and shut her eyes. Certainly, this was not how she had pictured a reunion between them to unfold, with the dryness of a business meeting. At a very minimum, he would have kissed her . . . and, preferably, he should have fallen to his knees and begged her forgiveness for leaving as he had. Either scenario should have concluded with his making passionate love to her in her bedroom atop that yellow coverlet that she truly must replace.

"Jess, are you insane?" Lily exclaimed from the doorway, wringing her hands and practically hopping from foot to foot. "He's back, and all you're doing is sitting there. For goodness sake, go after him."

"Don't worry, Lily," she wearily said, opening her eyes again. "I'll be seeing him in a few minutes. He happens to be the applicant for marshal that we're about to meet."

"Why, that's wonderful . . . isn't it?"

"I'm sure he'd make an excellent marshal, if that's what you're asking."

Lily stamped her foot impatiently. "That's not what I'm asking, Jess, and you know it. You've been mooning about ever since you came back to Brimstone—"

"I have not!"

"—and I know it's because of him. And don't tell me he came all the way back to this little town in the middle of nowhere just because he wants to be marshal here. He came back for you, Jess."

"Well, he certainly took his time about doing so," Jess retorted with a sniff, though a tendril of hope began to unfurl in her breast. With as much dignity as she could muster, she rose and straightened the sleeves of her green poplin. "The interview commences in a few minutes, so I'd best be going. Don't forget to take Jake to your uncle Chan's."

"I won't . . . that is, *if* you promise to be very partial and favorable when it comes time to vote whether or not to hire him. And maybe you should have a cup of tea first?"

That last question a laughing Lily called after her as Jess hurried from the bank in the direction of the Lucky Nugget. Jess, however, was not amused. Dear Lord, if Nick became marshal, she would see him every day from here on out. Depending on how he now felt about her, such daily encounters could prove either quite blissful or else soul-searingly painful. For her own feelings for him had not changed . . . that much she had realized from the moment he set foot inside her office doorway.

She made her way through the crowded saloon to the back room, to find that the others were already gathered on chairs behind a makeshift table that was made up of a plank and two whiskey barrels. Nick, looking quite at ease, was settled in the hard-backed wooden chair that Jess knew was Reba's. Hastily taking her seat beside that woman, who favored her with a sly wink, she nodded to Ted.

"Very well, now that we are all here," that man began, "let me first thank you, Mr. Devilbiss, for coming. As you must guess, we are eager to fill this post, and your qualifications are quite impressive."

He glanced down at the sheaf of papers he held. "There's your army experience, a previous stint as a deputy marshal, your years with the Pinkerton Agency. And, of course, we are all quite familiar with your role in capturing the Black Horse Gang and recovering the money from both our bank robberies. And you have several impressive letters of recommendation here, including one from the governor of Kansas. But, as a formality, the committee likes to ask a few questions. So if we might start with Mr. Barris, owner of the local mercantile . . ."

Jess barely heard his questions, or those of Mr. Kirby, who followed. Instead, her thoughts swirled like dust caught up in a desert breeze as she recalled those few days she had spent alone with Nick. Did he recall that time with the same excruciating surge of joy as did she, or was he eager to pretend that nothing had ever happened between them save what had been printed in the pages of the *Fire?*

"All right, Reba, you're next," she heard Ted say. "I believe, Mr. Devilbiss, that you have met Miss Starr, proprietor of this fine establishment?"

"I have . . . and it was a distinct pleasure."

Grinning, Reba popped up from her seat and leaned across the table toward him, the flounces of her orange satin gown rustling. She pursed her lips, painted the same bright shade as her dress, and raised a perfectly drawn brow. "I've just got two questions. Question number one . . . you married, Mr. Devilbiss?"

"No, ma'am, I'm not."

"Question number two . . . do you want to be?"

"If that's an offer, Miss Starr, I'll give it serious consideration."

Reba grinned even more broadly. "Hell, I say hire the man," she exclaimed, reseating herself amid a flurry of satin and a ripple of laughter from the rest of the committee members, save Jess.

She had bit back a sound of dismay at the first blunt query, and blushed at the second. Reba, she knew, had guessed the extent of her relationship with Nick. Now she suspected that the older woman had had a hand in making certain that Jess was the only one of the committee who had not known in advance the identity of this current candidate.

When the amusement subsided, Ted looked her way. "All right, Jess, er, Mrs. Satterly. You're the final one up. Do you have any questions for Mr. Devilbiss, here?"

Questions?

Indeed, she had all sorts of questions for him, none of which were ones she cared to share with anyone else in the room. She was aware that Ted and the others were staring at her, waiting. Nick was waiting, too.

Gently clearing her throat, she eased back her chair and stood. "Yes, I do have one question, Mr. Devilbiss. With your obvious talents and experience, you could find a post anywhere. Why on earth would you want to settle in a place like Brimstone?"

"That's easy, Mrs. Satterly," he softly replied. "I'd want to settle in Brimstone because it's a town full of promise . . . big enough so that a man wouldn't feel crowded living here, but not so large that he could lose his way in its streets."

Abruptly, she recalled what Nick had said to her that day before he had boarded the stage. *I think that Rory got lost somewhere . . . so lost that he couldn't find his way back. And I see that happening to myself, Jess. I'm getting lost, too.* But maybe, just maybe, Nick wasn't lost anymore.

"Thank you, Mr. Devilbiss," she murmured as she resumed her chair. "I believe that was my only question."

Ted nodded and rose. "Very well, Mr. Devilbiss, I believe that concludes the interview. You and I already spoke at some length this afternoon about the specifics of the job, so I think that is covered, as well. So, if you would step outside for a moment, the committee will take a vote."

"Tell Bannister I said to pour you a whiskey on the house," Reba called after him as he started for the door. "Tell 'im I said to give you the good stuff."

"Thanks, Reba," Nick replied with a smile and a nod as he left the room and pulled the door shut behind him.

"Man's got my vote," Kirby promptly spoke up in a rusty voice. "We'd be fools to let 'im go."

"Hold on," Ted said, glancing at the rest of them. "Let's

do this according to procedure. Everyone in favor of hiring Mr. Devilbiss as our new marshal, raise your right hand.''

Reba flung her flabby arm enthusiastically skyward, followed by the others. Jess looked down at her own hands, which were tightly clasped in her lap. *Raise it, raise it, raise it,* her inner voice urged, though her fingers seemed suddenly glued together.

''Jess,'' she heard Ted say in a concerned tone, ''is there some reason you don't think we should hire the man? If so, you'd better speak up now, in case what you say might make someone else change his vote. Otherwise, I'm going to walk out there and offer him the job.''

''Hell, she's in favor, too,'' Reba exclaimed, snatching her hand and dragging it upwards. ''Aren't you, Jess?''

''Yes,'' she whispered, then repeated more loudly, ''Yes, I say hire him.''

''Then it's unanimous. Let's go congratulate our new marshal.''

As a group, the other four left the room and converged on Nick, where he leaned against the bar, an untouched whiskey before him. Jess followed more slowly, watching as they shook his hand and pounded him on the back. The commotion drew the other patrons over, while Reba called for a round on the house, which brought a resounding cheer.

''But not the good stuff, Bannister,'' she told the bartender, grinning. ''Rest of 'em gets the usual, same as always.''

While the whiskey freely flowed, Nick glanced up and caught Jess's eye. He murmured a few words to Ted beside him, then broke away from the buoyant group and started toward her.

''Ted tells me the vote was unanimous,'' he said as he halted before her. ''But I want to hear it from your own lips, Jess. Do you want me here?''

''I'm sure you'll make an excellent marshal,'' she politely replied, repeating what she had told Lily.

Nick frowned. ''You know that's not what I mean. I need to know if there's a chance that . . . if there's a chance for us to start all over again.'' His cool blue gaze darkened. ''As soon as that stage pulled out of Tombstone, I knew I'd made a mistake, but it took me a while longer to actually admit it. In the meantime, I headed back to Kansas City and quit the agency, then spent some time trying to decide what to do next. I made it back to Tombstone just a couple of days after that run-in that the Earps and Doc had with the Clanton boys.''

He was referring, Jess knew, to the brief if brutal gun battle that had occurred there two weeks earlier behind the O.K. livery . . . the same place she had stabled Old Pete. Several men had been killed, and rumor had it that the fight had been less than a fair one. In fact, the *Brimstone Fire* had published several letters and editorials defending combatants on both sides of the fatal conflict, so that Jess wondered if even the Earps actually knew the truth of what they had done.

''Did you get to talk to Doc?'' she asked anxiously, sidetracked for the moment from her own problems. ''I heard he'd been injured.''

''Actually, he was pretty damn lucky. The bullet just creased him, but an inch to the other side and he'd be dead.'' Nick shook his head. ''The judge is still hearing testimony, so it'll be a while longer before anyone knows if they'll stand trial for murder or be set free. In the meantime, Virgil was fired as marshal, and the other boys lost their jobs as deputy. That's how I heard that Brimstone was still looking for a new marshal, too.''

''We're not looking anymore,'' Jess softly reminded him. ''And to answer your question, yes, I think there is a chance for us to start again.''

''I see.'' Nick gave her that same slow smile that once would have turned her insides to jelly. This time, however, it seemed simply to set her entire body on fire. ''Then why don't we start with supper at Chan's? Lily told me that she and the black hound would be waiting for us there, and that she'd have one of her brothers bring your father around, as well.''

''All right,'' she agreed, rather breathlessly, ''but why don't we take the long way there? I'm sure they'll wait on us awhile.''

Nick's smile broadened into a grin, and he took her arm. ''Jess, sweetheart, I'm sure they will, too.''

Epilogue

Jess stood at the edge of the shallow wash, where the same four boulders still stood sentinel-like around it edges. The scene was different from when they last had been there, for the spring rains had brought with them a burst of bright flowers—pink, white, and scarlet—that brought the tan and gray desert landscape vividly to life. The hole where the stolen bank loot once had been buried had been partially filled by those same sporadic rains that had washed the dislodged soil back to where it had been. As for the fact that two men once had died violently there, no sign remained save a mournful silence.

She sighed and took Nick's hand. ''I'm sorry; this probably was a terrible idea, after all,'' she conceded, feeling a shadow of the past events sweep over her.

She had been the one who insisted they make the trip, curious to pursue the idea that had occurred to her the last time they had been there. Now had seemed an appropriate time, for the weather was pleasant, and Nick's duties as marshal had been light of late. Besides which, in another few months she would be in no shape to bounce about on horseback . . . though Nick did not yet know that. She smiled. She would tell him her news later that night, when they were camped in the same clearing where they first had made love.

Now he shook his head and gave her a faint smile, though shadows of the past momentarily had darkened his eyes, as well. "Hell, sweetheart, it's your honeymoon . . . belated as it might be. And besides, I think I needed to come back here, just this once."

He stood with her silently for several minutes, letting the soft breeze weave through them. Occasionally, the roan and Old Pete would nicker to each other and, once, Jake barked at a passing hare. Otherwise, the only sounds Jess heard were the remembered voices in her mind . . . Rory and Len and Bobby, the Earps and Doc. But those voices were fast growing faint, and she suspected that on another visit to this place, she might not hear them at all.

Finally, Nick turned to her again, and she saw in relief that the shadows in his eyes were now gone, so that his gaze was the clear blue of the Arizona sky above. "All right, Jess; you said you had something to show me," he said with an expectant smile. "What is it?"

"It might not be anything," she warned, reaching into her boot and withdrawing the parchment that originally had taken them to Dead Squaw Canyon. Smoothing it open, she traced a finger from that point on the map to another, the spot where an *X* marked the supposed location of the Spanish gold.

"I noticed it that day we were here, though that was hardly the appropriate time to mention it. You see, I had thought it odd that the outlaw, Whitey, just happened to have a shovel on him when he decided to bury all that money from the first robbery. I wondered if maybe he had found a shovel that someone else had left behind, maybe when they were searching for the lost gold, and that had given him the idea to dig."

"Not a bad deduction," Nick agreed with a wry lift of his brow. "You would have made a fair detective, I think. So, let's take a look at those landmarks."

A few moments consulting with the map and his compass brought him to the same conclusion that Jess instinctively had been drawn to . . . that this wash with its four standing boulders was the same place marked on the map by two pairs of castlelike images. The *X* in question was between the second pair of tall rocks.

"Too bad Whitey didn't bury the loot there, instead," Nick wryly observed as he untied the shovel Jess had brought from the back of Old Pete's saddle. "He would have saved me some digging."

As the first time, his progress through the rocky soil was slow. Once, Jess insisted on taking a turn, determinedly clearing a section herself before handing back the shovel to Nick. Within half an hour, they had made substantial progress, but no convenient chest of treasure had yet to appear.

Finally, Nick paused and swiped at his brow with a bandanna. He'd already taken off his vest and shirt, the badge pinned to the former glinting in the sun where Jess had neatly hung them from a nearby shrub. At the sight of his lean, well-muscled form gleaming with sweat, she considered suggesting that they postpone the treasure hunt for a few moments. Nick must have seen the look she gave him, for he gave her that familiar slow smile.

"Deciding which you'd rather have right now, the gold or me?"

Jess blushed to be caught so blatantly staring, but she smiled as she replied, "It's a difficult decision, but I'll hold out for the gold. Keep digging."

His smile broadened into a grin, and he obligingly thrust the shovel back into the dirt. This time, however, they both heard the dull thud of metal connecting with something hard. "You've found it," Jess gasped in disbelief.

Nick shook his head, though she could see the excitement glittering in his blue eyes as he said, "Don't get your hopes up, sweetheart. It might be an old wagon wheel."

But a few moments' more careful digging revealed a crude wooden box, its splintered planks held together by rotting leather straps. Together, they eased the box out of its longtime resting place and onto level ground, the weight of it assuring Jess that something *was* inside it.

"What do you think," she breathlessly asked as she knelt beside Nick and he began unfastening the latches, "gold or jewels?"

"Why not both?" he answered with a grin and pried open the lid.

Jess blinked, not quite believing her eyes. Then, slowly, she turned to look at Nick.

"Sand!"

"Sand," he agreed, his lips quirking so that she guessed he was trying not to laugh. He reached a hand into it and let the tan grains sift back through his fingers. "I'd say that either those Spaniards had a pretty good sense of humor, or else someone beat us to the gold."

"I suppose you're right—"

She broke off abruptly, seeing a glint where Nick had dislodged the sand's surface. A forgotten gold coin, perhaps? she wondered, hardly daring to hope. Nick proved swifter than she, however, and scooped up the small object first. After a quick look at it, he laughed and dropped it into her open palm.

"As treasure hunters, I'm afraid we're not much good," he said. "It's a button, sweetheart . . . from a Confederate Army uniform, to be exact."

"So it is," she exclaimed, turning the dull bit of metal over in her hand. "I wonder . . ."

She recalled now that the old prospector, Mr. Johnson, had worn gray, army-issue trousers. She remembered, too, stories she'd heard from Ted and other former soldiers that certain of General Lee's troops were rumored to have come west in search of buried gold to help fund the cause. Perhaps Mr. Johnson had been one of those same Confederate soldiers, and they had uncovered this cache of Spanish gold almost a generation earlier. If so, then the old man had not lied about the map being genuine . . . he'd simply neglected to mention that the treasure already had been found.

"So, should we rebury this for someone else to find?" Nick wryly asked.

Later, as he shoveled in the last bit of dirt over the now-filled hole, he said, "I think this was my first and last treasure hunt. The work's too damn hard, and the pickings are pretty slim. If I'm ever desperate for cash, I think I'll just head to the bank and get myself a loan."

"Indeed?" Jess replied with a smile. "And what sort of collateral can you offer to secure that loan?"

"I don't need collateral." He grinned and drew her into his embrace. "That's one of the advantages of being married to the local banker."

"I see. And what's the advantage of being married to the local marshal?"

His grin broadened, and he pulled her closer. "Well, sweetheart," he murmured in her ear, "why don't I just show you?"

As he kissed her quite thoroughly, and then proceeded to other equally enjoyable things, Jess knew with sweet certainty that she had found the best treasure of all. Not the kind that could be spent or stolen, she knew, but the sort that remains buried safely in the heart for a lifetime.